"I wrote *Charlie Mike* for the men and women who served and those who waited and supported at home—they all fought the war.

Some fought on the battlefield while others fought the anguish of worry and loneliness on the homefront. They were all touched by the war. Their sacrifice in youth, tears, pain, and blood will not be forgotten."

Leonard B. Scott

"A moving and important portrait of a group of heroic young men who fought hard, and of survivors who came home to get on with the business of living."

Publishers Weekly

"An exceptionally fine addition to the literature on the Vietnam War. Scott combines romance, humor, tragedy, stupidity...to make this a first-class reading experience. ENTHRALLING FROM FIRST PAGE TO LAST."

Military Review

CHARLIE MIKE

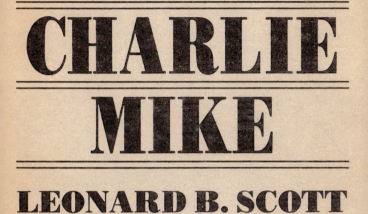

LEONARD B. SCOTT

BALLANTINE BOOKS · NEW YORK

Library of Congress Catalog Card Number: 84-91669

ISBN 0-345-34402-2

Manufactured in the United States of America

First Trade Edition: July 1985
First Mass Market Edition: June 1988

ACKNOWLEDGMENTS

Heartfelt thanks and gratitude to the veteran Rangers, pilots, nurses, Red Cross workers, and Vietnamese who shared their stories with me.

A special thanks to Betsy Badgett, who took an infantryman's scribbles and turned them into readable prose.

Thanks to the believers who supported and helped: Ann, Kathy, Wanda, George, Jim, Dan, Ernie, Owen, Rick, Judy, Debbie, Charles, and Pamela.

Charlie Mike
is dedicated

To the families and friends of the 58,008 fallen Americans whose names on a black marble wall represent the ultimate sacrifice paid to our country.

To an old World War II bomber pilot who gave his years to his country. He lay paralyzed in a veterans hospital when I read him my story. They said he couldn't understand. His eyes told me they were wrong. The old pilot passed away Easter Sunday, 1983. I'll miss you, Dad.

To my wife, Jammye, and children, Scotty, Stefne, and Robby, who have patiently stood by through the years.

To the American soldier, whose indomitable spirit will always prevail!

PROLOGUE

The rain forest was still and silent. Its muggy air stank with rot. The midday sun attacked the green canopy above, but the intertwined latticework of foliage allowed only the narrowest shafts of light to dapple the jungle floor.

Sergeant David Grady lay hidden with five other rangers among the fiddlehead ferns. They all wore camouflage fatigues, and their faces were painted green. Grady pressed himself closer to the dank earth, squinting to hide the whites of his eyes as seven North Vietnamese regulars approached.

The North Vietnamese, burdened with heavy packs, walked single file along a trail that twisted among tall, stately trunks of teak and mahogany. Everywhere, woody vines hung like thick cables. The men's uniforms were darkened by perspiration, and their rifles were slung over their shoulders. Had only two of them held their weapons ready, Grady would have let them pass, but their carelessness would cost them.

He tapped the man lying next to him, Specialist Fourth Class Greg Bartlett. Bartlett gently pushed back the safety clip of his detonator. Twenty feet away, hidden next to the trail, were deadly Claymore mines.

Beads of sweat trickled down Grady's brow and stung his

eyes. He couldn't help but think how young the approaching soldiers were, probably no more than eighteen. Bartlett pressed the detonator. The earth erupted in a roaring, shattering explosion of dirt, decayed leaves, jagged plastic and hundreds of steel ball bearings. The seven small Vietnamese were violently flung through the air. Their stunned bodies were ripped and torn as if made of paper. Leaves and branches fell like rain into the billowing debris as the green-faced men rose and fired.

Grady tapped Bartlett, then yelled to the others, *"Security!"*

Bartlett pulled his pistol and followed his sergeant as he cautiously approached the mangled bodies.

Grady hesitated. The smell—he would never get used to it. It was the odor of plastic explosive mixed with soil and blood, the overwhelming smell of death. He could feel it and taste it.

A gritty mist lingered over the scene as Grady passed the first blood-splattered corpse and knelt by the second. The dead man lay on his stomach, his legs sprawled at odd angles. He reeked with the smell of musty smoke absorbed from countless cooking fires.

Grady thought about how many men like this one he had seen shattered, ashen-faced, lying in their own blood. For ten months he had been killing them . . . ten months of setting up ambushes and waiting. At first he'd counted those he'd killed, but after a while it didn't matter anymore. He stopped counting at twenty-two. That was eight months ago.

He pulled off the soldier's pack and dumped the contents on the ground. He knew what he'd find. They all carried the same things: wadded clothes, a few tins of fish, a bag of rice, a hammock, and always a book wrapped in yellow plastic—not a real book but a cardboard-covered note pad used as a daily log or diary. Stuck between the thin rice-paper pages would be letters and pictures, but in this, each book was unique. Some men wrote poetry, others sketched, some even collected stamps. Each one wrote of his war experiences.

Grady glanced up. Bartlett was grinning at him boyishly.

Grady winked at his assistant team leader, then suddenly tightened, realizing his friend was about to turn a body over. Bartlett hadn't followed search procedure. He didn't have his pistol at the soldier's head, and he had not pulled the hands free to ensure that the Vietnamese held no weapon.

Greg Bartlett still held his grin as a single shot echoed through the silent forest before being answered by a succession of loud rifle cracks and Grady's anguished scream: *"No!"*

PART ONE

1

The screen door of the headquarters building flew open, and out stepped a thin, gnarled-looking sergeant wearing a black beret and pressed camouflage jungle fatigues. He took one look at the four replacements who were slapping red dust from their uniforms, and he barked "Ah-*tench-hut!*"

The new men immediately snapped into the rigid position. The sergeant circled the men, then halted and placed his hands on his hips. "I'm Sergeant First Class Childs, your actin' first sergeant. You people have all been to An Khe and went through our two-week Ranger course, *right?*"

Three of the four men responded loudly, *"Yes, Sergeant!"*

The fourth soldier raised his hand and stepped forward timidly. "Nnn . . . uh, no, Sergeant, I came from Eighteenth Replacement and—"

"Who told you to move, shitbird!" yelled Childs, stepping closer to the small, bespectacled private, eyeing him from head to foot. Suddenly the sergeant's eyes narrowed and his face reddened. He spun toward the door and hollered, "Dove, get out here!"

A tanned, curly-headed blond who wore a dirty green T-shirt came to the door.

"Yeah, Top?"

Childs pointed the private's chest where parachute wings should have been sewn.

"Dove, they sent me a puny-assed *leg*! Jesus H. Christ! Don't them replacement pukes know this is an *Airborne* Ranger company?"

Dove nonchalantly walked out, looked over the private and read his name tape.

"Top, this is Peteroski, the clerk-typist from Eighteenth Replacement. We had to trade a lotta shit and pull strings to get him, remember?"

Childs stared at the private. "But a *leg*! Damn, I didn't know it was gonna be a straight-ass *leg*!"

Dove rolled his eyes at the young private, then tapped his arm, motioning him to follow inside.

Childs resumed his position in front of the other three men and bellowed, *"Anybody else a leg?"*

"No, Sergeant!" the men yelled in unison.

Satisfied that there were no other surprises, Childs put his hands on his hips and began rocking, heel to toe.

"Welcome to Sierra Company, Seventy-fifth Infantry Airborne Rangers. Now, loosen up, this is the first and last time I will tell you the rules of this company. Should you violate, stretch, or disregard *my* rules, your ass will be on a plane to a leg-ass outfit in a heartbeat!

"*First*: Keep your mouth shut and your eyes open, and remember what they taught you at the mini-Ranger course. It *might* save your life until your team leader squares your ass away.

"*Second: No* smokin' dope, screwin' local broads, writin' letters to congressmen, or sendin' pictures of dead gooks to girl friends.

"*Third*: No fightin', fraggin', or gassin' LEGs, REMFs, or local friendlies.

"*Fourth*: No stealin' or lyin' to fellow Rangers.

"*Fifth* and last: *You are here to kill!* You can bet your sweet ass them bastards out there will do you in if given half a chance, so you *must* kill them first. *No doubts, no hesitation.* If for any reason—whether it be religious, lack of guts, or you're just not sure you can pull the trigger—*quit now!*"

Childs paused for effect and stared into each pair of eyes.

"People, that's the rules. Now, this afternoon you gonna meet the Ol' Man, Major Colven. He is the best there is. I've been in the Army twenty years, and I know. Don't be askin' him no dumb-ass questions. I'll answer your questions after his briefing; just nod and keep your mouths shut.

"People, your performance records and files arrived yesterday, and your assignments to teams have already been made. When I dismiss you, report to Pfc. Dove and he'll show you where to go. *People*, remember *my* rules and don't fuck up!"

Childs raised his hand and pointed to the door:

"Do it!"

A cloud of dust billowed as the three men ran for the door. Sfc. Childs shook his head and spun around to walk to the mess hall.

Pfc. Dove sat behind a desk, drinking a Coke, when the three men ran into the orderly room and stood at attention.

The blond smiled and said quietly, "Relax. Ol' Childs always does that. He's got the disposition of a rattler. Just stay out of his way and do what he says."

The three men took deep breaths and exchanged glances as Dove walked to the door and pointed across the road. "Jenkins, you're going to team One-Three and Donnelly, you're on One-Four. They're both in the first barracks, there. Get your duffel bags and go on over. Be back for the Ol' Man's briefing at Fourteen hundred hours. Good luck."

Dove walked back to his desk, motioning the third man to take a seat, and he picked up the appropriate file and silently read the name on it: Kenneth Meeks.

Dove eyed the big soldier. He'd seen the report on Meeks and was curious. The name sure didn't fit. Meeks was six two, broad-shouldered and narrow-hipped. His square jaw and deep, piercing brown eyes made him seem older than his twenty years. At the mini-Ranger course he'd become a celebrity when he had walked the "Death Valley" course without being "killed." Death Valley was a thick-treed stream bed next to the huge base camp of An Khe. The instructors always set up a series of ambushes and booby traps there to humble new students. No one had ever finished the course without being "killed" at least twice—until Meeks.

Dove glanced back at the file. "Meeks," he said, trying to keep the enthusiasm out of his voice, "your file says you have some college. By any chance, did you take courses in business or marketing?"

Meeks shook his head. "No. I was a poli-sci major."

Dove's face showed disappointment, then suddenly brightened. "How about animals? Do you know anything about pigs or chickens?"

Meeks stared at the young blond, as if wondering whether the strange questions should be taken seriously.

Dove saw the confused look and smiled. "Hey, I ain't hasslin'. I just have a little business on the side, and I'm lookin' for a qualified consultant. You know what I mean?"

Meeks returned the smile. He had suddenly realized who Dove was. At the Ranger school they had talked about a wheeler-dealer who raised pigs for roasting at unit luaus, and chickens for cutting and bleeding onto NVA flags he made and sold as war souvenirs.

Meeks stood and held out his hand. "Dove, it's a pleasure to meet you. You're famous at An Khe."

Dove grinned at the compliment and sheepishly shrugged his shoulders. "They talked about me, huh?"

"Sure did," laughed Meeks. "You, Sergeant Evans, and Sergeant Grady were the big names."

Dove headed for the door. "Speakin' of Evans and Grady, I gotta get you to your new team."

Meeks tossed his duffel bag over his shoulder and asked, "What team am I going to?"

Dove went to the door and pointed to the last barracks. "You're gonna be on my old team. You're replacing a man they lost three weeks ago. His name was Bartlett. He was the first man Grady lost as team sergeant."

Meeks slowed. "Grady? Grady of team Two-Two? The one the instructors talked so much about?"

Dove smiled. "Yeah, you're gonna be a proud member of team Two-Two, the Double-Deuce. Come on, now, we're runnin' late. Peteroski, you come too."

Rock Steady, seated in the shade of the barracks, set down his partially disassembled M-16. People were walking down the road toward him, but the rising midday heat waves distorted their images into shimmering blurs. Suddenly, as if by magic, the images came into focus. Rock smiled and stood up.

"Hey, Dove, what's happenin', man?"

Dove threw his thumb in Meeks's direction. "I brought you a cherry."

Rock quickly stepped forward and thrust out his hand. "I'm Rock Steady, assistant team leader. Sure good to see you."

Kenneth Meeks forced a smile, hoping the disappointment he felt didn't show. Rock Steady was not what he had expected. He'd heard stories about team 2-2 and had imagined its members to be strong, athletic types, but the man with whom he shook hands couldn't have been over nineteen, and he looked like a prisoner from a Nazi death camp. At about five feet nine, the soldier could not have weighed more than 140 pounds. He had sparse brown hair and a hawk nose that reminded Meeks of Ichabod Crane.

Rock backed up and suddenly froze. He pointed to Peteroski. "Is that what I think it is?"

Dove frowned and put his arm around the clerk's shoulder. "Yeah, he's a leg, but don't you say nothin'. This is my turtle! I'm gettin' short, and we need a typist."

Rock grinned. "Has Childs seen him yet?"

Dove narrowed his eyes and kicked at Rock, who backed away laughing, then stepped forward and put out his hand. "Pete, I'm Rock; good to have you aboard."

Meeks's opinion of Rock vanished the second Rock shook hands with the typist. For reasons he couldn't explain, he suddenly found himself taking to the thin soldier who had made the timid clerk smile.

Dove patted Peteroski's back. "We've gotta get back. Rock, introduce the team to Meeks; then get him back to the briefing room by fourteen hundred hours. The Ol' Man is gonna brief all the cherries that came in this week."

Rock slapped Meeks on the back and pointed him toward the barracks. "Come on, big 'un, I'll square you away." Meeks waved at Dove and Peteroski and followed Rock into the building.

At one end of the empty barracks was a small room. Rock pushed open the door and blurted, "Hey, guys, meet our new team member."

Three men were sitting on the floor, looking over large pictures done with crayon. Rock made the introductions as each man stood. The first to shake hands with Meeks was a huge black soldier named Benjamin Murray. He looked like a bear—a black, gentle bear with rounded shoulders and a round coffee-colored face. He held a constant grin as he pointed to the pictures. "My sister sends me them drawings."

Rock patted Ben's stomach. "Ben is our M-60 machine-gunner and our team watch. He always knows when it's chow time!"

The second member introduced himself as Sox, the radioman. He was of average build and had longer-than-normal thick, brown hair. He seemed shy and wore a Peace medal around his neck. The third soldier, a small Puerto Rican, was surprisingly handsome, with almost delicate features. His handshake was strong and his deep-set, large brown eyes sparkled when he introduced himself as Juan Ortega Isaacs Ramon Rodriguez, from Brooklyn.

Rock thumped the Puerto Rican's chest. "We just call him Pancho."

Meeks laughed comfortably. These men were all so young and easygoing that they didn't fit their reputations as hardened killers. That any of them could kill other men seemed impossible, but deep inside Meeks knew that the stories about them were true. He stole quick looks at each member. There were no clues, no visible characteristics that revealed what made these men different.

Rock looked at his watch. "Come on, big 'un, I gotta get you to Major Colven's briefing."

Minutes later Meeks sat in the hot briefing room with eight other new men. He had heard about "the Ol' Man" from others, and he eagerly awaited the appearance of the famous Ranger commander, Major John Colven.

Sergeant Childs walked in and barked "Ah-tench-*hut*!" and Major Colven strode in.

He was of medium height and stocky; his camouflage fatigue shirt strained to hold his huge chest and arms. Sweat rolled down his forehead as he removed his black beret, carefully rolled it and put it into his fatigue leg pocket. With his green eyes he looked over the assembled group. "Take your seats," he ordered. He then sat down as a young lieutenant began an intelligence briefing. Meeks studied the major from out of the corner of his eye. Colven had a large, pink, diagonal scar that ran from the top of his forehead down across his nose to the lower side of his face. That he'd gotten it from shrapnel in Korea in 1951, and that his stomach and legs also bore testimony to the jagged, tearing metal was common knowledge. He'd received a Distinguished Service Cross for continuing his charge up a nameless frozen hill despite those wounds. He had been a nineteen-year-old staff sergeant then and had subsequently risen to the rank of first sergeant.

Years later, when the Vietnam War expanded, the Army needed experienced officers, so Colven was offered a direct commission. This was his third tour. He wasn't handsome, but the scar was a badge that spoke for itself. He looked good with it. Meeks couldn't explain why, but he envied it.

After the lieutenant finished, Major Colven stood to begin his talk.

"Welcome to the Rangers. I try to brief my new men so that we're all on the same sheet of music. You are volunteers, as are all my men. Some come from field units; others, like you, volunteer at the replacement detachment when they get in country." He turned toward the map. "First thing you gotta know is *AO*. AO is nothing more than an area of operation, or the area we operate in. You see it there on the map, marked off with black grease pencil.

"The AO is broken down into smaller sectors for each platoon, then further broken down for each team. Think of it as a small town in which each team is given a specific block to work with. We are the Ranger company for the corps—the eyes and ears of the corps commander. If he wants an area checked to see if the dinks are building up or using it as a supply route, he calls on us. Vietnam is big. Most people don't understand how much land it covers. The U.S. and South Vietnamese army (ARVN) protect only a very small portion of the country. The rest is Indian Territory. Enemy units of any size must subsist largely off the land or near their supply routes. They stay where there is camouflage, food, and water. Our job is to find 'em."

The major walked to the blackboard. "It's not easy. Our mission is tough, dangerous work. We gather all the intelligence we can about an assigned area—prisoner and deserter reports, captured documents, diaries, the usual stuff— then we send a lieutenant up in the backseat of a spotter plane to fly over and determine the most likely spots in which to find the bad guys. He can't fly over the area but a couple of times, or the bad guys would figure out we're interested in that particular piece of real estate, but he takes as many pictures as he can and marks his map.

"I go over the pictures and select the platoon area. We have four platoons, with six teams in each platoon. That's on paper. Actually, we normally only have four teams per platoon at any given time, due to rotation, R&R, and sickness. And two of our platoons are in Phan Thiet right now with Task Force South." This was the first Meeks had heard about the company being split up. And from the look on Colven's face when he mentioned it, he wasn't too happy about the situation. "A team recons the area or sets up an ambush, depending on the mission.

"Four days is usually the max time we'll keep a team out. That's about all the time the nerves can stand without causing mistakes, and in our business, mistakes are forever. Now, how do we get our teams in undetected? The process is called an 'infill,' infiltration or insertion, and we do it by Huey helicopter—a Slick. The pilot can't see anything but the tree limbs, so he is directed by our command-and-control—C&C—spotter plane flying three thousand feet above.

"The LT gives the helicopter pilot a countdown, like, two kilometers out, one klick out, five hundred meters and so on. He is, in effect, the eyes of the helicopter. The chopper lands and you guys un-ass. That's all there is to it. In case of trouble, the guns will come in to cover. Guns are either Huey Charlie models or the new Cobra; we call 'em Snakes.

"Now, how do we communicate with the teams, since they're so far out? We use an X-ray. The X-ray is our communications site, and it's the most important element in our operation. We pick out the highest elevation close to the area of operations. We then helicopter in a commo—communications team—to the site with all their special radio gear."

Colven paused and stared into the faces of the assembled soldiers.

"That's a brief overview of how we operate. Your team sergeants will be giving you more detailed information. Men, we're not your everyday men off the block. We're Rangers, and we're special because we're damned good. Ranger is more than just a name: It's a way of life. You must live, eat, and breathe your profession. A Ranger can have no doubts about himself or his team members. He must give one hundred and ten percent of his body, mind, and soul to become the best he can possibly be, because he knows *his life* and the lives of his fellow team members *depend* on it.

"We are a proud unit, with a tradition of excellence and professionalism. It is up to you to keep up that tradition. It is an honor and a privilege to serve with you. Good luck to you all."

Childs snapped, "Ah-tench-*hut*!"

Meeks, who was closest to the door, sprang to his feet as the major strode down the aisle. He saw the major stop at the doorway and heard him whisper to Childs, "The third

shitbird on the left, second row, slept through my pitch.
Have him out by nightfall."

Childs responded immediately. "It's done, sir!"

Meeks walked back to the barracks thinking about the major's words '. . . Your life and your fellow team members'
lives depend on it.' *Heavy,* he thought. *Very heavy.*

He pulled open the barracks door. Rock was sitting on the
closest bunk, cleaning his M-16. Across the aisle, Rodriguez
was doing the same. Ben and Sox sat against the wall, taping
fragmentation grenades. Each man looked up with a smile or
nod as Meeks entered. Rock waved him over to his bed.

"Well, big 'un, did the old man give you his Ranger rah-
rah?"

Meeks smiled. "He's impressive."

Rock set down his oily rag. "The Ol' Man watches out for
us. He can be a real bastard at times, but he knows the business."

Just then the front door opened, and a broad-shouldered,
muscular sergeant walked in. He was about twenty-one and
stood five ten. His short, sandy hair contrasted with his
black beret, which was pulled low over his right eye. He
looked over his men; then his eyes locked on Meeks.

Rock quickly stood. "Grade, meet our newest member,
Kenneth Meeks. He's from—"

"I've read his file," said the sergeant without taking his
eyes off the new soldier.

Meeks was spellbound by the sergeant's strange gray eyes.
They seemed totally expressionless, and his voice was likewise cold, detached.

Grady's gaze turned to Rock and softened. "Has he got
his equipment yet?"

"No, Grade, he just got the Ol' Man's briefing."

Grady's eyes shifted back to Meeks and immediately
turned cold again. "Get him his equipment, take him to the
range, and get him qualified on all our weapons. Then drill
him on the lingo. I'll talk to him after chow."

Rock looked at his sergeant as if confused, then stiffened
and quietly said, "Sure, Grade."

The other men stared at the sergeant in disbelief as he
pointed at Meeks.

"The cherry is *not* a team member till I say he's a team
member." He turned to Rock. "I've got a mission brief tomorrow. We'll be going out in three days. If this cherry isn't

ready in that time, he's *out*!" The sergeant pivoted on his heel and walked out the door.

Ben exchanged glances with Sox and Rodriguez. Rock shook his head and patted Meeks's shoulder. "Sorry, big 'un. Grady been actin' kinda funny since we lost Bartlett. Don't think nothin' of it. Ol' Ben'll make sure you makes it."

Sox tossed his ruck on the floor. "Dig it, dudes: Grade said to get him qualified on the guns. It's fourteen-thirty; we ain't got much time."

Rock pointed to Rodriguez. "Pancho, get the weapons from the connex. Me and Ben will get his gear. Sox, you write down the lingo."

Rock smiled at Meeks. "Well, big 'un, looks like we got work to do."

Meeks's marksmanship with the team weapons earned him a nickname. When he fired the M-79 grenade launcher, he hit the target on every shot, and Ben made a big thing of it.

"You sure can thump them rounds out," he said.

Rock immediately picked up on the comment and called him Thumper. By the time he got to the mess hall an hour later, everyone was calling him by that name.

"Okay, Thump," Rock said over a cup of coffee. "This is just the start. You hang tough when you talk to Grady. Don't let him get you down. We'll get you ready in three days."

Rodriguez waved his fork at Meeks. "*Sí*, man, no problema. I teach you everything."

Ben shook his massive hand at the Puerto Rican. "Pancho, you can't even talk English. How you gonna teach anybody?"

The Puerto Rican immediately tensed and waved his fork at Ben's black, grinning face. "Man, who say I no speak good English?"

Ben leaned back. "I rest my case."

"Oh, yeah, man?" Pancho replied. "You test the Thumper and you see how good I teach him to talk." He pushed a piece of paper across the table.

Sox looked it over. It was a list of words, a compendium of the special vocabulary used by Rangers when they were out in the bush.

"Okay, what's a blue line?" Sox asked.

Meeks answered immediately. "A river or stream."

"Yeah. Now, what's a daisy chain?"

"Two or more Claymore mines rigged with detonation cord so they'll blow simultaneously."

Sox grinned at Ben. "I think Thump has got the lingo down, man."

Pancho nonchalantly looked over his fingernails. "I told you, man."

Sergeant David Grady sat in his room, absently paging through a two-week-old edition of *Stars & Stripes*, when Rock knocked on the open door. "Come in, Rock. You never have to knock. You know that."

Rock entered, letting out a deep breath. "Shit! Grade, after this afternoon I wasn't sure."

Grady shook his head apologetically. "I guess I did come on strong, but you guys gotta be more careful. You'd take in a damn cobra and try to make a pet out of it."

"We ain't talkin' about pets, Grade. Thumper is gonna be a real—"

Grady's face flushed. "You laid a nickname on him? Damn, Rock, what the hell you doin'? He's not a team member. He's a dumbass cherry who doesn't know his butt from a hole in the ground. He's got it or he doesn't."

Rock shook his head. "Grade, when I came to this team, you accepted me without all this stuff you're havin' him to do. You didn't have *any* of the team do it."

Grady looked at Rock and spoke softly. "You're right, I didn't. And three weeks ago I sent Greg home in a body bag. I'm not losing any more of you, Rock. I . . . I couldn't take it. Now, is that all you came for, to talk about the cherry? Because if it is, the conversation is over."

The thin soldier nodded sadly and walked out without another word.

Grady tried to take stock of his feelings. Why had he acted like such an ass to the cherry and the team? He remembered when he had first seen Meeks, he'd become inexplicably angry. He couldn't help it. The sight of him, the replacement for Greg . . . Just thinking the word *replacement* had made him mad. It wasn't Meeks. It was the idea of him taking such a good friend's place, a friend who had been killed by a man whom he, Grady, had passed by.

I should have searched the first man. I would have followed procedure and pulled his hand with the pistol free. Greg would be alive and . . . Damn, Greg, I'm sorry . . . so sorry.

Grady fought back tears and took several deep breaths. He'd gotten too damned close to his men. He should have known better, but it had just happened. He'd never done it before. It was just . . . just here in Vietnam that . . . Shit!

The sergeant spun around and rotated his shoulders back. Meeks wouldn't be on the team, by God, unless he pulled his own weight. Grady knew he was right in demanding it. Still, he'd been wrong in snapping at his team. They were his men and needed his friendship. . . .

A loud knock at his door broke Grady from his thoughts. It was Meeks, there as ordered. Grady sat down and snapped, "Enter."

Meeks walked in and stood in front of his sergeant, who leaned forward in his chair and looked up.

"Meeks, your record at the An Khe Ranger school is impressive, but it doesn't mean anything to me. I've seen too many cherries who could perform in school, but who couldn't cut it when real bullets started flying. The next couple of days will determine if you go with us on the upcoming mission. I'm going to push your ass and see what you got inside." Grady stood up. "Those men out there would accept you now because they think they could make up for your mistakes. They probably could, in many cases, but I won't take that chance . . . for their sakes.

"You're going out tonight and fire again. Ben will take you. Once you've completed your night-firing, Pancho will march you around the perimeter. It's five miles. You'll carry your rucksack with all your equipment, plus a twenty-five-pound bag of sand. That's all; move out and pack your gear."

Meeks stood steadfast, feeling an odd sensation he hadn't felt in a long time but was like an old friend. He tingled with an electriclike energy that flowed through his body, charging every nerve and fiber: The sergeant was challenging him.

"Sergeant Grady, permission to speak."

Grady raised his eyebrows. "Speak."

"Sergeant Grady, I don't want any team member to have to watch out for me or cover my mistakes. I agree with you. I have to prove myself. I wouldn't want it any other way."

Grady stared at the big soldier for several seconds, then motioned toward the door. "Move out," he said.

Private Wes Peteroski lay on his bunk, holding a new black beret.

"Dove, I'm not Airborne like you guys. Do I have to wear this?"

"'Course you got to wear it! You're in this unit, and it's part of our uniform," said Dove taking off his boots.

"But I'm only a clerk. Couldn't I just wear a regular hat?"

Dove tossed a boot to the floor. "Look, Pete, you're not just a clerk. You're important! You're my replacement when I'm driving the Ol' Man."

Pete shook his head doggedly. "I'm out of place here. Couldn't you-all find an Airborne-qualified clerk?"

Dove lay back on his bed. "No, we-all can't. Look, the Dove will take care of you. Just wear that beret and be proud of it. If anybody hassles you, let me know."

Pete lay back, too, and stared at the ceiling for a long moment. Then he shut his eyes.

"Dove?" He said.

"Yeah?"

"Thanks."

"You're welcome. Now shut up. I've got to wake up Sergeant Grady early tomorrow."

It was still dark when Grady felt a nudge and opened one eye. A smiling Dove stood over him. The sergeant shut his eye and rolled over.

"Dove, you'd better be a bad dream, 'cause you gonna die otherwise."

"Come on, Grade, the Ol' Man moved up the briefing."

Grady sprung from his bed, grabbing Dove. *"You gonna die!"*

The two arm-wrestled a moment, laughing and hitting each other with exaggerated blows. Grady finally pushed Dove onto the bed and looked at his watch. "Damn, it's only oh-six-hundred. When's the brief?"

"Ten minutes. Corps's got some good intelligence and wants it checked."

Grady yawned and bent over for his trousers. Dove took the opportunity to push him over and ran for the door. He just made it to the hall when a boot hit him squarely in the back.

Grady laughed loudly and retrieved his boot. Dove had been on his team when he first took over and was a good friend. "Dove, wait a minute and I'll walk over with you."

Dove nodded with a grin and walked down the barracks aisle to wait while Grady dressed. Rodriguez pulled himself out of bed and walked toward the door to visit the latrine.

"What's a matter, Pancho? You sure movin' slow."

The Puerto Rican pointed to Grady's room. "Man, Grade, he say march the cherry, but the cherry, he march *me*!"

Dove looked at the two empty beds. "Where is the big guy?"

"Grady make Sox march him this morning!"

Grady walked down the aisle, putting on his fatigue shirt and kicking the occupied beds. "Get up, girls! If I gotta get up, I want company!"

Ben and Rock stirred but no one rose. Grady shrugged his shoulders at Dove. "Guess I'm losing my touch."

The broad-shouldered sergeant pushed open the door and strode out. The blond fell in beside him.

"How's business?" Grady asked as they walked. "I heard you added a new line of merchandise."

Dove grinned. "The buckles from Hong Kong came in and they're perfect. They have a red star and everything."

Grady shook his head. "And I suppose they will be NVA buckles captured by the Rangers. Right?"

Dove sighed. "Grady, you have no imagination. The buckles were recovered from bodies of the elite NVA's Thirteenth Regiment at the battle of Dong Xuan."

"Dong Xuan? Where the hell is that?

Dove shrugged his shoulders. "I don't know. I made it up."

Grady laughed and put his arm around the smaller man's shoulder.

"You're unbelievable. When is the Ol' Man going to promote you?"

"Hell, Grade, I can't afford to get promoted. You know that!"

They walked fifty meters to the tactical operation center. The TOC was half buried in the red earth, and it had three large antennae protruding from the top, held in place by a spider web of guy wires. Three layers of sandbags were stacked along the outside, with six layers on top.

Inside, three of Grady's fellow team sergeants from the Second Platoon sat in chairs next to a radio operator who was monitoring the X-ray.

"'Bout damn time!" said one of the sergeants. It was Evans, Grady's closest friend.

Grady rolled his eyes. *Here it comes,* he thought.

"Where you been, Double-Dude? The ville again?"

"Evans, you damned hick, I'm too short to be screwin' around in the ville!"

Evans grinned slyly. "Short! Why, me and the boys, here, heard you was reenlistin' and becomin' a lifer." The other sergeants, Trapsell and Salazar, laughed.

"Okay, who told you? I thought it was a secret." He looked up with a grin. "I'm re-uppin' for life and becomin' a recruiting poster for the Rangers." In fact, Grady had only two months to go and would be going back to the University of Arizona to finish school.

Evans was about to retort when a familiar voice cut him off.

"Knock it fuckin' off, clowns!"

The four young sergeants knew who it was without looking: Sergeant Jerry P. Childs.

When he spoke, his voice was always a cranky bark, and his weathered face rarely showed any emotion other than a scowl. The younger sergeants disliked him personally, but professionally he couldn't be beat.

"You clowns always screwin' around." He walked between their chairs, looking at the seated buck sergeants. "Got you Deuce clowns a good AO."

Grady looked over at his friend Evans and rolled his eyes. Evans tried not to laugh.

"That's what you said last time, Sarge. All we got was three monkeys and two cases of jock rot," said Grady.

The sergeants all laughed.

"Fuckin' clowns," mumbled Childs.

Grady winked at Evans who quickly covered his grin with a cough.

Behind them, the small briefing room door swung open and Major Colven came out. Without looking at the seated sergeants, he bellowed from the side of his mouth, "Get in here, Deuce!"

The four men rose immediately, followed the major back through the door, and took seats inside.

"Corps wants information about this area." He pointed to the map behind him. "It's all virgin territory; nobody has ever worked it. The river here runs parallel to a major trail we found."

Colven motioned toward Grady. "You got the main trail. Sergeant Evans, you have this feeder trail, here. Sergeant Salazar, you have this one. Trapsell, you're going in here on this small tributary that feeds the river. The LZs are all marked; you can mark them on your maps later. Now, the good news: You ain't 'bushin'."

The sergeants moaned and looked at each other for consolation. Not ambushing meant a recon mission; they'd go in, set up, watch, and report enemy activity.

Colven smiled. "Now, now, prima donnas, even you all have to earn your long-range recon title." His smile turned into a serious look of concern. "We gotta find out how much traffic uses the trail, and we can't do that by killin' the first bunch we see. The enemy would just be alerted and divert the flow elsewhere. Now, for air assets, we have . . ."

Shit, thought Grady as Colven droned on, *The team's sure not gonna like this one. And on top of everything else, I gotta train that damned cherry.*

That afternoon, each team member began teaching Meeks an area of expertise. Rodriguez showed him how to walk point, what signs to look for, what hand signals to give and what ones to respond to. Sox instructed on radio procedures and how to encode and decode messages. Ben taught ambush and search procedures. Rock instructed on movement techniques, and laagering in a patrol base. Meeks had learned it all in Ranger training, but each unit had its own special way of doing things. Sergeant Grady was there to lead him through his education, step by step. "Procedure, Meeks! Procedure!" he yelled again and again.

On the next day came the final examination, a two-hour test of immediate-action drills and team procedures. Grady walked behind him the whole time, yelling out combat situations to which Meeks had to respond. He did near ambushes, far ambushes, and chance contact, and he established a hasty ambush and a deliberate ambush. After each drill, Meeks had to explain his actions and what the actions of the other team member would have been.

Afterward, Grady stood with his hands on his hips, eyeing the tired soldier for a few moments before motioning him to the shade of a nearby tree.

Meeks couldn't tell how he'd done. The sergeant never responded to his actions or answers, except for an occasional raising of an eyebrow or shake of his head.

Once in the shade, Grady took off his beret. Meeks took a deep breath and waited.

"Meeks," said Grady, wiping perspiration from his forehead, "you didn't do too bad. I'm going to let you go on the mission as a conditional member. I'll see how you do in the field and make a final decision when we get back. Go on back and rest up.

"And have Ben tell you about extraction procedures if we have to be lifted out by McGuire rig."

Meeks couldn't keep from smiling, and was about to say "Thanks" when Grady turned his back to him and snapped, "Move out!"

Rock, Ben, Rodriguez, and Sox paced back and forth in front of the barracks, waiting.

Rock blew out a breath in disgust. "Damn, it's like the movies. We look like dads waitin' on word if our ol' lady has had a kid!"

Ben shook his head, agreeing. "Wish I smoked right now."

Rodriguez put his hand to his forehead, shielding the sun, and pointed: "He coming!"

The four men broke into a run toward the approaching big soldier.

Meeks's face was stony somber, and his eyes stared at the ground as the worried men gathered around him.

"Well?" asked Rock.

Meeks raised his eyes and winked. "I'm going."

Ben threw his beret in the air and hollered. Rock and Rodriguez broke into huge grins and grabbed for Meeks's hand. Sox mumbled, "I knew it, man, I knew it!"

Grady stood in the distance, watching his laughing men pounce on the new soldier. He shook his head and turned around. He knew he had to take the cherry, no matter what.

The damned team had gotten too personally involved. If he'd failed Meeks, he'd have failed the men who worked and taught him. Still, he had to admit the cherry was good. He was exceptionally strong and had the ability to think on his feet. But more than that, he seemed to sense what was going to happen next. He had an uncanny ability to react to a situation as if he'd been through it before. He'd reacted like a veteran.

Grady stopped and turned again. He looked at the big soldier in the distance and said to himself, "We'll see, cherry, we'll see."

2

A lone sentry stood, tired, shivering, lost in his misery. Six dark apparitions moved silently toward him in the heavy morning fog. His heart skipped as he raised his rifle.

"Who's there?" The shrillness of his own voice surprised him.

"Team Two-Two, Sierra Rangers," floated back a whisper as the specters came closer.

The sentry exhaled a sigh of relief and his taut body relaxed. He stood motionless as the procession of phantomlike men passed close by.

Their faces were darkened, and laden with heavy packs they leaned slightly forward, their black weapons held diagonally across their bodies. No sound was created by their movement except the slight swish of fatigue material and the faintest crackle of the earth disturbed by their steps. The sentry lowered his rifle, placing the stock by his foot. They had disappeared in the swirling mist in the direction of the helicopter landing pad.

As Grady moved slowly along at the head of the team he thought of a foggy morning long ago in his previous life—the civilian life of David Grady, deceased.

David had been a loner since the age of ten, when love, with his mother, had died.

He remembered her hugging him when he was hurt, kissing his tears away, holding him to her breast, rocking him gently, always there with her special smile for her last-born. Her tender smile began in her eyes with a peculiar sparkle and then spread to her lips and always ended in a touch . . . a warm, loving hug or squeeze that he secretly longed for and could never get enough of. She was love: When they buried her on that foggy morning, they buried a young boy's heart.

David's father cherished his son and tried desperately to rekindle the boy's lost spark of life, but he couldn't penetrate the boy's shell. The unrestrained laughter David had always given to his mother was gone forever.

His father remarried eventually, but David couldn't accept his stepmother. He couldn't stand to see his father touch or smile at the replacement wife, so he stayed away from home as much as possible, fanatically dedicating himself to sports. The lonely days turned to years. The rift between him and his father became a crevice. His father had a new life, and David had his memories of his mother. As soon as he was old enough, David left home.

He had received a four-year baseball scholarship to college and played with an intensity and devotion that made him well known and respected. His reckless style and his total self-confidence were overpowering to men and women alike. The flash of his steel-gray eyes and his brief, ironic smile were charismatic, and yet, there was always a strange, cold reticence about him that made him seem inaccessible.

Life to David Grady was to be met head on. Life's barriers were not to be gone around or over; he preferred to go through them, to feel the power of conquering obstacles the difficult way. It was a strange satisfaction, and it drove him to even more barriers. His first two years of college provided many; the studies, the varsity baseball team, the women, were all slowly, methodically, conquered.

Then came an empty loneliness. His successes seemed hollow. He began a search. It ended on a winter evening in the school dormitory. The six-o'clock news was displaying the horrors of the Vietnam War, the Tet Offensive of 1968. David felt the queer sensation of another compelling quest: the ultimate barrier, one in which life itself was to be challenged . . . in which winning meant staying alive. David joined the Army the following morning.

The olive-drab ranks provided the new recruit with what he sought. He felt alive and whole again. He volunteered for the toughest duty and most difficult schools and became, in time, a soldier's soldier.

Then he was sent to Vietnam and was handed the cold blade of responsibility. David had always accepted and met every challenge by himself, alone, but now responsibility came in the form of five young men assigned to him as a team, his team. Success was no longer judged by what he alone did but rather by what they, the team, did. Five men. Some big, strong, some small, weak. Brave and cowardly, evil and good. They put their lives in his hands. Their smiles, their heartaches, all became a part of him. They were his new life.

David was no more. Now he was just Grady, team sergeant of Ranger team 2-2, the Double-Deuce.

Grady stopped at the top of the small hill that was the landing pad.

"Bag it by the revetment. The bird'll be here in fifteen," he said. "Ben, drill Meeks again."

The moving shapes veered right, walking the twenty feet to the corrugated steel blast wall that protected the north portion of the pad. Mist engulfed the men as they sat heavily with their weighted rucksacks. Grady continued walking. He wanted to be alone.

That's the way it always was now. He was either with his team or alone. He didn't feel he needed anything else, though during the last conversation they'd had, his friend Evans had tried to convince him how important a woman's love was.

"Ya love 'em till they scream out and claw your back, right?" Grady had teased.

"Naw, Grady, that's not love, that's frat talk from that lib-eral-ass school you call an institute of education."

"Now, wait a minute. You call that agricultural school you went to an educational institution?"

"Okay, okay, Grade, we're not talkin' about schools. You asked why I want to get married, so I'm trying to tell you."

"Sorry, you're right. I wanna know how to avoid that trap, so tell me the early symptoms."

"Aw, Grade, you won't feel that way when you find the right lady. She'll change your whole perspective about livin'."

"You call stayin' with one woman livin'? I call that boring!"

Evans shook his head. "You'll see. I just hope it happens soon. I don't want you wanderin' like some do, searchin' for somethin' all your life but never findin' it. Like your ideas about making money. You got it all figured, but let me ask one question: What is it you're working for? What is it you wanna buy that will make it all worthwhile?"

Grady had to think about that. What was it he really wanted to achieve? "Aw, hell, Ev, that's too far off. I'm just thinkin' about gettin' outta 'Nam; forget ten years from now!"

"See! See! You said it! You figure it's gonna take years to make it. Well, let me tell you, buddy, I got it all now. I'm gonna go home and marry Helen and have kids and have friends and laugh and play and love. . . . That's livin', Grady. That's what it's all about."

"I don't know. I'm not convinced. Hell, I can have fun at school and travel, seein' the country, experiencing new things and doing the things I wanna do."

"Sure you can, Grade, but who you gonna turn to and say, 'Isn't this a neat place. Hey, look at the Grand Canyon, isn't it somethin'?' Who, Grade? You'll be talkin' to yourself; is that what you want?"

"You know, Evans, your mind is warped. All you got on your mind is that woman."

Evans laughed. "You're right, buddy, and it's great!"

Grady shook his head. *That dumb hick. So simple—got it all figured. Except life is just not that simple. It can't be. It just can't be.*

Grady stopped at the edge of the hill. A light breeze brushed his painted face as he took off his heavy pack and rolled his shoulders back to relax. Before him the South China Sea's light wind was slowly pushing back the gray curtain of fog, revealing a small base camp and the sleeping port city of Nha Trang. Behind him the mist would linger in the greens and blues of the rice fields, foothills, and mountains.

The barbed wire and scarred earth of a perimeter fence confined a series of military posts and bases on the outskirts of the city. Everything within the wire seemed so colorless and temporary compared to the looming mountains to the east and the endless sea to the west. His own base camp consisted of low buildings of wood and corrugated steel sitting in regimental rows strung together by drooping electrical wires. Beyond the camps were the rusted and sheet-metal and clapboard shacks of the brothels and bars. Still farther away was the city and its white sand beach lined with royal palms, French châteaus, and elegant restaurants. They were all blemished by war.

The beach stank with raw sewage, and the palms were used as telephone poles. The châteaus were used as military headquarters, and the restaurant windows were covered with chicken wire and sandbagged.

The sergeant turned and looked at the mountains. Within their majesty was his war, the war few knew. No wire fences, trenches, or sandbags, only the battle of stealth and patience.

A faint sound caused the sergeant to shift his gaze north toward a sprawling air base. A small L-19 spotter plane lifted from the runway effortlessly, gaining altitude. Grady knew who rode in the plane's backseat: Lieutenant Bud Sikes, his platoon leader. Within thirty minutes Sikes would guide their helicopter to a small landing zone in the mountains.

The plane banked west and turned golden orange as the sun was reflected off the fusilage. The sergeant dropped his gaze to the unusual boulder hills just past the airfield. Nestled among them were the Quonset huts of the field hospital.

A slapping noise, almost like gunshots, caused Grady to look up. An olive-drab Huey was making its landing descent. He quickly looked back at his five waiting team members.

"Take off your damn boonie hat, Meeks!" he yelled over the roar of the beating blades.

Meeks quickly pulled off his soft cloth jungle hat and stuffed it into his pant pocket.

When the helicopter landed, the six men boarded the shaking, whining machine, and within seconds the engine screamed louder and lifted them up and away.

The helicopter circled a small hill two thousand feet below. Grady pointed the hill out to Meeks. "We're over the check point. From here, the bird dog will see us and guide the chopper into the LZ. When the bird drops to low level, get your ruck on and get ready."

A minute passed before the helicopter suddenly banked right and began a rapid, steep descent. Meek's stomach fluttered frantically, and he forced his eyes to close.

The Huey picked up air speed as it dropped—one thousand, nine hundred, eight hundred—the pilot watched the altimeter numbers roll—six hundred, five-fifty, five hundred . . . the vibrant jungle below seemed to wait in anticipation—three hundred, two-fifty, two hundred . . .

"Steer left," came the order from spotter plane overhead.

The pilot responded immediately, then glanced down at his air speed, ninety knots. He pulled the chopper's nose up slightly, clearing tree branches by only a few feet.

"On course."

Sergeant Grady rose to his knees and looked toward the front of the speeding aircraft. The co-pilot turned toward him, his dark visor reflecting the sergeant's green-black face. He raised his gloved hand, holding up two fingers. Grady nodded, shot his thumb up in acknowledgment of the two-minute warning, and then yelled over the engine noise to the others: "Two Mikes!"

Grady put on his seventy-five-pound ruck, then scooted out to the edge of the chopper. The wind tore at his legs as he positioned them over the side.

The pilot spoke through his helmet's small gray transmitter to the two door gunners behind the passengers. The gunners responded by grasping their mounted M-60 machine guns.

"Two klicks out," came Sikes's voice over the radio from the spotter plane.

The pilot shifted in his seat. Two thousand meters away was a small landing zone he wouldn't see until he was on top of it. The landing would require his every skill; he had to get the bird in and out quickly.

"One thousand meters."

The pilot squared his shoulders and took a deep breath. The door gunners swung the 60s to the front, pulling back the gun-charging handles.

". . . Five hundred . . . two-fifty . . ."

The aviator's right hand eased back on the cyclical control stick while his left hand pushed gently on the collective control. His eyes searched for the opening.

". . . one hundred . . ."

The tail began dropping in a flare. Grady scooted out over the edge, his feet touching the skids. He held his rifle in front of him with one hand while holding on to the lip of the helicopter with the other. He was looking for the landing zone. He'd have to make the decision whether to jump, depending on obstacles or uneven ground. The other team members scooted out and stood on the skids, ready.

"LZ your one o'clock."

"I got it. Going in."

The helicopter dropped quickly. Grady sighed. The LZ was a good one. The bird had settled within three feet of the windblown, waist-high elephant grass when Grady jumped into the stalks at a full run. The others followed. Within seconds the unburdened helicopter was gone.

Grady ran for the treeline, twenty yards away. The high grass was thick and hot. His running turned to wading. The swooshing, crackling sound behind him told him the others were following. Breathless, he reached the first trees and fell heavily to the soft ground. His knees hit and sank, the weight and forward momentum of the rucksack pushing his chest down heavily.

He spun around as the others ran past and fell close to him, forming a small circle with their feet inside and their bodies and weapons facing out. He couldn't see anything but the grass, but seeing didn't matter. He wasn't looking, he was listening.

Helicopter sound is a strange phenomenon. In dense vegetation one can hear a chopper but can't tell its direction unless the chopper comes directly overhead. The lower the bird comes in, the harder it is to tell the direction. The landing is crucial. If it takes more than seconds, one can detect, even at a great distance, differences in noise pitch and recognize a landing in progress.

Grady knew this landing had been perfect. No one, unless he was very close, would know they had landed. That's why they listened. If anyone was near, he'd come to investigate. They'd wait ten minutes, completely still.

Sox, the radio operator, whispered into his radio handset to the communications site, "X-ray, this is Double-Deuce. How you hear me? Over."

"This is X-ray. We have you Lima Charlie. Over."

"This is Double-Deuce. I got you same same. Out."

Lieutenant Sikes then called from the bird dog, "Double-Deuce, this is Two-Zero. Good huntin'. I'm gone. Charlie Mike, out."

Sox gave Grady a thumbs-up. The sergeant nodded, understanding he had good commo—communications. Sox had been a radio operator for five months. He was good at it. He'd picked up the radio lingo early. His team's call sign, Double-Deuce, never changed: It was a tradition. Two-Zero was his platoon leader, Lieutenant Sikes. He'd be flying in a circle a mile or so away after the insertion to make sure they had communications with X-ray. If they didn't they would have had to be pulled out.

A team can't survive without the radio—that's what Grady had told him, so that meant they couldn't survive without Sox. *There it is,* he thought. He smiled to himself; he had the radio lingo down pat. *Lima Charlie* meant loud and clear, *Charlie Mike* meant continue the mission.

The rustling of his sergeant getting to his feet snapped him out of his thoughts.

Grady took off his rucksack and glanced over at Meeks, who was lying beside Ben, watching, just as he'd been taught. *Good,* Grady thought, *maybe he has the instincts. If he's got those, then . . .* He shook his head and took out his map. The trail they were to watch was three klicks to the west. He knew the hard part would be getting there: Moving through brush was always dangerous. It meant making noise. Noise is what gave them away and got them killed. He pulled out his compass, which was wrapped with parachute cord, a "dummy cord," and tied to the buttonhole of his shirt-pocket flap. Every important item of his equipment was similarly tied to his person. One glance at the compass confirmed his map bearing. He reoriented the map, placing the compass straight edge along the grid lines superimposed on the map. Looking at his map, he knew the terrain would slowly descend and abruptly drop off into a large valley about a thousand meters away. They would move west and eventually run into the large, well-used trail that paralleled a river.

He refolded the map, checked the time, and leaned back.

A branch snapped. Every head and weapon turned toward the sound. Another branch cracked. Grady gently pushed off the safety and lowered his head. The sound was moving closer.

Rock raised his M-16 and peered around the tree he lay behind. The sound was moving directly in front of him and coming closer, but he couldn't see anything through the dense foliage. He lowered his rifle and looked over the barrel, straining his ears. Leaves rustled; the sound was moving closer. Rock moved slightly to the right and froze. The tall grass fifteen feet away fell toward him and a huge black boar lumbered out. Rock released the trigger and let out a gasp of air, then turned toward Grady and mouthed a word.

Grady looked at him questioningly. The others all relaxed, seeing his reaction but still not understanding. Rock looked back at the boar. Veering right, the animal walked within ten feet of Rock, who lay watching, spellbound by its size. Suddenly the pig dug its front feet in and raised its snout, sniffing the air, then shot its head toward Rock's position.

The others now saw the animal. It had massive shoulders and short legs. The black bristly hair was sparse and practically nonexistent across the shoulders and at the top of its head, where lay exposed gray skin scarred from countless battles. The eight-inch tusks protruding from its lower jaw were dirty yellow and brown-tipped. The right ear was mangled and flopped over.

The boar stepped closer. Rock, not sure what to do, looked at the others pleadingly. He glanced back at the boar and waved his hand as if shooing off a pest. The boar charged.

Rock could only open his eyes wider and throw himself behind his rucksack. The boar followed the startled soldier's movement and struck with a furious blow, jerking its head up and ripping the pack with its tusks.

Rock got to his knees and lunged, swinging the butt of his rifle. It struck the hog's head with a dull crack but moved the head only slightly.

Rock's forward momentum carried him to a prone position. The boar grunted and lowered its head for the finishing assault. Rock stared with horror into the boar's dark, expressionless eyes. He knew he was about to die.

Suddenly the animal fell to its front knees and squealed in pain, then, shaking its head violently, rose again.

Grady had pulled his pistol and screwed in the silencer. His quickly aimed shot hit the boar just behind the mangled ear.

The boar grunted hideously and now faced Grady, who stepped closer to shoot again. The boar lowered its head and attacked. Grady stood his ground and fired. The boar stumbled but kept his balance and threw itself at the standing soldier.

Grady jumped clear of the slashing tusks, but he was struck by the massive shoulders and knocked to the ground. The boar spun around, frothing, and charged again, but suddenly its front legs seemed to freeze and its three-hundred-pound body tumbled forward, rolling onto Grady's kicking feet. The dying animal raised its head to slash his victim but fell short. It shook spasmodically, then lay still.

Ben grabbed Grady and pulled him free. Grady stood weakly and, with a shaking hand, replaced his pistol. Failing, he let his hand fall to his side.

Rock bent over the boar, inspecting the tusks, then looked up at Grady and whispered, "Thanks, Grade. I thought I'd bought it for sure. These tusks will make a great necklace, huh?"

Grady's eyes widened as he shook with rage. He reached down and grabbed Rock's shirt and jerked him up to eye level. His raspy whisper came out in a spit. "*Necklace?* That thing almost killed you, and you want . . ." Grady's eyes slowly closed and he released his grip.

Rock stared into his sergeant's face, realizing Grady had been shaking in fear not for himself but for him, Rock. That was the way Grady was. He cared.

"I'm sorry, Grade, I just . . ."

Grady stepped back and took a deep breath. He looked at Rock and cracked a small smile.

"Don't you ever wave at another pig, or I swear I'll wring your neck with your new necklace."

Rock grinned and pulled his knife. "Grade, you want his tail?"

3

Rodriguez signaled for the team to stop and get down. He moved forward slowly and dropped to one knee. He was looking down into a deep valley of green hues. It was beautiful . . . and ominous. He beckoned to Grady to join him.

"Damn, I knew it dropped off," Grady said, "but . . ." He reached for his map as he looked down the seventy-five-foot sheer rock wall. *I see what happened,* he thought. *We drifted left.* Satisfied, he refolded the map and whispered, "Pancho, move south along the rim. We should hit a ridge up ahead that will take us down."

"Grade, we gonna take a break, no?"

Grady hadn't thought of it, but he knew the Puerto Rican was telling him they needed one. He winked. "Yeah." Smiling, Rodriguez signaled to the others to take five.

Grady sat down and watched as Rodriguez slipped off his rucksack and rummaged through one of its pockets. Seconds later he pulled out a Tootsie Pop. *Where'd he get that?* Grady wondered. *Got to be from his mama. She sends him more junk . . .* Grady smiled.

Pancho had been on the team now for almost six months. He and Ben had come in almost at the same time, he recalled. Rodriguez was from New York; his home was on the third floor of a crowded Brooklyn tenement. His features were like those of a woman, unblemished and soft, but he had a wiry, hardened body that moved like a cat's.

Rodriguez looked at Grady and motioned toward the white stick protruding from his mouth. "You want one, man?"

Grady shook his head with a smile. Just then Grady detected a movement out of the corner of his eye and instinctively turned his head. Ben was kneeling to adjust the sling on his M-60 machine gun. That gun and a small Bible wrapped in plastic were the huge black soldier's most prized possessions.

Grady checked his own weapon, a short-barreled Colt Commando Assault Rifle, known as a CAR-15. When he was handed the rifle ten months earlier, he had immediately known it was for him. There was a strange feeling he had every time he touched the weapon. It was like it became a part of him. He slipped his other weapon, his customized 9mm Browning Hi-power—the P-35—out of the specially made left-shoulder holster. The P-35, too, was special. He and Evans had each ordered one. Its extended, modified barrel allowed for a small cylindrical silencer to be screwed on in seconds. The holster held the silencer in a kid-glove compartment sewed to the outside. Grady pushed the clip release. The thirteen-round clip fell into his hand. He quickly inspected the green-tipped bullets. They, like the weapon, were special. They were subsonic, loaded to ensure they didn't exceed 1,088 feet per second. Bullets that exceed 1,088 feet break the sound barrier and give a telltale crack. These were quiet. Grady slid the clip back in and replaced the weapon in his holster.

He rose and checked his men. They were ready. He motioned toward Rodriguez, who nodded and turned south.

They heard it before they saw it. The rushing water fell fifteen feet before crashing onto huge glistening boulders that smoked with a thin cloud of mist. Miniature rainbows appeared in the wet cloud. Rodriguez stopped near the pool and dropped to one knee. It had been a tough hour of moving since their last break. His fatigues were soaked with sweat. He motioned to Grady to come forward. Rodriguez's camouflage-painted face was streaked. Grady knelt beside him. He didn't have to whisper; the crashing water made it difficult even to talk normally. "We'll take fifteen and give everybody a chance to cool off."

The water was clear and cool. Grady moved to the far side of the pool and stood guard while the others refilled their canteens and dipped their faces.

They had found the ridge, but the vegetation was thick and made their descent unbearably slow and laborious. On his map he had seen a blue line depicting a stream farther to the south. He'd directed Rodriguez toward it, hoping it would be easier traveling along its banks. His decision had been a good one. The stream led to a succession of pools. It was as if a giant hand had cut huge stairsteps out of the rock. The water poured from one step to the other. It was just what Grady had hoped for. The sound of running water would cover their movement. They would now have the advantage: the dinks wouldn't hear them.

Meeks stood from where he had been filling his canteen and carefully moved around the pool toward him. The M-79 seemed ridiculously small for him. He held it in one hand easily. The 79 was a small but lethal single-shot, breech-loading weapon that fired 40mm spin-stabilized grenades with a bursting radius of about five meters. The launcher also fired other types of rounds: high explosive, smoke, signal, gas, and buckshot. Greg Bartlett had always preferred the buckshot round when they moved, Grady remembered . . . he . . .

Meeks knelt beside Grady. "I'll spell you."

Grady nodded and began moving to the water. He stopped. "What round you got in it?" He motioned toward the 79.

Meeks raised his eyebrows slightly, and replied, almost as if he had been insulted: "Buck."

Grady turned toward the pool without speaking.

As they neared the valley's floor, the green canopy above became more dense while the ground became more open. The forest of sheer teak and mahogany trunks soared upward for a hundred feet, while around them thick woody vines twisted, attaching themselves with ugly tendrils, climbing always upward in the never-ending struggle for light. The stream broadened and became slow-moving and tranquil on its meandering trek to the river. Only a few tenacious rays of light penetrated the thick latticework above, and the small gold spots they made on the earth seemed to smoke as notes of dust rose upward and were softly illuminated. The dank smell of damp, rotting organic life was pungent and seemed heavy in their lungs. A pair of iridescent butterflies fluttered in front of Rodriguez as he waded carefully through the pebble-strewn stream. The sudden absence of sound was unnerving. They had become used to the gurgling, laughing water that rushed over the rocks from pool to pool.

The stream widened further. Ten meters ahead it veered left and its banks became steeper. Rodriguez raised his hand slowly. The team froze. He moved forward, hugging the near bank at a half crouch. His eyes saw it all in one glance: the bamboo poles stuck in the bank, the strategically placed flat rocks, the lighter-colored, packed clay: the trail.

Grady led. They moved confidently yet quietly. They had backed up fifty meters down the stream, then struck north. He was looking for a place to set up a patrol base. The root systems of the huge trees were above ground there. The roots looked like fins on the base of a rocket, but they snaked and twisted, rising as high as fifteen feet.

Grady stopped and pointed to a large tree directly in front of him. The huge roots that soared from it formed a *V* with one side curving back, almost creating an enclosed room out of the open area in the middle. Within its confines they formed a tight circle and lay down, listening. Five minutes passed before Grady rose and took off his ruck.

"Looks good here. We'll break up into three teams. Me and Meeks'll take first watch; Rock and Pancho, second; Ben and Sox, third. One-hour shifts. If we gotta run, the rally point is the base of the stream, where it meets the valley floor. Me and Meeks'll go out first. Sox, get a commo check."

While he waited for Sox to whisper into the handset, he noticed Meeks open the breech of his 79 and take out the flat-nosed canister shell of buckshot, then replace it with a long gray round—gas. I'll be damned, Grady thought, and nodded as the big man snapped the breech shut. Only old vets would have thought of gas. It was the right round to select; if they were seen and had to run, tear gas would slow and disorient the dinks and temporarily put up a smoke screen. Grady then turned toward Sox who held his thumb up. He'd made contact with X-ray.

Grady crawled out of the root enclosure with the cherry following. They went only twenty feet and stopped. Grady was satisfied with what he could see. The ground on which they lay was on a small ridge. The little bit of elevation gave them a good view of the trail only thirty meters away. There were several large ferns next to a low fin root that they could hide behind comfortably.

Grady reached out and carefully broke two lower branches off a plant in front of him to get a better field of vision. He then placed his CAR close to his body and mentally pictured grasping it quickly. Meeks watched as his sergeant placed two M-26 grenades and one smoke grenade in front of himself and straightened the pull pins. Meeks reached down for his own grenades, but Grady's touch stopped him. "If we're compromised, I throw these, and you shoot the gas, then we *di di*."

Meeks looked at him strangely. "*Di di*?" he whispered.

Grady nodded. "It's Vietnamese for *hat up, split, make tracks, sky*."

Time passed slowly. Grady glanced at his watch again, surprised. It was only six minutes later than the last time he'd checked. He looked at Meeks, who was staring out toward the trail, lost in thought. Meeks had replaced Barlett just as his dad had replaced his mother only eight months after her death. He could still see them walking into the house with their arms around each other and his Dad saying, "David, I want you to meet your new mother." *Jesus,* Grady thought, *you can't replace people you love like some broken china cup. You just can't. Didn't he—*

Grady tensed. He'd heard a faint sound. He pushed himself closer to the ground and waited.

Ten seconds passed before the NVA, North Vietnamese Army regulars, came into view. They were walking quickly and talking. The first one laughed, then the others did too. He counted five men wearing faded green uniforms with pith helmets. They all had packs and carried weapons. His chest suddenly became tight. For a split second he panicked, then he realized he had instinctively stopped breathing. He let the air out slowly and was about to tap Meeks when another group appeared, moving the same way, north to south. Their faces were stern. By their perspiration-soaked shirts he figured they had been moving hard. This time there were eight men, three with cloth rice tubes tied diagonally across their chests. The third soldier was an officer. He wore his K-54 pistol high on his hip. As they passed, Grady studied their packs, looking for mortar rounds. None of them carried any. They disappeared down the bank into the stream.

He leaned over to Meeks. "That was the enemy."

Meeks whispered calmly, "Some wore red epaulets. Were they officers or NCOs?"

Grady was surprised. He thought the cherry would be beside himself with excitement. Instead, Meeks had placidly asked about the damned red epaulets.

"The red tabs on the collars don't mean anything. It's the rank on them that counts. The second bunch had an officer or a high-ranking NCO; you could tell by the pistol he was carrying."

"What were those canvas rolls across their chests?"

"Rice tubes. They tie an end off and fill it with rice, then tie the other and sling it over their chests so the whole thing won't interfere with carrying their packs."

"Why didn't they all wear the same uniform?"

"They ain't got supply rooms like us. You'll see them wear everything, but on regulars you'll mostly see that mustard-green or gray shirt, and for pants, khaki, gray, green, and black pajamas. They wear sandals or sometimes Chicom tennis shoe–type boots, and on their heads, pith helmets or boonie hats like ours. In this group they were all carrying AK-47s."

Grady leaned back. Not bad, he thought. The cherry asked good questions—not bad at—

Another group was aproaching. Like the first bunch, they were talking. Suddenly their point man brought his weapon up and stepped off the trail, walking directly toward Grady and Meeks's position. Grady reached for his weapon. The small NVA soldier stopped and reached down and unbuttoned his pants while talking over his shoulder to the others. In a second he was directing a small yellow stream toward an unfortunate plant. Grady couldn't help smiling. When the soldier was finished, he glanced toward the trail just as the others were disappearing over the bank. He trotted off toward them, trying to button his pants and hold up his rifle as he ran.

It felt good to be back at his ruck and the protection of the "root room." Grady crawled to the radio and pushed in the bar on the side of the handset. "X-ray, this is Double-Deuce, over."

"This is X-ray. Over."

"Message follows."

"Send it. Over."

"Observed three separate units of five, eight, and five NVA moving north to south, location XJ869246. Time"—he looked at his watch—"fourteen-thirty hours. They were carrying AK-47s and packs."

"Roger, Double-Deuce, got a good copy, out."

Grady felt tired. He moved to his ruck and lay back.

Meeks watched as the sergeant relaxed. Grady reminded him of his brother. They would have been the same age. He wondered if Robby had been a leader like Grady. He looked down at his weapon, then shut his eyes, reflecting.

Kenneth Meeks and his one-year-older brother, Robby, were born and reared in the sleepy town of Herndon, Pennsylvania, on the banks of the Susquehanna. His father, Robert senior, was the owner of the one-car showroom Ford dealership on Main, and his mother, Claire, taught second grade at Herndon Elementary.

Kenny and Robby were inseparable. They could always be found hunting and playing together along the muddy river banks or in the forest behind their home. Many a night Claire would pace the worn linoleum kitchen floor, waiting for her boys to return for supper. Robert would put his arm around her and lead her to the table, telling her not to worry, because they had the two best woodsmen in the country in those boys.

When Kenny turned twelve, The Competition, as it came to be known, began. The two boys were on their way home from gigging frogs one evening when Robby stopped and eyed his brother.

"I'll race ya to the house."

Kenny looked up and shrugged his shoulders. "It's too far, Rob."

But when he'd passed his brother, he broke into a dead run. "You're on, pantywaist!"

Robby won that day, but not easily. Soon they were challenging each other to more tests of endurance and strength. Claire was at first concerned, as her boys returned battered and scratched from their grueling runs, but her concern dissolved with their laughter. The Competition drove them even closer.

Time passed quickly. The awkward years were gone. The boys grew into young men and became known as the Meeks Freaks. Their workout regime, running and lifting weights, would last two to three hours a day, each brother always pushing the other to his limits. Their Spartan training program developed their bodies to Herculean proportions. The Meeks Freaks led the Herndon Panthers to the state high school football championship during Kenny's junior year. The Harrisburg paper described the win in banner headlines as HERNDON'S MEEKS FREAKS STREAK!

Robby graduated and went to Penn State on a full athletic scholarship. The following year Kenny was the most sought-after high school fullback in the state, and when he graduated, he also selected Penn State. Rob was hurt his sophomore year. A knee injury ended his football career and his schooling, because, being unable to play, he lost interest in everything, including his studies. Rather than flunk out and be drafted, Rob joined the Army.

Kenny, in his sophomore year, won the starting fullback position from the returning senior and played first team the entire season. It was clear to all spectators and sportswriters that the young, muscular fullback was destined for greatness.

In January of 1968, Kenny was home for the semester break and the holidays. He was sitting at the dinner table with his parents when the knock came. When Ken opened the door, the world stopped revolving. The beribboned, uniformed officer didn't have to speak. Kenny knew Robby was dead.

He walked the snow-covered forest trails for two days after receiving the news. Then, returning home at dusk the second day, he stopped at a fork in the trail. It was the spot where as boys they would begin their race for home. As he shut his eyes to hold back the tears he suddenly heard laughter, at first faint but steadily growing louder. The laughter was of two boys running, falling, yelling at each other. It was the laughter of years of playing and hunting in their beloved forest.

Kenny found peace in the knowledge that his brother wasn't really gone. He would always be with him. As long as the trees stood and the river flowed, Robby would be there. He'd be alive in memories . . . forever.

When Kenny returned to school, he realized that the papers and the evening news now spoke of the war as a mistake. Leading politicians and movie stars were visiting North Vietnam to see American war crimes firsthand. Students and professors were eager to mouth antiwar rhetoric and recite lofty platitudes that he would not, and could not, accept, for they all concluded that his brother had died for nothing.

The anger and frustration he felt ate at him like a cancer. He loathed being around those who hid behind their college deferments, pointing their fingers and jeering at others who went when their government called.

On a warm spring afternoon he sat alone in the crowded student union, nursing a Coke. A long line of students stood behind a table of faculty and student leaders who had drafted a petition to the President. A large banner strung up behind their table proclaimed LET THEM KNOW WE DON'T SUPPORT THE WAR! Smiling coeds wearing gold T-shirts imprinted with the banner slogan moved among the tables, asking the lounging students to sign the petition. One of the girls recognized the star fullback and ran over to his table.

"Hi, Kenny. You're going to sign up for me, aren't you?" He looked up into the grinning young face, then stood.

The girl shrieked with joy, jumping up and down and yelling to the line of students, who all clapped.

The smiling girl led him for several steps before she noticed his eyes. Her smile vanished. Something was wrong: He was shaking and looked as if he was about to kill. The coed stopped, frightened, and watched as he strode past her up to the table and grabbed the petition away from the startled professor. He then turned defiantly to the shocked, openmouthed students and methodically ripped the paper to bits. There was complete silence as he glared at their faces. The last shred of the torn petition drifted to the littered floor as he walked out.

Kenny Meeks never changed his pace as he covered the eight blocks to the Army recruitment office, the same office his brother had entered a year and a half before. He knew he would break his mother's heart, but he knew, too, that he could not continue living without finding meaning for his brother's death. Robby died for something, something that Kenny Meeks was going to find.

"Hey, Sarge, it looks like we got us a hot one, huh?" The radio operator was looking over Sergeant Childs's shoulder as he plotted the information X-ray had just relayed from Grady's team.

"Yeah, Johnson, you'd better get the major."

Johnson smiled. He knew that asshole Childs was excited even though he didn't show it. He turned just as the major walked in. "The Ol' Man's here," Johnson said.

"What we got, Jerry?" Colven asked.

"It looks good, John." They'd been working together a long time, having known each other before the war. They used first names when the troops weren't around. It was an unspoken understanding. Childs pointed at the map. "Two-Two's sighted eighteen NVA, different-size groups moving south. Salazar's team watched five moving southwest from his location here." Colven moved closer to the map and looked at the locations Childs had marked.

"What do ya think, Jerry?"

"I'd say them dinks is up to no good. Look at this." He pointed at the map again. "From the sightings, the closest friendlies are here at firebase Dagger. Nothin' but two South Vietnamese companies protecting a couple of resettlement villages. I'd bet Dagger is them bastards' target."

"I'll give what we got to Corps." Colven grinned. "You know them flat peters will piss all over themselves hearing this."

"Yeah, John, I'm glad you're the one going up, not me."

Colven rolled his eyes. "Thanks, Jer, you're a big help!" He walked for the door. Seconds later Childs heard the major's booming voice: "Dove! . . . Dove, let's go!"

Rock and Pancho crawled back in excitedly. Grady looked up into Rock's wide eyes. "What we got?" Grady asked.

"Goddamn, Grady, we counted twelve. Six in each group. The first bunch was humpin' a .51-caliber machine gun, and the second was humpin' 82mm mortar rounds."

"Any officers?"

"Nope, didn't see none." Rock looked at Rodriguez, who nodded in agreement.

"Okay, I'll call it in."

Five minutes later Rock reached into the pocket of his rucksack and pulled out a green foil bag, his freeze-dried meal. The rations were fairly new. They were called Lurps, after Long Range Reconnaissance Patrol. He sat back on his ruck and meticulously arranged them in a neat row. First the foil bag with the freeze-dried food, then a white plastic spoon, two cornflake bars, the toilet paper, matches, coffee, cream, sugar, and Stimudents. He took out his canteen and reached into the right ruck pocket again for his bottle of Tabasco sauce.

He carefully tore the top off the foil bag and pulled out the inner plastic pack of freeze-dried beef and rice. He then unscrewed his canteen top and poured water into the bag. He raised the concoction to eye level and checked the mix. "More water," he said to himself and added a few drops. When he was satisfied, he carefully closed the bag, put it inside his shirt on his stomach, and lay back. The food would be really great if he could boil some water to heat it up, but no fires were allowed. He'd just have to let body heat do the work. The others were doing the same—eating and getting ready for the night. He looked up. Not much light left. He'd just have time to eat and lay everything out. Everything had to be positioned where he could touch it. Rock pulled the bag from his shirt and sat up. Three shakes of Tabasco, now just a little more stirring. He filled the spoon with the mush and lifted it carefully toward his mouth.

Grady glanced over and shook his head: What a character Rock was.

"Rock Steady, Sarge, that's my name," Grady remembered him saying nine months before when he'd first introduced himself.

"No, what's your real name?"

The hawk-faced soldier quickly glanced around, "It's . . . it's . . . Friedrich Heinemann," he said softly.

Grady had heard about Heinemann; he was a cocky loudmouth. The other team sergeants from the First Platoon had passed him around from team to team and finally pushed him off on the new sergeant in the Second Platoon. Heinemann talked like a used-car salesman, and walked as if he were disjointed: His arms and legs didn't seem to move in sync. But Grady liked him at once. Something about the young, awkward-looking kid appealed to him. His tailored camouflage fatigues fit him snugly, which accented his thinness. His brown eyes seemed unusually large and didn't fit his jaunty air. His face hadn't a wrinkle, but scattered pimples always seemed to be present. Rock Steady was unique in more than his appearance. He was an expert in everything: All you had to do was ask him. At first it had taken every ounce of Grady's resolve not to laugh when the ungainly soldier started his authoritative tirades, but with time Grady got used to them. That was Rock.

Grady looked over at the young soldier affectionately. Rock was lying with his eyes closed, but his hand was stroking the reassuring metal and plastic of his M-16. *A good Ranger,* Grady thought. *One of the best.*

4

Grady heard faint whispering and opened his eyes. He could barely make out the shape of giant tree trunks in the dark gray morning light. As he sat up slowly his damp poncho liner fell from his chest to his lap. Sox was talking almost inaudibly into the radio handset. In civilian life his friends probably called William S. Kaplan, Bill. His Jewish father and Greek mother had made a mistake in giving him Socrates for a middle name. Rock had started calling him Socrates, but Rodriguez couldn't pronounce it and shortened the name to Sox.

Kaplan had been drafted and was a self-proclaimed hippie from San Francisco. He had become an integral part of the team although he was only nineteen, and he was considered one of the best radiomen in the company. He had the ability to memorize countless radio frequencies and call signs with ease. He had an almost photographic memory, and this, combined with his unflappability, made him a perfect RTO.

Sox had made contact with the X-ray site and gotten a message from Colven to Charlie Mike.

Thirty minutes later Grady and Meeks lay in their reconnaissance position. Grady was pulling out his grenades when he heard voices coming from up the trail. Meeks glanced at him quickly, confirming he'd heard the voices too. Within seconds NVA soldiers appeared. The first two were like the others they'd seen, with AK-47s and regular green uniforms, although they wore cloth jungle hats instead of pith helmets.

The others were different. There were six of them, all stripped except for floppy boxer shorts. They were pushing antique-looking bicycles loaded down with equipment. Grady could see their small, sinewy muscles strain as they pushed their enormous loads. The bikes had large tires and the frames were reinforced with fitted bamboo poles. One long pole was tied to each of the handlebars, extending out to the right and providing a handhold to push the bike more easily along the trail. Each load had been balanced and tied on with strips of tire inner tube. Grady could see the base plates of several mortars and the telltale cylindrical brown cardboard tubes of mortar rounds tied to several of the bikes as they passed. The other bikes held large reddish-brown rusted ten-gallon cans. Following the bikes was a short NVA sergeant holding a walking stick. He seemed to be barking out short singsong commands to no one in particular. The first two NVAs disappeared over the bank. The others slowed, then stopped. From the sound of the voices from the stream, it was obvious they were having difficulty negotiating the far bank. The NCO walked past the others and disappeared from view. Then he reappeared on the bank and yelled at the remaining men, who immediately laid their bikes down and jogged down into the creek.

Grady could visualize the men helping push one bike at a time up the steep bank. The sergeant would be on the far side with his hands on his hips, watching and yelling. *Lifers*, he thought. *They're the same in every army.* One at a time the men came back and picked up the remaining bikes and pushed them down the bank. Grady lowered his head in thought. *It's big. Hell, they're carrying lots of gear and they're all going in the same direction. It's gotta be preparation for an attack somewhere. . . . But where?*

"That's it!" Childs said to nobody as he read the message from X-ray. Johnson, the radio operator, looked at the sergeant, thinking he'd been spoken to.

"Say what? Sarge," Childs looked up with his famous I-wasn't-talkin'-to-you-shithead looks, then back to the message. *Asshole!* thought Johnson as he turned back toward the radio. Childs picked up the phone handset and rung the crank several times.

"Rhoads? . . . Yeah, this is Childs. Get me the Ol' Man. . . . Chow? Well, go get him! Tell 'im Two-Two confirmed size. . . . Yeah, confirmed. . . . Oh, shit, Rhoads! Never fuckin' mind, just get him—*now!*" Johnson smiled to himself as the sergeant slammed the handset back and mumbled, "Goddamn hippies, can't take simple messages . . . can't do a fuckin' thing!"

The small old Vietnamese man held his ground and looked directly into the eyes of the irate blond GI.

"You cheap Charlie! You pay *ti ti* mon-nay for chi-kans."

"Look, we got a deal, old man!" Dove shook his finger in his rage.

"You cheap Charlie!"

"I protect your goddamn chickens and pigs, don't I? Nobody steals your animals, do they? Don't I pay you what we agreed?"

The old man squinted and shook his head. "You make bucoo mon-nay and give ol' Han"—he gestured to himself—"*Ti ti* mon-nay. Cheap Charlie! Cheap Charlie!"

"Okay . . . okay, forget it! I won't buy any more of your lousy *chi-kans!*"

The old man folded his arms. "No chi-kans, no sew girls."

"Now, wait a minute, that's blackmail. It's unfair. Understand, you ol' pirate? Unfair!"

"No chi-kans, no sew girls!"

Dove stepped back to collect his thoughts. *This old bastard controls the KPs for the mess hall, he's hired more girls than he needs, and the excess he uses as my sew girls to make my NVA flags. The bastard is gettin' paid to pay the girls for KP, which he doesn't, and he probably only pays them fifty cents of the dollar-ten I pay per flag. Plus, I buy his damn skinny chickens, which I pay to have guarded! Why, that son of a bitch . . . !*

"Okay, twenty-five cents more per chicken."

The old man yawned, showing his few brown teeth, then shook his head. "Seventy-five cent!"

"Damn you! Fifty cents."

"Seventy-five cent."

"Okay, seventy-five cents, but damnit, feed 'em more, will ya? They don't bleed enough to spot ten flags!"

Colven walked into the operations center and found Jerry Childs half smiling. Jerry Childs never smiled, at least not on purpose.

"What we got?"

Childs nodded toward the map. "Two-Two saw their mortars go by on bikes. Then a few minutes ago they called in again. They watched a slew of officers go by: One of them was a colonel."

Colven smiled. "A battalion for sure! Maybe even bigger. Jerry, tell Double-Deuce to pull back. And for God's sake, don't get compromised now."

"Go green, sir?" asked Childs.

"Yeah, go green. Now, give me all the information and I'll tell Corps."

"Two-Two, this is X-ray, over."

"Double-Deuce, go."

"Message from Hotel Bravo, over."

"Send it. Over."

"Go green. Await instructions. Do not—I say again, *do not*—become compromised. Over."

"This is Double-Deuce. Have solid copy. Out."

Sox tapped Rock, who was eating a C-ration can of peaches. "Better get Grady and Thump in here quick. We got a new mission. We're goin' green."

Minutes later Grady crawled back in with Meeks and the excited Rock. The others were already packed and ready to move. Meeks crawled to his ruck and hurriedly packed. He leaned over to Ben. "What's 'go green'?"

"It means we pullin' back to a safe area. They don't wanna take any chances we might get in contact."

Grady looked over his men. They were ready. "Were gonna move slow and easy. I'll be point. . . . Let's go."

The general's eyes shifted to his operations officer, who was speaking. Colven remained silent.

"Even if it's battalion size, we still can't do anything meaningful. Sir, we're committed to our operation in the south."

The general motioned toward the map. "All right, Howie, but what do we do with the major's information?"

The G-3 sat back. "I'm afraid we can't do anything right now."

The general shook his head and slapped the chair arm. "I'll be damned: We look for those bastards endlessly, and now we've found them and can't do a damn thing?"

The corps intelligence officer, who was seated behind the general, spoke up. "What about air, Howie? Surely we can bomb them."

"It's not that simple. Look at the map. They could be any-place. It's like . . . knowing your dog has one flea. You could kill the little bastard easy if you could just find it."

The group fell silent. Major Colven knew it was not his place to speak, but . . . hell!

"Sir!" His voice rang louder than he intended. The three men's eyes immediately swung to him.

The general, seeing the major's discomfort, spoke gently. "Yes, Major, you have something to add?"

"Sir, your problem is finding the 'flea,' using the colonel's analogy. If we can find the flea—I mean, determine his exact location—then we can bring our air assets to bear."

The general leaned forward, his eyes narrowing. "Are you suggesting that you could locate them?"

"It's possible, sir."

The general turned toward his G-3. "Howie?"

"Sir, if they could do that, we could really do some damage. What have we got to lose?"

The general spoke softly. "We could lose a few brave men who got into more than they could handle." He glanced at Colven for a reaction.

Colven knew what he meant. Was the leader of the Rangers volunteering his men for a mission that was over their heads? He looked into the general's eyes. "My men are professionals. They understand the risks . . . and *I* under-stand them."

The general had no other options. "Howie, make sure the major is given all the support he requires." He rose from his chair.

The major spoke quietly, as if it were only the two of them in the room. "Sir, they're good. If anyone can, my men will."

The general put his hand on Colven's arm. "For their sake, I hope so."

Grady stopped momentarily and looked up at the cascad-ing water that crashed at his feet. He was glad they weren't climbing back up the ridge. It was easy coming down, but it would be a bitch going up. He dipped his parachute scarf into the flowing water, placing it around his neck without wringing it. He knew he couldn't laager anywhere close to the splashing water. It would cover sounds that could foretell trouble. He decided to move along the base of the ridge where it met the valley floor. The cool water trickled down his back and chest as he turned to make sure that Meeks was behind him. He was.

As they paralleled the ridge, it became increasingly steep, forming a solid rock wall. The sides of the trees next to the rock wall were covered with moss, as if splashed with light green paint. Vivid orchids hung in festoons from the branches overhead; delicate fern fronds rose up all around them. The wall curved sharply to the east in the shape of a giant 7. They followed the wall of rock, which gave way to some huge boulders that formed dark caves. On top of the boulders the jungle had formed yet another garden that stretched upward and intertwined with the branches high above. Grady stopped next to a large boulder, black with dripping water, that lay on another, which created a small outcrop. This was it.

Camp was made quickly while Rodriguez knelt twenty feet away, watching and listening. It'd be a good laager. A small pool of water was trapped in a rock bowl next to the overhang, and an escape route on the other side of the boulder led to the valley. Grady was satisfied as he motioned Pancho in.

Grady briefed the assembled team: "All right, check your food supply and let me know how you stand. We conserve from now on. Keep movement to a minimum, and be sure and check your weapons and equipment. No tellin' how long we'll be here. I'll call X-ray and try and get an estimate. One man on security at all times during daylight. Rock, make up a schedule." He looked at their faces and smiled. "It could be worse."

Sox nodded. "Really, man."

Colven stood in front of the map, holding a blue grease pencil. Lieutenant Sikes sat with Captain Rowe from the aviation battalion, and Sergeant Childs sat behind them.

"I think we all agree the dinks have to be assembling somewhere in this area," said Colven, marking a three-inch blue circle on the map. "That means Double-Deuce is closest. Two-two has got experience, but the team's too big for snoopin' and poopin'. It's gonna have to split. You agree?"

"You're right, sir," said Childs, leaning forward. "The team's too damn big now for sure, but let Grady make the call. He'll know what's gotta be done."

"You're right, Jerry. It's his call." Colven looked at the mustachioed aviator captain. "You understand how our plan is to work?"

The captain looked up at the looming major. "What you described for us to do sounds awfully hairy. We've never—at least, *I've* never—done anything like you've suggested."

Colven's eyes widened, "I'm not suggesting shit! I'm tellin' you exactly how it's to be done! I don't want any pilot to think for a second there's leeway on how I want it accomplished. There *is* only *one* way!"

The captain flushed and pushed back as far as he could in his chair. He'd heard about the major and how he liked to run the whole show. "Sir, as you know, we fly support, but we do have some say on . . ."

Colven's scar turned purple. Unnoticed by the others, Childs leaned over to the nearby table and picked up the phone handset. Colven's eyes burned holes into the captain before him. He tried to contain his anger as he spoke. He failed.

"Captain, I will disregard your last statement because you are a junior representative of your battalion."

Childs whispered into the mouthpiece of the phone.

"You are obviously not aware of Ranger tactics and therefore are a liability to this operation," Colven continued. "*You* will call your battalion commander *now* and tell him you are incapable of dealing with us and would he please see fit to come over personally—like in about *five fucking minutes*!"

Childs handed the phone over the startled captain's shoulder. "Sir, your battalion is on the line," he said it nonchalantly, trying to contain his enjoyment. He'd seen the major in action before. Colven was holding all the aces and was establishing the command arrangements so that there would be no doubt about who was working for whom.

"Sir, this is Captain Rowe. . . . Well, no, sir, I'm not through. . . . Yes, but"—his eyes shifted up to Colven—"he wants to see you, sir. . . . Well, he'd like to see you now, sir. . . . Uh . . . well, sir, he's right here. I think you'd better speak . . ."

Colven held his hand out for the handset. "Hello, Sam. . . . Yeah, it's big, Sam, real big. The big brass are playin'. I think it needs your personal attention, like the time in the toilet bowl, remember?" Colven smiled. "Yeah, Sam, I know he's young. . . ." His gaze shifted down to the captain, who quickly averted his own gaze. "Sure, I'll need Snakes. . . . Okay, Sam, out here."

The major turned to Sikes. "Call the Headhunters. Tell 'em you'll need a pilot here at sixteen-hundred hours, and tell 'em I'll need a bird tonight at nineteen-hundred hours."

Childs stood. "Want me to inform X-ray to tell Grady of the new mission?"

"No, Jerry, this is one I gotta tell Sergeant Grady myself. That's why I need the plane tonight. I don't want a radio operator tellin' my team leader his mission might not bring him or his team back."

"Two-Two, this is X-ray. Over." The handset dangled on its long, twisting black cord around Rock's neck. He lifted it off his neck to his ear.

"This is Double-Deuce. Go."

"Double-Deuce, be prepared for new mission, break. You will receive message concerning mission at approximately nineteen-forty hours tonight. Over."

"Roger, X-ray. Solid copy. Out."

Grady looked at Rock unbelievingly as he repeated the message to him. "Nineteen-forty? Are you sure?" asked Grady. "Shit! Call 'em back and confirm the time. Then, if it's for sure nineteen-forty, collect the guys' ponchos and get a lightproof hootch rigged up."

Rock understood and smiled. "Wait until I get hold of Lieutenant Sikes. I'll explain to his young ass about after-dark messages and what a pain in the ass it is to build a lightproof hootch."

Grady nodded disgustedly. "He should know better!"

Nguyen Van Hoi sat leaning up against an old teak. He was tired. They'd been moving for three days, finally arriving only minutes before to the designated assembly point. His platoon sergeant had told the squad to rest until he found out their camp location. Van Hoi took off his faded jungle hat and ran his fingers through his wet black hair, then rotated his shoulders up and back, trying to relax his muscles. His pack had eaten into his shoulders badly. This assembly point meant rest for at least a day, until the others arrived. He leaned back against the old teak again and shut his eyes. Rest, then action again. Good. He and his squad needed it. The high morale of their last successes had quickly worn off in the boredom of the base camp. He hoped his friend Tuy would be close to wherever Hoi's platoon was sent. Poor Tuy, assigned to the heavy mortars. He smiled, envisioning his small friend carrying a large, heavy tube.

Hoi opened his eyes and looked over at his squad beside him. They sat next to their packs, watching more of their battalion arrive. He instinctively looked upward, checking. It was all right. The canopy above, though not thick, was adequate to hide them from the deadly Yankee planes. This move had been a good one. Not a single time did they have to freeze in fear or hide from searching planes or helicopters. His platoon commander must have been correct when he said that the Yankees were occupied in the south. The south. Just thinking of the designation made his body tense.

It was only five months earlier that he and Tuy, with twenty-one others, had left the small camp on the border and begun their march to the south. They'd traveled the western route that many called the Ho Chi Minh Trail. It had been the second week of the trek that the B-52s' bombs fell. He remembered vividly his screaming fear as he dived to the shaking earth. Tuy had grabbed him and forced him to a nearby gully, but not before the shock wave almost took his eyes and Tuy's hearing. Others who stayed on the trail in frozen fear died horribly. Some lost their eyes like seeds popping from pods. Others' ears gushed crimson blood that stained the hard clay. Eight were killed and three died later.

"Corporal Hoi."

He looked up, his platoon sergeant interrupting his thoughts. "Yes, comrade?"

"We are fortunate, friend. Our camp will be here." He pointed to the area just to his left. "As soon as your squad is set up, report to Sergeant Tin next to the river, and help with the fire pits."

Hoi rose, smiling at the older man before him. "Fire pits? Hot rice tonight, comrade?"

"Yes, young Hoi, your stomach will be full tonight with warm food, but only if you and your squad hurry."

"Yes, Sergeant, right away." Hoi clapped his hands and turned to his men. "Hot rice tonight, comrades!"

The major swung out of the jeep, stretched, then looked over at Dove. "Be sure and lock it up if you're going to leave it. I'm going to be gone for an hour or so."

"I'll have it parked by the tree over there, sir. Have a good flight, and be careful, huh?"

"Yeah, I'll take care." He glanced toward the large duffel bag in the back, "You take it easy on them REMFs too."

"Aw, sir."

Colven smiled, feeling a special love for his young driver, who would be leaving him in only a month. He felt suddenly sad at the thought and walked toward the small flight-operations building.

Dove excitedly hopped from the jeep and grabbed the heavy bag.

Tonight I'm gonna do at least a couple hundred bucks, he said to himself as he hefted the bag to his shoulder. He walked ten steps. Damn! He'd forgotten to lock up the jeep. He walked back quickly.

"Long time, no see, Major."

"It has been a while, Larry." Colven reached out and shook the young first lieutenant's hand. Wine had been sitting in the makeshift lounge, waiting for the major, for ten minutes. "You know where we're going?"

The sandy-haired aviator nodded. "Yes, sir. Bud Sikes filled me in by phone earlier. Two-two, huh?"

Colven took the mesh survival vest the pilot lifted up from the floor. "Yeah, the ol' Double-Deuce has come through again."

The two men walked through the door and out onto the tarmac. A single light bulb illuminated their approach to the small plane parked only twenty feet away. Colven stepped up and stooped as he squeezed past the front seat. He took the large flight helmet off the seat and carefully sat down. The young lieutenant made a quick inspection of the tail rudder, then hopped up into his seat and buckled himself in.

It wasn't long before the plane choked, coughed, then purred with life. The red lights of the instrument panel gave off a soft glow in the dark. Colven slipped an olive-drab helmet over his head, immediately shutting out the sound of the engine. He reached up, searching, then found the black cord attached to his helmet and plugged it into the coiled cord next to the small radio panel. An immediate click sounded in his ear phones. He reached for the panel and flipped a thin toggle switch. A red light magically appeared at his fingertips. He could now easily read a dial above, that was the size of a fifty-cent piece. He turned it clockwise to INT, internal communications, and stepped on the button on the floor by his left foot.

"Larry, you got me okay?"

"Sure enough. You sound good, sir. Looks like we got a good night for it."

Colven stared through the Plexiglas window, that reflected his own shadow, into the blackness, "Yeah, looks good."

The plane began to taxi down the side runway. Colven leaned back and relaxed. It had been a long time since he'd flown in the "pit." He smiled to himself, thinking of the word. He wondered if his lieutenants called it that. He'd done many an infill during his last tour. In fact, he had invented the whole system. The plane reverberated. He could hear the muffled sound of the straining engine, then felt the slight jerk that pushed him back in his seat. They were up in seconds.

Rodriguez stood outside the poncho hootch. He stooped and ran his fingers over the seams again. "Try again, man." He whispered as he held the extra poncho ready. His job was to stand outside the poncho hootch and ensure that no light escaped during the upcoming radio transmission. None did.

They had used the back of the outcrop and had cut several poles to hold the ponchos in place. Grady and Sox sat within the small confines of the hootch. Grady had his map and code book ready, along with a pad and pencil. Sox held the red-lens flashlight.

"How much longer, Grade?"

The sergeant looked at the luminous dial on his wrist.

"About five more minutes. This one sure better be good."

"Sir, I'm not sure about this."

"It's okay. I won't say anything to anybody about the weapons."

"Sir, you understand, it's not war souvenirs that belonged to the livin'. It's from the guys that are . . . well, that are not comin' back." Dove was almost crying.

"It's all right, take it easy." The Air Force lieutenant patted the distraught soldier's back.

"Thanks, sir, it's just . . . ah, you know . . . it's tough sellin' another man's property, but it's the only way I can get the unit fund out of trouble. I was responsible for it and I lost it. Damn hootch girls!"

"I know, I know," said the lieutenant, thinking, *You dumbass, you probably lost it gambling.* "It's okay."

Dove glanced at the bag, then at the lieutenant. "Thanks again, sir, for helping me." He stooped over, quickly opened the bag, and pulled out the two AK-47 folding-stock assault rifles. He handed one to the lieutenant and lovingly ran his own hand over the other.

"You said seventy-five dollars, right?"

Dove looked up questioningly. "I thought I said eighty-five . . . but if you say seventy-five, okay, I guess."

The lieutenant put the weapon between his knees and reached for his billfold. *You did say eighty-five, you dummy,* he thought with satisfaction.

"A hundred and fifty for the two, right?"

Dove smiled in the darkness while taking the money and handing the Russian-made weapon to the eager lieutenant. "Thanks again, sir. Really."

"No sweat. I'm glad I could help," the lieutenant said quietly. He looked around, then turned and walked back into the officers' quarters.

Dove waited until he disappeared into one of the doorways. "REMF!" he said aloud, then again, more quietly: "REMF." He wished he could be there when the Air Force desk jockey found out that automatic weapons like AK-47s were not considered acceptable by the Army as war souvenirs and had to be turned in. In fact, it was illegal to have them in your possession unless authorized. Dove had that feeling he always got after a sale: It was like winning the big game in the last seconds. *I love it,* he thought. *I really love screwin' them!* He reached for his small blue notebook.

The handset crackled, "Double-Deuce, this is Devil Six. Over."

Grady's eyes widened. "Six," he said aloud. "Damn, Colven himself. It must be important!"

Sox looked at his sergeant with a Glad-it's-you-talkin'-and-not-me look.

"This is Double-Deuce. Over."

Grady began taking notes, and talking to the major in whispers. Then, when radio contact was broken, Grady reread the message he'd copied. Mission: Find the enemy assembly area. What was it the Ol' Man had said? "Find it and we'll take direct action."

Sox decoded the grid coordinates of the suspected area, and handed them to Grady. Grady looked at the small paper, remembering the other words from the major: "It's all yours. Do it your way. If you want to get smaller, we'll pick up excess later. Good luck. Good hunting, Charlie Mike. Out." Get smaller. . . . No question about that, he would have to go in light. He'd have to split the team.

The thought caused an immediate tightening of his stomach. Damn, split the team. But he knew what had to be done.

Hoi swayed in his hammock and watched the darkness turn into morning's gray light. He could easily distinguish the other hammocks around him. Those of older soldiers were covered with pieces of American parachutes. Only comrades who had been to the south had them. They said flare parachutes were plentiful if one's eyes were sharp and one had the ability to climb unhampered. The Americans were extremely wasteful people, he thought, to drop flares in such numbers by parachute. The silk material was used as mosquito netting. He hoped to go one day into the American zone and find one. It wasn't so much out of need as it was a sign of service, to be shown with pride. Didn't the commander himself and a few of the senior sergeants still use French parachute pieces acquired in the earlier revolution? Yes, and they were admired for it.

He carefully shifted his weight and put one leg on the ground, then sat up. It was a fine place. The camp stretched from the river for some five hundred meters to a small rocky hill that jutted from the valley floor. The trees were not so tall there, only fifteen or twenty meters, but their branches easily hid them from any passing plane. Many smaller trees made the area more dense, but not so thick as to impede movement. He stood and walked toward the small knoll where his friend Tuy had been assigned with the mortars. Pale blue hammocks seemed to be everywhere. Equipment stacked neatly and in orderly rows filled him with confidence as he walked. Today they would go over the plans one more time, perhaps even rehearse. Others were up and moving throughout the encampment. He would have to hurry: He would be able to spend only a few minutes with his friend before having to return to work details.

Without opening his eyes, Meeks picked off an inch-long insect that was crossing his cheek. He lowered his hand, still holding the squirming invader, applied pressure, and heard the crack and pop of its thorax and abdomen. He wiped the carnage on his pant leg and turned over. Rock was completely wrapped in his poncho liner, still sleeping. Meeks tapped the place where he thought Rock's head would be. The cocoon moved, then spoke. "Is it light?"

"Almost," Meeks whispered.

Rock slipped the poncho liner from his head. "Is it time for Cap'n Kangaroo, Big Buddy?"

"Even better: It's time for Sergeant Grady."

The team gathered under the outcrop for a mission briefing.

Grady started with a question: "Who can't swim?" They all sat dumbfounded and exchanged confused looks with one another.

Grady shook his head. "Watch my lips, dummies. Whoooo . . . caaaan't . . . swiiiim?"

They looked at each other again.

Grady frowned. "Look, I need to know whether you can swim or not. Pancho," he said, pointing, "can you swim?"

The Puerto Rican shrugged his shoulders. "They no have pools on de block."

"Ben?"

"I . . . I'm sorry, Grade, I just never learned. . . . I . . ."

Grady patted Ben's shoulder. "No sweat."

Meeks nodded. So did Rock.

Sox looked at Grady meekly. "A little, Sarge." His face brightened. "But I can hold my breath a long time."

Grady stepped back. "We're breakin' up." Each man's face showed immediate concern. "Rock, as my assistant team leader, you're in charge. You and Ben, Sox, and Pancho are going back to the LZ and hole up. Me and Meeks are gonna move up the trail a ways and try to find the dink base camp. We probably have to cross the river, so I need a swimmer. I want you all to be ready to move out in ten minutes. . . . Questions?"

Rock got up. "Now, Grade, hell, you gonna need me, man, and—"

Grady held up his hand and stared into Rock's eyes. "Rock, I'm dependin' on you to take care of the team. You're not going to have the radio, just the emergency squawker, so it's gonna be tricky. I need your experience, Buddy."

Rock nodded. He didn't like it, but he understood.

The others knew Grady well enough not to argue. He'd thought it out, as always. He knew what was best.

Grady smiled. They looked like they'd lost their best friends. "Hey, lighten up. It's a chance to get *beaucoup* body count. We'll be that much up on Two-Four."

Sox grinned, "Yeah, there it is. We'll whip up on Two-Four, man."

Ben glanced up but didn't smile. He didn't like leaving friends behind.

Grady repeated, "Ten minutes. . . . Meeks, get your ruck over here. Sox, help him change the radio over to his ruck." Grady grabbed his pack and put it down beside Meeks. "Get rid of the Claymores, bush ax, two of those canteens; just keep two, your extra HE rounds and those smokes. Keep all your gas and flares."

Sox took all the excess and began handing it to the others. Grady walked over to Ben and Rock, who were studying Rock's map. "You guys take it easy. Remember, that emergency radio only transmits. It doesn't receive."

"Yeah, Sarge." Rock's smile vanished. "You take it slow, Grade. You ain't got the Rock or big Ben here to bail your ass out. Take care of Thump too. We kinda gettin' used to him, you know?"

Ben put out his hand. "See you in a couple days, ya hear?"

Grady shook the big man's hand, then Rock's. He fought a desire to hug his skinny friend, but instead he just smiled. "Yeah, guys, a couple days."

Ben watched Grady and Thumper disappear into the jungle then sat down next to his ruck. He took out his Bible and leaned back. He knew all too well why Grady had taken

Thumper. Grady knew who could swim. They'd been to the beach with Evans's team plenty of times. His asking was just an excuse. Grady was taking Meeks because he was new. He wouldn't take Rock or him because he wouldn't chance losing another friend.

Ben shut his eyes and clutched his Bible tightly. His friend was taking an inexperienced man, reducing his own chances for survival, out of love . . . love his sergeant would never admit to.

Ben prayed for Grady's safety, and he prayed that Thumper, in some way, would win his sergeant's affection.

5

Hoi wiped the dirt from his face with his sleeve. They had just finished the last of the fire trenches. It had been easy work. The ground was softer than where they had dug the day before. The large fire-pit holes were dug twenty meters from the bank of the river. They were two meters deep and were connected by a trench only ten centimeters in depth. The trench ran all the way to the river. Hoi's men had covered the trench with bamboo and vine strips, then covered those with large banana leaves, and finally covered those with soil. The fire in the covered pit would send its smoke out through the only escape route: the trench. Holes would be poked along the route, allowing small columns of smoke to escape. By the time the smoke reached the river, it would be almost dissipated. His squad members washed their hands in the cool, silty river water. The dugout embankment was two meters high and sloped gently to the water. He jumped down the embankment and joined his men.

Minutes later they were strolling back to their camp area. It was then that he saw it, off to his left. He hadn't noticed it yesterday. It was so . . . He couldn't think of the word. The squad continued to the camp as he stopped and looked at the rock formation, fascinated. He'd never seen one like it. It comprised five huge boulders that looked like elongated bird's eggs sitting in a row. Each top tapered to a different height, the middle one rising to ten meters. As he moved closer he could see many smaller boulders covered by thick vines and moss that seemed to support the royal others. It was a natural observation point, like the small hill that lay five hundred meters to the east, where Tuy camped. He stepped yet closer, then stopped. A strange sensation came over him; then he saw the rocks form a single distinct shape. It was a dragon's back. A sleeping dragon! He backed up slowly, hoping he hadn't disturbed the creature. A chill ran through him as he turned and hurried back to his men. A few minutes later he sat in his hammock, still trembling with the odd sensation. He looked to the south but couldn't see it, his view blocked by trees and undergrowth. *It is a terrible thing for a soldier to have such childish fears,* he thought, disgusted at himself. *Tomorrow I will go back and explore the rocks and end these stupid imaginings.*

The verdant stalks swayed with the motion of the two green-faced men as they stood up. They'd been lying silent for twenty minutes, watching the trail. It was time. They moved quietly. They would stay just a few feet off the trail, following it to the south, Grady in the lead. The trail led to the river, then paralleled it to the south. They had moved a hundred meters, when Meeks stopped. Grady turned. The big man was staring down the trail, then slowly sank to his knees while motioning toward his sergeant to get down.

Grady couldn't hear or see anything. At first he stood silently, then decided he'd do it—this time. He was only partially down when the first one appeared. He quickly sank into the green-yellow jungle floor. He could see only the intricate veining of the plants in front of him, but he heard the gentle slap of rubber-tire sandals. The slapping became louder. A slight but distinct sloshing noise could also be heard: water in partially filled canteens. He pushed the sound from his mind and concentrated on the slapping noise, which by now was fading . . . fading . . . nothing. Silence. He pushed the selector back on safety.

Meeks had done well. He obviously had that intangible gift, that other sense, that marked the naturals, the hunters, the killers. He could feel the movement behind him and looked up slowly. Meeks was watching him smugly. Grady gave him a thumbs-up, then turned. As he walked, he smiled.

"Why do people buy these buckles anyway?" Pete stooped and picked up a handful of the shining objects and let them fall back into the box.

Dove didn't look up from the small notebook he was writing in. "'Cause they wanna get a piece of the action they'll never see and don't really want to."

"Huh?"

Dove looked up at the new clerk typist. "Look, Pete, REMFs don't see our war, they just read about it in *Stars & Stripes*, comic books, and war movies. They don't know what it is, and they don't want to! They don't give a damn about us grunts. They don't care, man. The Dove gives them a chance to show off, to take the easy way, just like their kind always do. . . . The easy way. . . ."

"But Sergeant Childs said the buckles weren't even the right color."

Dove laughed and got up from his bunk. "He's right! Any grunt who ever greased dinks knows they don't wear brass belt buckles. They wear a tinny-lookin' thing." The blond reached down and picked up one of the brass counterfeits. "I had these made in Hong Kong. Not bad, huh? They're like our buckles but shorter, and I had them put this star here in the middle. What a deal, man. Two thousand buckles at fourteen cents apiece."

Pete looked up stunned. "Fourteen cents! My God, Dove, you're getting ten bucks for them!"

"Yeah, ain't it great?"

Pete stared at his new friend. His expression had changed to a hurt look. "Dove, I know you were on a team until you got your second wound, so you aren't a REMF, but me, I guess I am . . . aren't I? I'm just another rear-echelon motherfucker."

Dove placed his hand on the young clerk's shoulder. "You're a grunt at heart, and you ain't no shithead, which means to me you ain't no REMF, and I know REMFs! They are a people out to get by, to skate, smoke dope, make excuses, and always—*always*—screw with us grunts. Their main mission in life is to hassle us. They don't understand what we do, and don't care. They go by rules, regulations, SOPs, and dumb orders. They just ain't in the same Army as us. You'll know a REMF by the way he treats you."

Dove picked up his green bag and started throwing buckles in. "Pete, buddy, you gonna get to go with the Dove and see how it is." He shook the bag of rattling buckles. "We gonna screw us some REMFs!"

Pete hesitated, then smiled.

Grady held up his hand. It was time to rest. He'd learned long ago that once your mind drifted to your bodyaches, you were going only half speed. He and Meeks moved away from the trail, found a large tree, and sat down behind it.

"We're gonna rest for an hour or so," said Grady checking his watch. Fourteen-hundred hours. He motioned for Meeks to hand him the radio handset.

"X-ray, this is Double-Deuce. Over," he said into the receiver.

"Double-Deuce, this is X-ray."

"This is Double-Deuce. Commo check."

"Roger, got you loud and clear. How about me? Over."

"Got you same same. We're Charlie Miking. Out."

Both men were soaked with sweat. Walking with such concentration drained a man quickly, but their senses had become fine-tuned, and they'd learned the trail. They now knew its natural sounds, the creaks of the old trees and the swishing of the bamboo, the river sounds and those of the insects and birds. Every nerve ending tingled. It was a sensation most men would never feel. It was like fear but not fear, like elation without joy, a high without a stimulus. It was a hunter that could attack unseen and unheard. They walked a tightrope on which their balance was instinct and senses. If either failed, they would fall to certain destruction.

Both men had no illusions. They knew they had a fifty-fifty chance, but neither would rather be any place else than right there, where they felt so alive. Grady relaxed as the big man next to him cuddled his M-79 closer and closed his eyes.

Grady awoke to a gentle tap. Meeks was kneeling next to him, putting on his ruck. Grady slipped his arms through the lightened pack and rose slowly. Within minutes they were walking next to the trail and river. They moved for fifteen minutes, when Meeks stopped and snapped his fingers lightly. Grady stared at the cherry who was slowly lowering himself to a kneeling position on the ground and motioning the sergeant to come close to him. Grady checked the trail, then joined his companion, who picked up a dead fern frond and dropped it in front of him. It slowly settled only inches from his knee. He looked up at the questioning face of his sergeant.

"Do you smell it?"

Grady sniffed the air. Nothing. . . . No . . . a trace—yes, it was a trace of something burning: a fire.

Meeks pointed south. "Not much wind, but that's the direction it's coming from."

"We move extra slow now," whispered Grady as he got up cautiously.

In ten minutes they'd moved only a hundred meters. The smell was more distinct. Grady held his CAR out in front of him, watching the trail and where he'd step next. They heard a sound and froze. It was a conversation in progress not thirty meters away, although neither could see the source. They sank slowly to the ground. Another noise, more distant, like chopping, could be heard behind the voices.

Grady leaned over. "I'm going to see what we got."

Meeks shook his head. "Better let me do it, Sarge. I'm not sure how to operate the radio. If something happens, you'll need to report our location."

Grady stared into the cherry's eyes. He was really saying, *I'm better at this, Sarge.* Grady smiled. He *was* better. "Confirm what we got ahead and come straight back." He pulled his 9mm pistol from his holster, unsnapped the silencer and screwed it in quickly, then handed it to Meeks. "Take it easy."

Meeks exchanged weapons and crawled forward. Grady watched him for several minutes until he disappeared into the green vegetation, then turned and got his ruck ready in case he had to pick it up in a hurry and run. He glanced at his watch: 1520. Five minutes passed. He was reaching down for his canteen when he heard the whisper. He jumped almost straight up. My God! Meeks stood in a half crouch, looking for him.

"There's five of them about forty meters straight ahead. There are more behind them and there are some to our right. They've got blue hammocks strung up between the trees."

Grady grinned. Hammocks up at midday meant one thing: They were in a camp, maybe the assembly area. He looked at his watch again. Not much time to confirm the location before dark, but they might move the next day or even that night.

"We're both going out," he whispered. "We gotta confirm numbers. Figure out if this is the main camp. You'll be lookin' for heavy weapons: .51-cal. machine guns and mortars. And try to estimate numbers of men, got it?"

Meeks nodded in acknowledgment.

"We're going to move to the river and find a spot to dump our gear. In case it gets dark before one of us gets back, the river will be easy to find at night. I'm going to call X-ray and tell 'em what we got, our plan and our location. Then we'll move."

Meeks reached for the handset as his sergeant pulled his map out to confirm their location.

"Two-Four this is Two-Zero, Pop Smoke. Over."

"Roger."

Lieutenant Sikes was three thousand feet above the green canopy. His mission was to pull Evans' 2-4 team and Salazar's 2-3 team from their AOs.

First Lieutenant Wine, the pilot, pressed the transmit button on the control stick. "I got it! One o'clock."

He banked the plane, giving his rear passenger a better view. There it was, a thin column of yellow smoke rising from a small open area.

"Two-Four, this is Two-Zero. Got ya. Stand by."

Sikes flicked the toggle switch on the radio panel, changing to the helicopter channel frequency. "Red Devil Two, this is Two-Zero. Over."

"This is Red Devil. Go."

"Take up heading one-eight-zero. I'll pick you up when you're treetop. Over."

"Roger."

One of the two lift helicopters, Red Devil Two, and two heavily armed gunships circling an abandoned ricefield at two thousand feet headed south. The pilot of Red Devil Two could feel the adrenaline flow and smiled behind his green-shaded visor as he began his descent. He loved it! He loved buzzing treetops at max speed. All he had to do was fly, and not worry where. The guy above took care of that. This was what it was all about, he thought, as he leveled off, barely avoiding the top branches of trees passing at ninety knots. Up slightly, then down, following every fold of the terrain below him. Up, right, then down. In his excitement his co-pilot was murmuring *wheee*'s and *whooo*'s at each dip and upward motion. It was a free roller-coaster ride.

"Steer right," Sikes ordered from far above the speeding helicopter. The chopper pilot moved the stick slightly, descended, then pulled back up to avoid a rock face that loomed up ahead, then descended again to the valley floor.

"On course."

He glanced quickly at his air speed and heading.

"One thousand meters."

"Hot damn, baby, here we go."

"Five hundred meters."

He could see a trace of yellow smoke ahead.

"Two hundred meters."

"Roger, I got yellow smoke my twelve o'clock." He began his flare. The bird shuddered and dropped.

The right door gunner was leaning out and quickly depressed his transmit button. "Clear right!"

The left door gunner chimed in, "Clear left!"

The co-pilot said matter-of-factly, "Here they come."

The pilot saw nothing as he concentrated on the ground in front of him and gingerly placed the skids down. The door gunner counted as the running men jumped into the quivering helicopter: ". . . Two . . . three . . . four . . . five . . . six . . . *go!*" The pilot pulled pitch. The stalking gunships that had followed the lone Slick circled once while the bird made his pickup.

Sikes flicked the toggle switch again. "Two-Three this is Two-Zero. Over."

"This is Two-Three. Go."

"Stand by for pickup. Over."

"Roger."

Grady assessed their position again. They'd climbed down the embankment and followed along the river for only fifteen meters when he had located what he was looking for: an easy place to find, even at night. A large tree had been uprooted and fallen into the water. Its twisted, gnarled roots, scoured by countless monsoons, jutted out in all directions. At the base of the trunk, near the six-foot-high bank, a small indention had been carved out by past floods, causing an overhang. It was there that Grady stored their rucks and sat down.

He spoke in a whisper. "I'll follow along the river and check out down along the bank. You see how far the camp stretches to the west, then get back here. This spot will be easy to find. If it gets too dark and you can't make it back, lay low till morning, but for God's sake, try and make it back tonight. No matter what, though, you call X-ray and tell 'em what you found. If I'm not back by tomorrow, wait until oh-seven-hundred, then take the radio and get back to the spot near the creek where we holed up before. If you hear any commotion or shots during your recon, hide quick; then, when it's safe, get back here to the radio and report in."

Meeks put his hand out. "Good luck, Grade."

Grady took his hand. "Same to you. Take my CAR: That 79 won't help you."

Meeks took the rifle and slipped over the embankment silently.

The trail ran only a few feet above Grady's head. The tree's body lay half submerged, its branches rising from the water like outstretched hands. He pulled his pistol and rose. He'd climb the bank, stay close to the trail, and see if he could skirt around the men ahead without having to get into the water. He reached out, grabbed a thick root, and pulled himself up.

Meeks moved quickly. He planned to travel about four hundred meters due west, turn south, then work back east toward the river. He felt light and powerful. The small CAR-15 felt good in his hands. And Grady had finally treated him as a team member. That meant a lot.

Grady hugged the trail for twenty-five meters. He could hear the NVA chattering among themselves. They were close. He climbed back down the embankment and followed, hugging the five-foot-high steep bank. He didn't like it there; it was too open. Nowhere to go. If one of them came to the bank, he'd be seen for sure. He moved swiftly. Ten feet. Twenty. He could hear them clearly. They were parallel to him now. Holding his pistol up toward the bank, he stepped over washed-up logs and waded through small pools of water. He continued for five more paces, then inched himself to the edge of the bank and slowly raised his head. He was looking at four five-gallon cans sitting next to some sacks filled with rice. Thirty feet away two NVAs in shorts were busily handing down wood to an unseen man in a hole. He could hear more voices in the distance.

To the left he saw a strange-looking rock formation with plenty of vegetation. If he could get there, he'd be able to get a better look at the camp. He lowered his head slowly and began moving again, staying as close to the embankment as possible. He estimated he had to move only about fifteen more yards to be parallel with the start of the boulder formation. He took another step, then heard voices coming closer. He moved quickly back under the bank overhang and shouldered his way through the roots. He pushed and twisted, falling against the cool clay bank. The roots formed a thin curtain. His boot toes stuck out so he turned them up, digging into the sand. He held his pistol at his side. He couldn't bring it up or it would protrude from the curtain.

The voices became louder and then he saw the first man, who was carrying a pole on his shoulder with large cans hanging from each end. The soldier walked down the embankment path to the water's edge. Another green-clad soldier followed with a similar pole and cans. Both men squatted to fill their vessels with water. Then the first man stood up, his pole bending with the added weight.

Grady was afraid they could hear his heart, it was pounding so loudly. He knew that if either man turned around and faced him, he'd be seen. The root curtain was too thin to hide his shape completely, so he might have to step out and kill them. He thought how he would do it. He'd drop to one knee and shoot the closest one in the head. Then the other. If they were clean shots, the soldiers wouldn't have a chance to yell. Only the falling cans would make noise.

The first man turned upriver away from Grady and climbed the embankment. The second one lost his balance as he stood and fell back, breaking his fall with his left hand. Grady tightened his grip on the pistol.

The soldier steadied himself and rose up again. He began to turn toward Grady but lowered his head and turned quickly back to the bank and started walking with short, quick steps.

Grady let out a quiet sigh of relief and slid out of the root curtain. He crawled across the path and moved in a hurry down the embankment to the spot that was parallel with the rock formation. He raised his head slowly. A large tree stood a few feet away on top of the bank. Jumping slightly, he pulled himself over the bank by holding on to the tree's gnarled roots. He crawled to the first small boulders and lay in the engulfing vegetation, that grew around them. Then he rose slowly, trying to determine how he should proceed.

The large rock formation was a few feet ahead. It ran perpendicular to the river and stretched for thirty meters. He lowered himself and began crawling for the huge rocks.

Meeks's left foot had gone to sleep. He tried to move it back and forth to stimulate the blood flow. He had been watching a khaki-uniformed NVA sergeant give a first-aid class to twenty-one seated soldiers when he had discovered that his foot wouldn't move. Now, for the moment, he was stuck.

He had followed his plan and skirted wide, then moved directly south. He had crawled up a small creek, where he found small groups of camped soldiers on both sides. He had realized at once that this was indeed the battalion assembly area. It stretched from the river to the east for at least five hundred meters.

Just to satisfy his curiosity, he crawled out of the small, heavily vegetated creek to the bank and watched the NCO give his class. Behind the sergeant, in the distance, was a knoll strewn with boulders. If it was on the map, it would be a good reference point. Meeks looked at his watch. Seventeen ten hours. He had only an hour of daylight left.

Damn vines, Grady thought. He hated them. They grabbed, pulled, stopped his every movement. He'd stayed next to the huge boulders. They were covered with a wet carpet of two-inch spongelike moss that oozed as he placed pressure on it. He had crawled halfway down the rock formation, following the base by tunneling through the damnable web of rattan and strangler figs. Now a four-inch-thick wood vine blocked his way, so he tried to squeeze under it. He got half his body through, when suddenly there was no more rock behind him. He turned and looked into a black void, a cave. The opening was small and rectangular. He put his hand inside, trying to feel how far it went. He touched nothing. He reached into his shirt pocket, took out his pen light, and directed its beam into the blackness. The cave was small and wet. It went back five yards to a rock wall that dripped with moisture. The floor descended into a round cavern five feet deep. The near wall was made of glistening clay and white, hairlike roots.

It must fill with water during the monsoons, he thought as he backed out and flicked off the light. He crawled for five more minutes and came to a gap where the last huge boulder rested against its companion, forming a rock tunnel four feet high and five feet across at the bottom. He could see light from the other side, so he crawled in and immediately sank into six inches of cove water. The water made it easy to slide the twenty feet to the far opening. A large, thick bamboo stand partially blocked his view when he got there, but what he *could* see just a few yards to his right made his body quiver with excitement: a row of SGM machine guns mounted on wheels. Behind them were mortars, which a group of soldiers were cleaning carefully with small brushes. The cardboard tubes containing the mortar rounds were stacked several feet high. Blue hammocks were strung everywhere, some with parachute cloth strung over them.

Evans, you son of a bitch, I got ya, he thought, shaking with elation. *The radio. I gotta get back—gotta let 'em know.* He began to back up slowly.

"X-ray, did you get a solid copy? Over."

"Roger, Double-Deuce, got good copy on location of NVA assembly area. Will relay to base. Over."

"Roger, X-ray. Be advised we're movin' out of the AO soonest!"

"Roger, Double-Dude—take care. Out"

He had done it! He had accomplished the mission. Grady looked toward the river. The sun was low on the horizon. Where the hell was Meeks?

He sat back against the bank under the overhang and watched the river meander by. It was so peaceful. He wished Evans were there so they could share the excitement of it all. Evans . . . the coach . . . the hick . . . the friend.

Sergeant Stanley Evans had reported to the Rangers a month after Grady. He'd been to the Ranger school at Fort Benning, then, after a fifteen-day leave, had been sent straight to 'Nam. He still had his burr haircut when he reported the first day.

Grady had taken him under his wing, and they had soon become inseparable friends, though Grady could never really understand why. Grady wanted to go back home and play playboy bachelor and finish school. That was his fondest dream. Evans, the small-town boy, only wanted to work with his old man and marry his skinny hometown girl. Grady had talked to the guy until he was blue about Evan's higher

potential. Evans was a natural. He was one of those types
that men like to be around, a man's man, tall, good-looking,
broad-shouldered, athletic, very classy yet very personable.
Not temperamental, as Grady knew he himself was, but
calm and always in complete charge. He had a presence
about him that put people at ease. And as a leader, he was
good—a real professional who asked nothing of his men that
he wouldn't do. Grady could just see him in a three-piece
pinstripe suit, at the head of a business and making real
money. Grady smiled. He just couldn't see the guy in jeans
and plaid shirt, sellin' nails in his dad's hardware store. Yet,
deep inside, Grady knew he was envious. At least Evans had
someone to go back to.

Dirt fell from the overhang and splattered lightly on
Grady's wide-brimmed jungle hat. He brought the pistol up.
A jungle boot appeared, then the light was temporarily
blocked as the big man landed on the ground in front of him.
Something was wrong! Meeks fell against Grady's chest and
pushed him against the bank. The large body smelled of
sweat and decayed plants as he pressed harder. *God, he's
squeezing me to death,* Grady thought. They touched noses.

Grady could see only one eye and could feel the heat of
Meeks's breath. One quick whisper gave the answer to
Grady's question: "Dinks."

Dirt from the bank crumbled and fell down Grady's shirt
collar as he pressed as hard as he could against the bank.
The overhang was barely large enough for one, let alone two.
God, I can't breathe. More dirt fell from above, causing a
dust cloud around his face. . . . *Oh, God . . . God.* Then he
heard them, their voices and their movement.

Grady and Meeks waited for several long minutes. The
NVA seemed to be stopping on the trail above and setting up
camp. Meeks leaned back and slowly crouched. Grady took
a full breath.

Holding up the CAR, Meeks backed up into the water.
Slowly, very slowly, he sank to his knees and then to his
stomach. Grady replaced his pistol in its holster and picked
up Thumper's ruck with the radio. He would have to leave
his own. He turned and also began backing out. *Jesus,
they're close,* he thought. He went to one knee and hefted
the pack to his head, then lay down, grasping the straps, and
backed up still farther. He glanced to his right. The bank
tapered to nothing, leaving no place to hide. They would

have to move south toward the NVA camp. He felt the tree trunk to his left as he scooted out into the water, holding the ruck up to keep it dry. The sandy bottom fell away and he went down. He grabbed for the tree, pushed his head back up, and regained his footing.

Meeks reached over Grady's shoulder and grabbed the ruck. Grady had to submerge again to allow the pack to clear his head. They moved a few more feet, then froze. They could see the tops of Vietnamese heads on the bank. It was just a matter of time! They had to go, thought Grady as he slowly started climbing over the slimy trunk of the submerged tree. Thumper followed. In waist-deep water they moved southward, crouching down with only their heads and the green ruck above water. Five feet out. Ten feet. The water got deeper. They were able to stand and bend over. Twenty feet. Grady started moving in closer to the bank. It was only partially vegetated. They had to keep moving. The place where they'd been was full of their footprints. And of course they'd left a ruck. They'd have to keep moving south and hope they could pass by the campsite. It would be too risky trying to cross the river during daylight. They moved slowly. Behind them the sun was beginning to sink behind the mountains. Grady recognized details of the near bank from that afternoon. He began to feel more confident and moved more quickly. The dug-out portion of the bank where the men had drawn water was just ahead. Grady moved closer in and covered the path while Thumper passed behind him. The constant jabbering above was unnerving.

They kept moving. Then the bank farther down disappeared. Grady remembered the map. The entire area to the south was swampland. The NVA camp stretched to the edge of the last high ground before the river turned east about two kilometers down. Damn! He turned quickly toward the sun; there was still too much light to try and cross. They'd have to hole up till nightfall. Where? He looked back north. It was the only choice they had: the rock formation.

"This is an all-air show. I've shown you the exact location and how we're gonna do it. I believe it's a sound plan and, if executed correctly, it will maximize results. I can't emphasize enough how important timing is." Colven looked directly at the Air Force forward air controller (FAC) seated in the second seat on the aisle. "Tom, your fast movers have got to be on station and know what's happening."

The pilot spoke in a deep voice: "Sir, my people are ready. The jet jocks have already been chosen, and my boss is flying up to Da Nang tonight to brief them on your plan."

Colven smiled. "Good." He then turned toward the aviation battalion's operations officer. "Anything you wanna add, Shelby?"

"I don't, John. Looks good to me."

"Okay, I can tell you're ready. Remember, timing is the key. Gentlemen, that's all I have. Lieutenant Sikes will brief you on commo freqs and checkpoint locations. Good luck and good huntin'."

He walked down the aisle to the operations room, where Childs stood waiting. "What'd you think, Jerry? Should I have added anything?"

"Naw, the dumbshit prima donnas wouldn't understand anything too technical. All they think of is pussy and killin'."

"Damn, Jerry, you ever gonna cut these aviators any slack?"

Childs stared at his major for an instant. "Yeah, the same day you do. You know I don't trust nobody but grunts, and they best be Airborne Ranger grunts."

Colven took the sergeant's arm affectionately and turned him toward the map. "Let's go over it again, Jerry, and see if we missed anything."

"Ya think they're okay?"

"Sure, Ben, you know Grade. . . . Hey, what we eatin' tonight?"

The brown face frowned. "Whacha mean, 'we'?"

Rock smiled slyly. "Now, Ben, I know you carry more food than anybody."

Sox, hearing them whisper, leaned over. "Really. I seen him pack his shit. That big dude is a walking grocery store."

"Come on, guys. I'm bigger. I need a little more fuel, that's all."

Rock tapped Sox's arm. "Whatta ya say we make a big mulligan stew tonight, 'cause Ben's providin' two Lurps"— he looked at Ben with a grin—"and we'll all kick in one."

"Two? Come on, Rock, it ain't fair."

They all reached for their food. Rodriguez, lying on the other side of Sox, saw the others reaching and did the same. Rock took out a large plastic Ziploc bag and poured in his freeze-dried meal. "Give me yours." He held his hand out toward Sox.

"Whoa, man, hold it. What'd you just put in?"

"Chicken and rice."

"Okay. That's what I got too." He handed the bag to Rock, who dumped it in.

Ben threw over two bags. "I hope you moochers is satisfied. My mama gonna hear 'bout this: You guys starvin' her big, beautiful boy."

Rock held up the two bags. "A beef and rice and a chicken and rice. Man, oh, man, this is chow. Okay, one to go. Pancho, where's your meal?"

"Oh, wow, amigo, *aquí está*." He handed Rock the bag.

Rock looked up, shocked. "Chili? No, man, we ain't mixin' up no Latino chow here. This is class!"

He pushed the bag back toward Rodriguez, and Sox nodded in agreement. "Yeah, Pancho, really. No south-of-the-border shit."

The small man shrugged his shoulders. "Wow, man, I only got chilies."

"No wonder you fart so much," said Rock in disgust as he opened the chili pack and poured it in.

Sox watched in horror. "We gonna eat that, man?"

"Sure. Gimme some water. It'll be all right if I add a little hot sauce."

"No way. No hot sauce!"

"Yeah, Sox," Ben said, "we gots to have hot sauce."

"Not on my chow!"

"You eatin' what we fixin'," said Rock. "That's the rule."

"Ah, man, what a bummer."

"What's going on?"

Childs turned toward the voice and motioned toward the wall map. "Grady found a NVA base camp. Looks like he really got one up on you."

Sergeant Stanley Evans's partially camouflaged face showed concern as he stepped closer to the map. "They get out OK?"

"Yeah, he called in the location of the camp to X-ray and said he was gonna sky up."

Evans relaxed his shoulders with a sigh of relief. "I'll bet Grade volunteered for that mission. I'm gonna have to talk to that boy."

Childs snickered, "Evans, don't give me that shit. You know you would have jumped at the chance to get one up on the double deuce."

"Oh, hell, Sarge, the two-four woulda found that camp an hour before showboat Grady!"

Hoi was trying to contain his excitement as he spoke to his squad members. They were listening and eating rice and vegetables by the quickly fading light. Earlier they'd all rehearsed their attack and cleaned their weapons. The next morning they would move into position. Hoi had just returned from a squad leaders' meeting held by his platoon commander. Hoi's squad would lead the attack. "An honor, bestowed for your hard efforts," the lieutenant had said.

Hoi told his men of the following day's schedule. "We rise at first light and pack. The platoon commander will inspect at oh-six-forty-five, and we depart at oh-seven-ten behind Third Squad. Tonight we can have small fires if we want. We also—"

A voice called from behind him. "Corporal Hoi!"

"Here, comrade."

The platoon commander and sergeant walked up. "Corporal Hoi, we have a new order. I want you to move your camp closer to the river and fire pits. The commander wants hot rice for the men tomorrow. Your squad will keep the fires going at night. I don't like doing this, Corporal, but it will not be bad duty. Only one man per shift is necessary to feed the fires and haul water for the cooks. You will still have time to sleep if you organize properly."

Hoi stood. "Yes, comrade. My squad considers it an honor, but such honor might be shared with yet another squad to give us more time for preparation and sleep."

The lieutenant smiled, then looked at the platoon sergeant. "He is a smart one, isn't he? You are right. I'll see to it that you share the mission with Corporal Dim's squad."

"Thank you, comrade Leader. Thank you." Hoi's men smiled among themselves. Hoi had done well to ease their burden.

"Meeks, let's get out of here." Grady began crawling; he felt rested and ready for the long night move and swim. They got abreast of the last large boulder, only fifteen yards from the river, when he saw lights approaching.

Grady backed up slowly, trying to get out of the glow of the torch. Thumper could easily see Grady silhouetted by the fire's light and knew they'd have to retreat a long way to be safe. Back they crawled, ever so slowly, deeper and deeper into the protective darkness. They could hear more men coming. And someone was building a fire.

"We're trapped, Meeks," Grady whispered.

"What the hell, Sarge, couldn't be helped. We just ran outta luck, that's all." They lay close in the darkness.

"I could call X-ray and tell 'em we're here, and they'd call off whatever they got planned."

"I hate to think these guys would get away."

"Yeah, I know, but the way I see it, we only got two options. We can ride out whatever the major's got planned or call in and tell X-ray we're here; then they'd cancel their attack, and we'd have to wait till these guys leave."

"What's the chances of us stayin' here and not gettin' caught if we tell X-ray we're here?"

Grady thought a minute. The ruck he'd left hadn't been found yet, but the next day it surely would be, and so would the trail they'd made through the vines. "Not good," he answered.

"Well, Sarge, I vote we take our chances with whatever they got comin' in."

Grady smiled, unseen in the darkness. "That's my vote too."

Hoi lay back on his pack, watching their small fire crackle and send its red and gold sparks upward into the night. He looked at the rock formation. A cold chill ran through his body. He brought his legs up to his chest and turned back toward the fire. *I hope the fire doesn't disturb the dragon's sleep,* he thought. He shut his eyes for a few seconds, then opened them quickly. He thought for a moment he could hear the creature breathing.

6

Colven sipped from his second cup of coffee while looking at the large map across from him. Bud Sikes walked into the brightly lit room and narrowed his eyes at the glare.

"Oh, sir, up already, huh? I just came in to confirm freqs one more time." He walked toward the blackboard with the radio-frequency information.

Colven turned to his lieutenant. "Keep it under control, kid."

Sikes looked up from his note pad. "Sir, you've got a good plan. It's made for me. I'll run it right, don't worry."

Colven stared at the young officer for a moment, then nodded. He knew the lieutenant could do it. The kid was cool as ice. He thrived on the confusion and excitement of others. Sikes and he were alike in that way. He, Colven, loved it when others let fear and excitement overtake them. He enjoyed confusion and panic. He felt most alive and best as a leader when he was calming the scared and directing the lost.

Sikes put away his pad and walked for the door. Colven watched him and spoke quietly. "Be careful, kid."

Bud glanced over his shoulder and winked as he raised his hand and gave his major a thumbs-up.

Larry Wine was already at the Bird Dog. He had just topped off the wing tanks when the jeep's headlights hit his aircraft. The Ranger lieutenant got out and walked quickly

to the plane, carrying his survival bag. Wine thought about
Bud Sikes and smiled to himself. The kid was good, but he
had a definite weakness: snack food. That guy ate more
cookies, candy, and crackers than anybody he'd ever met.
Sikes scooted in behind him, put on his flight helmet, and sat
down. He immediately plugged in his headset and depressed
the floor transmit button.

"Larry, you got me okay?"

"Yep, you sound good. What'd you bring for us to eat,
kid?"

"Us? Us? You fly-boys make more on your flight pay than
I get in a year. And don't call me 'kid.' The major is the only
one who gets away with that!"

"Aw, now, kid, don't get sensitive on me. Sit back and eat
something while this fly-boy finds you the *en-na-my*!"

Grady had watched the blackness turn to gray. He tapped
Meeks. "How many star clusters you got for your 79?"

"Two."

"Good, I'm gonna crawl past you. We're going to a small
cave I found the last time I was here. It's our only chance to
ride out what's comin'"

"X-ray, this is Two-Zero. Over."

"This X-ray. Over."

The small plane soared lazily over a bald hill. The tip of
the brilliant orange sun was just peeping over the dark land.
"You got commo with Double-Deuce for pickup?"

"Negative. We've had no commo since they said they was
leavin' the AO yesterday. Over."

"Roger. Out." Sikes didn't like the sound of that. It meant
Grady's radio was on the blink. He'd have to assume they'd
rejoined the others at the original insertion LZ. That was the
standard procedure. He'd pick them up after the big ball
game.

"Rebel Lead, Matador Lead, Blue Bird, this is Two-Zero.
Y'all ready for the ball game? Over."

"This is Rebel Lead. Roger, we're inbound to checkpoint.
Will arrive in two Mikes," came the first reply.

"This is Matador Lead. Roger, we're over you now," came
the second.

Larry Wine and Sikes instantly looked up, searching. A
thousand feet above, the Cobras circled.

"Two-Zero, this is Blue Bird. I'm inbound and have a visual on you. Be advised I have a pair of Fast-Fours ten miles to the north, itchin' to go. Over."

"This is Two-Zero. All stations are advised ball game starts in five Mikes. Out."

Private Nguyen Huong felt nature's call. It was barely light as he swung from his hammock, placing his feet into his sandals. The river would be a good place to relieve himself, he thought as he got up and walked the four feet to the embankment. The huge upturned tree roots loomed out of the gray mist that rose from the slowly moving water. He jumped down, landing in the soft sand, and immediately unbuckled his pants, turned toward the bank, and squatted. His trousers had fallen halfway down, when suddenly he caught them and yanked them up quickly. "Sergeant Khue!" he yelled excitedly, "Sergeant Khue!" Seconds later the sergeant and several others stared down at the excited private and the American pack he had found.

Grady cut the last vine and pushed it back. He'd cleared an area in front of the cave opening so he and Meeks would have clear firing lanes if needed. He put the radio against the boulder and turned it on. "X-ray this is Double-Deuce. Over."

"This is X-ray. Say hey, Double-Deuce, where have you been? The big boys been worried. Over."

Sikes heard the whispered call from Grady to X-ray and immediately broke in: "Break, break! Double-Deuce this is Two-Zero."

"This is Double-Deuce," said Grady in a low whisper as he screwed the silencer into the pistol barrel.

"This is Two-Zero. Sit tight on the Lima Zulu until I get done with the ball game in thirty Mikes. Out."

Grady quickly pressed the transmit bar. "Two-Zero, be advised we're not on LZ, we're in *bad guy* AO. . . ." Sikes felt like vomiting as he heard the rest of the whispered words. ". . . We couldn't get out. We'll mark location of eastern end of camp with 79 star cluster. Camp runs from river to the west for five hundred meters. Over."

Sikes hit the floor button. "Negative! Negative! We'll abort. Over."

"No way, Two-Zero. We're gonna open up anyway! They're going to find us in *ti ti* time. You gotta come! You're our only chance. We have a cave to protect us, so come on! We'll mark when we hear you come in."

Sikes cussed under his breath, knowing he had no choice. "Deuce, I'll be coming in low down the river. Look for me: We're coming in quiet."

Grady understood. "Roger. Let me know when you're close.

Sikes's hands shook. He took a deep breath and depressed the floor button. "Double-Deuce, we're comin' in four Mikes. Out."

Hoi squatted with his squad near the fire pits. They were all packed, waiting with Dim's squad for the lieutenant to inspect them. One of Dim's men rose and began walking toward the rock formation. Dim turned. "Where are you off to, comrade?"

The soldier smiled. "Nature is calling." The others laughed as he walked quickly toward the boulders.

"You find a spot to get a flare through?" Grady whispered.

Thumper pointed to a small opening through the low canopy.

"That'll—"

He suddenly stopped whispering, hearing someone approaching. A small soldier stepped high over the vegetation, looking to his left and right and walking directly at them. Grady slowly raised his pistol. The soldier stopped next to a small tree and unbuttoned his pants. He looked up at the strange boulders. As the warm fluid shot from his body he froze and the flow ceased instantly. His eyes widened only slightly when the bullet struck him just above the left brow, and his head snapped back. He fell heavily against the tree, then dropped as if he were a rag doll. Grady rose up slowly; there was no sound except for the voices of other soldiers talking farther away. He quickly looked around him, then spoke from the side of his mouth. "The shit has hit the fan." The big man nodded and looked up at the opening.

Private Huong ran behind his sergeant toward the camp headquarters, holding the GI pack. Hoi stood as the men ran by, recognizing the sergeant from Third Company. The sergeant didn't speak as he passed.

Corporal Dim yelled toward the rock formation. "Come on, Nhuan, the earth is wet enough!" The men laughed as Dim shrugged his shoulders at the smiling Hoi.

Bud Sikes leaned forward in his seat and looked down at the river. There was no other option but to follow their plan. He ran it over in his mind again for the hundredth time. The Bird Dog was to drop down and fly just above the river. The two Rebel Huey gunships would follow five hundred meters behind, and a thousand meters back, the Cobras would follow the Rebs at an altitude of a thousand feet. When the spotter plane got close to its target, it would shut off its engines and glide. The slow speed would allow the plane to bank over and drop white-phosphorous marking grenades. The Rebels would then swoop in and blow the top of the jungle canopy off with their rockets. The Snakes would then dive and fire fléchette rockets, eighty-five-pound missiles that explode and shower thousands of little finned nails over their target. The Air Force forward air controller would bring in his pair of F-4 fighter bombers once the gunships had made their last rocket runs to finish off the camp. The success of the plan had depended on his spotting the camp. Now it wouldn't be a problem. Grady would mark it for him, poor bastard.

Sikes glanced at his watch and depressed the floor button. "All stations: Let's do it!"

They were five miles north of the camp when the plane plunged downward, followed closely by the Rebel guns. The Air Force FAC pilot's stomach quivered and goosebumps rose up on his neck as he watched the plane and helicopters below him streak directly over the center of the shimmering river.

"Nhuan!" yelled Corporal Dim as he looked toward the rock formation and got up, disgusted. He shook his head and mumbled as he trudged off to find his private. Hoi laughed at Dim's distress but stopped when his gaze fell on the gray boulders. They still frightened him.

The stocky NVA corporal yelled loudly again and took several steps farther up the riverbank before turning toward the boulders. He waded into the ferns and vines for several meters then abruptly stopped. He saw the path in the vines and grabbed for the AK-47 on his shoulder. Grady's pistol spit. Dim's vision blurred and his body fell toward the twisted vines. He tried to put his hand out to stop his fall, but it wouldn't respond.

"Double-Deuce, stand by!"

"Roger," said Thumper as he took the 79 off safety. He was ready to start popping flares as soon as they were called for.

With the engine off, the plane rocked gently as it glided silently down the river. Sikes strained forward in the seat harness, searching for the camp. "We're close, I know it. It's gonna be just ahead. . . . It's gotta be just a little . . . just a . . . there! Shoot it, Deuce!"

Thumper raised the M-79 and fired. *Thump!* The blunt-nosed round shot upward disappearing through the opening in the branches.

Hoi jumped to his feet at the sound. His men spun and grabbed for their rifles. Someone screamed out behind him, "Helicopters! Helicopters!" Hoi yelled for Dim, but the sound of the sputtering engine of a plane passing directly overhead drowned out his frantic call.

The signal round burst 150 meters above the canopy. Three glowing green flares sparkled, then fell, leaving white trails.

Two helicopters rose suddenly and banked right as another flare burst overhead.

Hoi stood motionless, staring at the serpent's back as his men screamed and ran in horror from the deafening sound of the attacking helicopters. He fought the chilling terror that stiffened his body and tried to yell again for Dim, but his words came out only in a hoarse whisper. Raising his rifle, he ran for the evil rocks.

Three rockets from pods on the left and right side of the lead gunship ignited in puffs of white smoke and swooshed forward.

Grady shoved Thumper toward the cavern. A single screaming soldier was running directly toward them. Grady twisted around and fired his CAR-15. The soldier was propelled backward, contorted in midair, and fell heavily on his side. Grady rose up higher to fire again, when the ground in front of him suddenly heaved upward and swallowed him in a shattering roar.

Six more 2.75-inch rockets with ten-pound warheads snaked across the morning sky and disappeared into the smoking green forest.

The ground shuddered; the trees cracked and snapped; the air was split by deafening noise and filled with smoke and cordite. Hysterical men screamed, running everywhere. Leaves, branches, and wood chips fell like rain on the huge boulders.

Grady's hand twitched, then his eyes fluttered open. Everything was in a dirty haze. He couldn't feel or hear. He was dying, he knew it. *Mother! Oh, God, Mother, I'm dying!* A hand roughly grabbed his shoulder and pulled him backward.

"Help me, Grade! Push with your feet, damn it!"

The voice came out of the haze. Grady could see a blur of colors, and his nerve endings screamed in agony at the tugging. He moaned loudly.

"Grade! Help me!" Meeks frantically pulled his sergeant toward the cavern entrance, fell, got to his feet, and yanked again. Grady's vision cleared and he shook his head to stop the dizziness. Then his stunned body began to respond, and he pushed to help. Finally, Thumper pulled Grady through the cave entrance. He grabbed the radio and Grady's CAR, then he, too, fell in headfirst.

High above them, six eighty-five pound rockets flew out from their pods in firy orange balls, then exploded five hundred meters from the ground, unleashing thousands of miniature steel spears that screamed toward earth.

Grady opened his eyes. It was still and dark, but the sounds outside were those of hell. He shook and rose, supported by Meeks. Suddenly the sky outside exploded in a succession of thunderous cracks. The earth lurched in agony. The fléchettes had struck. Grady looked out the opening. It was smoking mayhem. Leaves, branches, dirt, and flesh were pulverized into a gritty mist. The lush plants that used to protect and conceal the boulders were stripped of leaves and lay cut, bruised, dying.

The blood-curdling screams that cut through the mist made his skin crawl. The sound of beating chopper blades became louder. He turned and looked at Thumper with a savage grin.

"This is Reb. We're going in for a second run!"

"Roger, Reb," said Sikes, releasing the floor button. He'd never seen anything like it—the precision of such destruction. He watched in awe as the two Hueys made their second rocket, attack this time west to east, toward the river.

Then the radio crackled, "Snakes inbound!"

He saw the Cobras diving and involuntarily held his breath. The Cobras' rockets left their pods and flew forward, spitting fire and smoke.

"Two-Zero, be advised, fast movers inbound! Over."

Sikes swallowed hard, his mouth and throat completely dry.

"Roger." He could hear the Rebels talking on their freq, ". . . controls sticking. Gonna have to put her down soon. . . . Got a couple rounds in the hydraulics, Bill."

"Roger, Reb, head southwest. Dagger is only ten klicks away. You got that made easy. We'll follow."

"Roger, Wild Bill. Hey, some show, huh?"

"Jesus, Reb, was it! Ya see 'em running? They looked like mad piss ants at a picnic."

A group of NVA soldiers ran with a platoon leader to their RPD machine guns. They would be ready for the helicopters to pass again. The ground suddenly seemed to jump up and the air was filled with a strange buzzing noise, like that of hornets. The lieutenant turned toward his men. Two lay twisted in agony. He bent over the closest one to help. A steel wire with small fins protruded from the squirming man's skull. Other small, bloody entry holes peppered the man's jaw and neck. The other soldier sat on the ground, holding his foot. A small steel arrow was sticking out of the top portion of the foot just behind the toes. The lieutenant grasped the tiny fins and yanked up. The small spear came out easily. Men lay all about him, some dead, most wounded. The smell of death choked him.

Hoi lay on his back, conscious but stunned. His body seemed heavy. The air was thick, making breathing difficult. He didn't feel pain, but he knew he was wounded. He tried raising his head. It seemed too heavy. He'd seen the helicopters pass over and heard the horrible thunderclaps and men yelling, shooting, dying. It was as if he were looking at pictures in a book—unreal, not happening, just images. The sun's rays broke through the large gaps in the stripped trees above and penetrated the smoke and grit. He tried to raise his head again. Suddenly his shoulder felt as if it were being ripped from his body. He vomited, choking on his own bile. . . .

"This is Black Ace, Lead. We're turning final. Got fuel for two passes. Thanks for smoke and invitation to party. We're going hot *now!*"

The FAC turned his head in time to see the jets flash under him for their run. He depressed his transmit button. "They're going in *now*, Two-Zero."

Bud Sikes had seen their approach. They were beautiful, but he wasn't happy. The thought of his own men in that inferno tugged at his insides. The first Phantom 4 streaked over the river. Its five-hundred-pound olive-drab bomb had been released seconds ago. It followed the bird as if it were unwilling to leave its protection, but then the fighter-bomber pulled straight up and the bomb fin section blew back, forming a metal wind drag that cut its forward speed in half. The plane was a mile away when the iron "snake-eye" bomb penetrated the thinned canopy branches.

Grady was pulling himself out of the cavern, holding on to the white roots, when the earth erupted and shuddered, throwing him into the lower wall, then jerked him back, slamming his body into the far rock wall.

The first bomb hit two hundred meters east of the rock formation, the second, four hundred meters. Their craters dug out giant red gashes in the earth. Everyone and everything living within fifty meters was killed, maimed, or dying. Clouds of debris hung thick in the air.

Grady opened his eyes. His lungs craved air. He tried to get up and fell. The diffused dusty light of the opening grinned at him. He tried again and fell. The cavern was filled with dust and mud that covered his body. The near wall had partially collapsed. He kicked and yanked, struggling, his lungs bursting. He threw himself at the opening and pulled himself out. He lay gasping . . . one breath . . . two . . . a third. His chest pounded. His nostrils were full of blood and dirt. He wheezed through his open mouth . . . a fourth.

Meeks! He shook his head violently, trying to clear the spinning, and crawled for the opening of the darkness.

Hoi turned his head. The pain had passed. The ground had shook him back to consciousness. He was staring at the battle-scarred boulders. Large pieces of rock were chipped out of the dark gray stone, leaving whitish-gray scars. His eyes had deceived him. He thought he'd seen a dark spirit crawl from the rocks. He shut his eyes. He opened them again, the spirit was gone.

"This is Black Ace Lead, we're turning final. Coming hot to trot second shot. Over."

"Roger, Black Ace, first pass was super! Do it same-same. Out." The Air Force FAC banked his spotter plane east to get a better view. Bud Sikes looked down at his hands. He'd seen enough.

Grady felt around in the darkness. He was on his knees. The cavern was still filled with thick rock dust that made him gasp and choke. A leg! He jerked it, followed it up, pulled, scraped wet mud, then jerked again. The heavy body moved slightly. He took hold of Thumper's muddy shirt. He stood and pulled upward. Again the body moved, then jerked, making Grady lose his grip. He heard Meeks choking. He reached down and pulled. This time it was easier. Meeks had drawn up his feet and was kicking.

The bomb crashed through the hundred-year-old mahogany's upper branches and struck the ground twenty meters from its ancient base, burying its ugly iron skin into the root-filled soil. It exploded. The great tree shook. The top third of its thick body snapped and fell crashing into the billowing debris cloud climbing upward. Its lower branches flew skyward, splintered. Red earth and its own root flesh tore at its bark, stripping and tearing. Seconds later the old one creaked and moaned, but stood.

The third and fourth bombs fell four hundred and seven hundred meters from the river. Grady had just gotten Meeks up when he was rocked forward with the blasts, but he managed to stay on his feet and shoved the big man toward the opening.

"Two-Zero, this is the Red Reb. Sorry we left the party early, but I got a couple rounds in my bird's innards and am limping to Dagger. Over."

"Roger, Reb. I monitored your freq. Are you gonna make it all right? Over."

"Roger that, Two-Zero. I got the altitude now. I can always autorotate if need be. We had fun. Invite us back, hear?"

"Roger, Red Reb, take care. Out. Break, Matador Lead, this is Two-Zero. Over."

"This is Matador. Go."

"Thanks much. Great job!"

"No sweat. We're RTBing. Great day! Out."

"Blue Bird this is Two-Zero. Over."

"This is Blue Bird. My fast-movers did good, huh?"

"You bet. Thank 'em for us. We'll give a bomb-damage assessment tomorrow when we go in."

"Roger that, Two-Zero. Good working with you. See you back at base. Out."

Sikes looked down at the smoking jungle below. He knew the answer before he pushed the floor button, but he had to try. "Double-Deuce, Double-Deuce, this is Two-Zero. Over." *Oh, please,* he prayed as he shut his eyes and listened.

"Double-Deuce, Double-Deuce, this is Two-Zero. Over." Nothing. "Double—" He stopped. There was no need—he knew it.

Hoi saw them emerge. Huge men with green faces. He shut his eyes, then opened them quickly. They were still there. He tried to raise his head. Pain raced through his body, making him shudder and moan uncontrollably. His eyes squinted as he gritted his teeth. He forced his eyes back open and watched the giant men.

Grady put on the ruck, then handed Meeks the CAR. "Let's go!" he whispered loudly, and shoved the shaky-legged soldier forward.

Grady hooked one arm under Meeks's and began moving toward the river. Five feet from the bank he heard voices. He released his grip and pulled out his pistol. He crept to the edge, looked over, and found himself staring into the face of a young NVA soldier who was just about to pull himself up. Two more stood behind him. They had hidden in the water along the protecting bank. He moved the pistol slightly and fired point-blank. The man's face showed no expression of pain or surprise as the bullet left a dark hole in his right cheek and jerked his head and body backward. The men behind were splattered with blood and frothy gray matter as the bullet passed out the back of the man's head, blowing away the lower portion of the skull. Grady raised the pistol and fired again. The projectile caught the side of the second man's raised hand, penetrated, and struck him in the mouth. Grady twisted and fired at the third soldier, who was turning for the river. It hit him in the left side, knocking him into the shallow water. Grady spun around, grabbed Thumper, and pulled. They both landed in the shallow water. The third NVA soldier lay on his side, kicking and twisting in agony, trying to breathe. The bullet had passed through both lungs, and they were quickly filling with blood. The water around him was turning crimson.

Grady headed south. He motioned Thumper to get down, then, holding the pack just above his head, he lay in the water.

"Let the current take us down and keep as low as possible," he whispered.

Meeks nodded and submerged himself quickly.

Hoi watched them until they were out of view. Now he heard voices coming closer.

"Here is another one!"

Hoi looked up at a tall lieutenant who was bending to kneel beside him. Lieutenant Le Be Son inspected the wound, then smiled. "You are blessed, friend. Your wound is clean. It will be very painful for you, but you will live to tell your grandchildren." He rose. "You"—he pointed to a soldier walking in a daze out of the still-smoking forest—"come here!" Son turned toward the sergeant next to him. "Gather the ones returning from the forest. Assemble them all next to the river." The sergeant nodded and went to do as he was told.

The dazed soldier approached. "Yes, comrade Leader?"

"Stay here with this man until the medical orderly sees him. Place a bandage on the exit wound."

Hoi looked up at the lieutenant. "Green faces. They came from the rocks." The lieutenant glanced down at the mumbling man.

Two sergeants ran up the trail.

"Lieutenant! The battalion commander is wounded. He wants an officer to come to him."

Son looked surprised. "Are there no others?"

The older sergeant lowered his head. "The deputy is dead, as is the plans officer." He looked back up at the tall lieutenant. "You are the first we've seen."

Son thought for a moment, then spoke to the younger sergeant: "I want you to count the dead and wounded and report to me at headquarters." He turned to the older one. "I have men gathering those who escaped. I want you to organize them. They will be sent to the river. Set up an aid station next to it and place the dead"—he looked around, searching—"there, by those large boulders." He pointed to the rock formation. Both sergeants nodded and trotted off.

Hoi spoke again. "Lieutenant, green-faced ones shot me."

The lieutenant was lost in thought, but the word *shot* grabbed his attention. He looked down at the wound with renewed interest—a gunshot, not shrapnel or tiny metal arrows. He knelt quickly. "What did you say?"

Wine banked the plane right. The campsite far below was still smoking. Sikes had called Major Colven and given him a situation report. He now waited for another set of gunships and a Slick to pick up Rock Steady's bunch. He looked down again at the rising smoke. Tomorrow they would send in teams to check the damage. The dinks would all be gone. They'd take their wounded and bury their dead. They always did. Tomorrow the teams would find the graves and count them. Maybe they'd find the American bodies. The dinks wouldn't bury them. If there was enough of them left to find. He shook his head and stared at the back of Wine's helmet. . . . *Damn!*

Colven got up slowly from his chair. The attack had lasted ten minutes. Ten minutes of coordinated death. It had been executed perfectly, thanks to two young Rangers who had sacrificed themselves. . . . Shit! The thought of Sergeant Grady being in the melee ruined the whole success.

Childs watched his major and walked to the map. "It couldn't have been aborted, sir. They knew that. It happens that way. You'd better call Corps and tell 'em the good news."

Colven looked up at the sergeant. "You know, Jerry, sometimes you're a real sonofabitch."

Childs glared at Colven. "I get paid to be a son of a bitch. You get paid to command!"

Colven stared back. The old bastard was right. Colven couldn't show his feelings. He had to Charlie Mike. During his first tour he'd lost many men, but he'd been in the field and hadn't had time to worry about them. He'd had to think of the living and try to keep them alive, and this was no different. He reached out and put his hand on Childs's shoulder. "Thanks." He turned toward the radio operator. "Get Dove. Tell him to bring the jeep up." He looked back at childs, "Get me two—no, three—teams ready for tomorrow's damage assessment. I'll lead it. And call the aviation battalion. I want debriefs from the pilots on what they saw. . . . And better find out about the gun that got hit. You'll be coming with me to brief Corps: Bring the maps and get Evans for me. I wanna tell him about Grady myself." With that he strode into the briefing room and shut the door

Childs sighed inwardly knowing the major was his old self again. He spun around to Johnson, the radio operator, "Well, you heard him, get Dove!"

Johnson sprang up from his chair and jogged for the door. "Asshole," he mumbled to himself as he bounded up the steps.

Sox sat with his feet up. "Hey, Rock, you think them explosions was the Air Force doin' its thing, man?"

"It was more than just Air Force. You heard them choppers, didn't ya?"

Sox stood up. "Well, I hope Grady and Thump are okay."

Ben shifted his M-60 from his lap, "Yep. I was hopin' them boys be joinin' us by now."

Sox looked at Rock. "Man, you sure you weren't supposed to turn the squawker on when you heard them choppers?"

Rock looked up at him, shaking his head. "We don't turn it on till the Bird Dog passes over us low. Lieutenant Sikes put us in here, so he knows where to find us. When he comes over, I'll turn it on for five seconds to let him know we're here, then we'll pop smoke."

Ben looked at the others. "Anybody got any chow?"

The lieutenant knelt down beside his battalion commander. The older man's jaw muscles tightened, and sweat rolled in small beads down his dust-caked cheeks. He lay on a hastily spread plastic ground sheet that held a dark pool of quickly coagulating blood. His stomach was wrapped with fresh bandages, but already a small red stain was beginning to appear. His eyes opened as the lieutenant knelt.

"It is you, Le Be Son."

"Yes, comrade Commander, of the Second Company."

The commander attempted to smile, but bit his lip as a wave of pain swept through him. The lieutenant looked up at the medical orderly. He shook his head. There was nothing he could do.

The old one opened his eyes again. "You must organize quickly, Son. . . ." He now shut his eyes. "Send runners to the field hospital to prepare for the wounded. Reorganize the units; redistribute the weapons. Fill all the leadership positions quickly, and be sure the scouts are far out in front of you when you move to the hospital."

"Sir, the Americans were among us. They had green faces and hid in the boulders by the river."

The commander opened his eyes upon hearing the words and stared up at the lieutenant.

"Green faces?"

"Yes. They must have guided the flying ones to us."

The commander's eyes rolled downward. "I know of the green-faced ones. They have inflicted wounds on my unit before."

Son had been with the battalion only six months and wasn't aware of the previous attacks. "Who are they, Commander?"

The old man's eyes didn't move. "They are commandos. They must be watched for." He looked up at Son. "They observe and they kill—silently. They are like the cobra. They strike a deadly blow, then they are gone, leaving the dead for the ancestors."

He grimaced, then opened his mouth, taking in more air. The spot on the bandage was increasing in size and becoming darker. Son leaned over. The old man's voice was fading. "Do not be disheartened, Le Be Son of the Second Company. We will fight again. They have won this day only. We have time . . . time to"—he opened his eyes wide, tears rolling from them—"to achieve a glorious victory . . . a glorious . . ." He stiffened. His body convulsed. Blood appeared at the corner of his mouth.

Son looked up at the orderly, who knelt quickly and placed his hand on the commander's neck to feel for a pulse.

The orderly stood, shaking his head. "He has joined the ancestors."

"Lieutenant."

Son looked up at the young sergeant whom he'd seen on the trail earlier. He held a pad of paper and looked distraught.

"Yes."

"You sent me to count the dead and —"

"Yes, I remember. Tell me."

The soldier looked down at his pad, then back at the lieutenant apprehensively.

"Go on."

"I counted forty-six dead, ninety-three wounded. Twenty-one are critical, comrade Leader."

The lieutenant stared at the young sergeant, who bit at his lip, waiting for a reply.

"Thank you, Sergeant. You did well."

"Captain Thieu Ky and Captain Vinh are at the small hill to the west. I told them you would be here."

Son stood up quickly. "Are they injured?"

"No, comrade, they were on the small hill and found protection. The hill was barely touched." The lieutenant nodded, relieved at the news that there were senior officers who could take charge. He looked down again at his commander and bent over, pulling the green scarf from the dead man's neck and wrapping it around his own. Forty-six men. The men with green faces had caused the tragedy. He looked back at his commander. *I will avenge the deaths, old one. I will have the glorious victory you talked of.* He turned to the men around him. "Move the commander to the rocks with the others."

Evans knocked softly on the briefing-room door. He knew something was wrong by the way Childs looked at him when he walked in.

"Come in," said Colven, who was seated behind a desk.

"Sir, Sergeant Evans reporting." He walked in and stood three paces from the major.

"Sit down, Stan."

Evans's heart sank. The major never called his team sergeants by their first names. It wasn't impersonal; It was a

status symbol of their leadership. So when the major used
his first name, he knew it meant bad news. Very bad news.
He tightened his stomach muscles and waited.

Colven looked into the sergeant's eyes. "Grady didn't
make it out. He called the air on himself. . . ."

Evans heard the explanation of what happened through a
fog. He sat motionless, with no expression except for an occasional nod to help the major in his difficult task. It was
over in two minutes. He got up and thanked the major for
telling him and exited quickly. He reached the fresh outside
air just in time. *Grady! Grady, why . . . ?*

Evans looked around, searching. He wanted a place to be
alone. The barbed-wire perimeter fence was off to his right.
He headed quickly for its solitude. He'd prepared himself a
long time ago. It was a part of the job. You knew friends
would die. It was a price some had to pay for membership in
a unit that dealt in death. He smiled through the hurt. *You
won, didn't you, Grady?*

They had been close, like brothers. They'd gravitated toward each other because they were alike—both completely
dedicated to their teams but with no one to confide in. It was
strange. The team members were your family, yet you always
kept a piece of yourself back from them. There was a line
you drew in your mind that, as a leader, you could not cross.
You couldn't share your intimate thoughts—the ones that
exposed the real you, your dreams, fears, expectations—
with your men. You kept those for very special people: He
and Grady had that special relationship. With Grady, Evans
could relax and be himself, just Stan Evans from Beloit,
Kansas. Grady had no real home where he could be buried,
no friends or family back in the States to grieve for him. He
had always claimed not to care, laughing his situation off
with an "I don't need the hassle." Now it was too late.

Evans remembered how mail call had always been the
worst for his friend. Grady never got mail. He and Rock
would always leave the mail-call formation together, knowing
there would be no letters. Evans had often thought that was
the reason Grady cared for Rock so much: They shared their
loneliness.

Evans stopped and took in a deep breath. He would return
in a few minutes. It would be over. He would put the
thoughts of his friend in a special place. He wouldn't carry
his remorse. It affected thoughts, actions, decisions. It could

eat away at a man's mind. He was a team leader. He wasn't allowed the luxury of remorse. His mind had to be clear, with no distractions. His life—his teams—depended on it. Grady had understood; he had known. They had discussed it when Grady lost his 79 man, Bartlett.

Evans turned back toward the camp, wiping the tears away. *I'm going to miss you Grade . . . really miss you.*

Grady lay on the soft ground, exhausted. Meeks lay next to him, white and shaking with fatigue. They had stayed in the water and waded to the south for two miles. There, where the river turned west in a wide arc, they'd found a spot shallow enough to cross. Now, on the far bank, they rested under the protection of the trees.

Thumper tried to spit. His tongue was too dry. He felt the way he had back in school when the coach ran him until he passed out. The coach kept asking him how he felt, trying to break him. Meeks remembered he wouldn't give him the satisfaction of telling him he was tiring, and he kept running till he dropped. His body felt the same now. His muscles seemed elongated and rubbery, and normal breathing was impossible. His head was still pounding from the blow on the rocks. He got to his knees and dry-heaved.

The lieutenant stood watching as cold chills ran up his angular body. The site before him sickened his insides. They had stacked the dead in the gap between the last boulders and had used the cave to store the remaining bodies. Captain Vinh had ordered it. Burying them would take too much time. He wanted to move out immediately. Besides, it would take almost every able-bodied man to help carry the wounded. The distance to the underground field hospital was over twenty kilometers, and the men's strength could not be wasted on the dead's graves. "The ancestors will understand," he had said. Lieutenant Le Be Son walked back to the trail, where his newly assigned men squatted next to the wounded, who lay on hammocks tied to bamboo poles. He recognized the soldier who had told him of seeing the green-faced ones lying on the last stretcher. A smiling soldier was holding his hand. He squatted down next to the wounded man.

"How are you feeling, comrade?"

Corporal Nguyen Van Hoi was surprised to see the lieutenant, but was gladdened by his concern. "I feel much better. My friend Tuy is here with me."

The lieutenant looked at the bucktoothed private and smiled. "Your friend is fortunate to have a companion to tend to his needs during the journey." He glanced back toward the rocks. For the first time he saw the strange shape: It looked like a . . . a dragon's back. Yes, a sleeping dragon. He spoke to Tuy as he rose, "Be sure your friend is secured to the stretcher comfortably. We're leaving soon." He looked back at the boulders. *Yes, it does have a look of a dragon's back. The sleeping dragon will protect the dead.* He felt better about the dead among the rocks, knowing they would be protected.

The men on the trail began moving. Hearing the activity, the lieutenant adjusted the AK-47 on his shoulder, then touched the green scarf around his neck and tucked the ends into his shirt. Revenge would come in time. Time. Yes. Then glorious victory.

Private First Class Winters turned the radio off. Lieutenant Sikes had given them permission to go off push as soon as he had extracted Rock Steady and the remainder of Double-Deuce. Sikes had told them to rest, since there were no teams out on patrol to monitor. That's why he liked Sikes, he said to himself. He always thought about giving them a break when he could. Hell, it was tough duty on the rocky mountaintop—six men constantly changing shifts of guard and monitoring the radio. Tonight they would sleep; tomorrow they would monitor the assessment mission, then get picked up. He walked over to his poncho hootch and spoke to Sergeant Wilkes, who sat beside a large boulder, eating.

"It's off, Sarge. What time you wanna go on in the morning?"

"Oh-eight hundred hours. The assessment is going in at ten hundred hours. We'll pack up most of the gear tomorrow morning so we can get picked up as soon as they're finished. Hey, you want a bite?"

Dove drove in silence. Colven, seated beside him, spoke softly. "I'm sorry about Grady. I know how it is to lose a close friend."

Dove nodded without speaking. He was afraid to say anything or he might cry again. *Hell of a note,* he thought, *me crying.*

It had been Grady who had carried Dove to the chopper the time he was hit. That was six months ago. Dove had been on Grady's team from the first. When Dove was sent to Japan to recover from his wound, Rodriguez had taken his place. It was Dove's second Purple Heart, so he had been assigned as Colven's driver when he returned. Colven knew Dove still considered the Deuce to be his platoon and that he was very close to Grady and the team.

The jeep turned into the corps headquarters compound and came to a slow stop in front of the entrance. Colven stepped out and took the maps given to him by Childs, who was sitting in the back.

"Park it in the same place as usual," Colven said. "And take it easy on the REMFs, okay?"

Dove looked at his major and forced a smile. "Aw, sir."

Grady jerked awake. He looked around quickly, then sat up. Dumb, Grady! Real dumb, sleeping like that. He glanced at his watch. Son of a bitch! Thirty minutes! Thirty minutes' lying here like a wimp! *They could have walked right up on us.* His mouth was dry; his tongue felt swollen. He reached for his canteen. Meeks lay in front of him, asleep. Grady moved the warm water back and forth in his mouth while looking at the still man. *Poor guy. His first mission and he gets a real lulu.* Grady reached down, still smiling, and tapped Meeks's shoulder. He rose immediately and looked into his sergeant's face with its strange grin.

"You feelin' better now, big guy?"

"Yeah. Can I have some of that water?" Meeks sat up and took a swallow, and, like Grady, swilled it around before swallowing. He handed the canteen back. "Thanks."

"No, drink more: You need it. We got plenty." Grady opened the rucksack, took out the twenty-five-pound radio, and flipped up the flexible antenna. Meeks got to his knees and crawled next to him.

"Is it okay?"

"I hope so. It's our ticket outta here." Grady put the handset to his ear and pushed the transmit bar. "X-ray, X-ray. This is Double-Deuce. Over. . . . X-ray, X-ray. This is

Double-Deuce. Over. . . . Break. Two-Zero, Two-Zero. This
is Double-Deuce. Over. . . . Any station, this is Double-
Deuce. Over. . . . *Son of a bitch!*"

He got to his knees and checked the frequency setting
again, then the handset connection. "X-ray should be
monitoring," he whispered. "X-ray, X-ray. This is Double-
Deuce. Over. . . . X-ray, X-ray. This is Double-Deuce.
Over. . . . Why the hell aren't they monitoring?"

The big man shifted on his knees and mumbled, "They
probably think we're dead."

Grady's eyes widened. "My God, that's it!"

Colven shook his head. "When did all this happen anyway?"

The corps operations officer, Lieutenant Colonel Ranklin,
stood up from his cluttered desk and walked to the doorway
with Colven following. "Last night we got the word. The
general left this morning."

Colven walked behind the balding colonel, still shaking his
head in disbelief. The colonel had taken him into his office to
explain. General Collier, the corps commander, had received
word his wife was hospitalized with terminal cancer. He'd
received permission to leave immediately to be with her. The
deputy corps commander, Major General Wayland, had as-
sumed the corps commander's duties. Colonel Ranklin had
warned Colven that Wayland was not like General Collier
and to watch out for him. Colven had gotten the distinct impression that the colonel didn't like the new general. They
turned into the large briefing room and walked to the front
chairs, where the new general sat listening to the G-2, the
intelligence officer, who was giving him an update on the
recent operation against the NVA battalion. The general
turned toward Colonel Ranklin.

"Very interesting operation you have here, Colonel. Does
the major have us some results?"

Ranklin nodded. "Sir, this is Major Colven, our Ranger
company's commander. He will explain how the operation
went this morning."

The general eyed Colven as approached the map. Colven
was about to begin when the general leaned forward.

"Why is a major commanding a company and not a captain?"

The general's question caught Colven by surprise. He turned toward Ranklin for help.

"Sir," the colonel said quickly, "the corps Ranger company is larger than a regular division Ranger company, and it has a corps area rather than a division area."

The general nodded, then looked back to Colven. "Major, I'm not interested in how you elite types planned this morning's operation. I just want to know the results."

Colven stiffened. "We don't have the results, sir. We'll get those tomorrow when my assessment team goes in."

The general turned and looked behind him. "Where is my personnel officer?"

Colonel Ranklin said quietly, "He's not here, sir."

"Well, I want him! Somebody call and tell him I want him up here right now!"

The intelligence major went to the telephone.

The general got up from his chair and walked to the window. He was tall and thin. His thin, light gray hair was combed to the side. He had a cold, detached air about him and seemed uncomfortable, shifting from foot to foot. Colven glanced at Ranklin, who rolled his eyes, then shook his head to indicate that he didn't understand the need for the G-1 (personnel officer) either.

Minutes passed in awkward silence. The men waited without speaking.

Finally an overweight lieutenant colonel walked down the aisle of chairs toward the general. "Yes, sir, you called for me?"

"Yes—yes, I did, Charles." The general sat down in his chair and turned toward Ranklin. "Let Charlie sit there, will you?" His tone was a command, not a request. The colonel rose slowly and the other colonel sat down.

"Charles, this is . . . uh, what was your name again?"

Colven flushed. "Colven, sir!"

"Yes. Major Colven. He is my Ranger commander, and tomorrow his people are going into an enemy base to check the damage they inflicted in an operation this morning. I want a public-information team to accompany the major and get us some good pictures and a story for the *Stars & Stripes* . . . and maybe some stateside papers."

Colven took a step forward and spoke firmly. "Sir, that's not possible."

The general looked at the major with indignation. "What are you talking about?"

"Sir, our method of operation is secret. No pictures of my men or stories on how we operate are allowed!"

"I'm the corps commander! I can say what is secret and what isn't!"

"No, sir, we're talking order of battle, our method of operation. It's directed by the highest authority."

Colonel Ranklin stood. "That's right, sir, it's policy: We don't give order of battle to any press."

The general stood, staring at Colven, then shifted his stare to Colonel Ranklin. "All right. Then, I want photographs of the bodies as proof of the attack. They will be used in a briefing for the region commander. If, of course, there are bodies, and"—he shot an icy look at Colven—"if the elite major, here, will permit it!"

Colven was about to tell him *"Hell, no, they can't go,"* when Colonel Ranklin stepped in front of the two men. "Yes, sir, we'll get the pictures." He turned toward Colven and gave him a pleading look.

The major headed for the door.

"Now, Charles, tell me: When was the last time this corps made the *Washington Post*?"

Colven walked into Ranklin's office and grabbed the folded map Childs sat holding. "Let's get the hell outta here!"

Childs got up slowly and shook his head knowingly. "So, the new honcho is a shitbird, huh?"

Colven was already to the doorway. "Yeah, A-number-one classical."

Childs picked up the other maps, let out a sigh, and strolled for the door. "He's gotta be a leg," he said quietly as he walked out.

"Not much, is it?"

Meeks shook his head, agreeing, and picked up the only food packet. "I'll fix this and we'll split it, okay?"

Grady nodded and started putting the other articles back in the rucksack. They had made an inventory of all their equipment. Meeks had lost his M-79 in the cave, so the only weapons were Grady's pistol and the CAR. The ruck held the meal, a poncho, one smoke grenade, the radio, an extra battery, and two canteens.

"They'll send in a unit tomorrow to check the air attacks' damage. We'll be able to signal them and get out of here then."

"Will it be our guys that check out the camp?"

"I don't know. Could be anybody—ARVNs, legs, or Rangers. There'll be a show at first. The gunships will come in and make a few rocket runs. Then the unit will go in."

"How do we signal them, Grade?"

"Very carefully." He smiled. "We'll try the radio first, but if it's not our guys, we won't be on the right frequency. So then we go to plan B, which is, we move back up the river and get within five hundred meters of the camp, then pop a smoke grenade. The C&C bird will come down and investigate. When it does, we wave like good ol' American boys and *voilà*, we're out."

"What happens if they don't come in tomorrow and check the damage?"

Grady looked up slowly. "Well, Thump, then we got ourselves one hell of a walk!"

Meeks stared in disbelief. "What'd you call me?"

Grady leaned back, "Your ears plugged?"

The big man grinned from ear to ear and lay back against a tree. His sergeant had finally called him Thump. Meeks shut his eyes and treasured the feeling. It was like that first time he had beat his brother in a race home so many years ago.

Night was coming quickly, but it would provide the men little respite. Lieutenant Le Be Son rose from the shallow grave he had just covered. It had been the fifth hastily dug grave he and two others had dug in the past three hours of movement. There would be others. Son wiped the sweat from his forehead with his green scarf, then looked about, searching. He wondered if the green-faced ones were watching.

"Lieutenant, we must catch up with the others."

Son turned toward the soldier who had spoken. "You must speak softly, comrade. The forest has ears. The column will be stopped ahead for a rest."

"Yes, comrade, I am foolish. Forgive my loudness."

The lieutenant stepped onto the trail and brought his AK-47 around. He held it to his chest, at the ready. "Now, my friend, let us go."

7

Colven swung open the door to his small hootch and walked out into the cool morning air. His ruck was over one shoulder, and his M-16 was in his hand. He walked toward the TOC. His jeep was parked out front; Dove sat in the front, asleep. He wore his boonie hat, and his face was camouflaged.

Colven slapped the young soldier's shoulder. "What the hell you doin'?"

Dove jumped, startled. "Oh, shit, sir, you scared me."

"What are you doing, Dove?"

"Waitin' on you. The major's driver is his bodyguard in the field, sir, and the Dove doesn't shirk his responsibility."

He had proclaimed it proudly. Colven stared at the young driver and knew he meant it. He cracked a slight grin. "Okay, but clear it with Childs. We only got room for twenty-four."

"Yes, sir, I already have. I'm on your bird."

Colven shook his head, threw his ruck into the back, and walked into the TOC.

"We're going!"

"You're not going, rag bags! You're goin' back to your hootch and taking off your shit!"

"Sarge, we're going!"

"Yeah, there it is!"

"*Sí.*"

Childs turned his head on the four men. They had met him when he walked down to inspect the assessment team: Rock, Rodriguez, Ben, and Sox all stood with weapons and rucks ready. They had received word as soon as they had returned to the Ranger camp. Evans had been waiting for them and told them the bad news about Grady. The reaction was the same for all of them: They wouldn't believe it. They refitted immediately and waited. When Childs came down to inspect the teams, they were ready. They were going to find Grady and Thumper.

Childs had to turn away to collect his thoughts and emotions. The men had gotten to him. Their determined faces ate at his heart. He pointed at Rock. "Okay, you go, rag bags, but you do what I say. No searches unless I approve them. Got it?"

Rock nodded and was about to thank him, when Childs turned and walked for the assembled men waiting for him. He took two steps, then stopped and looked over his shoulder. "Well, shitbirds, you gonna stand there? Move your asses!"

"You get half. Chew it slow. If the birds don't show up, it's all we'll get for a while."

Thumper watched as Grady pulled the shiny Buck knife from its black sheath and cut the Lurp cornflake bar in half. They'd slept well and awakened at first light. Grady had tried the radio again, with no results, so they crossed the river, under the cover of the white-gray mist that rose from the warm water. They moved upstream only a couple hundred yards before stopping. Grady explained he didn't want to get too close. "If the guns see us, they'll shoot first and ask questions later." They sat under a large sugar palm next to the bank, waiting.

"You got a girl friend, Grade?" asked Thumper, chewing the crumbly bar.

"Sure, plenty of them."

"But anyone special?"

"No, not really. Never found one that could keep up—you know what I mean?"

"Yeah, same here." Thumper grinned. "I guess I never had the time to really give any of them a chance."

Grady looked up. "What do you mean?"

"Aw, you know. I was playing football and all. Big jock. I really never wanted one that would mess up my mind, distract me, you know?"

Grady nodded, remembering his conversation with Evans. "I did the same at school. I played baseball and never thought about keeping a girl around very long."

Thumper sat back against the palm. He had had a special girl once. He really messed that one up. She had somehow gotten to him, but then he had fought it. He said and did things to hurt her, and she left him. He remembered how her tears made him feel so helpless. He didn't know what to do or say. It tore him up inside and made him angry at his own weakness. He worked hard to drive her from his mind after that, but although his body would ache with fatigue, his heart never strengthened. It still twisted at the thought of her. He opened his eyes and brought the CAR up to his lap. He wished he could have at least told her he was sorry.

Hoi shut his eyes as the throbbing pain in his shoulder spread to his head and made him grind his teeth. He didn't remember the night. Tuy had told him he had passed out and had been fortunate not to hear the screams of pain and silence of death. Poor Tuy, Hoi thought, he looked so tired.

He opened his eyes again. Tuy squatted beside him, talking to the tall lieutenant whom he remembered from the day before. The lieutenant looked very weary too.

Lieutenant Son, seeing the wounded soldier's open eyes, smiled. "You are over the hard part of the journey, my friend. Doctors have come to meet us and have brought medical supplies. You will be attended to in a short while."

"Thank you, Lieutenant."

Son walked toward the new arrivals. It was good that they had met the column or many more would have been lost, he thought as he walked down the trail, which was littered with stretchers. The underground hospital was only a three-hour march. They would make it before nightfall. Several of the doctors walked toward him, accompanied by nurses who carried large packs.

"How many more, Lieutenant?" one asked as he got closer.

Son motioned tiredly down the trail from where he had come. "As far as you can see, friend."

The doctor reached out with a delicate hand. "Get some rest, Lieutenant. We won't be leaving for a while."

Son smiled wanly, sat against a moss-covered trunk, and shut his eyes. The screams of the night were forgotten as he drifted into a deep sleep.

Bud Sikes nibbled on a Cheez-It cracker as he pushed up the toggle switch to contact X-ray.

"X-ray, this is Two-Zero. Over."

"Two-Zero, this is X-ray. How ya doing?"

"Doing good, X-ray. You packed, ready to sky? Over."

"Roger that. We're set."

"Good, X-ray. Stay on push until this little ball game is over, then it's bye-bye time."

"Roger, we'll monitor. Out."

Sikes pushed the toggle switch down and looked out his right window as the lead gunship dropped its nose for the first rocket run on the campsite.

Grady heard the familiar whooping noise of the helicopters and smiled. "I told you they'd come."

Thumper grinned, handing Grady the handset. Grady took a deep breath. "X-ray, this is Double-Deuce. Over. . . . X-ray, X-ray, this is Double-Deuce. Over. . . ."

Winters stared at his handset unbelievingly, then he heard the call again. "God damn!" he yelled. "God damn! Sarge, come 'ere quick!" The sergeant ran to the excited operator, who was pointing at the handset. "It's Grady! I know his voice, it's him! *He's alive!*"

The sergeant took the handset from the excited soldier, put it to his ear, and immediately heard a familiar voice: ". . . Any station, any station, this is Double-Deuce. . . ."

His eyes widened as he pushed the transmit button. "Double-Deuce, Double-Deuce, welcome back. . . . God damn, you scared us. . . ."

Colven winked at Dove who was looking at the photographer, a young Spec-4, next to him. The poor guy was holding on to the frame of the circling helicopter with a death grip. He had been sent along with a Public Information office lieutenant. Colven had laid down the rules to the PIO lieutenant as soon as he'd arrived at the TOC.

"Lt., we're a special operations force. No pictures will be allowed of the operation or of any of my men. You can take all the pictures you want of the camp, but not my people, understand?"

"Yes, sir, sure do. Don't worry, I know the rules." Colven was prepared to dislike the Lt., but he wasn't a bad sort. The photographer was green and scared. It was his first assignment, and he'd never been in a helicopter before.

The co-pilot turned and held up one finger. Colven nodded and put a finger up for the others to see. The helicopter dropped suddenly and took up its approach heading.

Sikes had the Slicks circling the river only five klicks away from the NVA camp. When the gunships gave him an all-clear, he had them follow the river down to a sand bar close to the camp. The second set of guns led the way, just in case.

The landing went smoothly. He could see the men run from the chopper like frenzied black ants. He tried to contact Colven. "Devil Six, Devil Six, this is Two-Zero. Over." No response. He glanced at the toggles on the panel. "Son of a bitch!" He had left the toggle down on X-ray and the major. He flipped it up and immediately heard X-ray getting a commo check from Sox:

". . . Roger, I have you Lima Charlie. Let me talk to Six: I have good news. Over."

"Roger, stand by." Sox ran awkwardly with the weight of the radio toward the major.

"Sir, it's X-ray. They got a message for you."

Colven took the handset. "This is Devil Six. Go."

"Six, be advised Double-Deuce team leader is alive. He called a few Mikes ago. We're trying to make contact with Two-Zero for pickup."

Colven smiled and repeated the message so Sox and Dove, who stood close by, could hear. "Roger, X-ray. Understand Double-Deuce team leader is alive and called you Mikes ago. He is awaiting pickup. Over."

"That's a Roger, Six. Out." Colven handed the handset back to Sox, who stood open-mouthed, staring at the major.

"Pass the word back," Colven said, "and let's get up to that camp."

"Really, sir!" Sox turned with a huge smile and ran toward the others, hardly noticing the weight of the radio. "I knew it!" he said to himself as he ran. "I knew it!"

Sikes had monitored the radio message. He hooted out his happiness, then hit his floor button. "Double-Deuce, Double-Deuce, this is Two-Zero. Over."

"Hiya, Two-Zero. This is Double-Deuce. We're hungry and wanna go home. Can you help? Over."

Rodriquez, walking point for the assessment team, slowed as he saw the smoke of the rocket hits drifting upwards. He moved cautiously, feeling cold chills run up his back. Before him the gritty mist was dissipating and revealed the broken, shattered earth. He stopped as his stomach knotted uncontrollably. He could smell and feel the unmistakable aura of death.

8

". . . In conclusion, sir, the total loss to the NVA battalion was fifty-one killed, and we can assume from that number of deaths that twice as many were wounded. Sir, this concludes my briefing."

"Excellent, Major! *That* is what I call *results*!" Smiling, the General stood up and turned to his staff. "Gentlemen, this will go down into the history books of this corps. We can be proud!" He turned toward Colven. "Thank you, Major. That's all."

Colven stood unmoving for a second, then realized he was being dismissed. He came to attention. "Yes, sir."

The general waited until the major was gone. "Charles, I want a press meeting set for this afternoon, and two days from now I want an awards ceremony as a follow-up. Find out who we can give medals to." The general looked at Colonel Ranklin. "You know the big operation we've got coming up? I think this Ranger company can help us more than you planned."

The balding colonel nodded. "Yes, sir, but you must realize they require a lot of aircraft assets. During this kind of operation, air assets will be stretched awfully thin."

The general shook his head. "That won't be a problem. Get them in and brief me on your plan by Friday. Charles, what kind of pictures did we get from the P10 team?"

"You gonna eat your bread?"

Rock looked up at Ben's inquiring face. "Man, I'm sure glad I ain't your mama and gotta feed your big ass. Here." He tossed the slice of bread at the grinning face across from him.

"Thanks, Rock, but you gotta watch your language. It's gettin' real bad."

Rock rolled his eyes back. "Sure, Ben, I'll work on it for you."

"There it is, man!" Sox put in. "You're gettin' nastier in your old age. Why, Grade, you should'a seen Rock when he thought you guys bought it. He acted like he was a hotshot team leader."

Rock glared at Sox while shaking his head. "That's bull-shit. Don't believe a word, Grade. I wasn't actin' shit. I *was* a hotshot team leader!"

The team broke up in laughter. Other men in the mess hall looked over at the six seated men, who were obviously enjoying themselves.

Grady leaned back in his chair, happy. They'd gotten back yesterday to a lot of back-slapping and hugging. They had fallen asleep by the time the assessment team had returned, but it didn't stop Rock and the others from attacking him and Thumper with bear hugs.

Evans had come in later in the morning and yelled out in front of the team, "Grady, you cheated! No fair! You gotta have the whole team with you to count. As far as Two-Four is concerned, we're even. And remember, Double–Douche Bags, Two-Four is goin' to get more—and shut the door—on Double-Deuce for eeever more!" It started a yelling match that ended with Evans walking away, laughing.

Grady smiled, thinking about it. Rock winked at him in a prearranged signal, and Grady tapped the water glass in front of him to get the team's attention.

"Men, as you know, one of our members lost his weapon." They all turned toward Thumper, who lowered his red face and stared at his empty place. "Yes, Double-Deuce, he *lost* it on his first mission!" All of them moaned and shook their heads dramatically. "Yes, fellow team members. But, Thump, we want you to know we took care of you. We turned the loss in to Finance, and money will be taken out of your pay immediately to pay for another. That, however, will take a while, so we have provided for our newest member. Rock, will you please bestow the honors?"

Rock stood. "My fellow team members, as you know, I am a man of few words. . . ."

"Aw, shit," said Sox loudly. Rock glared at him, then continued, "It gives me great pleasure to give this"—he bent down and took a new M-79 from a bag from under the table—"to our forgetful friend."

Thumper sheepishly took the new weapon. He didn't know what to say. The team clapped and hooted. He stood slowly, embarrassed by the attention from the men at other tables, who had now turned their chairs around for the presentation and were joining in on the moaning and clapping.

Rock held up his hand for silence. "And, big forgetful one, we have an accessory to go with your new weapon." Rock bent down under the table and pulled out a five-foot piece of thick chain that weighed at least twenty pounds. "This is your dummy cord! One end goes through the trigger housing, and the other around your neck. We don't think you'll *forget* your M-79 again!"

The mess hall rocked with laughter. Thumper glanced at Grady, who winked. Thumper smiled back, then addressed the others. "I would like to thank you all, but I *forgot* your names." The mess hall broke up again.

Grady stood and held up a carton of milk. "Men, a toast to the cherry!"

"*To the cherry,*" echoed through the building.

The team sat down again, all smiling. Grady leaned over and produced a small box, then spoke quietly. "Kiddin' aside, Thump, the team and I are real proud of you. We thought maybe you should have this, since you can't hold on to your 79."

He handed the box to Thumper, who looked up at the men's faces for an indication of whether this was another joke. They returned his with strange smiles. He opened the lid and stared at a .45 automatic pistol. Grady took a shoulder holster from his leg pocket and handed it to Thumper. "It was Bartlett's. We thought you deserved it."

Thumper lowered his head again to hide the emotions that flooded him. Words wouldn't come.

Ben tapped Grady's shoulder. "Say, boss, where is your ruck? I didn't see it with your gear."

The others immediately began verbally harassing their team leader, who became red-faced and proclaimed loudly,

"Look, shitbirds, I can dish it out, but I can't take it. Okay?"

Laughter and bantering were exchanged, allowing Thumper to win control of his feelings. At least he hadn't cried—and he wouldn't, he told himself. He hadn't since his brother's funeral.

Dove dropped the major off at the TOC then pulled the jeep up to the small administration shack where Pete sat typing.

Pete looked up from his typewriter. "How'd you do?"

"Super! We musta made a couple hundred, easy. I'll tell ya, Pete, if I could go back to that NVA camp right now, I'd do it. I left fifteen, maybe twenty, pith helmets there. I just couldn't carry any more. The old man was pissed! You should' a seen him when I climbed on the bird with those two bags of helmets."

Pete smiled, then suddenly stopped typing and looked up. "Dove, I'm confused about something."

"What'sa matter?"

"I keep getting mail for guys that aren't here. Where are the rest of our guys, anyway?"

Dove sat down next to the clerk. "Look, we got two platoons here, the First and Second, right?"

"Yeah."

"The Third and Fourth are in Phan Thiet with Task Force South. Our home base is in An Khe, and that's where our Ranger school is. We got Sierra Rangers scattered in three places. Simple."

"Well, it sure messes up the mail, I can tell you that."

"No sweat, buddy, we got *you* to keep us straight."

"Yeah, well, I understand about the three locations and the platoons being in different areas; it's the poor headquarters platoon that really gets screwed. The Headquarters guys, like the commo guys and the cooks, sure get messed around."

Dove smiled. "See, Pete, that's why I like you. You're worried about guys gettin' a fair shake. That's good, it means you're watchin' out for them. Hey, I'm going selling tonight. Ya wanna come?"

"You bet!"

Corpural Nguyen Van Hoi lay on a rice straw mat on a woven bamboo strip bed. He looked up at the earth ceiling and the lone light bulb that dangled from a thick black wire that stretched taut above him. He raised his head slightly and saw other light bulbs spaced evenly apart as far as he could see down the long tunnel. His breathing became difficult. He lowered his head and breathed more easily.

He remembered little about the previous day and their arrival. Or was it yesterday? He had been unconscious and couldn't even tell it was day without seeing the sun. To his left were others lying on similar beds. He could turn his head to the left with little pain, but to turn to the right was excruciating. He had been awake for some time, watching, listening. He had determined that the tunnel had one entrance, to his right. Everyone seemed to come and depart from that direction.

"Well, Corporal, you seem better." He shifted his eyes to the right without moving his head. A nurse was looking at his bandage.

"How do you feel?"

"Very well, thank you," he lied.

"The doctor will be pleased with his work. Are you comfortable, comrade?" She'd noticed his eyes had shifted up to the ceiling.

"Forgive my weakness, but the bandage restricts my breathing a little."

The nurse smiled. "It is not your weakness; it is my ineptness." She leaned over and quickly checked. He was correct: it was too tight. "I'm going to sit you up and we will rewrap your bandage. You must keep your upper body stiff when I pull you to a sitting position. Use your left hand to support yourself. All right?"

"Yes."

She came around to his other side. For the first time he could see her without straining his eyes. She was very beautiful, he thought as she moved closer and put one hand behind his neck and the other on his left shoulder. Her hands were soft and warm.

"Now, tighten your stomach muscles and help me as I pull. Ready? Now."

He rose easily. She wore a dark blue man's uniform with no rank insignia. Her sleeves were rolled up past the elbows.

"Is that more comfortable for you?"

He was enjoying the attention she was showing him as she unwrapped and rewrapped the long gauze pieces. "Oh, yes, you are very kind. It is much better."

She came around the bed again and helped him lie back. "Your wound was clean. The doctors said you were shot with the burning bullets that glow. You were fortunate, because it cauterized the many small vessels that would have caused much bleeding and damage to the muscle." She backed up from his bed. His eyes followed. "You will be able to see the sun soon."

She turned and walked down the aisle. *Like the lotus,* he thought, *beautiful and delicate in the midst of a muddy puddle.* He looked up again at the light bulb. The pain was dull and deep. He closed his eyes. *What is her name? From what village does she come? How long has she. . . .?* The pain slipped back to another chamber in his mind.

Lieutenant Son placed his chopsticks alongside his mess kit. The meal had been quickly eaten. They were leaving in a short while.

They had arrived yesterday afternoon. The hospital had been ready, but it had been overfilled, so they were given no time to rest. Instead they collected bamboo and large leaves to build temporary huts for the overflow of patients as well as cut camouflage foliage to hide the new activity. He'd been very tired but strangely excited. He'd heard many stories and read many accounts while a student at the university about the famous Toa Bat Hospital, built during the first revolution. It had been a large cave, but the villagers from Toa Bat had expanded the cave into the major tunnel complex it was today. Their exploits, as well as those of the doctors and nurses, were an inspiration to all liberators, he thought as he packed his last belongings. The village three kilometers to the west had been destroyed years ago; the remaining people had moved into the hospital and become its orderlies, cooks, and food gatherers. The People's Party had given the village the "Determined to Win" banner every year since 1965.

"Lieutenant Son!"

The lieutenant looked up, seeing a senior sergeant approach. "Lieutenant Son?"

"Yes."

"You are to depart in five minutes." Son stood, holding his pack and weapon. "We leave sooner than expected, then?"

"Yes, they want us to leave the area quickly. There are too many to hide if aircraft come looking."

Son walked several steps to a trail where his platoon waited. The battalion was to be split. Most would return to their base camp to the north and await replacements. Lieutenant Son and one platoon were being assigned to the Forty-seventh Regiment in the Con Trang Valley. He was very happy when Captain Vinh told him. The Forty-seventh was a famous unit and had many battle banners. It would be a long march but a good one. The route had many rest stations that would provide opportunities for his men to regain their strength and fighting spirit.

He took off his jungle hat and faced his platoon. "Fellow soldiers, we go to join the famous Forty-seventh Regiment. We leave many friends." He reached into his pack pocket and pulled out a handful of thinly cut pieces of green cloth. "Today I wear this"—he held one of the pieces up—"to show they are not forgotten." He tied the cloth around his forehead quickly. "The cloth is from our battalion commander's scarf. I proclaim this platoon the Avenger Platoon. I shall wear the mourning band for all to see. I will take it off only when the deaths of my friends . . . your friends . . . have been avenged!"

Corporal Tuy took the handful of green cloth pieces and handed them to the other platoon members.

Le Be Son raised his weapon. "We go forward today renewed with the knowledge of ultimate victory!" He placed his weapon in the crook of his arm and began walking down the trail to the south. The men rose without speaking, one at a time, and followed.

The heavy lieutenant colonel paced outside the general's door, looking at the sheaf of papers in his hand. They were all completed and needed the general's signature.

The goddamn aviation battalion had changed one of the pilot's names and erased it, then rewritten it in pencil. Didn't they know the regulations! *Okay, I've got two Silver Stars for the Rangers that directed the air attack. And a Air Medal for Valor for a Lt. Sikes. And I've got twelve more Air Medals for aviators. The corps commander has the authority to award them. Let's see . . . that's stated in Army Regulation 672-5-1, "Military Awards," Chapter One. Good, I've got it. If he asks, I'll have all the answers.*

The colonel strode to the desk, where the aide sat reading *Life*.

"How much longer?"

"I don't know, sir. The new deputy is still in there with him."

The colonel nodded. He remembered the new deputy corps commander had come in that morning. . . . What was his name? Burlington? No, Burton. Yes, Brigadier General Burton. An infantry type. *Great, that's all we need, another fire-breather. I bet the—*

The door opened and the two generals walked out in conversation.

"Get settled, Glen, then I'll get the staff to brief you on what's going on."

"Great, Sam, the sooner the better. You know me."

The colonel rolled his eyes. Shit! A fire-breather for sure.

"Come on in, Charles. Glen, I'll see you at dinner." The general was smiling. He shut the door and turned toward his G-1. "How many?"

"Sir, we've got two Silver Stars and fifteen—no, thirteen—Air Medals."

"Any West Pointers?" asked the general as he walked to his desk.

The colonel looked up from his papers. "Beggin' your pardon, sir?"

"West Pointers! Graduates!"

"Uh, well, I don't know that, sir. I—"

"Find out, Charles. It's good for the school. You know, 'Corps Commander Awards Medal to Lieutenant Hero, Class of 19——' and so and so." The general sat down, still smiling. "Plus, Charles, it's good for this old grad too. You know what I mean?"

"Oh, yes, sir, I understand. I'll find out as soon as I get back to my desk. I wanted to—"

"I was thinking, Charles," the colonel interrupted, "those Rangers wear camouflage fatigues and black berets. I'm going to look like a desk commander with my regular green jungle fatigues and ball cap. That's a very negative image, you know?"

"Well, yes, I—"

"So I've made a decision. The staff and I will all wear pistol belts and helmets. I've talked to the logistics officer and checked. The Rangers are issued three sets of camouflage fatigues and two regular. Charles, I want you to inform Major Colven that his men are to wear their green fatigues and helmets for the ceremony."

"I don't know, sir. The Ranger uniform is—"

"And, Charles, don't worry about the aviators. Their flight suits look unmilitary anyway, so let them wear whatever. What else do you have for me?"

The colonel was about to object but saw that the general had turned and was looking out the large window behind him.

"Uh, nothing, sir. I'll get the word to the major and get the information you wanted immediately." He backed slowly toward the door. He got halfway there when the general turned around and smiled.

"Thank you, Charles. You've been most helpful."

"Uh, yes, sir." Now he turned quickly and walked out.

"You scared me."

"Aw, hell, Ev, you know I wouldn't get myself greased until my boys whipped your guys good."

"No, Grade, I really . . . well, I don't wanna talk about it. How was it?"

Grady leaned back against the sandbags as the fading day bathed everything in soft gray. *Evans isn't in a joking mood*, he thought.

"It was the most horrible thing I've ever experienced, Ev. The noise, the destruction . . . It . . . it was hell." He looked at Evans. "I mean real hell! I've never experienced anything like it."

Evans stared at his friend, then shifted his gaze to the barbed wire in front of them. "What'd ya think about?"

"Death, and how easy it is to call it out and confront it. Ev, I was ready to die. Ain't that some shit? Me, the playboy who's gonna make a million, acceptin' death so easy. Why do you think that is, Ev?"

"I don't know, Grade. You're the only one who can answer that one, but I'm glad you made it. Hell, don't worry about it. I guess you proved it isn't true that your entire life passes before your eyes in living color when you're about to die."

Grady laughed. "Hell, it better not have. I woulda got horny!"

A lone guard walking the perimeter heard the laughter of the two men just ahead. "Hey, who's there?"

"A ghost and a hick! . . . No, a hick and a horny ghost!"

The guard lowered his rifle and mumbled to himself, "Goddamn pot-smokers." He turned and walked in the other direction.

Their laughter floated through the stillness as the darkness spread over the land.

Thumper reached out, lovingly grasped the cool metal next to him, and brought it to his chest. His fingers gently caressed its every ridge and depression. He thought about the men who had given him the gift. He felt a closeness to them he couldn't put into words. They were friends . . . genuine friends who cared and were concerned about him. The pistol was a wonderful gift, but it was their smiles and the knowledge that he was accepted as an equal that was the best gift of all.

9

aptain Bob Celeste, Larry Wine's alternate, ran his hand through his prematurely gray hair. "We're givin' Larry a break today, Bud. You've put a lot of hours on that guy lately, and with him gettin' that medal and all, well, I thought a day off would be good for him."

Sikes snickered as he stepped through the open door of the small plane and squeezed past the back control stick. "Bob, you know how you pilots are. It'll take weeks for you all to retrain him."

"Get in! You're in for a ride for that remark! You gotta learn, boy. Us pilots don't get mad: We get even!"

Bud placed his goody bag on the floor and adjusted his survival vest before pulling the shoulder straps over his shoulders and hooking them into the seat belt.

"Where we going today, Bud?"

"North."

"Up to where I spotted those trails?"

"Yep, you got it. You know, Bob, you're smarter than most aviators. I don't begrudge your flight pay at all; it's your base pay they oughta keep."

"Sikes, you know what I like about you? Absolutely nothin'!"

Minutes later the small plane soared skyward. Sikes watched from his window as the sun climbed the Vietnam morning sky. The sun turned the dark land below into subdued shadows, then into vibrant forms. He watched, amazed, still not jaded after countless mornings such as this.

He was feeling high. The days had been good. He felt strangely aware of everything. Colven had told him yesterday, "Kid, you did good in the air, real good. I was proud of you. Hell, ya did it better than I could have." The major had walked away then, leaving Sikes with a warm feeling that he hadn't been able to shake.

Sikes smiled to himself. Grady and Meeks had made it back. Grady was a soldier of the sort he, Bud Sikes, wanted to be. Grady was a leader, strong, good-looking, tough, yet reckless too. The manner—the confident, reckless manner in which he walked—was like a magnetic field around him that drew other men to it. He knew the right words and the right moves. Sikes had been jealous of him, but Grady had a way of taking you in and turning your jealousy into respect. You wanted to get yet closer and know the man better because you knew you were in the presence of something beautiful that men, only a special type of man, would understand. He felt good. Yes, because he knew that, although he was not a Grady, an Evans, or a Colven, he was one of them— one of the men who understood the feeling. He was a leader too—he knew that now.

The propeller cut and threw the sky behind it. Captain Celeste banked the plane right and brought the nose up slightly.

"Hey, Bud."

"Yo."

"What we got to eat?"

"Cookies."

"What kind?"

"Oreos."

"No chocolate chip or pecan sandies? How about ginger snaps?"

"Or-e-ooos."

"You'd better write your mom or girl friend and tell them you need some *real* cookies—homemade. Man, that sounds good . . . homemade. Jesus, what I'd give for a batch of the homemade peanut butter cookies my mom used to make."

Sikes felt guilty. The word *home* reminded him of the letter in his shirt pocket. He had received it the day before, but he had been too busy with a debriefing to read it. Then he'd forgotten it.

Sikes loved his mother. She was a gentle woman, unassuming and quiet. She was the foundation of the family. The pillar. He wished she and his dad could be there for the awards ceremony. They would be very proud. No, they were already proud. The ceremony would just confirm what they already knew. He was a Sikes, doing his duty as his dad had done his in World War II and as his older brother had done his three years ago during his tour here in 'Nam.

The letter. It would be like the others he received weekly. His mother would tell him what was happening in the sleepy town—"the latest gossip," she called it. Dad would give her clips from the *Charlotte Observer* sports page to include, and she'd invariably tell him what girls were still available in town. By last count, it was seven.

"There it is!" Bud looked out the left Plexiglas window. "Those low hills to your ten o'clock are where I spotted the trail. I'm going to drop down and show you. As you can see, it's too open for you guys, but you'll get an idea of how used it looks. Farther up in the mountains is where you guys could operate."

"Sounds good, Bob. Let's take a look."

Chuong had sounded the alarm several minutes before, when he had seen the plane on the horizon. His small unit had been waiting for an opportunity since yesterday noon when they'd received word. A runner had arrived from Central District Headquarters and informed his deputy platoon commander of the misfortune of a Battalion of Northern Liberators. The underground hospital at Toa Bat was overcrowded, causing men to be quartered aboveground. The situation was very dangerous. The American planes must be lured away from the hospital area. The outlying units were ordered to engage Yankee aircraft on sight. The Americans were predictable and the scheme had worked many times before. Once fired upon, many planes would appear and reappear for days. The deputy commander had asked for volunteers from the heavy machine-gunners. All had stepped forward, but he, Chuong, had been honored.

He scanned the sky beyond the small plane. It was a Yankee trick to bait a gunner with a small fish. When he made an attempt to snare the small one, the eagles would strike from high above. Today there were no eagles.

His newly dug firing pit was covered with an old camouflage net. Chuong motioned to his assistant gunner to be ready to throw the net aside, then positioned himself in the pit. The machine gun was on a solid ground table. The pit was dug in a *U* shape around the weapon. He could elevate the gun and swing from side to side easily. The small plane dropped its wing and began its descent. It would not be long. He would destroy this Yankee pirate.

Sikes could see the series of low hills coming up quickly through his left window. They were the first of many that gently rose and joined the dark mountains several kilometers farther north. The land in front of the hills was divided into brown, deserted, geometrically shaped rice paddies.

Sikes saw the trail immediately. It was light brown and about two feet wide. He followed it with his eyes. It ran along the bottom of the first hill, then into the green vegetation, and finally disappeared. He leaned closer to the window, searching. His eyes caught the movement first. A patch of green suddenly flew up and back, exposing a mound of red soil and . . . *My God!* He stomped on the floor switch. "Get up! Get up! Machine gun!" He turned to look back when the first green traces streaked by.

Celeste jerked the nose up. The backseat control stick slammed into Sikes's knee. He winced and moved his leg quickly out of the way. The left Plexiglas window suddenly exploded, showering him with plastic crystals. "Oh, God!" he screamed as the plane shuddered and more glass exploded. Sikes's faceplate wasn't down, and the wind blew the particles into his face. His body flew upward but was restrained by his shoulder harness, which groaned with the strain. His right leg jumped out and up as if exploding.

"You hit it, Chuong! You hit it! I saw the glass glisten as it fell."

"What happened to the belt?" Chuong yelled as he jerked the feeder tray up to clear the jammed round.

The excited assistant gunner had watched the plane and not the gunner. When Chuong spun the gun up and fired, he'd held the belt at an angle, causing it to bind. "I'm sorry, Corporal. I—"

"No matter, we have done what we were told. Take the tripod. Hurry! More planes will come!"

Chuong lifted the heavy weapon, being careful not to touch the hot barrel, and ran for the trail. The assistant collapsed the tripod and ran to catch up, then stopped. The plane was heading directly for the mountain. He smiled, then continued to run.

Sikes pawed at his face, brushing the plastic slivers away. "Bob!" he screamed. He tried to open his eyes but still felt shards on his eyelids. Quickly he put his fingers up and brushed them away and tried again. His body was shaking uncontrollably. The billowing wind from the broken windows blinded him, forcing his eyes shut. The pain of his leg made him feel weak and sick.

"Bob, oh, God, help me!"

The faceplate! He remembered and grabbed for the top of his helmet, pulling down the plastic visor, then opened his eyes.

"We're too low! Bob! Bob!" He frantically grabbed the control stick in front of him and pulled back. The small plane responded immediately, its nose rising. Pain swept through him, making his tight stomach go into spasms. He looked up to see Celeste. What he saw was a mountain looming ahead. *Go right! Right!* He saw the clear sky. He jerked the stick right. The plane rocked over precariously. *To much!* He pulled it back and the plane righted itself. *Easy, goddamn it! Think, Bud! Think!* He pushed the stick gently with shaking hands. It turned slowly. *We're not going to make it. We're not . . .* The mountain came closer. He could see the trees— the limbs, individual leaves. *Oh, God, we're not goin' . . .* Blue sky.

"Bob!"

Celeste lay forward in the straps to the right of his seat. Bud could see the back of his helmet. Then he saw the right Plexiglas window beside Celeste. It had two holes through it with spider-web cracks that ran out to the frame. Blood was splattered on the glass. *No!*

The plane was still turning. He pushed the stick to the center. Celeste's body moved back to the middle of the seat, suspended forward in the harness.

Sikes himself was bleeding. He forced himself to feel for the wound and drew away his hand, which was covered with a deep crimson ooze that blew off his fingers and splattered on his chest and visor.

Feel again, Bud. How bad? He put his hand down again. The bottom of his pants was soaked and stickly. He felt, then touched the material, which was stuck to his leg just below the knee. The hit had taken a piece of his upper calf. It was bad but not that bad. He was relieved in a gruesome way. He hadn't lost his leg—just a piece!

Sikes sat up, then looked down at his leg again. *My God! The floor! No! No!* The green floor was streaked with streams of thick, deep-red blood that was quivering its way to the rear of the plane with the vibration of the engine. The blood was Bob's. *Oh, God!*

Sikes looked at the land below. *Think! Okay, the mountain's to the north. I must be traveling northeast. I need to be traveling southwest.* He turned and spotted a reference point to his rear. *Now, when I turn, I need to line up on that. Then I'll at least be going in the right direction.*

With slight pressure he pushed the stick to the right. It didn't feel right. It was as if he were slipping as he turned. Why? He'd seen them fly enough. *Think! They used the pedals . . . the rudder! No sweat, don't need that.* Larry had talked about it once before. He had said it stabilized the turn or something. The plane made a gentle but awkward turn. Sikes lined up the large hill he had designated as a reference point and brought the stick to the center. *Good, now I . . .* a wave of futility ran through is mind. *Why prolong certainty? Why? I can't fly. I can't land if I get there. I'm going to die!*

Sikes closed his eyes for an instant, fighting. *No! I'm going to try, damn it! I gotta try. Relax, now. Relax.*

Radio . . . I can at least talk to someone and tell 'em I'm . . . No, X-ray is gone. I'm too far away from Ops. Maybe the aviation freqs! He picked up his left foot. The black congealed blood clung to his boot soles. His foot slipped off the metal button the first two tries, then finally depressed it.

He tried for several minutes, using all the toggles. Nothing. He looked out of the jagged window to his left. One piece of clear plastic was blowing back and forth, bending and straightening. Bending and . . . A plane! Just a speck. But it had to be a plane! He pushed the stick over and headed for the speck.

Captain Leyland Weinburg was tired. It was time to go home, he thought as he placed his map in the compartment door of the Air Force spotter plane. He saw the Army Bird Dog approaching and tried to raise it on the FAC frequency, but it didn't respond. He pulled out of the lazy turn he had been making and headed for home. The Army plane passed by his left side. He raised his hand to wave and stopped.

Jesus! Weinburg thought. *It's shot to shit!* He hadn't seen the pilot, but the rear-seater was waving frantically. Something was wrong! He turned immediately and pushed the throttle forward to catch up.

Sikes had seen the plane turn. *Thank you, Lord! Thank you!* At least now someone would see where he went down. All the rice paddies and roads to the south would provide plenty of spots to glide in. *Well, I might survive the crash.* Bob had said once they could take a pretty good crack-up and make it, 'cause they came in so slow, . . . Bob . . . poor Bob.

Captain Weinburg inspected the damage. From the angle of the holes, the pilot was probably dead. Also, a bullet had struck from the bottom, near the rear passenger compartment. Whoever was in it was lucky. Jesus, how could he say lucky? If only he could talk to him. He slapped at his chest. The emergency radio! Weinburg pulled the small radio from his flight vest and quickly depressed the small rubber tit on the side. *Come on, baby, if you're monitorin' emergency freq like you're supposed to, then . . .*

Sikes jumped, hearing the first loud beeps as they rang through his earphones. It was loud, obnoxious, beautiful. Then he heard a voice.

"Army Bird Dog, use your emergency radio. Give me your frequency. Give me a freq."

Sikes understood immediately. He reached into his vest and pulled the small radio from its plastic bag. He'd never used one! Shit. Shit. It had instructions on the front. He read quickly, then found the small button to push and squeezed.

"Air Force, Air Force, freq is . . ." He had forgotten! *God! Think!* ". . . freq is . . . thirty"—he strained—"thirty"—*I got it*—"is thirty-six-point-five-five Fox Mike. Over."

"Army Bird Dog, this is the Air Force," came a voice over the FM receiver. "How you hear me?"

Sikes almost laughed with joy as he answered, "This is Army, *loud and clear*. Over."

"You look like you took some rounds. Are you okay? Over."

"I'm hit in the leg but okay. Pilot is dead. Over."

"Roger. Are you a pilot? Can you fly? Over."

"Negative, but I ain't doing too bad so far. Are we headin' in the right direction? Over."

"Almost, Army. I will lead you. Don't worry. Between now and then, I'm going to give you some cheap flying lessons. I'm going off push for just a second to notify the airfield. I'll be back. Out."

Childs was sitting in the operations room when the telephone rang. He leaned over casually and picked up the handset. "Sierra Rangers."

He listened for a full minute. He had dropped the report and moved closer. "Yes, sir. I'll notify the major right away and put a radio on freq to monitor. . . . Yes, sir. I'll be here. The major'll probably go to the airfield. . . . Yes, sir. Thank you!"

He tossed the phone down and ran to the door. Twenty-five meters away, two Rangers were walking toward their barracks.

"Hey, you! Shitbirds, come here!" When they turned, Childs recognized both of them: Walker and Rose from team 1-3.

"Hurry up!" They both double-timed. Childs pointed at Walker. "Go get the major. He's in his hootch. Tell him it's an emergency. You"—he pointed at Rose—"go over to the headquarters barracks and find me a radio operator. Tell him to get over here. It's an emergency. Go! *Go!*"

Both men turned and ran. Childs walked two steps, then turned back around. "Dove! Dove!"

". . . Okay, Army, she's running fine, so we're not going to touch the controls, at least not until before you land. The black knob behind the radio panel is your throttle, remember?"

"Roger, Air Force, we went over that ten minutes ago. How much further, I . . . I'm not feeling too good."

"Hey, Army, no sweat! We're close, baby, close. Hang in, now! Real close. It's straight ahead, Army. I can almost see it. You got it made now, Army. Now, let's go over again how we're gonna land."

Sikes was slipping. His eyes were fixed straight ahead. It hurt too much to shift his eyes left or right. His body seemed weighted. Every movement took a conscious effort.

"Air Force, I'm not going to make it. Thanks, I . . . I . . ."

"Your ass! Army, look at it! There it is! Look, Army, look! We're going straight in. Here we go. Push the stick right. Good. Gently, now . . . a little more . . . too much! Steady, now . . . gently. Okay, now, Army, you gotta bend over and flip your pedals up. They're in the floor to your front. Just reach down and flip both of them up. That will activate them. Acknowledge, Army. . . . Talk to me!"

"Got . . . it. . . . Push pedals up."

"Roger, Army, do it now!"

Sikes leaned forward. The shoulder straps stopped him. He reached for the buckle release. His hand seemed to be in slow motion as it finally grasped the metal finger and pulled. It didn't release. He concentrated, then pulled again. It came free. His head fell to the side. He rolled it to the front, then leaned forward. The floor was covered with coagulated blood. He would have to put his hand in the blood to flip the pedals over.

"Army, I can't see you. Have you flipped them? Army! Goddamn you, Army! Sit up! Army!"

Sikes's earphones were screaming. *The pedals . . . the pedals, Army . . . pedals!* He reached out, his fingertips disappearing in the purple stickiness. *The pedals, Army . . . pedals.* He put his hand up and grasped the side of the cockpit and pushed, slipped, then tried again. He had pushed the pedals up easily. Now he was trying to sit straight. His right hand grasped the side of the metal wall. Then he lifted. He'd made it.

"Army, grab the stick! You're too low. Goddamn, Arm—"

He reached out and grabbed the stick and pulled back. It took both hands. They both shook with weakness as he stared at his bloody hands.

"Okay, we're going in. Don't talk, just listen. We're a little low. We're gonna be touching down a little short, but no sweat, Army, we'll just kick up some dust. You're on course. . . . Push the stick forward. . . . Good, now pull the throttle back. . . . Pull it back *now*, Army, *now*, Army! All the way! . . . Good, Army, good! You're lookin' good. You're almost there. A little back, back, back! Good . . . a little more . . . good. Five hundred . . . Four hundred . . . two hundred, Army. Good. . . . Push it forward gently, gently, gently. You're there! Now . . ."

The wheels touched twenty yards in front of the runway, jolting the plane. Sikes fell back, holding the stick. The plane lifted. He shoved the stick forward again. The plane hit hard, bounced, hit, bounced only a few feet, then struck again. It streaked down the runway at full speed. Sikes's head rolled left, then forward.

"*Brakes!* Hit your brakes, *Armeeeeee!*"

Sikes heard the echo in the darkness. He lifted his left foot. The right wouldn't listen! *Come on, right! Oh, hell, screw you, then!* He pushed. His body suddenly flew forward through a black void.

Colven watched in horror. Dove was screaming beside him, "Jesus! Jesus!"

The plane ran down the runway for five hundred meters, then abruptly turned left. The left wing struck the tarmac with a screeching noise that raised the hair on the major's neck. The left strut snapped and the fuselage fell to the pavement, then jumped up as the propeller struck the red dirt and shattered. The left wing snapped in half, spinning the fuselage back into the ground.

It now lay still. A red dust cloud billowed upward.

The yellow crash truck stopped with screeching brakes. The red powder it had kicked up choked and covered the men who ran for the twisted plane.

A Spec-4 got to the bird first. It lay tilted with the right side up. He grabbed the single door handle and swung it open. The smell of blood and feces sickened him. He grabbed the slumped-over pilot and pulled him toward him to unbuckle the seat belt. The lower portion of the pilot's face was gone.

The Spec-4 vomited. An older sergeant pushed the retching man aside and looked into the aircraft. He pulled the dead pilot up. The second man lay in a ball against the back of the pilot's seat. He'd been thrown forward. The sergeant climbed up into the plane to get to the blood-smeared man. His foot slipped on the sticky floor, and he fell to his knee. He reached out and pulled the man's shoulder to him, then felt for a pulse on his neck.

"We got a live one here! Help me get him out."

Two more men from the crash crew moved into the doorway, but only one could assist in the tight confines of the cockpit.

The ambulance arrived and two medics hustled to the side of the plane's door. As the first man was pulled out, a half bag of Oreo cookies fell out of the plane and onto the runway.

Colven stepped from the jeep and walked straight to the plane. Two men were getting ready to lift a man lying on the ground onto a stretcher. Another held an IV bottle that was attached to the wounded soldier by a long, thin tube. Colven moved closer, shielding his eyes from the glaring sun. He saw the camouflaged fatigue pant legs. The kid!

"On two! Ready? One . . . *two*." The four men lifted the stretcher together and walked for the ambulance. Colven walked beside the blood-splattered lieutenant. He was so pale. Christ! His eyes were half open, but only the whites showed. He looked dead. Cookie crumbs were stuck to the dried dark blood on his chest, stomach, and legs. Bud!

They lifted him gently and placed the stretcher in the metal rack.

"May I ride with him?" The black medic turned as he shut the first door. "No, it's . . . oh, sure, Major, hop in!"

The nurse picked up a pair of stainless-steel scissors from the desk top and poked them into her fatigue-shirt pocket, then patted her waist pocket and felt the stethoscope there. She turned toward the narrow full-length mirror on the door. *You're getting fat, dear. These damned fatigues don't help either,* she thought as she sucked her stomach in and turned sideways, looking at herself. *They make me look ten pounds heavier.*

She let the air out with a sigh and brushed her auburn hair back with a quick push of her hand. She hadn't wanted to cut it so short, but it got so hot, and . . . The heck with it!

She opened the door and walked out into the covered breezeway. She would never get used to living in the compound, she thought as she strode slowly down the cement walkway.

The compound was a concrete box with a large courtyard in the center. In it were twenty rooms, which all faced the open yard. The outside back wall was made of solid cement blocks, and the room walls were wood and unpainted Sheetrock. The rooms themselves were semiprivate, with two nurses in each room. The latrine was on the north side of the compound, and the kitchen–TV room was on the south side, along with the narrow exit passage, which was the only way in or out. Like a prison, she thought. The courtyard could have been a bright spot in the drab scene, but a bunker had been built in the dead center of it.

She walked past the booth where the ever-smiling MP nodded at her. "Now the obstacle course," she mumbled, and she zig-zagged back and forth through the barbed wire maze that led to the asphalt road. There she stopped and took a deep breath of fresh air.

She was standing at the top of a small knoll. Their compound was the highest point in the Seventeenth Field Hospital complex, the whole of which nestled against a rocky hill. The scene below her wasn't exactly what she had expected when she volunteered for war duty. She had had a vision of an old French plantation turned hospital: high ceilings, overhead fans, like in *Casablanca*. . . .

She took one more deep breath, then began walking down the hot black road. To her left was the main section of the complex, in which were five rows, three deep, of different-size Quonset huts. It contained everything from a mess hall to a one-hole latrine. *Yeah, Jean,* she thought dryly, *real close to a French plantation.*

To her right she heard the patio parachute pop in the gentle breeze. There, she thought, was the reason she had gained those extra pounds: the club. She loved it. It was small but neat. The outside patio had been completed a month before. The 102nd Engineer Construction Company had built it, along with a large brick grill, picnic tables, and benches. Ever since, they had been cooking out every chance they got. The food was cheap and the drinks cheaper.

She finally turned toward the next to last building. WARD B was stenciled on the door. She was about to reach for the handle when she heard the ambulance siren. That was odd. Most patients came in by helicopter. The landing pad was just on the other side of the last Q-hut, which housed the emergency room. It was probably the usual rear-echelon injury—an overdose or cuts from barbed wire—or more likely a sports injury. She shook her head as she opened the door. She had never seen so many sports injuries in such a small place. She remembered a thin black soldier telling her as she wrapped his ankle, "Hell, lady, you can go like *all out here*. I mean, really *all out*! So what, you get hurt: It's outta da field, ain't it?"

Jean walked down the aisle of the partially filled ward. Things were slow, thank goodness. Fourteen beds on this end, all enlisted. The other end was for officers. Their beds were spread a little farther apart. Her small office was just past the doorway, in the middle of the building. She almost got to the open door of her office when the double doors of the right hallway opened.

"Say, Captain O'Neal, they need you in ER *stat*."

She looked at the long-haired orderly. "Where's Lieutenant White?"

"She's up at X-ray."

"Okay, Jim, I'm on my way. Hey, go back and tell Val—I mean, Captain Weathers—where I am."

"Yes, ma'am."

Jean was angry. White should never have left ER. She should have sent an orderly with an ER X-ray patient. The patient must have been cute. She pushed through the doors. In the middle of the room was a cluster of excited men gathered around a gurney. She recognized the two medics. They were both a mess: there was blood smeared all over them and they stank. There were a couple of other strangers, one in a flight suit. Dr. Robeler was bent over the patient's head, making his preliminaries. Jean waded into the middle of the group.

"Okay, out! Everybody out right now! Give me the IV bottle!" She turned to a black medic and took the bottle. "You stay till the corpsman gets back. Get me that IV bar, huh?"

"Yes, ma'am."

The medical specialist went over to another gurney against the wall and pulled out a metal rod, which he quickly brought over and inserted in the gurney. Jean hung the bottle hurriedly and then noticed the patient's condition. Damn, he was a gory sight, but she'd seen worse. She pulled out her scissors and began cutting off his pant leg.

The doctor looked up at Jean. "He's lost a lot of blood, but we don't know his type. He's not wearing tags.

"A-positive."

The doctor and Jean both turned toward the voice.

"He's A-positive," Colven said.

He was leaning up against the wall next to the door. She hadn't seen him there.

"Okay, let's start whole blood," said the doctor as he moved beside Jean and looked at the leg wound. The long-haired orderly walked through the door.

Jean glanced up. "Get me two bottles, *whole*, A-pos, *stat*." The orderly rolled his eyes and hurried out.

"Jean, get him cleaned up and into the cutting room. I've got a broken ankle down at the other end. I'll tell surgery he's coming."

Jean backed away from the gurney to let the doctor pass. Two more corpsmen walked through the double doors. They were smiling.

"Where the hell you been?" she asked tartly. Both of the men kept smiling.

"Hey, it's chowtime, Captain," said the taller one.

Jean stepped directly in front of him and pointed a finger at his face. "You leave together again, and I'll have your ass, Simkins. Understand?"

Their expressions changed at once. The tall one nodded sheepishly. "Yes, ma'am."

"Now, push this patient over to one. Josh, you go down to six and help the doctor." The tall one grabbed the end of the gurney and started pushing. Jean started to follow, when she felt a tap on her shoulder. She turned, surprised. It was the one who'd been leaning against the wall, the major. He wore camouflage fatigues like the patient's. . . . The scar on his face looked like an old one; it was so . . . unusual.

"How is he?" the major asked her.

"He'll be fine. We'll get him into surgery and cut out some of the damaged tissue." She began to turn back around, but realized he was pleading with his eyes.

Strange, she thought. It wasn't the look she would expect from such a man. He surprised her even more by reaching out and touching her arm.

"Captain, watch him close: He . . . he's . . . well, he's a special kid."

She blinked and turned her head away. She felt oddly uncomfortable. She moved so that his hand fell away.

"Major, all our patients are special," she said, but more coldly than she had intended.

His eyes narrowed, his jaw tightened and his gaze dropped to the floor. He spoke matter-of-factly, but she could tell he was hurt.

"Of course. I'm sorry," he said, and made to leave.

"Major." She stepped closer and looked into his eyes. "I'll watch him, Major. Don't worry. I'll take special care." She winked.

His eyes widened only slightly as he reached out and touched her arm again. "Thank you." He rolled his shoulders back, took his black beret out of his pant pocket, and strode for the double doors. They swung out in one powerful push and he disappeared.

Jean heard his booming voice in the hallway:

"Dove! Dove!"

The tall corpsman shook his head. "Get a load of John Wayne. Man, what a lifer."

Jean didn't answer. She glanced over at the black medic who was watching them. "Come on over here. You can help. You guys did a good job stabilizing him. What happened to him, anyway?"

The medic leaned over and began unbuttoning the wounded man's shirt. "You got yourself a hero, here, Captain. He flew a shot-up plane back and landed it. Well, he cracked it up, but he got that sucker down."

The tall orderly snickered. "No big thing, man. They get paid for flyin' and landin' planes."

The medic looked up at the corpsman, then back at the wounded man. "Not him. He ain't no pilot."

"What?"

"He ain't no pilot. He's a Ranger."

The orderly shrugged his shoulders. "Big deal."

Jean read the soldier's name tape—SIKES—then wrote the name on a clipboard. "Simkins, get a bag." She turned again to the medic when the orderly left. "What happened to the pilot?"

"Dead. Shot through the face and abdomen. He leaked pretty bad."

Jean waved her hand in front of her nose. "I can tell."

Simkins returned and opened the plastic bag, then threw in the shirt, flight vest, and boots. Jean and the medic pulled the man's pants off. He wasn't wearing a T-shirt or underwear. The medic threw the pants into the bag, and Jean began cleaning the man with a wet sponge. She motioned toward the bag. "Mark it for me. He's Sikes, First Lieutenant, Seventy-fifth Infantry, Rangers."

Colven stared stonily ahead as the jeep rolled down the road that headed back toward camp.

She had understood. At first he thought he had misjudged her, but when she looked at him the second time, he knew he hadn't. She was a professional. She knew he was one pro asking another for a favor. He smiled, took a deep breath, and looked at Dove.

"The kid's gonna be okay."

Dove turned toward his major, smiling. "Good, sir. I was worried." He looked back at the road. "You know, sir, the Lt., he don't land too good, does he?"

Jean backed away from the table and rinsed the sponge in a pan of water. She looked over at him. He was good-looking. Kid—that was what the major had called him. But he wasn't any kid, that was for sure. Five ten, maybe eleven, and 170 or 175 pounds. Muscular chest and legs. Light brown hair. His nakedness didn't bother her. He was a patient. She had seen hundreds. He was just a patient . . . no, he was special. She had made a pact with a man she had never seen before. She had made a commitment. She wasn't sure why. She had never done anything like it before.

The word had spread quickly through the Ranger camp. The kid Lt. had been hit. At first only a few had gathered around the entrance to the TOC. Later, when Childs walked outside to wait for the major, he had had to yell at people to get out of the way.

"Hell, the whole company's here," he mumbled, then spoke to a passing Ranger. "What you doing here?"

"Nothing, Sarge, just bored."

"And you?"

"Me? Aw, ain't nothin' else happening."

Childs knew better. They wouldn't tell him, but he knew. They were waiting for word.

The jeep pulled up to the entrance. Colven got out and walked straight for the door without speaking. The gathered men moved in closer but made a path for him as he walked. Their eyes all searched his expression. He got to the doorway, then stopped and turned slowly.

"Sergeant Childs, I almost forgot: Inform the men tomorrow at morning formation that Lieutenant Sikes landed his first airplane today and fucked it up. Tell them I don't want any Rangers trying to land planes in the future. The Lt. should be around in a week or so to sign his statement of charges for the damages." Colven then winked and walked into the ops center.

Childs smiled to himself. The major . . . always trying to be a hard-ass. He could hear little bits of conversation as he walked for the ops door.

"Hey, how come us Rangers touch somethin' and we destroy it?"

"I heard the lieutenant got shot in the ass and bled chocolate-chip cookies, man."

"Shit! I had dibs on his CAR."

"Yeah, well, I was gonna get that CARE package his mom sent today."

Big Ben walked by, "Did somebody say they had some cookies?"

The heavy G-1 colonel walked into the general's office and stopped in front of his desk. The general looked up.

"Yes, Charles?"

"Sir, I need your speech for tomorrow's awards ceremony back. We need to make some changes."

"Changes!"

"Yes, sir, one of the awardees, a Lieutenant Sikes, won't be there. He got himself wounded in a plane this afternoon. He's in the Seventeenth Field."

"Shot! Didn't he know about the ceremony? What the hell are they doing, sending men out that have ceremonies coming up? Damn, I wanted that picture of me pinning the medal on a fellow graduate. It would have made the Academy paper for sure. Damn!"

"Sir, Lieutenant Sikes isn't a graduate of West Point. Lieutenant Wine, the aviator, is the graduate."

"Wine, you say? But didn't you say this man was shot in a plane?"

"Sorry, sir. Sikes was a passenger in the plane."

"Wine will be there, then, right?"

"Yes, sir, he'll be there."

"You got the word out about the uniforms, didn't you, Charles?"

"Yes, sir, it went out this morning."

"Good. Good, Charles. Now, you should know Major Collier of the Rangers came in to—"

"Colven, sir."

"Whoever. He came in asking for his company to be sent to An Khe for refitting and some special training of some kind. That will include the platoons down in Phan Thiet. I've approved the move. It works well with the plans we have for him later. He said he needed some officers to fill vacancies. Can you help him out?"

"Yes, sir, but the Rangers request officers that are Airborne- and Ranger-qualified and who have good records. Well, sir, those kind are in high demand from all our units."

"Don't worry about all the qualification crap, Charles. An officer is an officer. Get him a couple when you get a chance."

"Yes, sir. I'll take care of it."

"Good. Now, be sure you brief the photographer tomorrow. I want good pictures."

"Yes, sir."

Jean had been on the ward for an hour when they pushed the lieutenant through the double doors.

"Where you want this one?"

She glanced down the aisle with the eight empty beds. She had only one officer patient, a colonel who'd had hemorrhoids removed. He was on the far end, lying on his stomach with his buttocks elevated.

"Put him here, on this end." The bed was directly across from her office. She would be able to keep an eye on him.

Sikes had been dressed in hospital *greens*—light green pajamas. She took the chart off his bed. She was to call the on-duty doctor when the patient regained consciousness, and she wasn't to give him any medication until the doctor prescribed it. His head was bandaged, as was his leg, which was elevated on rolls of towels. He looked much better now, she thought as she brushed his hair back off the bandage. *Wonder why you're so special to your major, Lieutenant Sikes—kid.*

Colven was reading the message for the second time when Sergeant Grady and Private First Class Meeks walked in smartly and executed a right-face. Grady saluted. "Sir, Sergeant Grady and Pfc. Meeks report."

"Stand at ease. Naw, screw it, sit down." Both men looked at each other, then behind them. The only place to sit was on the major's bed.

"Read this." Colven handed the piece of paper to Grady, who read it, then gave it to Meeks. The message read: *Subject: Award Ceremony, 5th Corps Headquarters. All personnel attending ceremony will wear the following uniform: Fatigues, OD in color, standard issue.* He read down the list of a basic soldier's uniform to include olive-drab T-shirt and underwear. Then he read the last line: *The above uniform will be worn by all participants and awardees. There will be no exceptions.*

Colven paced the floor in front of them.

"What do you think of that?"

Grady looked up. "Sir, I don't have any regular fatigues and my helmet is in Ah Khe, with the rest of the gear we don't use."

Meeks added a quick "Me, too, sir."

"I can find you uniforms and helmets, if that's the only problem. Is it the only problem?"

Grady spoke up. "Sir, I don't wanna get my award wearing a REMF-ass outfit. Can't you have them just send the medal over here, and you give it to me or something?"

Colven looked at Meeks. "What about you? What're your thoughts?"

Thumper glanced at Grady, then up at the major. "Sir, I'm new, but I was thinking, when they gave me my camouflage fatigues and black beret after the Ranger introduction course, it was kinda like an award for being something special. The way I see it, I'd have to give up that award to get another one, and you know, sir, this award they're going to give me—well, it's just not worth it."

Colven shrugged his shoulders. "It's your decision. You both deserve those medals, regardless of what uniform you wear to receive them in."

"Sir, would you and the team have to wear regular fatigues if we decided to go?" Grady asked.

"Yes, we would."

"No, sir!" Grady stood up. The thought of his team and the major having to wear regular fatigues, to give up their pride for him . . . No way! "I'm feeling sick, sir. I'm sorry. I guess I'd better report to sick call. They can just send the damn thing to me in the mail or keep it!"

Meeks got up with Grady. "Sir, I think I have what Grady's got. Have 'em send mine too."

Colven stared at his two men. "You're not getting Silver Stars through the mail! I promise, you'll get them the right way. I promise. Now, get the hell outta here. You might make me sick too."

"Yes, sir," said Grady, smiling. He saluted crisply and the two men turned for the door.

Jean was sitting in her small office. The radio next to her was playing softly. AFVN (Armed Forces Vietnam Network) was playing golden oldies. She glanced up and looked through the large plastic window in the partition that gave her a view of the enlisted ward, then looked over her shoulder through the other, smaller window to check the lieutenant. He was moving his right arm. She put her pen in her sleeve pocket and got up.

"Well, Lieutenant, how are you feeling?"

He moved his head slowly and tried focusing his eyes. He moved his left arm, which held the IV.

"Whoa, there! You shouldn't be moving that arm."

He blinked twice, gazed at her face, then at her collar. "Ma'am, do you . . . have . . . my letter?" His speech was slow and slurred.

"What letter, Lieutenant?"

He focused his eyes again. "My . . . folks sent me . . . a . . . letter, ma'am. I'd like to have it . . . please, ma'am."

"Where was it?" she asked curtly.

He moved his hand to his chest and tapped his breast. "In my . . . shirt . . . pocket."

"We bagged your stuff, but I didn't see the letter. Your unit will be picking up your belongings."

He spoke in a whisper. "I . . . I . . . just wanted to . . ." He turned his head slightly; a tear trickled down from the corner of his eye.

"Are you in pain? I'm going to call the doctor. You need something to help you."

He didn't move. His eyes stayed shut. "No, thank you, ma'am."

"Well, just yell if you change your mind." She checked the IV, then went back to her desk. She hadn't checked the shirt pockets, she thought to herself. It wouldn't have mattered. It would have gone into the bag anyway. She sat down and looked over at him. *He's in pain, but the macho bastard won't ask for something to ease it. He will; they all . . .* She caught herself. *Some of them do that: They hold out for a while, then finally they ask—they beg—for it when the hurt gets that bad.*

She picked up the telephone to call the on-duty doctor as per his instructions.

"You shitting me? 'Not going'? What do you mean, 'not going'? We're gonna make a killin' at that award ceremony. The place will be full of REMFs."

Pete shook his head. "Dove, the major told Childs what I just told you. I was there at my typewriter and heard the whole conversation."

"Not going? I'll see about this!" Dove kicked the NVA canteens that were neatly tied and laid out on the floor. "They can't get away with it!" He walked down the aisle of the long deserted barracks toward the far door, talking to the walls the entire way: "The bastards! How dare they! I'll . . ." He walked out the door. Pete reached down and put the canteens back in their place.

First Lieutenant Bud Sikes opened his eyes and stared at the curved corrugated steel above him. He remembered hitting the runway and bouncing. Then there had been a blur of motion and blackness. . . . His leg was bandaged, and he had obviously hit his head. It was bandaged too. The letter—he wanted it desperately. His mind ached for a place far away where troubles were few and smiles plentiful. The familiar, neatly penned lines of his mother's handwriting would speak of people he loved. It would help him drown the images of the floor, the blood . . . *oh, no . . . my God . . .*

"Hi, Jean!"

Jean looked up. It was her friend and roommate, Captain Valerie Weathers. Val had come to relieve her. She was a tall, pretty black girl who had a perpetual smile.

"Oh, hi, Val. It's time, huh?"

" 'Course it's time! You usually meet me at the door. What's up?"

Jean stood up. "Nothing, I was just calling about some letter a patient left in his fatigues."

"The unit picks all that up."

"I know, but the unit hasn't come yet. I guess I'll go over and look through his fatigues."

"Are you kiddin'? That stuff is kept in the last building, honey. Why, I wouldn't walk that far for O. J. Simpson. Well, maybe for O.J., but sure not for anything I've seen around here."

"Now, Val. . . ."

Valerie glanced over at the lieutenant. "Hey, Jean, what we got here?" She walked over to the lieutenant's bed. He was sleeping. She came quickly back to her desk. "Oh, my, Jean dear, we have got us a hunk. Who is he?"

Jean pulled his file from a wall basket and handed it to the inquisitive nurse. Jean was trying to look busy while Val scanned the record.

"Whoo-wee, honey! A Ranger lieutenant, no less! You know what they say about them?"

Jean tried to ignore her, then slammed her pencil down, giggling. "Okay, Val. I can't take the suspense. What do they say about *them*?"

Val put her hands on her hips and cocked her head to the side.

"Well, honey, they say: Rangers do it at night/With all their might!/That women love their gun/The one made for fun./But during the day/To the women's dismay,/They kill for fun to earn their pay!"

"Gross."

Val winked and bent over to whisper. "And, honey, I got the night shift. Whoo-wee!" She broke up again.

Jean couldn't help but laugh. She loved Val. Val was crazy, but she was a friend and always good for a laugh.

"I'm leaving on that one," Jean said, smiling. "Oh, Val, if *that* Ranger attacks you tonight, be sure and log it."

"Oh, Jean!" Val called out as Jean walked toward the swinging doors.

"Yeah?"

"Which one of these patients are you gettin' the letter for?" She smiled brightly, innocently.

Jean turned away, embarrassed, and walked through the door.

"Dove!"

The unmistakable voice resounded across the camp. Many a Ranger smiled, envisioning Dove jumping to get to his jeep and find the Ol' Man.

Colven waited, his hands on his hips, watching the sun dip below the horizon. The sound of the approaching jeep broke his trance. Dove pulled up beside him. He walked around the hood of the jeep and sat in the front seat.

"Go by ops and pick up Childs."

"Yes, sir."

"Well? Did you get 'em?"

"Sir, doesn't the Dove always take care of you?"

Colven laughed. "Yeah, Dove, you do, but one day I'm gonna go to jail because of it."

Dove smiled and handed Colven a package of chocolate-chip cookies.

When Jean opened the plastic bag, she was almost overcome by the smell. She held the bag away from her, and reluctantly put her hand in, and withdrew the shirt with her fingertips.

The letter was in the left pocket. She pulled the damp, crumpled paper out and stuffed it into her pant pocket, then picked up the shirt with two fingers and put it back into the bag.

Val was right: it was a long walk. She would have to hurry back to get to the club on time to see the movie. *True Grit* with John Wayne was the advertised feature. She'd seen the movie at Fort Sam Houston during her basic course. It was one of her favorite pictures.

When she finally walked through the swinging doors of the ward, she was surprised to see three men, Rangers, around the lieutenant's bed. The major was in the center. She recognized him immediately.

Val was standing against the lieutenant's bed. She looked over at Jean, grinning.

"See, gentlemen, reinforcements! Now, as I was telling you, be cool. He's still not really ready for visitors"—she smiled—"but I hear us girls can't tell a Ranger no."

The men seemed embarrassed and only made feeble attempts at smiles.

"Okay, guys, he's all yours," Valerie said, and left them alone.

Sikes looked up at them with a tired grin. They were all talking at once as they gathered around him, except Colven, who was staring at the young nurse he had seen that morning. She saw him looking at her and smiled. He immediately approached.

"How's he doing?"

She spoke sincerely. "Your kid's doing fine, Major."

Colven smiled and turned toward the lieutenant's bed. When he approached, the others stepped back. He reached into the Claymore bag around his shoulder and brought out the package of chocolate-chip cookies. "Kid, we knew you couldn't make it through the night without a snack." They all laughed.

The lieutenant shook his head drunkenly. "Thank you, sir."

"Sure, kid. Hey, we're gonna let you sleep. The rest of the guys will be here tomorrow. There's a FAC pilot who especially wants to meet his first flying student. I told him to come by."

"I want to meet him, too, sir. Sir, you'll make sure he's—"

"Taken care of? You bet, kid. I put him in for a Life Saving Medal this afternoon."

The lieutenant smiled again but was obviously having difficulty keeping his head up. Childs took a step back, then turned toward the lieutenant. "Better get your ass back quick. Them shitbirds in your platoon will turn to shit, ya know."

The sergeant turned away and walked for the door.

Dove leaned over to the lieutenant's ear. "Watch these REMFs, sir. If you need somethin', let the Dove know. I'll take care of it. Watch 'em, sir."

Colven stood at the end of the bed. When Dove went out, he patted Sikes's leg. "See you tomorrow. Get some sleep." He looked at Jean. "You take care too."

Valerie poked her head out of the office door. "Y'all come back now, hear?"

Now the room was empty of visitors. Jean picked up the package of cookies and set them on the small dresser beside the bed. The lieutenant had his eyes closed. She took the crumpled letter and put it in his right hand. She had just enough time to make the mess hall before it closed and get a good spot for the movie.

"Bye, Val."

"Honey, you'd better watch that Ranger." She threw her head in the direction of the lieutenant. "Them kind sneak up on you."

Jean smiled. "Val, you're so full of it. That's why I love ya."

She pushed open the swinging doors, thinking of John Wayne. The movie would at least be a respite from the olive-drab monotony of this damn place . . . for a few hours, anyway.

Sikes felt the pressure of the letter being placed in his hand. He opened his eyes and saw her back as she walked away. He felt the dampness of the paper as his fingers explored the texture. The major and the others visiting him had made him feel good. He hadn't realized seeing them would make a difference, but when he saw those camouflage fatigues and familiar faces, it had triggered an emotion of . . . He couldn't think of a word except *love*. Love? That wasn't it . . . but, yet . . . maybe it was a type of love—a love of kinship, mutual respect, and trust. His eyes closed slowly. Having the letter in his hand was enough for now. His feelings for the men who had just left flooded him with fond memories. Dove and his REMFs, Mr. Scrooge Childs, and the major . . . the major. Sikes had never met anyone like him. Every man in the company came under his spell. The major . . . Sikes's mind floated into an abyss of darkness and painless sleep.

The lieutenant colonel had just received the message while at the Corps Officers Club and hastily excused himself from the visiting delegation from Maryland. He hurriedly asked for the phone and was directed to the club office. He dialed the number given to him in the message. The phone rang only once before it was picked up.

"Sierra Rangers."

Before the voice on the other end could identify itself, the lieutenant colonel said gruffly, "Get me Major Colven."

"Who is this?" Sergeant First Class. Childs said in his meanest voice.

"Colonel Rite, G-1 Corps. Get me Colven."

"Sorry, sir, Major Colven is indisposed at the moment. Can I take a message?"

"I got a message that said you Rangers would not be participating in the awards ceremony. I want to know *why*!"

Childs smiled to himself. He'd been waiting for this call. "Sir, I'm familiar with that situation. I can explain, if you want."

"Go on."

"As you know, sir, we have only two platoons here. The other half of the company, our headquarters, is in An Khe. Unfortunately our supply section is over there too. In short, sir, we don't have the uniforms you wanted us to wear."

"I will call the Corps G-4 and have those uniforms delivered by tomorrow morning. I want those awardees there!"

"Oh, I'm sorry, sir. I thought we were talking about the Ranger contingent that was to represent the unit. You didn't receive word about the misfortune of the awardees?"

"I know about the lieutenant's getting shot, but what's wrong with the others?"

"Sir, the message was hand-carried this afternoon to your office, explaining that both Sergeant Grady and Pfc. Meeks contracted a severe case of post-hyperreactive-tension syndrome."

Dove had come up with that one. At least the shitbird was good for something. "It's unfortunate, sir, but the doctor has them on restricted bed rest."

"What? Post-what syndrome? Oh, shit! Never mind. You've undoubtedly got a signed medical slip to cover your ass. Okay, Colven got me on this one. But warn your major: He'll pay for this!"

"Sir, I will of course relay your message to the major and your condolences to the sick awardees. Was there something else, sir?"

The colonel slammed the phone down, startling the petite Vietnamese cashier at the desk. "Shit!" He was thinking quickly. *I'll tell the general tomorrow. I've got to come up with something better than post-whatchamacallit. Just as long as that West Pointer's there, he'll be happy.* He took a deep breath. *Colven, you shouldn't let pride get in the way of your career.*

"Lights!"

Jean smiled to herself as the humming projector threw the white tunnel of light onto the painted wall.

It was a typical movie night. The film had broken for the third time in ten minutes. The usual catcalls, insults, and questions were directed at old Sergeant Henry, the projectionist, who cussed the machine, the movie, the Army, and the hecklers, then started over again.

Jean sat on her Japanese futon, looking down the small grassy slope at the fuzzy cowboy figures moving on the painted white wall that served as a screen. Patients had priority on the few benches, and they sat up front. Staff such as herself sat on the gentle slope, which afforded a good view and a place to stretch out and relax. Susie Mercy had brought a whole blood cooler filled with beer and ice and sat next to Jean with her most recent boyfriend, a pilot from the Medevac helicopter unit assigned to the hospital. Susie would probably be using Jean's room later. Susie's roommate was a religious woman who wouldn't hear of men being brought into their room for an immoral purpose, as she called it. But Susie wouldn't think of disappointing a pilot.

The pilots did very well dating nurses. The helicopter pilots especially could provide the benefits of their profession. Free helicopter rides to almost anywhere in Vietnam and, of course, lots of money, which they spent freely. But they were a high-risk group. Their numbers had been reduced by six since Jean had been assigned—young, laughing men who didn't return.

She knew she couldn't handle it—getting involved with one of them and seeing him daily, then sweating out his missions.

Colven stood in front of a blackboard in the briefing room. Childs sat in a T-shirt, drinking beer and holding a note pad. Colven had a Budweiser in his hand and leaned on the podium.

"We're leaving, lock, stock, and barrel. I wanna be in An Khe in three days. Jerry, you take care of the vehicle transportation. I'll have to handle air transport myself."

Childs nodded. It was nothing new. They moved almost every two months. They would get out as much as possible by air. What was left would go by vehicle convoy.

"I want you to call the first sergeant and tell him we're coming in," Colven went on. "And I want everything ready. I don't want any screw-ups with chow or bunks. We're going to do some reorganizing and refit. Tell the first sergeant I want supply inventoried and a maintenance report of vehicles on my desk when I get there. I want the Ranger school to be prepared to teach the company classes in adjusting artillery fire, directing close air support, and advanced first aid. Lay on enough ammo for everyone to qualify with all weapons. And I want gas training. Okay, now it's your turn. What else?"

Childs looked up. "We need each of the teams to inventory their shit for sure, John. I think we're gettin' slack on team SOPs. I know for sure we need some more training on daisy-chaining Claymores, and we got to have a refresher course in RTO procedures."

Colven nodded. "Inform the first sergeant."

When Colven was satisfied that Childs didn't have anything else to add, he continued, "Tomorrow we're going to dress in our best, and I'm treatin' you to a steak dinner at the hospital O Club after visiting the kid."

Childs stared at the major suspiciously. "What's the occasion? You never sprung for chow in your whole life!"

Colven walked for the door. "I'm celebrating leaving this damn place; plus, you're paying for the beer." He walked out and quickly stepped back into the doorway. "And the beer costs more than the steaks!" He disappeared just as a beer can ricocheted off the door frame.

"Lights!"

The movie was over. Susie had left with her pilot during the third reel. Jean picked up her futon and saw that Susie's cooler was still there. She began dumping the ice when First Lieutenant Tom Lambosco walked up and asked if he could be of "some assistance to a damsel in distress." She smiled. He was one of the medevac pilots and was known for his love-'em-and-leave-'em routines.

"Sure, Tom. I'd appreciate it."

She picked up her futon and began walking to the nurse's compound. Tom followed carrying the empty cooler.

"Jean, you're lookin' good, especially from back here."

Jean blushed. "You walk in front," she said tersely.

He made a face at her as he passed by. He was tall and awfully good-looking, she thought. His black mustache and hair and his olive skin made him sort of dashing.

"Jean, when're you flying to Saigon with me? We got a maintenance flight next week."

"No, you know I have to put in for a leave earlier than that."

"Well, how about in two weeks? They have the best restaurants in the land."

Jean kept walking, pushing him forward. She knew it was expected of nurses to spend the night with their pilots on these Saigon trips. The BOQs were always filled with VIPs, so that meant a local hotel, at which the pilot always had a reservation.

It was a good arrangement. Fun for a night. Lately she had thought about taking a pilot up on it, but she was not quite ready yet.

"Let me think about it, Tom."

The pilot shook his head. "Jean, I promise, you won't regret it. They have one restaurant . . ."

They passed the MP shack and entered the courtyard. She hadn't heard what he'd said. She knew Susie would be using her room, so she slowed down before reaching it and turned around.

"Thanks a lot, Tom, for helping. You coming over tomorrow for steaks?" She already knew the answer. Wednesday night was half-price-steak night, and the Evac pilots' hootch was only a couple of hundred meters away.

"Sure, Jean, I'll be there." He put down the cooler and gave her a light kiss on the cheek. He always did that. It was just his way, and she liked it.

"See you tomorrow, honey," he said. He walked a couple of steps and turned. "You think about it, Jean. I know a place with great lobster."

He smiled, then walked down the sally port. Jean watched him, wondering if she would go. The screen door to her room was covered with a straw mat. All the rooms had them in case of heavy rains. In this case, however, it was a prearranged signal to Jean that Susie was inside. Jean went back to the cooler, pushed it up to the door, and put the futon on top. She stood next to the door for a few seconds, listening. She could hear her tape deck playing the new *Hair* album. "Aquarius" was playing. She turned and walked down the walkway. She would check on the lieutenant one more time. What the hell. She had the time, and she had a promise to keep.

Sikes was awake. He raised his head slightly. The lights were off except for the one in the nurse's office, where he could see the pretty black nurse thumbing through files. She had just sat down after making rounds. His throbbing leg had awakened him. He could also feel the IV needle; it was uncomfortable. His letter was still in his hand.

The swinging door opened, letting light flood into the ward for a moment. He heard a woman's voice: "Hi, Val."

"Well, looky here, a friend has come to look after things so her roomy can go to the potty, right, honey?" She gave Jean one of her pleading expressions.

Jean laughed. "Yes, I've come to save a friend."

Val rolled her eyes. "Susie's using the room again, huh?"

Jean smiled, embarrassed. "Well, you know, these summer romances . . ."

Val got up and tossed her pen onto the remaining files. "Well, I hope that girl uses *your* bed this time, honey! I'm tired of sleeping on wet sheets." Jean blushed. "I'll tell you what. I'm gonna make that girl order a rubber sheet from Sears. You just wait and see." Valerie walked out of the office and headed for the swinging doors. She looked through the partition. "You just wait and see!" She walked on through the doors.

Jean stood at the desk, smiling. Then she turned slowly and looked at the lieutenant. She could make out only his shadow against the white sheets. Suddenly she left her station and went to his bed.

She checked his IV and leg bandage, then moved around the bed and saw the letter she had put in his hand earlier. It might disturb him if she took it. She stood over him, staring at his face in the darkness, then reached out and pushed back a lock of hair that had fallen over his head bandage. *What makes you so special?* she wondered. A few seconds passed. She walked to the desk, remembering what Valerie had said: "They sneak up on you, honey."

Sikes felt her presence. He could hear her breathe and smell her light fragrance in the darkness. She looked at him a long time. He hoped she wouldn't leave. Her smell was so different and wonderful, he almost smiled with pleasure. When she walked away, he felt saddened. He watched her in the lighted office until the swinging doors opened again and the black nurse returned. They exchanged a few words he couldn't hear, and then she left, but not without first giving him a last look. He had forgotten about the leg.

Childs walked through the barracks, yelling, "Get out of them fart sacks, shitbirds! It's morning and *moving* day!"

"NCO call in ten mikes, my hootch."

They were moving to An Khe. No one was surprised. Their unit changed location so often. Still, the Rangers got up sluggishly. They knew Childs would yell no matter what they did.

Childs walked through the last barracks door. "God damn it, Dove, this place looks like a fucking NVA supply dump!"

Pete and Dove rose slowly from their beds. "Aw, Sarge, my inventory is a little overstocked, that's all," Dove complained, yawning.

Childs weaved his way through the piles of equipment, which were all tagged and priced. "The major wants to see you ASAP. Pete, start typing up three-day passes for First and Second platoons. Don't put a location, and don't tell anyone!" Childs threw a cold glare at Dove. "You'd better not say a fucking word, Dove, or I'll report your ass to the Better Business Bureau!"

"Aw, Sarge."

Childs started marching out. He stopped and picked up two NVA buckles. "Dove, I need these for trading material. How much?"

Dove yawned. "Take 'em, Sarge. Don't worry about it."

Childs smiled to himself, thinking that Dove, the big flimflam man, never screwed over a fellow Ranger. "I'll pay ya payday."

Dove was looking for his pants. He just waved his hand at the sergeant, leaned over, and grabbed a boot. Childs walked out, putting the buckles in his pocket.

"Sir, you wanted to see me?"

"Get in here, Dove! Dove, I won't be needing my jeep this afternoon or my jeep trailer. I understand you have excess equipment, and I thought you might want an opportunity to unload your surplus."

Dove smiled broadly. "Oh, yes sir. Thank you, sir."

The major stood up from his desk and looked at his blond driver. "You know, I haven't told you how much . . . Aw, never mind, Dove. Get out of here! And get rid of all that shit! I don't want to carry half the NVA equipment in Vietnam to An Khe."

Dove walked hurriedly to the door. "Thank you, sir. Thank you." Once out the door, he started running toward his hootch. "Pete! Pete!"

Nguyen Van Hoi was on his feet. A soldier and the pretty nurse who had stopped the day before were walking him down the tunnel corridor. He would finally see where the entrance was. His shoulder hurt, but he felt much stronger. His legs were shaky with weakness, which embarrassed him, but he was slowly regaining strength in them.

The tunnel was long and had four major connecting arteries. Fellow soldiers lay in beds for as far as he could see down each of the corridors. He saw many people, old and young, carrying food, tea, and bedding, and helping the nurses. An old woman who was sweeping looked up and smiled at him. His eyes filled with tears at the thought of the people who had given so much of themselves for the reunification. The busy entrance was ahead. The sunlight was a welcome sight. They walked out the large door. A huge camouflage net stretched from the entrance to huge trees thirty meters distant. The net was suspended by bamboo poles spliced many times and was at least five meters high. A wide trail ran in front of the tunnel entrance and descended the gradually sloping hill that overlooked a beautiful valley below. The trail and area beyond were full of activity. They took a winding path to the right and started following it up the hill.

There was virtually no ground vegetation, only the large trees and their triple-canopied branches. A series of bamboo huts appeared in front of him, among which walked many bandaged patients. He recognized several and called out to them.

The nurse took him to the first hut for processing and set him down gently on the rice-straw-matted floor. She smiled and told him good-bye, patting his shoulder. The sergeant, sitting at the desk, asked several questions, then assigned him to hut three. He told him he was fortunate, for a troupe had come to entertain the wounded that day, and he would be able to attend. Hoi smiled. He had not seen a troupe before. It would be great fun.

Jean came on duty and saw several officers, including an Air Force pilot, gathered around the lieutenant's bed. She checked all the other patients first. It took longer than she thought it would, because of two new patients who had been brought in that morning. One Fourth Division sergeant had accidentally shot himself with his pistol while cleaning it, and the other was an overdose case. The lieutenant colonel with hemorrhoids was feeling better and wanted to talk. She listened politely while watching the men come and go from the lieutenant's bed. She made several light comments to the colonel, then excused herself to check the lieutenant. She walked over and stood in front of several enlisted Rangers. One was talking about a pig that had attacked someone called the Rock. Hardly a common topic of conversation, but they were all laughing. Strange bunch, she thought.

"Well, Lieutenant, you seem to have lots of friends." The lieutenant felt better. She could tell by his quick eyes and his color.

"No, ma'am. These guys are just here checkin' to see if they're still in the will."

They all smiled. Sergeant Grady quickly added, "That's right, ma'am. Had he bought it, I'd gotten the lieutenant's CAR-15, and Rock here would get his collection of fu—" He stopped short, realizing his error."—*Playboy* magazines."

She knew what he had been going to say: fuck books. She had heard it many times before. In fact, that's what the girls called them too. She wouldn't embarrass the sergeant by looking shocked. She inspected the lieutenant's IV and bandages.

"The needle goes, after this one," she said to Sikes, pointing to the bottle over his left arm.

Rock stepped closer. "Ma'am, I hope that's liquid C rats, 'cause that's all the Lt. could handle."

Sox shook his head. "Man, it's not Cs. It ain't OD. It's clear. Looks like bug juice to me."

They all laughed again. Jean decided she liked them. "Well, it's time you guys said good-bye for now. I have to clean this guy up."

Rock grinned. "Aw, ma'am, can't I watch? I never seen big people play doctor!"

Grady hit Rock jokingly and started dragging him out. The others were laughing. They all said good-bye to the lieutenant and headed for the door. She heard one of them say to the sergeant, "I wish I could get washed by that round eye. You see her big . . ."

They walked out. It didn't bother her. In fact, she took it as a compliment. She did have nice breasts, she thought, if only her damned tummy and rump weren't growing out of proportion.

"Those yours?" she asked the lieutenant, nodding toward the departing Rangers.

"Yes, ma'am, they're in my platoon." He smiled, then quickly added, "I hope they didn't offend you, ma'am. It's just that they haven't been around wome—lady officers."

"I'm used to it. What's a CAR-15?"

The question surprised him, then he remembered Grady's remark. "Oh, ma'am, that's a short version of an M-16 rifle. It's actually called a Colt Commando. It's got a shortened barrel and stock and . . ." He looked at her. "I'm sorry, ma'am, you didn't want to hear a weapon-characteristics history, did you?"

She smiled. "Not really." He lowered his eyes to his chest. "Ma'am, thank you for getting the letter for me. It meant a lot to me at the time."

She was embarrassed. She hadn't realized that he knew who'd retrieved it. She turned, irritated. "Don't call me ma'am! We're the same age. Call me anything but that, okay?"

The lieutenant was surprised by her tone. "Yes, ma'—Captain. I didn't mean to—"

She walked toward her office without looking back. *Well, goddamn, what are you supposed to call them?* he wondered.

A short, fuzzy-headed doctor walked through the swinging doors and straight into the nurses' office.

"Let's go. I don't have much time!" he snarled.

Jean turned to face the impatient doctor. It was Captain Locke. Nobody liked him. He was the most unfriendly American she'd met in Vietnam. She gathered the files and followed him down to the end of the ward.

He started on her immediately:

"Captain, when was the last time you annotated these files? It seems you missed a round."

"No, Doctor, you're early by an hour. I would have started my prerounds by now."

"Not likely."

He poked his patients with his stubby fingers, causing many to cry out or moan. He seemed to like it. Jean hated him more every time he grabbed a soldier. They worked their way up to the sergeant who had accidently shot himself in the foot. He was only an empty bed space away from the lieutenant. The curly-headed doctor cupped his hand around the young sleeping sergeant's foot and squeezed. The sergeant awoke with a deep moan. The doctor squeezed again.

Jean was fed up. "Doctor, is that necessary?"

He looked up; giving her a cutting stare, he dropped the sergeant's foot and took the nurse by the arm. He pushed her to the empty place between the beds. His hand dug into her bicep. "You don't ever question me in front of patients, you bitch!" He spit the words out of a clenched jaw. He turned and went directly to the lieutenant's side.

Sikes had heard the other men moan and gasp with the doctor's prodding. At each sound of pain he became angrier. He had watched Fuzzy-Head operate on the last two men. When the man had grabbed the nurse, that had done it. Now the doctor reached down and felt the leg bandage and applied pressure. Sikes didn't flinch. The doctor stared into the lieutenant's eyes and squeezed again. Sikes's eyes bore through him without giving him the satisfaction of a reaction. He reached up to touch the lieutenant's forehead bandage. Sikes's right hand shot up and caught the doctor's in midair. He bent the startled man's hand back, making him groan and shift his body to alleviate the angle of pressure. "What the hell . . . are you . . . doing?"

Sikes applied more pressure. The captain raised his other hand to his cramped arm. "Stop. Stop!"

Sikes spoke slowly. His jaw muscles rippled. "I thought you wanted to play games." His eyes were wide and wild.

Jean held her breath. He was going to break the doctor's hand; she knew it. She couldn't move.

The doctor was whimpering, "Stop, please, stop . . ."

Sikes smiled cruelly. "Guess you don't wanna play anymore, huh?"

"No. No . . . no more."

Sikes kept the pressure on. "You know, where I come from, officers don't call ladies names. You do that again, or make a soldier so much as whisper from pain, and I'll knock your gawddamn head off. Understand?"

The doctor nodded, sweating and writhing in agony. Sikes, his eyes narrowed and his chest heaving as his breath came heavily through his nose, released him. Jean was still scared. She thought he would grab the doctor again and kill him. His right fist was clenched, and the veins in his arms were standing out over his taunt muscles.

The doctor cradled his injured hand and backed quickly away from the bed. His voice was a high-pitched whine; "Stupid grunt! I'll have you court-martialed! I'll report you for this!" The doctor was leaning over his sore hand; perspiration rolled off his forehead. Sikes watched, hoping he would come close again.

The doctor looked at Jean. "You saw that. He attacked me. That . . . that idiot attacked me!" His eyes were pleading, and he was spitting out his words. Saliva formed on both sides of his mouth. He looked at the lieutenant, then down the ward. Every eye was on him. He looked back at Jean, then ran through the double doors.

Jean stared at the lieutenant, whose eyes hadn't left the swinging door. "Now you've done it!"

Sikes shot a glance at her that made goosebumps rise on her arms. His eyes slowly widened, and his rigid body relaxed. He took a deep breath, looked at her again, then abruptly turned his head. She stood shaking. She had never seen a man give a look like the one the lieutenant had given the doctor. And for an instant, only an instant, those eyes of hate had fallen on her. It was like looking at an animal about to strike, an animal that would go for the throat. She stood there for another few seconds, trying to make sense of what had occurred. Down the ward aisle the men were still staring at the lieutenant and her, and smiling. She walked toward the sergeant who was trying to sit up.

"Lie back down, Sergeant. It's all over."

"Who is that guy, Captain?" The sergeant nodded toward the lieutenant.

"Oh, just a combat-fatigued soldier."

"Fatigued, my ass! You think he broke the doc's hand?"

Jean was embarrassed. She didn't know whether to cry or laugh. "I don't think so. I didn't hear any bones crack."

"Well, I ain't takin' no shit off that doc again! He'll never squeeze me like he did, or I swear I'll do the same thing that guy did. Jesus, it was somethin', wasn't it!"

Jean heard herself say, "Yes, it was somethin'." Then she hastily began settling down the others.

"First Lieutenant Wine, Larry R., 438-12-6834, United States Army, is hereby awarded the Air Medal with Valor device for . . ."

"How much again for flag, canteen, and buckle?"

Dove had four men around the jeep's trailer, including the master sergeant who just asked the price.

"Forty dollars, Sergeant."

"He displayed exceptional courage during . . ."

"Okay, deal!" Dove was parked in the parking lot of the corps headquarters. The awards ceremony was being conducted a hundred feet away in a large grassy field next to the corps headquarters building.

". . . flying his L-19 light observation aircraft with exceptional . . ."

"Can I see one of those flags and pith helmets?"

"You want a battle flag? I'm sorry, the flag has blood on it. The guy had it in his shirt and, well, you know. He kinda leaked on it."

"Let me see that one," said the tall specialist.

Dove reached toward the trailer, but Pete had already pulled the flag and pith helmet out and handed it to him. Dove winked at Pete, who looked down quickly, trying not to laugh.

"Ladies and gentlemen, awarding the medal to Lieutenant Wine is General Samuel . . ."

"Okay, I'll take these two." The specialist held the flag and helmet up.

Pete spoke matter-of-factly, interrupting the money exchange. "We only have a couple of NVA buckles left." He reached into the barracks bag that held ten more buckles and pulled out the cloth-covered buckle. "You said we'd keep two for ourselves so that leaves only one." He pulled the buckle from the dirty cloth and turned the red star toward the specialist.

"Let me see one of those." The soldier fingered it gingerly.

"Does that one have a name on the back? Sometimes them dinks do that," asked Dove casually.

The specialist turned it over. "Hey, this one's got a name. How much for the buckle?"

Nguyen Van Hoi sat back against a large tree. A light breeze was blowing over the hundred assembled patients, soldiers, and village volunteers who sat among the shaddock trees and watched the Nam Bo modern drama troupe perform a play called "Huong Buoi," "Scent of the Grapefruit Flower." In fascination he watched the painted faces and graceful dances. His eyes had wept at one of the beautiful songs. The story was so real, he thought. It related to the struggles of a coastal village in the south called Hon Dat against the U.S. puppets. As the conclusion of the play, the hospital commander presented the troupe liaison officer a small banner signed by the hospital staff. The director wept when he received it. He said it was the greatest honor the troupe had received—"the thanks of those who had given so much for the revolution." The commander asked them to sing one more song. Hoi and many others joined in the applause for more.

The troupe sang two songs and then walked among the wounded and shook their hands. Hoi was very happy. Can Truong, who had played the peasant girl, had shaken his hand and spoken to him.

"Thank you for your spirit," she said sweetly. Hoi sat against the tree for a long time. Most returned to their duties, but Hoi wanted to treasure the moment of such a good day a little longer.

"Now, what the hell happened?"

Lieutenant Sikes was looking up at a lieutenant colonel, a major, and two captains he had never seen before. Behind them was Fuzz-Head with a bandaged hand. Fuzz-Head spoke out behind them. "He attacked me! He's crazy!"

The lieutenant colonel told Fuzz-Head to be quiet, that he had already heard his story.

Jean stood to the side. She had removed the IV a few moments before they all came in. She and the lieutenant had not spoken. He was not intimidated by the high-ranking officers, Jean noted. He talked to them as he talked to his friends,

although he added a polite "sir" now and then. He told them
exactly what had happened. The colonel and other officers
showed no emotion, just nodded attentively now and then.
When he was finished, they thanked him and went over to
the sergeant, who used a lot more invectives. Several times
the colonel had glanced at Jean to ensure she was not embarrassed by his colorful verbiage. The officers went to each
patient in turn. Some said nothing; others were happy to
have the attention. Captain Locke was sweating and doing a
lot of mumbling.

The colonel turned to Jean. "Can you add anything?"

"No, sir," she said quickly.

The lieutenant colonel took her aside, leaving the others
by the door, and put his back to the officers as he asked
quietly, "How long has Locke been doing these Gestapo ex-
aminations?"

Jean was blocked from the others' view. "About a week
ago he started getting bad, sir."

"We've had complaints before. Too bad the lieutenant
didn't break his damn hand and solve our problem, eh?"

He winked at her, then turned around and joined the others. Fuzz-Head was excluded. A few minutes later the others
left, taking Locke with them.

The colonel ran his hand through his thinning hair and
spoke to Sikes. "You know, son, I run a good hospital. I'm
very proud of my people, just as you're proud of your unit. I
have, as you have, a few, just a few, who don't fit and, well,
won't fit. I'm afraid you've met one of my few. Words won't
say the 'I'm sorry' that I feel, but I apologize for him and
this hospital."

He stood, a sincere man—a professional who had been
betrayed by a fuzz-head, thought Sikes.

"Sir, I understand." He smiled at the colonel and wanted
to say more but couldn't find the words.

The colonel smiled. He had heard what he wanted to hear.
He patted the lieutenant's arm. "Thank you, son."

Childs was on his second beer. He was pissed. He'd given
the young NCOs a quick class on load plans, load lists,
weight restrictions, and the marking of centers of gravity of
vehicles. He'd turned them loose to screw it up, so he, the
senior NCO of the fucking place, could come and save the

whole mess by his leadership and organizational abilities. They'd done it perfectly!

"Goddamn, I'm a dinosaur!" He threw the can across the hootch.

Lieutenant Le Be Son was watching the sunset. His body was relaxed, his feet and ankles sore. The trail had been steep and angled. His tendons and ligaments had been stretched from negotiating the difficult trail. His men were exhausted, but they were all very happy. They had made it to the first rest station. They would stay there and rest for two days. It was a wonderful camp. The Mnong villagers had welcomed them with rice and green tea. They were mountain people of the Meo minority. He had seen several of their guides and scouts while at the base camp, but never before had he seen a whole village. The group was quite small, perhaps only twenty in number—only four families. The others, Ton explained, were farther north in their large village. They were a stocky people and rounder of eye than most Vietnamese. Their skin was a browner color. The women were thick-chested and wore many brass bracelets and necklaces. The toothless old women smoked long, curved pipes full of pungent tobacco. Son was fascinated with the construction of the huts. The village huts were only twenty meters from the "guest" huts, but almost identical. They were not affixed to the ground but elevated by Sayo wood supports. Chickens scratched under the huts, and many intricate brown and black baskets were stored there. The floors were supported by hardwood poles, then covered with rice-straw mats.

The roofs were angled steeply with several crossbeams. The thatch of the roofs was tightly packed and thick. Kehn Ton, the support village leader, had shown them the cooking fire in the clay-packed corner of the hut. Son was surprised that one could cook on the matted floor, but Ton had shown him how they packed the fire area with gray clay and then placed over it many coats of red river clay. The result was a layer as hard as rock that insulated the wood from the heat. The side of the hut close to the fire swung out for the smoke to escape through.

Outside the huts, fresh water flowed from an ingenious water system. Large bamboo poles were split down the middle and hollowed out completely. In a stream forty meters up from the camp they had constructed a dam. The resulting overflow fell into the first of many of the bamboo troughs that snaked down the hill toward the village. Near the camp where the ground fell away, the troughs were supported by crisscrossed pole A-frames. Plugged holes, burned in the bamboo, were unplugged when was a need for cooking or drinking water. The last trough ended at the edge of the village, where the remaining water, cascading down from its two-meter-high A-frame onto a flat rock, was used for washing and bathing. Ton showed them the five-liter cans at the side of each hut that were used as refuse for body waste. The cans would be picked up daily and packed off to small fields nearby, where the contents were used for fertilizing the crops. Ton explained that the fields had to be kept very small or they would be spotted by the iron birds. "The iron birds," Ton told them, "would call more such flying metal birds that spoke thunder and death."

When the tour was completed, the men cooked their food and went to bed early to ease their body aches. Only Le Be Son remained awake, sitting on the doorsill of the raised hut. He sat with his back against the hardwood frame with his legs dangling over the split-wood floor.

His eyes were fixed on the mountains where the sun had just vanished, leaving only a pale red glow, like a fire's embers slowly dying.

Unseen by Son, a small girl looked up at the tall valley dweller, staring, wondering. He glanced down and saw her in the faint light. Their eyes met. Her eyes were large and unafraid. He pushed off the lip of the elevated floor and landed lightly beside her. She blinked as she brought her small arms up to her bare chest as if bashful and turned from him. He knelt quickly and smiled. He couldn't speak to her. He didn't know her tongue. Only Ton, of all the villagers, spoke his language. She turned slowly, keeping her arms up to her chest, and looked at his smiling face. So beautiful, he thought, a true perfect one. Her face was so small and delicate, her features so soft and enjoyable to look upon. She walked closer to him, watching his eyes. Slowly she extended one small hand upward and touched the green band tied around his forehead. She looked deeply into his eyes. *"Con sea? Con sea?"*

Major Colven stood at Lieutenant Sikes's bedside. ". . . So we'll be leavin' by C-130, starting tomorrow. The move should only take a couple of days. I'm going to talk to the hospital commander about releasing you to the An Khe hospital so that you'll be close to the company. We really need the break. It'll give us a chance to get back to basics and get the whole company back together. Hell, I haven't seen the Third and Fourth platoons in a month."

Sikes was glad to have Colven there. The major was talking more than Bud had ever heard him talk in the six months he had known him. Sikes nodded and added a couple of "yes, sir's" now and then, just to let on that he was interested.

"You know, I'm worried about the Third Platoon because—"

The swinging doors opened and Jean walked in. Colven noticed that the lieutenant seemed to stiffen when he saw her.

Jean came straight to the bed. "Good to see you, Major. You seem to have King Kong occupied."

Sikes bristled when she said it. Colven gave her a quizzical look.

"Oh, he hasn't told you, huh?"

Sikes stared at her pleadingly for a second, then looked up at the major. "Sir, I had a little trouble—"

Jean interrupted, smiling. "Let me tell the major. Please."

Sikes could tell by her smile that she wasn't mad anymore, but he still didn't trust her. After all, she was a woman, totally unpredictable. Plus, she was a damn captain and the same friggin' age as he, no less.

"Well, Major," Jean began, "your Ranger lieutenant . . ."

Sikes couldn't believe what he heard. Jean portrayed the event as a humorous story. By the time Jean was finished, she and Colven were almost hysterical.

"I personally didn't think it was so darn funny," said Sikes, folding his arms across his chest. They went into another spasm of laughter.

"Damn, kid," Colven said, "you gonna give the Rangers a bad name if you only sprained his wrist."

Sikes frowned and mumbled, "That son of a bitch, he was . . ." He looked up at Colven's laughing eyes and shook his head. "I'm sorry. His hippie hair just got to me, I guess."

They all laughed again.

Jean glanced at her watch. "Hey, I've got to get going." She looked at Sikes but avoided his eyes. "Thank you for doing what you did this afternoon."

The lieutenant lowered his head, embarrassed. "No sweat, I guess it was a really dumb thing to do."

Colven couldn't help but notice the discomfort they displayed when they were together. Strange, he thought. It was as if they were trying to avoid each other. Maybe they were embarrassed by the presence of a senior officer. "I guess I'd better get up to the club and check on Jerry or he'll drink the place dry." He leaned over and patted the lieutenant's shoulder. "I'll drink one for you, kid."

"Thanks, sir, make it a Bud—nice and cold, huh?"

"Sure, kid, Bud it is." The major and Jean walked to the door.

Sikes watched as they left. He felt better. His leg throbbed a bit, but he was feeling stronger. It was good seeing the major laugh. He couldn't remember his being so relaxed. But the nurse, she was . . . aw, hell.

He leaned over to the small cabinet and pulled out the package of cookies.

PART TWO

10

The C-130 banked right and began its descent just as the awakening orange sun cast its glow on the eastern sky.

The dull camouflaged plane glided down, touched the runway, and immediately reversed its engines in a thunderous roar. The bellowing ungainly bird sped down the gray strip, finally slowing and turning onto the taxi ramp.

Dove, sitting in his jeep, uttered a low whistle. He turned to Sergeant Grady, who was leaning on the hood.

"Well, Grade, here we go again, huh?"

Grady nodded as he turned toward the lounging men assembled behind him. "First chalk, saddle up!"

Half of the reclining men got up to put on their stuffed rucksacks.

The plane rolled past the large group, stopped, then began backing up. Its tail ramp opened as it moved. A forklift placed three pallets of equipment onto the plane's ramp and backed up. The load master pointed at Grady and motioned.

"Follow me!" yelled Grady as he moved toward the ramp. The engines were still running and the hot blast of air they created forced the approaching men to hold on to their berets and lean forward.

A minute passed and Grady emerged from the back of the plane as the doors began closing and the ramp came up. The young sergeant jogged for several strides, then slowed to a gentle stroll as he approached Dove in the jeep.

"One down, Dove, buddy. Three to go."

The operations center was bare. Childs walked through one more time. Satisfied, he marched out toward the barracks. Two red dust-covered two-and-a-half-ton trucks in the middle of the road were being loaded. He saw Sergeant Evans and waved him over.

"You got all the commo gear on one truck, huh?"

Evans wiped sweat from his forehead. "That's right, Sarge. It'll be on the third flight."

"How much has gotta go by convoy?"

"Not much. We got rid of a lot of shit, but I figure two deuce-and-a-halfs will do it. It's all ammo, Claymores, smokes, M-60 ammo."

Childs nodded. You didn't give munitions away. He didn't want to use the convoy, but it was just one of those things. It meant leaving a sergeant and one team behind to ride shotgun. Evans and his team had been picked.

Jean pushed through the double doors and saw that Lieutenant Sikes's bed was empty. Her heart skipped a beat. She looked up and down the ward. Valerie was not there either. She walked into the office hurriedly to search the patients' records. Sikes's file was still there. She sighed in relief and walked out toward the enlisted patients. The door on the far end opened, and in came the lieutenant in a wheelchair. Wearing a big smile, Valerie followed behind.

Jean spun around and walked back toward the office. She was surprised by her reactions. Thinking he was gone . . . then seeing him again . . .

Sikes pulled the wheelchair up beside her.

"Hey, Captain, wanna ride?"

She turned, still disconcerted by her emotions. Sikes grinned broadly. The green V-neck shirt he wore exposed his neck and shoulder muscles, heavy from exercise. He obviously knew she noticed. *Damn him,* she thought.

"Sorry, Lieutenant, I don't ride with strangers."

Valerie walked up. "Well, I do, big boy, but the two of us would bust that little chair."

He laughed loudly. Jean glanced at his exposed chest, which was covered with light brown hair and glistening with perspiration. *Damn him!*

Lieutenant Le Be Son bowed to the toothless old woman who stared at him while blowing unpleasantly odorous tobacco smoke from the corner of her mouth.

Son had been summoned by her only minutes before. Ton had quickly told him of the old woman, whose name was Ba Trua. She was the "dominant one" and wanted to gaze upon him.

Ton explained that in his tribe, the Mnong, the "old one" was the leader of the family. Ba Trua was the mother of the village clan, all of whose members bore the last name of the mother. The men served as judges and could rule, but only at the matriarch's pleasure.

The woman spoke to Ton, her tone soft yet authoritative. Her voice lowered and tapered off as if she were ending in mid-sentence, too tired to speak. She exhaled a light blue cloud of smoke and looked at the officer.

Ton nodded and began translating. "This is Mother Trua of the Beh from the Mnong. The mother has called you because a daughter spoke of the tall valley dweller in the guest hut. The daughter is favored. Her inside spirits have been awakened and desire knowledge."

Ton paused and looked toward the woman, who immediately began speaking again.

Son listened intently to the unusual sounds emanating from the almond-skinned, wrinkled woman. Her thin gray hair was pulled back tightly and tied with a dull scarlet cloth that hung to her thin shoulders. Her tunic was old, just as she was, and had been repaired many times. Her eyes were intense and seemed younger than her body. They danced as she spoke.

Ton nodded several times and translated for the lieutenant when Ba Trua had finished.

"The mother will talk to you because the daughter favors you. The mother knows you are possessed with good spirits and will talk from the inner eye that is truthful. The mother speaks from her inner eye to you and says 'Welcome.'"

Le Be Son nodded to the woman as Ton continued. "The village is poor. The crops are small because of danger from the iron birds. To the north, her clan is wealthy and has sacrificed many buffalo. The spirits of the soil, the moon, are in need of a sacrifice, but there are no goats, no buffalo, no dogs. The spirits understand and let the people live, but only through difficult work. The Mnong clan is great, but the times are bad. Many sons and daughters have been planted with the magic beans that twist. Many mothers are alone and do men's work. The few men are afraid to hunt and cut and burn fields for growing, afraid the iron birds will come. The times are bad for the mother. The times are bad for the Mnong."

Son could feel the pain in the old woman's words as she stared at him as if looking through him.

"The mother asks when the iron birds will go away. When will the village be able to join the others in the north?"

Ba Trua took the pipe from her mouth and waited.

Son looked up at her questioning face. "Ba Trua, the times are bad for all. The people are like the bamboo: They have been cut and bruised by the foreigners and their puppets. The bamboo roots have gone deep and traveled far, but they always sprout again, not in one place, but in many." He smiled, full of confidence. "The Mnong will be able to join their clan soon."

Ba Trua replaced the pipe in her mouth and rose quietly. She walked to the corner of the hut and took a piece of dull scarlet material that hung on the wall. She walked back and resumed her position, holding out the small rectangular piece of cloth. She spoke again. Ton translated, speaking very softly.

"The mother gives you a gift. It is a piece of the cloth the favored daughter was placed in when she was born. All the clan have such pieces, but none may wear or show the cloth to anyone except the mother and the ones she marks as favored. The mother wishes you to wear it on your clothing. She wants nothing in return and would be offended if offered. The mark is to keep the bad spirits away while you are on your journey to help the Mnong."

The old woman handed the cloth, cupped in both hands, to the lieutenant. He accepted with both hands and bowed. The toothless woman rose and began to walk toward the fire, but she stopped and looked back at the young officer with the strange green cloth tied around his forehead. Her look was sad. Then she lowered her head and shuffled on.

The two men left the dimly lit hut and walked down the steps cut into the tree trunk that served as a stairway.

"The mother is old and will be planted in the earth soon," said Ton, sadly. "She hopes to be planted in the north."

Lieutenant Son looked back at the small hut, then down at the gift. Time. Time was the ally of their efforts, but time was an enemy to the old. They had no time left. The lieutenant walked with a heavy heart back to his hut. He would sew the cloth onto his jungle hat.

Corporal Tuy shook his head, disgusted. He had heard many bad stories about the mountain people collectively called the Moi (Savages), but he had considered the stories exaggerated tales—until now.

They *were* savages! They were so backward and stupid. He and two other soldiers had helped one of the village boys pick up the urine bucket. The boy was the first child they had seen except for one small girl, who followed the platoon leader like a dog. The poor boy's mouth was bruised, swollen, and almost black. His front teeth had been filed to the gums. Savages! Tuy and the soldiers found Ton and asked the reason. Ton had said that all the young men had to have their teeth filed. It was a rite of manhood. No woman would have him unless he had thus proved his manhood.

Tuy and the two men were walking back to their hut and expressing their disgust when a group of new soldiers appeared on the trail. The three men stopped and watched as the tired men assembled in the village. A senior sergeant among them pointed at Tuy.

"Come here, Corporal."

Tuy obeyed reluctantly. He knew none of these men and didn't like the tone the senior sergeant used.

"Who is your leader?" the sergeant asked.

"Lieutenant Le Be Son. We're on our way to the Forty-seventh, Sergeant."

The sergeant smiled. "The Forty-seventh?"

"Yes, Sergeant. They are in Con Trang Valley."

The sergeant laughed. "You had better fetch your leader, friend. You are fortunate. We are the lead scouts of our battalion, and I think my commander will want to see your leader. It seems, Corporal, you have found the Forty-seventh."

Lieutenant Son was writing in his diary when Corporal Tuy ran up to him.

"Comrade Leader, you are wanted."

The lieutenant placed his small book and pen on the ground by his pack and walked to the busy camp just below the village. Many soldiers had arrived and were already hanging their hammocks. He was guided to a seated man with a dirty khaki jungle hat.

"Sit down, my friend, sit down." He was an older man, in his fifties at least. His pants legs were rolled up like a peasant's. "I am Duc Thang, your commander."

Son was astonished. How could this frail one be his commander? The Forty-seventh was still a three-day march away.

"It is very fortunate that I find you here. I had not received word of your coming." The old one took a cup of tea from one of his soldiers and offered it to the lieutenant. Son refused.

The commander took a sip of tea and continued. "Your men tell me you are to join the Forty-seventh."

Le Be Son nodded.

"I am truly blessed by Buddha." Duc Thang looked into Son's eyes and smiled. "Oh, my liberator friend, don't be disheartened at this old man's body. My spirit is strong and my determination is stronger." He patted the lieutenant's shoulder. "Now, drink with me, and I will tell you how you happened to be in the right place at the right time."

Lieutenant Bud Sikes wanted out. His leg was itching, but the throbbing was gone. They had taken the bandage off his head, and the stitches would come out tomorrow. Hospital life was getting to him, and he was out of cookies.

Jean finished her rounds and walked to his bed. She saw that he was bored. "The ward gettin' to you, huh?"

"It's going to drive me nuts, Captain. I'm ready to leave—now! I could walk on a crutch easy. I could—"

"Forget it, Lieutenant. The stitches come out tomorrow. The head is no problem—it's so hard—but the leg wound was deep. There's always a possibility of infection, so you have to stay."

"Don't they have pills?"

"Yes, we have pills, but in this country infection is a killer. In fact, it kills more young men here than bullets do. It spreads so quickly, it's hard to control with medication. Anyway, I'm taking you to dinner tonight."

His eyes rolled up at hers. "Dinner? You mean you're stayin' and serving chow here tonight?"

"No, Lieutenant. I'm taking you to dinner at my place."

"Is that legal? I mean, feeding an inmate at a guard's house and all?"

"Yes, it's legal, silly! Now, here's the deal: We're not exactly eating alone."

"What do you mean, not *exactly* eating alone?"

"It seems one of your Rangers gave a case of Lurps to the head nurse in exchange for a spool of surgical hose. We've had the food for weeks and finally decided to have a dinner and call it Ranger Night. You know, eating Lurps like you all do? Well, it seems nobody knows exactly what the stuff is, except that it's food. We need an expert to help us. That's where you come in."

Sikes's smile had gotten wider as she talked. "Captain, you have come to the right man. Now, you got to first plan this shindig so that all the proper ingredients are present. Get pen and paper, 'cause the kid is gonna show the U.S. Army Nurse Corps what eatin' Ranger-style is all about."

11

Grady was watching the sun begin to touch the mountains. He was tired. Sergeant Evans sat with him.

Grady sighed and turned toward his friend. "What are you guys going to do for the next couple of days?"

Evans smiled. "We're gonna screw off, just like you would. I'm gonna take the team to the beach and get some rays, and we're gonna get fat, chowin' down on REMF food."

"You lucky bastard. We'll get back and be under ol' Childs again. He'll make us clean those damn barracks twenty times. You know how he is."

Evans grinned. "Yep. Just think of ol' Two-Four as you're moppin'. We'll be kicked back, baking in the sun and drinking beer."

Grady smiled and fell silent again. Evans stretched his legs out along the pebbled ground and leaned back on his elbows.

"You know, Grade, we're really gettin' short. It's hard to believe. I don't even like to think about it. It's like waitin' for Christmas when I was a kid."

Grady picked a slender shoot of grass and put it in his mouth. "I know what you mean. It's gone by so fast . . . until now. The time sure seems to drag now."

"Grade, I got a letter from my family, and they've got me all signed up to coach a Little-League baseball team."

"Coach?"

"Sure, Grade. You think a Ranger team is tough to control, you should see a dozen eight- and nine-year-olds learning how to play baseball."

"That's right. You like the coachin' stuff. Well, I guess if you're livin' in a small hick town, there's really nothin' else to do."

"Aw, Grade, there you go again. But I'm telling you, it's such a good feeling seeing those kids improve and become real boys. You know, you should try it. You've played college ball and could really help some kids get started right."

"Hell, Ev, baseball is baseball. Anybody can teach fundamentals to a bunch of kids."

Evans shook his head and leaned forward. "You're wrong. It's not just baseball you teach: You teach them leadership. They watch you, Grade. The little farts are smart. They don't always act like it, but they really watch and try to emulate. You're the kind of guy who would be a perfect coach. You care, and you'd take the time."

"Ev, you're full of it, man. Just because you were so impressed by your old coach, you think every kid responds the same way."

Evans turned and watched the disappearing sun. "If one kid feels the way I did—has the memory of a coach who was hard but fair, overlooked my weakness and saw only my strong points, made me feel good about myself, pushed me, but always let me have the freedom to fail—then, Grade, it's worth it."

Grady knew Evans was serious, and he knew Ev would be great at coaching. Grady felt that if he had a son, there was no man he'd rather have teaching his boy. But damn if he would admit it out loud.

"Okay, Ev, you've convinced me! Soon as I get back to school, I'll volunteer to coach the university's girls' freshman softball team. Now, that's a bunch I want to have respond to this coach!"

Evans laughed. "You're hopeless, Grady. If your head were cracked open, I wouldn't be surprised if all they found was a thousand little pussies running around."

"*Two* thousand!" laughed Grady, hitting his friend's arm.

The roar of the last C-130 landing drowned out their laughter. They rose and walked back to the last load of waiting men who were resting beside the runway.

Evans had brought his team to the airfield to help pack the pallets. Now his team sat with the Double-Deuce, trading insults and war stories.

Grady yelled over to the waiting men. "Saddle up, Deuce."

Evans put out his hand to his friend. "See your big ass in a couple of days."

Grady took Evans's hand and shook it warmly. "We gonna get all the good bunks. You and the Two-Four will probably have to sack it in the first sergeant's latrine."

"Oh, Grady . . . oh, Grady, buddy, anything but the . . . the . . . the first sergeant's latrine!" Evans wrung his hands as if pleading, then broke into laughter with the rest of the men. "You best get going. I wouldn't want Sergeant Childs to miss his chance at yelling at the Double-Douche at least once tonight."

Grady picked up his heavy ruck and CAR-15. "Ev, I hope you sunburn your ass!"

Evans and his team started for their waiting truck. Grady watched them for a few seconds, then yelled so the others would hear, "Hey, Two-Four, you'd better practice. The Double-Deuce is cuttin' no slack up north!"

Evans turned and yelled back, "I got a case of Bud that says the Two-Four drops the first one. Put up or shut up, Douches!"

Grady let the statement sink in for effect. "Okay, Two-Four, it's a bet! The day Two-Four drops one before the Deuce is the day I give you rag bags a case!"

The blast of the plane's props caused Grady to put his hand up to his beret. The men of the 2-4 were loading their truck. Evans opened the cab door and pulled himself up. He looked back at Grady, who raised his hand slowly and shot Evans a thumbs-up. Evans slid into the cab, extended his arm through the open window, and returned the gesture with a wide grin. Grady threw his friend a quick salute and turned for the waiting plane.

"Evans, I love ya."

Evans lowered his hand slowly and watched the sergeant disappear into the tail of the aircraft.

"You ready, Sikes?" Jean was waiting for him when he came out of the latrine on his crutches.

"Captain O'Neal, lead on. I'll pull rear security. He waved at Valerie, who was sitting at the desk.

She got up quickly and came over. "Now, honey, I want my boy back home by eleven, or I'll send Daddy out with the shotgun."

Bud winked. "Now, Maw, you know I don't allow no hanky-panky on the first date."

Jean laughed as she pushed the door open and held it for the hobbling lieutenant.

Bud walked out. Val leaned over to Jean and whispered, "Remember, they sneak up on you, honey."

Jean's reaction surprised Val. Instead of one of her usual quick retorts, Jean looked embarrassed and just shook her head as she joined the lieutenant.

Major Colven walked off the plane to stretch his legs rather than wait for his vehicle and trailer to be unchained. It was a beautiful evening, he thought, as he glanced at the orange sky where the sun had just disappeared.

"Good to see you, sir." Captain George Treadwell, the executive officer, saluted smartly as he approached.

Colven ignored the salute and held out his hand. "Good to see you, too, George. You look good. Phan Thiet did right by you?"

"Yes, sir. Sir, first sergeant has got things all squared away at the camp. There've been no problems. Your new ops officer, Captain Shane, has got a super record. You're gonna like him."

"Good." Colvin turned toward the plane just as Dove drove out, steering with one hand and putting his blue notebook back into his shirt pocket with the other. The crew chief appeared at the ramp, flipping a brass object into the air and catching it.

Treadwell laughed. "I see Dove hasn't changed any."

Colven shook his head, smiling. "As long as there's a REMF in the country, Dove will never quit."

"Sir, you riding with me?" asked the executive officer.

Colven shook his head as Dove pulled up beside him, wearing his usual wide smile. "George, I think I'll put my life in danger with this crazy bastard they call my driver."

Colven got in and patted Dove's shoulder. "Big Daddy is home, and he ain't gonna get no ass, so he's just gonna have to kick some. Take us home, son."

"Yes, sir!" Dove popped the clutch and sped down the taxi ramp. He loved it when his major felt good, and he especially liked it when he called him "son."

Bud Sikes had died and gone to heaven. *Fourteen women. My Gawd, fourteen.* He counted again just to remember for posterity. They were every size and color, and they were dressed . . . well, comfortably.

They were all jammed into the large kitchen that doubled as a party area. Bud was feeling no pain. He was on his third beer and sitting in the seat of honor when Jean motioned toward the huge smoking pan on the stove.

"It's time, ladies," he said as he started to rise.

The women opened the case of food and handed out the Lurp packets. Bud realized within seconds that there was only one way to save a lot of confusion.

"Ladies, may I have your attention."

One of the nurses yelled back, "You can have more than that, Lieutenant."

Embarrassed, he took another sip of beer for courage. "Ladies, we're gonna do this the right way—the Army way!"

The nurses booed loudly. Undaunted, he counted, "Give me two ranks here. Let's go, line up!"

The women giggled and milled around awhile but finally assembled into two uneven rows.

"We're gonna do this by the numbers, so there's no scre— mess-ups."

The women giggled.

"At my command, tear off the top portion of the bag. . . . No, the other end!" He pointed at a large nurse in shorts who was holding the bag upside down. "Ready? Tear! Good. Now we're going to take out the contents and prepare to file by and get water. . . ."

Jean giggled with the other nurses as the lieutenant explained how the dried food required water and had to soak for several minutes. Then, one by one, they filed by as Bud poured the proper amount of water into each bag. While they mixed the goo and waited the requisite five minutes, he explained the use of condiments—Tabasco, soy sauce and other assembled items. With only a minute to go, several of the girls complained about the wait.

"Now you know what's worth having is worth waiting for," he said. "Don't think about it. Think of something else."

A buxom redhead walked toward him, suggestively shutting her eyes and puckering her lips. "I am, I am."

The nurses laughed again at the red-faced lieutenant. Finally the time came, and he led them in a countdown: "Five . . . four . . . three . . . two . . . one . . . *chowtime!*"

Some tore right into the mush; others only nibbled. Jean found hers to be quite good. But whatever any of them thought of the food, Bud was certainly a hit. Jean watched him as several of the girls made moves on him. He was obviously loving it.

"Your lieutenant is some dreamboat."

Jean turned toward the familiar voice, shaking her head. "Susie, he's not *my* lieutenant."

Sue looked at her, genuinely surprised. "You're kiddin' me. He's glanced over here at you at least ten times. Everybody here has noticed it. Even Sylvia has backed off—says she can't compete."

Jean dropped her gaze to the floor, embarrassed. "It's your imagination, Sue. He's not interested in me."

The cute blond shook her head. "I swear, girl." She glanced over at the lieutenant. "Probably just as well. His kind will break your heart."

Jean shot her head up. "Why did you say that?"

"Look at him. He's your sincere kind. They're the worst. He's a one-woman man, but he also loves his profession, and they never mix, you know?"

Jean smiled. Her friend was trying to protect her.

"Don't worry, Sue. He's just a patient."

The petite blond patted Jean's arm. "Sure, Jean. Just a patient."

Bud prepared another meal and crutched his way over to Jean. "Pretty Captain, would you escort this cripple over to a hungry trooper?"

She looked at him quizzically. He held out the packet. "I gotta take care of the troops. It's for Val."

Jean grinned. He didn't forget his friends—another point in his favor. Taking the food, she began leading him to the door. Several of the nurses catcalled about their leaving early. It wasn't fair for Jean to hog the guest, they said.

Bud yelled back, "I shall return. Keep the beer cold!"

When they delivered the *Lurp* packet to Val, she was so surprised at his considerateness that she gave him a big kiss—much to his embarrassment.

Then Val took a large spoonful of the food and gulped it down. She chewed for several seconds before suddenly falling back, grabbing her breasts, and pulling out her fatigue shirt.

"My God! I'm growing hair on my chest!"

He leaned over to see for himself, but Jean pulled him back.

When they set out again for the nurses' compound, Jean walked beside him in silence. They passed the MP booth and back into the party room. It was empty.

"What a bunch of party poopers," he said aloud, looking for a beer in a forgotten cooler. There was none.

Jean shrugged her shoulders. "Come on down to my room. I've got a few beers left in my small fridge."

"Well, all right! Can't turn down an offer of a beer in a woman's room." He winked at her.

She blushed but led the way.

The room was homey, he thought, as he stood in the center of the tiny place. The two beds both had matching blankets and sheets from stateside. A small refrigerator sat against the far wall, and judging from the assorted bottles, pictures, and other items on its top, served as a table. Next to the door was a bookcase that held paperbacks, tapes, a Panasonic reel-to-reel, and an amplifier. The cement floor was covered with a large, expensive Oriental rug. There wasn't a military thing in view except each girl's extra pair of boots under her bed.

Jean opened the refrigerator and pulled out two Pabsts. "The opener should be behind you, next to the tapes."

Bud saw it immediately. It was a fancy Coors opener with a large plastic handle. She handed him his can.

On the near wall were colored posters taped to the unpainted Sheetrock walls. One of the posters was of a couple holding hands and walking through a waist-deep field of yellow flowers. It said "Togetherness is happiness." The other poster was an American Airlines travel poster depicting a Colorado mountain snow scene.

"You from Colorado, Captain?" Bud asked.

"It's Jean. Please call me Jean, will you?"

He smiled and took her beer can. "Okay, Jean, but you gotta call me Bud." He held out the opened can to her. She took it and raised it as if to toast.

"To Bud and Jean—regular people."

"Hear, hear."

Jean sat down on the thick rug and motioned for him to come sit on the closest bed. "I'm from Golden, Colorado, Bud. Home of Castle Rock and Coors beer."

"You like it there?"

"I love it. It's not that far from Denver. Have you ever been there?"

"Drove through it, I think, my sophomore year. We got a busload of us to go skiing. Isn't Loveland Pass the ski resort up that way?"

"Sure is. Best skiing in the country."

"It was pretty. Froze my ass off, though. I spent more time on my rear than on the skis."

Jean laughed as she got up and walked to the bookcase to turn on the reel-to-reel. "Aquarius" immediately filled the small room. Jean turned the volume down and browsed through her collection of tapes.

"I bet this bed is yours and that one is Val's," he said.

She glanced up surprised. "How did you know?"

He grinned as he put his hands on his hips. "'Cause, honey, your feet ain't that big." He motioned with his head toward the huge fluffy slippers under the other bed.

Jean resumed her previous position on the rug.

"Amazing, Mr. Holmes. Pray, tell what else you have deduced."

Bud thought a few seconds. "Well, my dear Watson, the rug came from Hong Kong, purchased on a recent R&R. It obviously belongs to the nurse called O'Neal. It's classy, like the lady. The reel-to-reel is also hers and was purchased through the Pacific Exchange Catalogue, as were the amp and speakers. The popcorn popper belongs to the other woman, and the black gentleman in the picture on the refrigerator is either the other woman's gentleman friend or her very young father."

Jean sipped her beer. "Not bad, although I didn't go to Hong Kong. Another nurse bought it for me there. And that's Val's boyfriend." She brushed back her hair. "Please continue."

Bud looked around the room until his gaze fell on Jean. Her light brown eyes were wide and searching. The slightly dimpled chin, which gave away her every emotion, seemed to be quivering. She was a strong-willed woman, he knew, yet she was sensitive too. Very sensitive, he thought as he spoke.

"I have deduced that Captain Jean O'Neal likes her profession, but it bothers her to work on a ward where so many young men lie broken. Also, the captain has a secret. She wears a special face when she works. She also uses a special tone of voice—authoritative and short; a special way of laughing—forced; and a special way of making conversation—light, meaningless small talk. The real Captain O'Neal takes off her secret face when she leaves the ward."

Jean stared at him without expression. "Am I that bad, Bud?"

"No, you're really good, Jean, but it's obvious you don't like to get to know the patients. Maybe it's the training you all get, huh?"

Jean lowered her head. "No, it's not in the training. It's . . . it's coping, I guess. I don't want to know any of you too well." She looked up at him. "It hurts too bad when you leave or when your wounds turn bad. I just can't take that too many times, you know?"

Bud nodded. He really did understand. He'd lost enough friends in the war to know exactly what she was talking about.

"How do you cope, Bud? How do you do the things you do and keep your sanity?"

Bud shifted his eyes to the hypnotizing revolving disks on the tape player. He spoke quietly while watching their slow rotation. For some reason an image of the blood on the floor of the airplane came back to him, but he instantly blocked it out. "I don't think about the death and the hurting. I think about the challenge of it. The excitement that comes from it is so . . . It's a release of such . . . Hell, I never could explain it." He broke his fixation and turned toward her. "I guess I joke a lot to . . . to cope. Laughing is better than crying, I suppose."

She hesitated, then said "Bud, does it ever bother you that you like it?"

He studied his empty beer can, opened his mouth to answer, then paused and looked questioningly into her eyes.

"Yes." His answer was a whisper. "I guess it makes me wonder what kind of a person I am." His eyes shifted back to the can.

Suddenly she rose and sat on the bed beside him. His eyes never acknowledged her. Only his hand betrayed him as it reached out and took hers. Jean leaned back, resting her head on his chest.

Bud sighed deeply, absorbing her fragrance and closeness. It was just too good to be true, he thought, as he leaned his head back on the wall, trying to comprehend the strange feelings that were overwhelming him.

The couple remained motionless, afraid to move and break the spell. The tape came to the end of its reel and automatically stopped with a metallic *clunk*.

Bud opened his eyes and began to rise. Jean moaned and held his hand tighter.

"I better get goin', Jean. It's late."

Jean moaned again as she snuggled closer, obviously not wanting him to go, but after a moment she released him, and he stood awkwardly on one leg. When she stood, he slipped a strong arm around her and pulled her close to him. They stood inches apart, looking into each other's eyes, searching. Bud leaned forward and gently kissed her. Her lips were soft and willing, and her body trembled as she hugged him closer.

Oh, Jesus, Bud, he thought, fighting back his desire. "Captain O'Neal, thank you again for a wonderful evening, and if ever again you need a Ranger to help fix a Lurp, well, you know where to find him." He bent over and retrieved his crutches, then turned and moved toward the door.

"Bud," she said suddenly.

He turned around.

"Thank you for everything."

He smiled. "My pleasure, ma'am. Anytime."

The night slowly gave way to dawn, revealing the faint silhouettes of waiting men who squatted around their standing lieutenant.

Le Be Son adjusted the green mourning band on his forehead before putting on his jungle hat with its new scarlet patch. It was time. "We go," he said.

Son began walking down the worn path. He felt strong. The coolness of the mountain morning was refreshing and a good sign. His pack was light. The commander had instructed him and his men to travel light. They would be returning in several days, victorious, to claim the rest of their meager belongings. The light of dawn gradually revealed the long column of men as they wound down the steep, tree-covered trail. Son smiled. Revenge was near.

The old woman stroked the sleeping girl's hair, receiving strength from her strong spirits. The girl slept with the woman to give her the needed power to fight the black spirit that closed one's eyes forever.

The valley people were gone. She'd heard them preparing and finally departing, leaving the Mnong to their mountain again. The girl would be heavy-hearted when she learned of their leaving. She had found a strong spirit in the tall valley soldier.

The old woman's wrinkled brown hand patted the child's forehead. She brushed a lone tear from her ancient eye. The young were hurt so easily. They did not understand. He would return, only to leave again. He was a valley dweller. The child would learn the bitter truth and become less of a child. She was Mnong. Only the mountains stayed forever . . . only the mountains.

Captain Ed Shane pushed open his screen door and stepped out. He'd gotten up early to read the recent after-action reports before talking to his new boss, Major Colven. Last night's meeting had lasted only a few minutes. Colven had wanted to be briefed by his executive officer, Captain Treadwell, and the first sergeant before assembling all the officers for their scheduled meeting.

Shane took a deep breath of the morning air as he gazed down the gently descending hill to the hills on the other side of the small valley. He could just make out the large perimeter fence and huge observation towers that silhouetted the tops of the brown, barren landscape. He shook his head, remembering his last tour. He hadn't had the opportunity to enjoy many mornings such as this one.

He was turning for the shower building when Captain Treadwell stepped out of his room and yelled to him. "Hey, Ed, wait up and I'll give you the nickel tour." He jogged up to Shane and clapped him on the back. "We'll shave; then I'll show you around."

They walked a few paces before Shane turned and looked at the long white cinder-block building. It reminded him of a cheap motel.

Treadwell stopped. "The officers sleep on that end." He pointed to the near end of the seventy-five-meter-long structure. "The old man's hootch is on the end. The senior NCOs sleep from door six, there, all the rest of the way down."

"Where's the latrine?"

"It's behind the shower point. You can't see it from here. It's another fifteen meters down. You going to it?"

"Sure. A morning sit-down is good for the soul, you know."

"Well, you'd best be careful. It's the first sergeant's latrine." Treadwell smiled. "You'll see what I mean when you get there. The first sergeant doesn't like flies. You haven't met Top yet, but when you do, you'll understand."

Shane and the executive officer parted company and Shane walked around the shower building. What the hell was Treadwell talking about? he wondered as he approached the rear of the small gray outhouse. It looked like the rest of the standard Engineer-built rear-area latrines: wood three-quarters of the way up, screening around the top quarter, and a flat tin roof. There was gravel spread around the building, and the telltale hinges on the back meant it was the usual burn-type latrine. The rear was designed to swing up and allow access to two fifty-gallon cans, cut in half, and positioned under the wooden toilet bench above. The barrels were periodically withdrawn, partially filled with diesel fuel, and set on fire. The pungent smell of burning body waste was all too familiar to any soldier who had been in country for any length of time.

Shane strode around to the front of the building, and there he stopped in awe. The door was a common screen door, but nailed to it were eight sections of inner-tube. *My God,* he thought as he grabbed the door handle and pulled. Nothing happened. Using both hands, he pulled harder. The door gave only a fraction. Shane put his foot on the wall to bring his leg muscles to bear. The door opened slowly. *Now what?* he wondered. He gingerly slid his body through the opening, keeping his back braced against the doorframe while holding the steel trap open with straining arms. Once in, he released his hold. The door shut with a loud clap, shaking the entire building.

Damn! He wiped the sweat from his forehead. The inside was spotless and freshly painted. *So this is the "first sergeant's latrine."*

Captain Treadwell had shaved half his face when Shane walked in and took the sink next to him.

"I know you warned me, but damn!"

Shane chuckled as he swirled the razor in the sink of water.

Colven walked out from behind a partition with a towel wrapped around his waist. "So you've been introduced to the first sergeant's latrine, have you?

Shane smiled. "Yes, sir, I sure have."

"You'll like Top. He is unquestionably the best I've ever seen."

Shane watched the major from the corner of his eye as he dressed. He couldn't help but notice the deep white scar on the major's stomach. Unlike the pink one on his face, the stomach scar was ugly and disfiguring. *Damn, he must have really been hit bad,* he thought as he picked up his razor.

Colven put on his pants and turned toward Shane. "Ed, I read your file. You were with the Herd your first tour, huh?"

"Yes, sir. I was with Bravo Company, 503rd, in '68."

"Were you with them at Dak To?"

"Yes, sir. I was the company commander."

"That where you were hit?"

Shane lowered his eyes. "Yes, sir. I was wounded the third day of the attack."

Colven nodded while putting on his shirt. He knew all about Dak To. Some of the worst fighting of the war had occurred there. The 503rd had lost almost forty percent in casualties during the battle.

He glanced up at the captain again. His record was impressive. Shane would be promoted within the year and probably take over the company when Colven left.

The captain was not quite six feet tall and looked older than his twenty-eight years. His body was thin but raw-boned. Only his confident eyes revealed his strength. Colven smiled to himself. They were the eyes of a leader.

Shane and Treadwell walked back to the white building and stored their shaving gear, then strolled down the red clay-packed road to the main camp.

"The base is built on three plateau steps. We're on the second step. You see behind the BOQ?" Treadwell turned and pointed behind the white building to where the grassy slope continued up for fifty meters past the building. "Up there is the first step. We call it the Golf Course. You can't see it from here, but on top is the largest helicopter landing field in the world. It's flatter than a pancake and stretches for almost a mile."

"Do they land planes up there?" asked Shane.

"Nope. The airfield where you came in last night is a good three miles away, at the southern end of the base."

"Damn, how big is this base?"

"Big! It takes an hour just to drive around the perimeter road. They keep the Rangers away from everybody else. The main camp is where the Fourth Division and most of the support units are located. We're on the most northern end."

The two men continued walking, kicking up a light dust cloud. The slope leveled as they walked. Treadwell pointed out the operations center and the low, rectangular wood-and-tin buildings that were the barracks. Typical of most troop housing, they had been built with plywood panels and were screened halfway up.

The two men strolled along the road until it abruptly curved left and fell from view down a sudden drop-off.

"Down there is the third step. You see what I mean now about three steps?"

Shane nodded, looking back from where they had come, down into the valley directly below.

"The mess hall is that long building below us. The road you see on the other side is the main drag that leads to the base. On the other side of that, where you see the rappeling tower, is our Ranger school."

"What's that?" Shane pointed to a small area behind the mess hall.

"That, my friend, is the Dove's private pig stockyard. You met Dove yet?"

"I don't think so."

"He's the major's driver—quite a guy. Before he came to the Rangers he was in the 173rd. He got wounded and when he was in the hospital some REMFs stule his money and class ring. He's been gettin' back at them ever since. If you ever need anything, talk to Dove. He's got connections everywhere. Let's go. I'm starved."

They wound down the steep trail to the valley floor and on to the back of the mess hall. They walked to a side entrance and were about to enter when a booming voice rang out from within.

"All right, Rangers, this ain't Howard Johnsonses! This is *my* mess hall. Eat your good Army chow and mooooove out!"

Treadwell smiled at Shane. "The first sergeant." He turned and pulled open the door.

They had entered through the officers' and senior NCOs' entrance and walked into their designated eating area. Directly across from them was the serving line, where Rangers were lined up and holding plastic trays. To their left was the main eating area.

A short, broad-shouldered black soldier stood a pace back from the line of waiting men, yelling.

"You ain't tourists, Rangers! Quit askin' for a choice! They got eggs scrambled, period. None of this sunny side crap. That's what queers and see-vill-yuns eat. Moooove out!"

The first sergeant's fatigues were starched as stiff as cardboard. His black jump boots sparkled and creaked as he shifted his weight forward and back. He stood, hands on his hips, legs spread apart. His tailored uniform hugged his narrow waist and abnormally large shoulders, accentuating his obviously fit body. Shane couldn't believe such a loud voice could come from such a small man. It wasn't a yell; it was a well-modulated, experienced bellow.

The first sergeant shifted his stance and, glancing behind him, saw the two officers taking seats at the near table. He immediately turned around and marched straight for them.

Shane was impressed. Top strode like a man in charge.

"Captain, it sure is good to have my Rangers back. The first sergeant likes his boys home."

Treadwell motioned toward Shane. "Top, you met our new ops officer, Captain Shane?"

The ebony-faced soldier grinned broadly, showing his large white teeth, and extended his hand. "No, sir, but it's always a pleasure to shake hands with an old veteran from a fine Airborne unit like the 173rd Sky Soldiers. I'm First Sergeant Demand."

Shane stood and took the strong hand of the bantam first sergeant. "Good to meet you, Top."

"Captain Shane, if you wants somethin', you just let your first sergeant know."

"Sure will, Top."

"If you officers will excuse me . . ." The first sergeant came to attention, clicked his bootheels, executed a flawless about-face, and marched back to the food line.

"Moooove out, Rangers: This ain't Howard Johnsonses!"

Dove checked the pens one more time. He was showing Pete his "farm."

"Mack did a good job taking care of 'em. Remind me to pay him an extra ten."

Pete nodded. "Same setup as before, Dove?"

"Yeah, basically. I think we're good on flags for a while, so we won't activate the sew-girl operation. Our buckle inventory is high, so we'd better push them a little harder."

As they started back up the road, a thin-looking soldier came toward them. He waved.

"Hey, Dove, I've been lookin' all over for you. I'm finally gettin' out."

"Glad to see ya made it, Beep."

Pete thought the man looked sick. His gaunt, pale face was stretched tightly over his high cheekbones.

"Dove, I wanted to thank you for the money and all." The soldier looked at the ground, obviously upset. "It really is gonna help me . . . and . . ."

"Hey, you'd do the same for me. Right?" Dove stepped closer and patted the soldier's arm. "What are friends for, man? It's only money."

The soldier reached down and took a small yellow puppy from the pocket of the leg of his fatigues. "Dove, I can't give you a thing to repay you, but I got this pup from a nurse at the hospital. I want you to have it. I know it ain't much, just a dumb gook mutt, but I wanted to give you somethin'."

Dove took the small dog, holding it out from him. "Hey, Beep, thanks, buddy. I really appreciate this, man. Now, look, you'd better get going. You don't wanna miss your freedom bird, man. You take care of your little girl back home, and send a letter to let me know how she's doin'."

The soldier smiled. "Sure will. I can't thank you enough, Dove."

"Don't worry about it. Now, get going, and take care of that new daughter."

Hopkins turned and jogged up the hill. Dove put the dog down quickly. "Damn dog. Can't stand the things. Sure is ugly, ain't it?"

"What was all that about?" asked Pete, watching the soldier disappear up the road.

"Pete, you and me is partners, right?"

"You bet."

"Well, partner, ol' Beep was in a bind. He knocked up a broad before comin' to the 'Nam. They never got married, and she had the kid a couple months ago. The kid got sick and of course didn't qualify for government hospitalization, so I just helped out a little. We take care of our own. Nobody else gives a shit. Hey, you want the dog? I don't know nothin' about 'em."

"No, thanks, Dove. He gave it to you."

Dove looked down at the yellow mongrel and pushed it out of the way with his foot. The little ball of fur rolled over in the dust and returned to its feet awkwardly. They had gotten five feet up the hill when it began whimpering.

Pete watched Dove from the corner of his eye, waiting. Dove walked two more steps. The puppy began a long, sorrowful wail. Dove stopped.

"Shit."

He spun around and walked back to the little animal, which rose up on all fours, wagging its tail.

"Come on, you stupid mutt." He reached down and gingerly picked up the puppy. "Maybe I can sell you to some REMF."

Pete waited for his friend with a smile.

Jean reached for the newest patient's file to make the necessary entries. She leaned back before opening it and looked through the small window at Bud. He was sitting up, writing. What was it she felt for the lieutenant? she wondered. She liked him, but why? Physical attraction? He *was* good-looking. He made her feel good when she looked at him. Her desires suddenly embarrassed her, and she quickly looked back at the file. *I would have made love to him. Yes, I would have done it, so it's got to be physical attraction, pure and simple. Physical attraction. But then, I . . . oh, hell.*

Lieutenant Le Be Son wiped the sweat from his nose. His legs felt the familiar ache. His pack, which he'd earlier thought was light, dug unmercifully into his shoulders. He watched the soldier in front of him shift an RPG-40 awkwardly on his shoulder. The shoulder-fired rocket was heavier than his AK-47.

They'd marched for six hours without rest. The trail was good, but the quick pace was taking its toll. He looked at his men behind him. They were tired, he could tell, but none would ask for a respite. They had determined faces and wouldn't quit. He was proud of them. The men all along the trail in front of him began stepping off the path to relieve themselves. Break at last, he thought. He turned and gave the rest signal to his men and sat down next to a tree. A moment later, in front of him he saw feet wearing Uncle Ho's rubber-tire sandals. He looked up. It was his commander staring down with a smile. He started to rise.

"Stay seated, friend." The colonel squatted down beside him. "We have moved fast, friend. I'm sorry, but the pace is necessary for a while longer. We must arrive before dusk so that assignments and positions are made before dark."

"Yes, comrade Leader. I understand. Do not worry about us. We can keep up."

The old leader smiled. "My friend, tomorrow you will have the opportunity for the revenge that you seek."

It had been many years since the colonel had fought for revenge. Revenge was a short-lived emotion that consumed the body from within. He had long ago lost the need to justify killing by working up emotions. It was just killing, surviving, then killing again. But as he looked into the eyes of the young lieutenant, the death of passion suddenly seemed sad. If only an old man could become young again!

"Sir, I'm Sergeant Evans of Sierra Rangers. I was told to report to you about the convoy tomorrow."

The lieutenant looked up from his desk at the lean, hard-looking sergeant. Without speaking, he got up and walked to a large poster board covered with acetate.

"Yes, you're numbers thirty-six and thirty-seven. Look over here, Sergeant." He pointed to a long line of small black rectangles that represented vehicles; there were numbers marked on them in yellow grease pencil. "Tomorrow you are to be in position here"—he pointed at the chart— "no later than oh-six-forty-five. The others behind you will pull in about oh-six-fifty. Convoy departs oh-seven-ten sharp. Usual uniforms: steel pots, flak vests, and one C-ration meal."

"Sir, we don't have helmets or flak vests."

"No sweat, just be there on time."

Evans saluted and walked out of the tin transportation office to his waiting truck. His team was sitting in the back of the truck. Evans yelled at them as he approached.

"Who's for going to the beach?"

The back of the truck erupted in yelps of joy.

The sergeant swung himself up into the cab and punched the smiling black driver lightly. "Amos, I guess it's time I taught you to swim, huh?"

"Damn, Sarge, you better. I almost drown in that big water yesterday. I'm gonna wear blown-up rubbers around my waist today, okay?"

Evans laughed as he leaned back and threw his feet up on the dash. The large truck lurched forward, and the men in the back began singing the Beach Boys' "Surfin' Safari."

Sergeant Jerry Childs paced back and forth in front of the Second Platoon, shaking his head. It was a bad sign, thought Rock, as he followed the angry sergeant with his eyes.

Childs abruptly stopped and faced them. His eyes narrowed and he took in a deep breath.

Here it comes, thought Rock. *Here it comes!*

"You clowns lookin' and actin' *slack*! Today we start to change that bullshit. I want a full layout inspection of platoon and team equipment, here, on the road, in one hour."

Childs put his hands on his hips and began rocking heel to toe. "You shitbirds embarrassed me! I took the new ops officer, Captain Shane, through the barracks a few minutes ago, and guess what we found? A fucking *trash heap.* A damn pigpen. Great impression you made, shitbirds. Well, I got somethin' for you. We're gonna correct your slack, trashy, hippie civilian ways—*today!*"

Captain Shane stood in the doorway of the Second Platoon barracks and listened to Childs chew out the platoon. The platoon area didn't really look that bad, but he knew the sergeant wanted to keep the platoon busy. Slack time was always dangerous. They could lose the all-important edge.

Shane turned and strolled down the aisle to the back door and pushed it open. Straight ahead of him was a well-worn path to a gray latrine twenty meters distant. Two large connexes were facing him. One was open. He looked in. It was full of NVA weapons, including a large .51-caliber machine gun. There were uniforms, packs, helmets, and rice. A hand tapped his shoulder. When he turned he faced a blond, curly-haired pfc. of about nineteen, who looked like a California surfer.

"Oh, sir, I didn't know it was you. I thought it was one of the guys needin' something'."

Shane hadn't met him before. "You in the Second Platoon?"

Dove was smiling. "Not now. I used to be in Double-Deuce. I'm the major's driver. I'm Dove, Sir, I guess you're wondering why I'm in the connexes. Well, this is where I store some of my inventory. Sergeant Childs lets me use this one 'cause the platoon doesn't need it, so—"

"Okay, Dove, no need to explain why you're here, but what the hell is all that stuff for?"

The puppy bounded from behind the connex and playfully jumped on Dove's leg. "Sir, I trade and sell the stuff to REMFs. . . . Down, dog. . . . We buy beer and stuff for our parties and . . . *down,* damn it!"

The captain bent down and patted the playful puppy. The dog immediately began licking his hand.

"You want him, sir?"

"Naw, I won't have time for one." He made a quick examination of the puppy and rose. "She seems healthy enough."

"She? You mean it's a broad?"

"Yep, you got a little bitch, there, Dove."

Dove shook his head, surprised, then eyed the officer with interest. "Sir, you know much about animals?"

"Well, I lived on a farm."

"Damn, sir. I need your help. Ya see, I got these pigs . . ."

Childs yelled "Do it!" to the platoon and walked toward his hootch.

Rodriguez shook his head, "Oh, wow, man, an inspection! It's like stateside!"

Grady turned to Rodriguez. "Shut up, Pancho. We need to check out our gear anyway."

"Yeah, but inspection? I can't take the pressure."

Rock put his arm around Rodriguez. "Don't worry, Pancho, I'll help ya."

"Wow, man, I'm screwed for sure now."

Grady shook his head. "Let's go, shitbirds. Pancho, you'll be first, so you won't have to worry so long."

"Oh, wow. Thanks, Sarge."

"Well, what do you think, sir?"

"Dove, your hogs are wormy."

"Wormy? What's that mean? They gonna die, sir?"

"Naw, but these hogs are full of 'em. It's just a part of the food cycle."

Dove was amazed at his find in the captain—a real pig expert. "What can I do, sir?"

Shane thought a minute while watching the little dog, which was trying to get into the pigpen, obviously fascinated by the gray-black animals that rooted around in the muddy pen.

Shane knew a scavenger when he saw one. It was obvious Dove was the "in" man of the unit. Shane had seen them in every organization—one man who had the knack and gumption and knew how to subvert the Army's red tape of acquiring both nonauthorized and authorized equipment.

"Dove, I'll make you a deal: I'll get your hogs and that dog of yours dewormed in return for a minor favor."

Dove was surprised. He hadn't thought the captain would be so quick to realize he could exact a price for his services.

"What's the favor, sir?"

"I need a couple of fans for the Second Platoon barracks. The guys need a breeze in their hootch to help keep it aired out. Think you can swing it?"

Dove smiled. The new captain wasn't after a personal favor. It was for the Deuce. He'd be a good one for the Rangers.

"Sure, sir. I'll get you two by tomorrow." The small dog was now chewing on Dove's boot. "Sir, now tell me about food for these pigs."

"Hogs," the captain corrected.

"Hogs," Dove said, smiling.

Major Colven stood in the Fourth Division G-3 office. The operations lieutenant colonel had a map on his desk and was looking at a large area that Colven had just encircled.

". . . No problem with me, John. Nobody's worked the area in a long while. We're more to the east."

"Sir, do you think you'll be able to help us out with aviation assets?"

The colonel looked up, smiling. "Shit, John, we're sittin' on our ass in this new Pacification program. Our aviation guys are so bored, they'll jump at the chance."

"Thank you, sir. We appreciate your help."

"No, *we* thank you for clearing the area for us like you guys do. Oh, John, why don't you bring your officers over to the club tonight. We got an act from Australia coming in that's supposed to be great."

Colven collected his map. "Thank you, sir, but we're involved in a major training program. On the other hand, if you've got any pull with the G-1, I sure do need some movies."

The colonel picked up the phone. "I'll call him now. He's a classmate; plus, the asshole's got my Shirley Bassey tape. When do you want the movies delivered?"

Ed Shane was walking back from the "hog farm" and decided to walk behind the troop barracks to see what was there. The captain strolled slowly, examining the new area. Off to his left, past the latrines, was a low gray compound of some kind. He judged the compound to be three hundred meters away. Probably a prisoner detention compound, he thought, seeing the high chain-link fence that surrounded it. A soldier passed by him on the way to one of the latrines.

"Hey, what's that compound over there?" asked Shane as the soldier passed.

The Ranger looked in the direction the captain was pointing. "That's the Red Cross girls' billet area, sir."

"Red Cross?"

"Yes, sir. You know, the Doughnut Dollies. They got a bunch up here. They got a Red Cross building down in the main base."

"Hell, it looks like a prison."

"It's to keep us horny Rangers out, sir." The soldier grinned. Then, as if reading the captain's mind, he quickly added, "Them women don't mess around with none of us grunts. I hear they only go out with the big REMF brass."

Shane smiled. "Thanks for the info. What's your name?"

"I'm Johnson, sir. Headquarters RTO."

"Thanks, for filling me in. Oh, good luck gettin' into the latrine."

The lanky soldier laughed as he turned and walked to the small outhouse.

12

Sarah Boyce couldn't sleep. She tossed and turned, then finally sat up and got out of bed. She paced the cement floor barefoot twice before stopping to look in the large mirror above her chest of drawers. The puffiness over her high cheekbones and the spider web of minuscule red veins around her pale blue irises told her she still bore the effects of her crying.

She raised her head slightly, still looking into the glass, and pushed back several loose strands of her dark-blond hair.

Why? Why had she come here? A few unruly short hairs wouldn't stay in place despite her coaxing. She gave up with a sigh of frustration.

Her Red Cross uniform lay in a wad on the gray steel chair across the room. The sight of the chair depressed her. It was like everything in this place—government-issue. Gray metal bed, small, uncomfortable mattress, scarred chest of drawers, tiny dented refrigerator, horrible tacky lamp.

She walked over and picked up the wadded light blue pinstripe culottes, shaking them out to their full length. She looked them over, made a face, and flung them across to the battered chest of drawers. They fell to the floor.

Her uniform was so ugly—the tacky black loafers, the tacky black purse, the sack they called a dress. *I might as well have joined the Army, for God's sake!* She stood, shaking her head, then suddenly spun around, bent down, and reached under the bed. She pulled out a brown Gucci leather suitcase and placed it lovingly on the bed. She ran fingers over the rich leather and opened it slowly.

Neatly folded and stacked in color-coordinated sets were the clothes of Miss Sarah Boyce of Mount Vernon, Virginia—clothes she was not allowed to wear except in the compound, and then only because the chief administrator had relaxed the rigid rule. Her slender fingers ran over the brightly colored polo shirts and specially designed slacks and shorts. Her fingers dug deeper and felt the old Bass Wejuns she adored. Just touching them made her want to cry, but she was determined not to cry again. She slammed the suitcase lid, stood up, and slipped on her sandals. She was wearing her unauthorized khaki hiking shorts and khaki shirt with epaulets, which her dad had sent a month earlier. Her dad didn't know the rules.

"Safari clothes," he had called them in his letter. Sarah shook her short hair and grabbed a blue bandana, tying it around her neck. She glanced one more time at the drab room and, making up her mind, crossed into and through the small living room in three strides and opened the screen door.

An MP guard stood, lighting a Salem outside his booth at the entrance to the Red Cross compound. When the door of hootch seven opened, he looked up. Sarah walked past him and made for the jeep parking lot.

"Ma'am . . . ma'am," he called after her.

Sarah stopped and turned toward the soldier. "Yes? What is it?" she snapped.

"You forgot about you-all's rules? I mean, about goin' out dressed like—"

"I'm not going anywhere," she interrupted, turning back toward the empty parking lot. "There's no place to go."

"Bitch!" she heard him rumble and then "Screw her" as he walked into the booth and sat down, picking up his half-read book.

Sarah walked ten more paces and stopped. There really *was* no place to go. Their compound was the farthest away from the main base—at least a mile. She looked north at a white building and barracks across from her. Well, the farthest after those people over there. She guessed they were really the farthest. She looked down the road. Not a single tree, not a bush, just dead yellow grass and God-awful red dirt.

Her gaze fell on the white buildings again. There was something unusual about that place, a peculiar noise she often heard while walking down the road to relieve the boredom. It was the sound of a door slamming. Once, she'd seen where the sound came from—the small gray outhouses. Very peculiar, she thought, that such small buildings would make such a racket. She shifted her stance and looked at the slope that wound up to the large flat helicopter landing field. She couldn't see it but knew it was there, because she had landed there several times when she and Mary Ann went out to present a program to an outpost. Her shifting gaze abruptly stopped. She took a step closer. A tree. At least, she thought it was a tree. She hadn't seen it before. How about that! A tree—green—something alive. She stepped off the road and started up the slight bank toward the ridge to investigate.

Once on the small ridge, she could see it was not just one tree but several. They were just below the crest of the hill. The yellow grass cracked as she walked. Thirty yards short of the trees, she stopped, pleasantly surprised. She'd only seen the tops of the trees. They were actually nestled in a small depression in the middle of the top of the ridge, where the ground suddenly dropped away to a small field of luscious green grass. The small verdant field was enclosed by higher ground on three sides and ran up to a slight rise where three large, round pink boulders sat. Without hesitation she walked down into the cool, inviting ankle-length grass and climbed up the bank to the boulders. Once on the bank, she sighed in ecstasy. It was like a little manicured park. The coolness of the shading branches and the smell of wood and green, vibrant life was so refreshing.

The tree bodies were thick and gnarled in a beautiful way. The long twisting limbs extended out rather than up, as if purposely to hide their beauty within the tiny hidden valley. Her valley—a hideaway, a secret place only she knew of. She walked slowly within the dark shade. The ground was barren except for a thin, light yellow-green moss that carpeted the ground beneath her steps. Breathing deeply, she walked back toward the round boulders and looked over them.

Barely visible to her left were the tops of the white buildings. Directly in front of her were the distant barren hills.

Escape, Sarah. You've escaped—for a while, at least. She closed her eyes slowly.

Sarah Boyce was the only child of a well-to-do Virginia family that traced its lineage back to the late 1700's. Her father, Robert Boyce, was a robust, dynamic man who was always in motion, always competing, and always demanding. His family long ago had sold out their tobacco lands and turned to manufacturing. Boyce Textiles International was among the ranks of the *Fortune* 500.

Robert Boyce had one weakness—his daughter—and he made certain the girl lacked nothing. The best private schools, the best clothes, and the best cars had all been hers.

In Sarah's early teens the Boyces lived in England while her father opened the European office for his expanding company. Her time in the English educational system taught Sarah independence. She, like girls of the upper English class, boarded at school and saw her parents only on weekends. Sarah never told her parents, but she hated the separation and loneliness. During her first month, she silently cried herself to sleep every night. In time, however, her young heart hardened and she turned inward for strength. Sarah learned that she was strong and didn't need anyone. The scars of separation eventually healed, but they would never be forgotten. And she never wanted to experience that hurt again.

The Boyces returned to Virginia on Sarah's fifteenth birthday. Her later teen years were her fondest memories. The days were filled with laughter and countless joys, playing tennis and sailing the Potomac and Chesapeake. She had many acquaintances but no real friends; it was the way she wanted it. She eventually attended Radcliffe College; then, for eight months following graduation, Sarah searched for something to do. It was a secret quest that drove her incessantly. First she tried teaching; then she worked as a congressional aide and for a while thought she had found her niche; but when she was promoted to liaison officer, she found herself flailing again. She couldn't deal with people. The congressional staffer brought her in and counseled her on her inability to understand others. That day Sarah walked out of the huge Rayburn Building contemplating suicide. She knew she couldn't kill herself, but she also knew there were other ways to end the emptiness. She needed to get away and find a place where she could cleanse herself and start a new life. She walked aimlessly.

While crossing Seventeenth Street, she saw a large white marble building with a red cross affixed to the top, and she wandered inside. She soon found herself sitting in the personnel office.

"What could I do in the Red Cross?" Sarah asked the elderly gentleman interviewer after briefly describing her background to him.

His eyes kept their friendly expression as he spoke. "Miss Boyce, right now we have a program called SRAO, Supplemental Recreation Activities Overseas. You meet the requirements, and the job pays well. Of course, you must be interviewed by your district headquarters, but if you're looking for fulfilling work overseas, this is the program you should apply for."

Three weeks later she was accepted, and only then, at dinner, did she tell her parents about her plans. Their reaction stunned her.

"What! A Red Cross girl! My God, what have you done, baby?" Her mother began crying.

Her father tossed his napkin down for emphasis. "You can't go through with it, by God!" he said. "You can't go over to some god-forsaken country and hand out candy to a bunch of strangers in uniform. I know you. That's not the sort of person you are."

"What sort of person am I, Daddy?"

"You're . . . well, you're just not that damn sort, that's all."

Sarah still had time to back out, but her father's reaction solidified her decision. Her own father had as much as told her that she couldn't handle this type of work. She would show them! She would show them all!

The familiarization course lasted two weeks. It went by in a blur and she understood none of it. Soldiers, insignia, rank, rules, uniforms, Red Cross history and traditions, Vietnam history and customs—all of it meant nothing except that she was leaving, escaping. Yes, escaping from the old Sarah Boyce.

The new Sarah became the old Sarah the minute she got off the plane in Vietnam. The country was beyond belief, so dirty, so disgustingly filthy. Saigon, where they landed, was a stinking pit. The streets were filled with brown small people who begged and yelled at them nearly every hour of every day for the entire week they remained there to receive orientation. Then she was assigned to An Khe in II Corps, which turned out to mean that she was leaving this squalor for even worse conditions. An Khe was not even a town. It was a cardboard and tin hodgepodge of makeshift bars, sleazy brothels, and cheap tailors. And, of course, it was the huge sprawling base just behind the outskirts of the clapboard village.

Sarah tried, but she soon realized the whole adventure was destined to be a disaster. The only bright spot was her relationship with the other girls. It took a while, but slowly she grew fond of them. They knew she hated the work and understood. All of them went out of their way to help her—something that had never happened before—especially unflappable, gregarious, constantly smiling Mary Ann, Sarah's first real friend. Mary Ann had been concerned about her and had driven her back to the compound this afternoon when she had started crying again at the center.

The job itself was stupid—fixing Kool-Aid in the too-heavy jugs that had to be lugged around and cleaned, and playing dumb games with the soldiers. Mary Ann could make them laugh, but that was Mary Ann. Sarah couldn't do it. All the soldiers did was stare at her in an unfriendly way.

Well, after three months in An Khe, she made her mind up. She was quitting. Her letter of resignation was in her desk drawer. Next week, when she had completed exactly three months, she would submit it and leave the wretched place, thank God.

For now, she was thankful to have such a comfortable place under the trees to rest for a while.

The Deuce Platoon was in a horseshoe formation. Sergeant Childs stood in the middle.

"I'm going to call off a piece of equipment, and you'll hold it up," growled Childs. "First, strobe light and case."

Within seconds every man except two held up a small orange distress light.

"Now, turn them on."

Childs took the names of the men who didn't have them. The others depressed the small buttons on the bases, and within seconds low whines could be heard, then the familiar *click, flash, click, flash.* Six men hit and shook their lights and depressed the buttons again. They looked as if they had been caught with their hands in the cookie jar. Child's inspected each soldier's light and wrote on his clipboard "Six inoperative."

Grady was pissed. His strobe was among those that didn't work.

"Pull out your pin-gun flares," barked Childs.

They reached into their rucks, some rummaging longer than others. Four held empty hands out.

"Each of you insert one flare."

They looked at the sergeant quizzically.

"Now spread out. You're all to fire at my command. Pull back the handle until the locking—"

Soooooawish! A flare shot skyward, bursting brightly above them.

All eyes turned to Ben. "My . . . finger . . . slipped . . . I—"

Childs cut him off with a knife-edge stare.

"Ready . . . fire!"

Swoosh, swoosh. Flares arched skyward. Red, green, white, yellow. Four men had to try again. *Swoosh.* One more projectile flew up. The other three didn't work.

"Each team hold up their bush axes."

Only one appeared. Childs stared into each man's eyes as he walked slowly around the small formation.

"I'm going to leave for two hours. Then I'm going to return and start the inspection over. You clowns are not prepared. The past fifteen minutes is erased, forgotten by me, but it had better not be forgotten by you."

Childs paused. There was a special reason for his harshness. It had happened on his last tour. He had taken an ambush out one night about a klick away from his platoon. They were initiating on eight NVA who had walked into their kill zone, when one of the enemy got lucky and sprayed them with AK fire before going down. His, Childs's, RTO was hit in the leg. The slug severed an artery. Childs got a Medevac up but couldn't get it into an LZ big enough to get him out. The RTO bled to death. The man who was supposed to bring the bush ax had forgotten it. They could have saved that RTO if there had been an ax to clear one small fucking tree.

Childs put away the painful memory and renewed his promise to himself that he would never lose a man that way again. "The individual and team SOPs will be strictly enforced. Supply will be open to make up shortages and for battery pickup. Better check detonator and magazines. I want team leaders to stay away from their teams for one hour. This is a personal thing for every man." He looked at each of them one more time. "Do it, clowns!"

Grady walked into the barracks, disgustedly threw his ruck onto his bunk, and walked out. He stood on the road a moment, then headed up the road toward the ridge and clump of trees where he and Evans used to sit for hours, talking. It was a place he could always wind down in after a mission. He needed to now. He jogged down into the familiar green field of grass to the boulders on the other side. There he sat, looking out to the far hills. Damn, he'd really screwed this one up. He'd let his team down. He'd taken the whole thing too lightly. Goddamn it! If only he— He heard a crack.

He froze before instinctively grabbing for his pistol. He didn't have it. It was locked up in the weapons connex with all the other weapons. Shit! He turned slowly and pulled the short Buck knife from its sheath on his belt, trying to control his shaking hand.

He stood slowly. He could see nothing. Whatever had made the noise was directly behind the boulder. His mind raced. He could back out slowly and get his weapon, or he could check it out. It might just be an animal, but it could be . . . He remembered just three months before, when NVA sappers had infiltrated the base and blown up thirteen helicopters on the pad above. None of the sappers were caught. They—the Rangers—and every available man on base searched every inch of the camp. They found several places where the saboteurs had holed up for days, probably reconning and mapping before their attack. Maybe, just maybe, they'd come back. Grady took a deep breath to ready himself. He took a step closer and leaned over the boulder.

He saw the flash of sandled feet and lunged over the rock. He noticed the blond hair while he was still in flight. He had time to fling his hand out, but he couldn't stop his momentum. He fell directly on top of the screaming woman, then instantly rolled off and regained his feet.

Sarah's head had struck her knees. Her head down, she whimpered, "Don't rape me. Don't rape . . ." She looked up slowly, her blue eyes searching.

"Gawd damn, lady, what the hell you doing here?"

Her eyes widened, and she whimpered. Mumbling, he cursed and shook his head.

"Gawd, lady, you scared me to death! What the hell you—"

"You attacked me!"

Her voice surprised him. It was like a low, angry growl. She regained her feet. Her hate-filled eyes bore through him.

"Look, lady, I don't know why you're here, but I thought you were a sapper."

Angry tears began to trickle down Sarah's pale cheeks. Grady stepped forward awkwardly, and she jumped back.

"You come closer, and I'll scream!"

Grady bent over and picked up his beret. "Scream all you want. I told you what happened. It's your own damned fault for being where you're not supposed to be."

She stiffened and quickly wiped away the tears on her cheeks. "Not supposed to be! I can be anywhere I want, mister! I'm a Red Cross worker. I have every right to bloody well go wherever I want!" She straightened her back and rubbed her neck.

"The hell you can! This is my AO! You can't go gallivanting around—"

"Your what?"

"My territory!"

"That's why you attacked me?"

"I told you, I didn't attack you. I thought—"

"Never mind. Just apologize to me, mister!"

Grady rolled his shoulders back, blowing out a breath of air in disgust. "The hell I will! Forget it." Grady turned his back on her and walked around the boulder to sit down in his original position. He would have apologized if she hadn't demanded it, but she had.

"Well, I'm waiting." She had come around the boulder and stood two feet away from him.

Grady glared at her. "You can wait till hell freezes over."

"A real gentleman soldier, aren't you," she said, and stomped down the small slope without so much as one look back.

Grady didn't watch her until she was halfway up the far

bank. *Great move, Grady,* he said to himself. *First round eye you've seen in months and you jump on her. Real smooth. Man, you gotta get back in practice before you get back home. . . . Apologize! Who the hell does she think she is?*

Lieutenant Son, the commander, and another officer, Lieutenant Trang, who had planned the attack, had been watching the road for thirty minutes. The time was now right for an ambush. The puppets had been clearing the road at first light every morning, and so had established a definite pattern. They drove up the road in a truck with a large roller attached to the front, designed to set off pressure-detonated mines. The convoys didn't pass until between 0820 and 0845, leaving plenty of time to put in explosives. The only problem was that helicopters scanned the area from about 0700, and their pattern was irregular and unpredictable. Le Be Son looked over the lip of the foxhole at the road below. His heartbeat quickened. His first glance told him they were in a poor position. Everything was wrong. The road below made a *U*-shaped curve, but at a flat portion of the road, not on an incline. On the other side of the road, the land fell away steeply to a valley. Except inside the *U*, there was little vegetation for cover. The Yankees had cut and burned it all.

The angle of the bank was at least eighty degrees. He could see no way for an assault force to negotiate the bank except by using ropes or by sliding, and how would the supporting forces position themselves? The only way to shoot at a convoy would be from the lip, and anyone there could easily be seen from the air. He was concerned that Lieutenant Trang, as a tactician, might be a brave fool.

Trang drew a likeness of the road in the dirt at their feet. It depicted the big *U* in the road, as well as the spot where they were sitting.

"Comrade Leader, the plan is simple," began Trang. "The convoy will come from the east at about oh-eight-thirty. We will let a third of the trucks pass by, as the Americans seem to put more firepower at the front. When truck number twenty-five arrives here"—he pointed to the left top of the *U*—"we detonate the 175mm shell implanted on the side of the road. Then we immediately detonate the other 175mm shell on the other end of the *U*. This will block all support from other U.S. vehicles and soldiers. Our support element will rise on the first detonation, run from the trees, and attack with rockets and machine guns. The bugle will then blow to begin the assault. At the bottom of the *U*—here—is where your men will be, Lieutenant Son. We have cut out two large sets of steps leading to the road. This has taken much time and effort. We did not know you would be with us. We planned for only two squads for the assault, but now, with your additional men, the assault will have great power. The two squads were going to split and take eight trucks each. Now, comrade, we can destroy twenty trucks. The time you have is short. Yankee helicopters with guns will be upon us within ten minutes of the first detonation.

"Supporting fire is to last only a minute, so you, my friend, have only five glorious minutes.

"The vegetation is thick here." Trang pointed to the inside of the *U*. "The Yankees will not be able to see you. A trail has been cut from here to the valley floor below, some four hundred meters distant. The valley floor is easy for travel. You should try to link up with all your comrades there after the attack."

The old commander took the pointing stick from Trang and looked at Le Be Son. "My friend, once the detonation and supporting fire have stopped, you are on your own. The support must move back quickly to safety. I have positioned one machine gun to the far left to fire at the oncoming Yankee flying machines. It will help you get to the valley. You will move your men across the road just before dusk with the two squads from Trang's platoon. The road ceases to be used after eighteen hundred hours. You can then position yourselves for the attack tomorrow. Make sure your soldiers know where to find the escape trail. Should the ambush not take place for some reason, wait until evening and return here. Should we be discovered by the Yankee air, immediately take your men to the valley floor. We will all"— he took out his map, which was encased in a plastic bag— "meet here tomorrow evening." He pointed to a spot down the valley about eight kilometers away. "I will be with Lieutenant Trang. You have much to do, my friend."

The commander smiled at the young lieutenant. "Tomorrow your mourning band will become a band of victory."

Le Be Son returned his colonel's smile. He had misjudged the position. It was a good plan for the ground selected. With them on the other side of the road, it would be a horror-filled day for the Yankees who tried to escape the fire of the support soldiers. If they tried to take refuge down Son's embankment, his men would be waiting.

"Go, my friend," said the commander. "The revenge you seek is at hand."

Grady inspected the team's equipment quickly while in the barracks. Everything looked better this time. He checked his watch. They had ten more minutes. "Okay, let's move it outside." The team began packing up their equipment.

"Ben, did you talk to your finger about slippin', man?" asked Sox.

"Aw, Sox, don't blame me. I just got big fingers."

Rock turned to the huge black man and pointed toward Ben's hands. "Ben, you didn't wash your hands. Childs's gonna check your hands for sure."

Ben looked toward Grady for confirmation, but Grady only rolled his eyes.

Ben grabbed Rock by the neck. "Aw, Rock, you funnin' me again." He laughed, hugging the startled soldier closer with his famous "li'l hug."

The pressure Ben put on Rock's neck felt as if it were breaking the top vertebra. The others were laughing at Rock's bulging eyes. Ben released him, and Rock, trying to catch his breath, began walking, still hunched over in the awkward position.

Rodriguez picked up his ruck and walked toward the door, followed by Sox. He passed the winded Rock. Pancho shook his head. "Oh, wow, Ben gonna have to marry a woman wrestler, you know, man?"

"Really," said Sox as he passed.

Thumper helped Rock put on his ruck. Rock gave his friend a pained expression.

"What I say?"

Thumper smiled, shaking his head.

Childs was pleased. The platoon's inspection had gone well. His only concern was that many of the men had taped their rifle magazines together. He had taken Sox's weapon and held it up to the platoon.

"This looks good. They do it in all the commando movies. The only problem is, your weapon is designed for the weight of only one magazine. All of you who have taped your mags will need to take your weapons to the armory and have the springs checked.

"Tomorrow we're scheduled for range firing. It's about three klicks away. We're going to zero personal weapons and familiarize with all others. I also wanna blow all our old Claymores and det cord. We're gonna hump it to the range. The walk will do us some good." He frowned. "Plus, this rear-area good life makes you start thinking REMF. We're gonna all start getting the edge back on. Okay, that's it. You've got ten minutes to store your gear and fall out for PT. No shirts; just fatigue pants and boots. Do it!"

The formation broke and the men walked toward the barracks. Ben ran up to Grady, looking worried. "PT? PT, Grade? What about supper? It's suppertime, Grade."

The sergeant reached over and patted the worried man's stomach.

"Ben, I'd say the PT might do you some good."

Ben glanced down at his midsection and back up at his team leader. "Really, Grade?"

Sox passed by and patted Ben's stomach. "There it is."

A faint chant could be heard outside of the mess hall. Ears strained and faces turned as the noise level became hushed.

> *"Sergeant, Sergeant, look at me!*
> *I'm an Airborne Ranger in the infantry!*
> *Rough and tough, mean and lean!*
> *I'm a bad mother humpin' fightin' machine!*
> *Hoo . . . ha . . . hoo . . . ha . . . hoo . . . ha . . ."*

The running men's voices faded. The sounds in the mess hall resumed.

"Quick time. . . . March."

The two-mile run was done at a slow pace, but it took its toll on the platoon which hadn't run in months. One man at the front threw up at the side of the formation. He started a chain reaction, and three more fled quickly to the side. Their bodies glistened with sweat. Their fatigue pants were soaked. Several held their sides in agony. Even Childs was breathing heavily. He hoped he could make it to the latrine before puking.

"Platoon . . . halt! Left . . . face!" Childs stood in front of the formation. "We'll take it slow for a while ladies. Tomorrow, same thing, oh-six-hundred. Dis-*missed*."

Thumper held on to Rodriguez who had fallen over on him. "Wow, I made it, man. I think!"

Grady was proud of his team. Nobody had fallen out. He wished Evans's team had been there. He knew they had several weak ones.

Rock turned toward Sox. "Hey, that wasn't bad. You know, I used to run track in school and won . . ."

Sox bent over, throwing up. Rock turned to Ben, who was watching the sick radioman. ". . . a bunch of medals in the mile run. In fact, I was the best . . ."

Ben hunched over and began vomiting too.

Rock hurried to Grady. "You know, I ran track in school and . . ."

Jean was about to go off shift. She looked at her watch again, making up her mind, then she tossed the clipboard down on the desk. She took a deep breath to gather all of her inner strength and, taking four steps, stood in front of him.

"You wanna come over again tonight, Bud?"

"The girls are eatin' Lurps again?"

"No, this time it's just us."

Bud shifted his eyes to the ceiling. "I don't know, Jean. You know how Ma Valerie is. She doesn't trust me." He glanced at her from the corner of his eye.

Jean smiled. "I'll get you about seven."

Sarah sat on the worn love seat, her legs under her, drinking a Coke, when Mary Ann walked in with her usual smile. Mary Ann was tall, almost six feet, and she had raven-black hair put up in a bun.

"You feeling better, huh?"

Sarah nodded and was about to speak, but Mary Ann suddenly lowered her arm, letting her bag fall to the floor, and ran to the small refrigerator. "God, I need a beer."

She swung the door open and touched a cold can to her face while searching the top of the refrigerator. She looked for several seconds before turning toward Sarah. "My God, Sarah! I can't find the damned opener."

Sarah shook her head as her friend took a fork and punctured the can with one violent stab. She let Mary Ann take a sip of her beer before dropping the bombshell.

"Mary Ann, I was attacked today."

"What?" said the large woman, seeing that her blond companion was serious.

"Yes, I was attacked by a soldier just a little ways from here. I . . ."

Sarah explained the whole incident while Mary Ann sat beside her, sipping her beer.

"My God, Sarah, who was it?"

"I don't know. A soldier."

"What was his rank, for heaven's sake? Oh, right. You still don't know rank, do you?"

"No, but he wore a black beanie and a splashy green-colored uniform."

Mary Ann smiled. "A Ranger. Was he good-looking?"

"Mary Ann, he *attacked* me! I didn't look at . . . Well, he was an athletic-looking sort."

Mary Ann laughed with her usual deep hee-haw, shaking her head. "You slay me, Sarah. 'The athletic sort'!" She bellowed again.

"What are Rangers?" asked Sarah.

"Rangers are our neighbors next door. They are a special unit of handpicked soldiers who snoop around in the jungle." She paused, took a sip of beer, and leaned back in the old love seat. "They're a good bunch of guys."

"Well, then why did he attack me?"

"Probably for just the reason he told you. We did have trouble here with sappers, you know. We had soldiers running all over the place, looking for those sappers. It sure was scary."

Sarah put her Coke can down. "You know, Mary Ann, I think it's time I learned rank. I want to be able to go over there one day and tell that Ranger what I think of him."

Bud and Jean walked to the doorway. Val followed.

"You two, the time is now seven P.M. I want that lieutenant back in his bed at—"

The smiling couple strolled out without turning around. Bud inhaled the fresh night air and the fragrance of the auburn-haired nurse who walked beside him.

"You're quiet tonight, Bud."

"I didn't wanna spoil it."

"Spoil what?"

"The feeling."

"What feeling?"

"The night air and you."

"That's nice, Bud. Thank you."

"No sweat. I've been reading a spicy novel and memorized a bunch of lines. In fact, I wrote a few here on my hand in case I forgot." He held out his hand to her.

"I think you've been around Valerie too long."

The MP at the compound booth heard the laughing couple as they approached. "Evening, Ma'am . . . sir."

Bud nodded as they passed. Jean stepped in front of him and hurried ahead to stop him in front of her door.

"Don't come in and don't look till I tell you."

"Okay. Watcha gotta do?"

"Just wait."

She disappeared inside. Bud leaned up against the wall, waiting. He heard the tape player start and the refrigerator door opening and closing. Two minutes passed.

"Okay, come on in."

He pushed off the wall, but it took him a moment to maneuver with his crutches to the door.

"Well, I'll be damned!" he said as he entered.

Between the two beds was a small sheet-covered table and two chairs. The lights were extinguished, but two tall red candles resting on can lids on the table illuminated the small room in a golden hue. A bottle of Mateus and a plate of yellow cheese and grapes rested invitingly on the table. Jean stood in the candle light, wearing a dark strapless Hawaiian flower-print dress that exposed her smooth white shoulders and deep satiny cleavage.

Bud was spellbound by her beauty as the glow of the flickering light danced over her body. He was afraid to avert his eyes for fear it was a dream and she would vanish in a blink.

"Well, what do you think?"

"Uh . . . huh?"

"What do you think?"

He moved closer on his crutches, drawn to her loveliness, wanting to touch the vision before him.

"Bud?"

"You are ravishing, Jean." The words came out in a trembling whisper.

"Not me. The table, the food, the wine. For heaven's sake, I worked hard to . . ."

She stopped as he leaned forward to kiss her quivering lips. Jean's yielding body trembled with electric excitement as he passionately embraced her.

Jean opened her eyes and pushed away from him, breathless. "I'd better cover the door."

He still held her hands and stared longingly into her liquid brown eyes as she backed away.

"Bud, why don't you pour the wine for us while I shut the screen."

Bud let her hands go. Shaking his head to clear his thoughts and taking a deep breath, he picked up the cold wine bottle and began to pour.

"Jean, where in the world did you get this stuff?"

She lowered the mat and walked back to the table to cut some cheese. "Oh, I've been saving the wine and food for a special occasion. Sit down and I'll bring the rest out."

Bud handed her a glass as he sat. "Am I a special occasion?"

She looked up coyly and raised her glass to him. "Yeah, kid. You're a real special occasion."

Sarah pushed open the screen door and marched quickly to the MP booth. A single light bulb hung above the guard shack; countless moths circled it. The MP sergeant looked up and rose to pass her out the gate, when she suddenly stopped in front of him.

Sarah was relieved. It was just as Mary Ann had said. The soldier's name tape was above the left pocket, and his rank was on his sleeve and his collar.

"Hello, Sergeant Todd."

"Ma'am." He looked confused.

She then bent forward slightly to see his shoulder patch. "You're in the Fourth Division, correct?"

"Yes, ma'am, the Forty-fourth MP Company."

Sarah's gaze shot up at him. "How can I tell that?"

"Beggin' your pardon, ma'am?"

"How can I tell you're in the Forty-fourth by looking at your uniform?"

"Oh, you can't, ma'am. You learning about uniforms and rank, huh?"

"Yes. Oh, what's that insignia above your U.S. Army tape?"

Sergeant Todd looked down at the right side of his chest. "Ma'am, this one is jump wings, and this one is the CIB, the Combat Infantryman's Badge."

"Oh, yes, I see the little gun now. Interesting. Well, thank you, Sergeant Todd. Have a pleasant evening."

"Thank you, ma'am. Same to you."

Sarah smiled gleefully as she turned to go back and report to Mary Ann that her first test had been a stunning success.

Jean poured the last of the wine. "I'm sorry it wasn't much of a dinner, but—"

"It was super. I haven't had summer sausage like that since . . . hell, I can't even remember that far back. Plus, your company makes it unforgettable."

"Is that a line from your hand?"

Bud lifted his hand, inspecting it carefully. "Let's see. 'It's better with company' is number . . . four."

"What's six?"

He glanced down again, looking at his hand. "Oh, I can't tell you that one yet. Not ready yet."

"Well, what do we do to get you ready?" He rose slowly, put his glass down, and hopped around the table to the bed behind her. He sat down.

"You have to come here so I can whisper it to you."

She smiled as she joined him, placing throw pillows behind them and leaning back. "Well, what is it, Ranger?"

He leaned over to her ear and nibbled it tenderly.

"Bud . . . Bud, that's not—" Her words were interrupted by his warm kiss. That rekindled the fire within her. Their lips separated as he brought his stiff leg up onto the bed.

"Bud, I really like being close to you," she whispered.

"Not as much as I like being close to you. That's number five, by the way."

Jean giggled as she pushed him back on the bed and rubbed her hand across his chest. "My God, I like touching you." Her eyes followed her hand as it pulled back his V-neck hospital shirt farther and she playfully curled the light hair on his chest. Her breathing became heavier as her fingers explored from his chest to his trembling stomach.

Bud shut his eyes. Her gentle caress was fueling a fiery furnace inside that was burning beyond his control.

"Jean, I can't take this, honey."

She stopped and stared into his yearning eyes.

"Good," she whispered huskily as she lowered her hand still farther.

The luminous candles flickered and danced to the music and the muffled sighs of their stirring pleasure. The candle flames suddenly fluttered as a dark, flower-print dress sailed to the nearby chair.

Sergeant Jerry Childs strolled through the darkened barracks, checking his men one more time before going to bed. They all were asleep. He pushed open the barracks door quietly and began walking back to his hootch. He was passing the headquarters barracks when he heard a scratching noise. He stopped and opened the door to investigate, and was instantly attacked by a two-pound yellow ball of fur that jumped up on his legs.

"Get down, ya little shit," he whispered loudly.

The puppy wagged its tail and ran to the side of the building, sniffing. Seconds later she squatted, relieving herself.

Childs shook his head and began walking back to the hootch, mumbling, "Dumb ass dog. Got no business in a . . ."

The puppy returned to the door, pawing frantically, and began a low whine. The sergeant stopped, sighed disgustedly, turned around, and retraced his steps.

"So you want in, huh? You dumb-ass mutt." He squatted down and patted the small animal, which ran playfully in small circles at his feet, excited at the attention. The sergeant opened the barracks door. The dog looked up at him, then bolted inside. Childs stood holding the door open and watched the black shadow scurry down the aisle to the third bunk and attempt to climb up and join the sleeping soldier.

The small animal tried two more times before sitting down on its haunches, whimpering.

"Dumb shit. You ain't got a lick of sense." Childs walked into the barracks and lifted the whimpering puppy up to the bed.

"You and that flimflam surfer boy deserve each other. You're both . . ."

The puppy trotted up to Dove's head, nestled by her master's chin, and looked up at the mumbling sergeant, who

leaned over and pulled the soft poncho liner up over the
blond's shoulder.

"Dumb shits. I swear, the Army is turning to shit because—"

The gruff sergeant straightened up, paused, leaned over
one more time, and patted the dog's head. "Don't tell nobody, ya dumb little . . . ya little . . . aw, shit!"

The sergeant withdrew his hand and turned for the door.

"Gawddamn flimflam surfer boy and dumb-ass dog. . . . I
swear, this fuckin' Army ain't—"

The puppy held its head up for several seconds, listening
to the fading steps before lowering its head to the sleeping
soldier's neck and shutting its eyes.

Bud lay on his side and stroked Jean's glistening sweat-
soaked body. A pool of perspiration lay between her breasts.
His fingers coaxed the clear liquid down her stomach to her
navel, where it formed another pool.

Jean's eyes were closed. She was too spent to move.

Bud leaned over, kissed her wet hair, and whispered,
"Nurse, IV with ringers *stat!*"

She smiled without opening her eyes and reached up and
pulled him down to her breast. "Bud?"

"Yes."

"What was six?"

He smiled, "Six . . . six was 'Ma'am, could I have a little
more wine, please?'"

She opened her eyes, squeezing him closer and giggling.
"No, silly, what was it really?"

Bud rose up on one elbow and looked into her eyes. "Six
was 'Thank you, thank you for an unforgettable evening,'
but I'm still saving it, Jean."

She looked at him questioningly. He smiled as he moved
closer. She felt him and smiled back, pulling his body onto
her as he whispered, "Because the evening isn't over yet."

13

Sergeant Stanley Evans raised his arm in the blackness. A faint luminous blur appeared. He brought his wrist closer, and focused his eyes: 0520. Just ten more minutes of sleep. Damn! The light-green glow disappeared as his arm fell to his chest. A part of his mind demanded the security of more blissful sleep, but already thoughts and visions were crowding his awakening brain.

The sounds of his men sleeping and the crickets chirping became louder, more distinct. The sergeant pulled back his warm poncho liner and stared at the corrugated steel ceiling.

A convoy . . . of all the damn luck. . . . At least he would see some more of the country. It would be just another day, a day like yesterday and the day before that and . . . no that wasn't true. Evans smiled. Yesterday was not like other days, it had been special. He chuckled remembering how his men had run naked into the inviting blue South China Sea. They had such a good time yesterday, laughing, playing and joking. They had acted like small boys for a whole wonderful day.

He could still see Elk's awe-struck face as the thin soldier turned toward him in the chest deep water. "Wo-Wo Women!" he stuttered excitedly. Two nurses wearing fatigues and carrying large bags had walked from behind a sand dune and now sauntered down the beach. The nurses stopped ten yards from the water's edge and began undressing in front of the staring men.

Amos and Chico hunkered down in the shallow water; both were non-swimmers, afraid to venture deeper. When the first nurse began unbuttoning her fatigue shirt, Amos crouched even lower, his eyes glued to the disrobing women. A wave temporarily engulfed him. Evans got ready to rescue the man, but to his surprise Amos didn't miss a button. He emerged spluttering, but fixed his eyes on the women again. Not a man moved a muscle or an eyelash. All were afraid any movement might stop the unbelievable event unfolding before them. Real Women! *Round Eyes!* The Nurses calmly chattered to each other, apparently used to the presence of men at this beach.

The men were not disappointed when it became obvious that the nurses wore bathing suits under their uniforms. A woman undressing, exposing bare shoulders, legs, thighs, was more than enough for men who hadn't seen such an erotic unfolding since home.

The nurses spread their blankets, turned their radio on, and sensually oiled their bodies. Then the men's predicament sank in.

"Wha-wha-what we gon-gon-gonna do, Sa-Sa-Sarge?" asked Elk.

"How we gonna get our clothes, Ev?" asked Bull.

Howdy Doody, named for his uncanny resemblance to the famous puppet, added, "Yeah Ev, how we gettin' out of here?"

The team sergeant studied his men's anxious faces. They were genuinely worried, pleading for direction. Elk wrapped his arms around his chest.

"Wha-wha-what ever we-we d-d-do, hu-hu-hurry I'm c-c-cold."

"No sweat guys, I'll just talk to 'em." The worried men heard their Sergeant's confidence and relaxed a little. He waded in closer.

"Hey Ladies . . . Ladies!" One of the nurses turned down the radio and looked at the yelling soldier in the waist-deep water.

"Ma'am, could you all move down the beach! We're . . . well, we're nude and—" The other nurse bolted upright. "Our clothes are behind you!" The two women exchanged quick words. The dark-headed one stood up carefully.

"You men are supposed to wear bathing suits to this beach!"

"Yes ma'am, I know, but we didn't have the time or money to—" Aw shit he thought.—"Could you all just move down, please?"

The women turned to each other, then the dark headed one turned back.

"No! It stinks down there. And we've got oil on: we don't want to get sandy. You'll just have to come out and leave. We'll turn over and won't look!"

"Aw ma'am . . . please!"

"No, soldier! You people should have obeyed the rules!"

"Shit . . . Ok, ma'am, we're coming in!" The two women turned over and lowered their heads. Evans turned around.

"Ok, guys let's go!"

"No way, Ev!"

"Not me!"

"They'll look, Sarge!"

Evans shook his head in disbelief. It was the first time his men had ever refused his orders.

"Come on 2-4, we ain't gonna let a few women stop us, are we?"

"They'll look" whispered Howdy Doody, his wet red hair glistening.

"Well guys, you can stay here until you wrinkle up and the sharks get you. Or, you can follow me. I'm goin' in!"

"Aw Sarge!"

"Come on, 2-4, the last one to his clothes has got to join Grady's Ladies!"

The Sergeant turned and began wading to the beach. The men looked at each other then broke for the shore. Their clothes were thirty yards past the women at the base of a large white sand dune.

Howdy Doody and Bull swam up to their sergeant. Black Jack and Elk were close behind. Amos and Chico stood up as the first two men ran past. Evans slowed, allowing his team to pass to ensure no one chickened out. It was then the absurdity hit him, his men running full speed, their bare buttocks and arms flailing, Howdy Doody yelling, "Don't look!!, Don't look!!"

Evans began laughing. He couldn't help it.

"Don't look! Don't look!" The red haired soldier circled far to the right of the women. Evans broke from the water and ran faster, trying to catch up.

The first men got to their clothes breathless, digging through the piles in a panic. Amos pulled his pants up, grabbing the zipper while looking up to see if the women were peeking. He caught himself in the zipper and screamed. Bull grabbed the first pair of pants he found—they were Elk's. Elk picked up the remaining pair and hopped on one foot kicking one foot through. He fell back in the sand, got up and hopped again. Bull's size 36's swallowed him. Bull couldn't get Elk's size 28's over his large white buttocks. Tears streamed down his face, blinding him. The dark-haired nurse yelled indignantly, "Aren't you finished yet?!"

"N-Na-Na-NO!" Bull was pleading with Elk to give him back his trousers. The thin soldier grasped the oversize pants with a death grip. Bull finally grabbed a fatigue shirt and wrapped it around his waist.

"Now can we turn over!" yelled the nurse.

Evans looked over his sweaty, sand caked men, then back toward the women.

"Yes ma'am. It's ok now!"

The dark haired nurse rose to one elbow, "You men leave now and don't swim nude again!"

"Yes ma—" He stopped and turned toward his men. "Guys, we ain't goin' anywhere."

"Say what?!"

"Huh?"

"To hell with them", said Evans as he straightened his back "We were here first! I say we go back and finish our swim!"

"Yeah!"

Howdy Doody cocked his head. "In our pants?"

Evans began emptying his pockets. "You bet, we can wash off some of this sand."

Chico began dancing to the beat of the women's radio. He stopped, seeing the others emptying their pockets. "Alll-right, let's do it man!"

Within seconds they were ready. Bull leaned over to Howdy Doody and squealed, "Don't Look! . . . Don't Look".

The men doubled over in laughter. The freckled red head shot Bull his middle finger. "That's not funny Shithead!" They all laughed again. Rico danced suggestively towards the nurses, singing with the music.

Evans yelled, "The last one in buys the beer!"

They dashed for the beach, Amos ran bow legged, while Bull waddled, his pants still stuck halfway up his white cheeks.

Now Evans laughed aloud and got out of bed. "Crazy mothers," he said to himself, shaking his head. He slipped on his pants then found a boot and put it on. His men still lay sleeping. He picked up the other boot, smiled, then threw it up against the closest metal wall locker with a loud bang.

Evans stood and squealed loudly "DON'T LOOK! DON'T LOOK!" his voice reverberating down the dark aisle.

The men's laughter drifted over the empty compound interrupted only by a lone disgruntled voice "SHITHEADS!"

Sergeant Childs pulled on his boots and stretched his sore, stiff legs. He took a couple of deep breaths, then walked to the door, pushing it open. "Hello, day . . . I'm gonna whip your ass!"

"Wow, man, he coming. . . . Oh, sheeet, man. I don't wanna do it, man. I don't wanna do it!"

Thumper patted the Puerto Rican's back. "Aw, Pancho, you'll do fine."

"Wow, can I hold your belt, man? You know, drag me?"

"Sure, Pancho."

Rock was moving his body as if he were shaking off fleas—"loosening up" he called it.

"I'm ready, I'm ready, baby," he said. "This is like when I ran in front of the formation at Airborne school."

"Shut up," Grady whispered. Childs was approaching.

"Platoon . . . 'Tench-*hut*. Left . . . *face*. For-ward . . . *march!*"

Childs moved to the other side of the formation to march alongside. He noticed that Dove and Pete were in the back. He was going to say something but then decided against it. If they wanted to be in his platoon, then more power to them.

"Double time . . ." A groan rose from the formation. ". . . *march!*"

Childs began the cadence chant. The running men repeated the words back loudly:

"Up in the mornin' at the break of dawn!

Up in the mornin', singing our song!"

Their feet pounded the hard clay in unison and they all clapped as their left feet struck the ground with a resounding slap.

"I'm a badass Ranger, can't you see!
An Airborne Ranger in the infantry!"

Colven rose from his desk when he heard the first command barked by Childs and looked out his window. The platoon had just turned and begun to move down the road. The major smiled and began hurriedly unbuttoning his shirt.

"If I die in Vietnam,
Write a letter and tell my mom!
Fold my arms across my chest,
Tell my mom I did my best!"

Colven joined the back of the running formation.

Dove turned around and yelled at the small yellow dog trying to keep up.

"Go back, ya dumb dog! Go back, bitch! . . . Aw, shit!"

He broke from the formation and ran back to the loping puppy, picked it up, and ran back to his position beside Pete. The major looked at his driver holding the bouncing pup.

"You gonna carry that dog the whole way?"

"Shit, sir, she'd just try and follow, and some damn REMF would get her."

"She'll get heavy, Dove."

Pete turned his head. "I'll spell him, sir."

Colven smiled. He knew he would offer to carry the dog too.

"Here we go! . . . All the way! . . . One way! . . .
Everyday! . . . Ranger! Ranger! Ha, Ha . . . ha, ha!
C–one-thirty, rollin' down the strip—
Ranger Daddy gonna take a little trip!
Stand up, hook up, shuffle to the door!
Jump right out and count to four!"

The running formation turned onto the main road toward the sprawling main base. The early-morning mist still lingered in the valley's recesses and pockets.

Lieutenant Le Be Son stretched his back. The night had been a miserable one for sleeping. He had dozed off leaning against a giant teak, which offered little respite from the chilly air. His body still shook; the warm sun was just beginning to rise above the mountains. He would welcome the sun's heat, he thought. He moved to his position and waited. It would not be long before the puppets would drive by. To keep his mind off his shivering, he thought of the plan again. He and his men would stay back in the trees just ten meters away from the lip of the embankment. They would let the puppets drive by. Once gone, one squad would move up to the road and stand guard while men from the other side slid down and planted big artillery shells. They would camouflage the wires and run them back to the firing positions on the high ridge. Then his squad would return to their position with him. Later, when the convoy began to pass, his platoon would position themselves at the steps that had been carved in the earth. Lieutenant Trang's two squads would spread out along the embankment and destroy anyone who jumped from a truck and took refuge over the steep bank. When the support element on the ridge ceased shooting their rockets and machine guns, at the sound of the bugle he would lead his men up the steps and assault the trapped convoy. He smiled at the thought. Once the support fire began, he planned to move up the steps as close to the top as possible, then charge at the first bugle note.

In the distance he heard the distinctive sound of a big truck approaching. The engine was straining as it pushed the large, heavy mine-clearing roller. Forgetting about his sleepless night, he lowered himself to the ground. His every muscle and fiber longed for the impending action. He touched the green band on his forehead and smiled.

Jean rolled over and turned off her alarm. The sheets were still damp and cool against her bare skin. Bud had left her during the night. She couldn't remember when he had gotten up. She thought about their passion and his tenderness. How would he feel about her this morning? The thought of seeing him in a short while worried her. *How should I act? What should I say? Will it be different? . . . Oh, Bud, it was so . . .*
She got up quickly.

The Deuce Platoon was running back up the hill toward the barracks. They had completed three miles. Colven held the small dog. Dove was supporting Pete by the arm.

"Up the hill! . . . No sweat! One way! . . . All the way! You bet! . . . Ah-ha! . . . ah-ha! . . . Quick time! . . . March!"

Two men bolted from the formation and began vomiting along the side of the road. One of them was Rock Steady. The platoon continued marching up the road. Childs felt good. He marched ramrod straight, bellowing from the side of his mouth:

> *"Get your heads up!*
> *Eyes up off the ground!*
> *Get your shoulders back!*
> *Let me hear a sound!*
> *Count cadence, delayed cadence . . . count cadence*
> *Count!"*

The formation sang back: *"One . . . two . . . three . . . four. . . . One- two! . . . three-four! . . . One-two! . . . Three-four!"*

"Pla-tooon . . . *halt!* Left . . . face!

"You got twenty minutes to clean up and get chow. . . . Not bad, ladies, not bad. Next formation oh-eight-hundred. Full rucks and all weapons . . . *Do it!"*

The formation dissolved quickly.

"Wow, no sweat, man. I do good, no?"

The pale Sox was about to nod but suddenly doubled over as gagging bile fought its way up his throat.

Pancho shook his head and leaned over his friend.

"Hey, it's cool. Pancho, he take care of you man."

Thumper and Grady both started to jog over to Rock, but Thumper tapped Grady's arm. "I'll get him, Sarge."

Grady stopped and smiled at the muscular man's concern. Then he turned and saw Ben approaching.

"Hey, Grade, do you think I lost weight?"

"Sure. I can tell already."

"Good, 'cause I starved to death yesterday. Today I'm gonna eat eggs and bacon and cereal and—"

"Whoa, Ben, you'd better take it easy, we gotta long hump yet this morning."

"I won't go back for thirds! I promise, Grade, I promise."

Thumper squatted down beside Rock and put his hand on the sick soldier's back.

"You okay, Rock?"

Rock looked up. Clear drool hung down from his mouth and his eyes looked swollen. "I made it, didn't I, Thump?"

"Yeah, Rock, you went all the way, Buddy. It was a tough run; it got to me too." He coughed several times and took in two loud breaths of air. "I didn't think I was gonna make it. . . . Come on, let's help each other to the showers and cool off."

Rock nodded while wiping away the long, stringy globs of saliva.

Thumper, acting as if tired and forcing heavy breathing, gently lifted Rock to his feet and walked him slowly to the shower building.

Rock swayed and leaned over on Thumper's arm. "You know, Thump, I used to run track at school. . . . I ran all the races. Why, the coach once told me . . ."

Thumper smiled, listening to Rock, knowing his skinny team member was feeling better. He also knew that Rock had never finished school and, for sure, had never run track. It didn't matter. Rock was a friend. It was an understanding. It wasn't written or spoken, but it was there. They were a team, and they took care of their own.

Dove walked slowly, watching the still chalky-looking Pete from the corner of his eye. Behind them the yellow dog bounded and hopped playfully.

"How ya feelin' now?"

"Better, thanks. Gosh, it's been a long time since I ran that far. . . . I'm sorry you had to help me up the hill. I would have quit if you hadn't grabbed me, you know?"

"No you wouldn't. That's why we're partners. You ain't no wimp-ass quitter. You're a fighter. . . . Hell, that dumb-ass dog is what did it. She got heavy, didn't she?"

"You bet. Good thing the major took her up the hill. I was dyin'!"

"Me, too, Pete! Me too."

Dove turned around and looked down at the puppy. "You big dummy!"

The ball of fur attacked Dove's boot, fell over, then sat on its haunches and looked up.

Dove shook his head and pointed at the mongrel.

"*You* . . . I'm sellin' you to the first REMF that'll take ya." The puppy rolled its head from side to side and attacked the soldier's boot again.

Grady stood at the back of the barracks. The men had all gone to morning chow. He wanted to be alone a few minutes. He followed the ridge with his eyes to the tops of the trees that marked his and Evans's spot, their secret AO. *Ah, Evans, hurry up and get here. I'm missing great opportunities to razz your ass. Half your team would have fallen out for sure*. The sergeant laughed to himself, thinking how his men would have three days of PT under their belt when the 2-4 pulled in. Boy, would Evans's men suffer then! He stood gazing another minute, then glanced over at the Red Cross compound across the slope and thought immediately of the girl.

Her eyes were light blue and a little too far apart, he remembered. They were so angry. Her thin nose was slightly upturned, and her long thin neck was much too long. Her wheat-colored hair had been cut too short but had been fixed in an aristocratic way. She'd had that polished aura of a socialite. Her perfume—he still couldn't believe his senses had picked that up just as he made his leap: He actually smelled her before seeing her golden hair. What the hell *had* she been doing there?

She was obviously a bitch. He'd seen plenty of her type at school. The sorority kind, holier than thou, pushy as hell. . . . Yeah, he'd seen her type before. But she wasn't beautiful enough to get away with it. She was only pretty. And so damn arrogant.

Grady shook his head and cleared the woman's image away. His stomach growled as he walked quickly for the road.

The convoy departed on time and moved steadily for fifteen minutes. Evans sat in the cab with Amos, the driver, a gangly black man. In the back, lying on a tarp thrown over the ammo boxes, was his team.

The land on both sides of the road fell away to solid brilliant green rice paddies. The conical-hatted workers standing knee-deep in brown ooze tended their staple crop. Huge black water buffalos dotted the geometric dikes as farmers coaxed the animals to plow their flooded fields. The sergeant leaned forward, trying to take mental pictures. It was beautiful and he wanted to be able to describe it to Helen and his folks in a letter. The paddies stretched for miles to low blue hills in the distance.

Amos turned slightly, still watching the road. "There's the mountains, Sarge."

Evans broke his trance from the side window and turned to look out the windshield. Directly ahead loomed the infamous Dai Das, the major mountain range of Vietnam.

"How many times you drive this road, Amos?"

"This trip'll make eleven, Sarge. . . . Me and ol' Highway 21 is good friends now. We'll be headin' northeast till we hit Ban Me Thuot, then we'll head due north and follow Highway 14 to Pleiku, then take a right on Highway 19 to An Khe. It'll take all day, Sarge. Ya might as well sit back and relax."

Evans unbuckled his web belt. He took his CAR-15 from the seat and inserted a full magazine, then took two of the new round M-33 grenades from his ammo pouch and put them into his pant pocket.

Amos glanced down and saw the grenades. "What are those, Sarge? I ain't seen them kind before?"

"Oh, these are the new Mike-33s." Evans held one up so Amos could see it. "You throw it like a baseball. It's got a coil steel spring in it. When she blows, the spring shatters, sending out hundreds of steel fragments. It's got a kill radius of fifty meters!"

"Man, Sarge, that little thang is bad!"

"You better believe it. It'll sure do ya' a damn damn."

Evans put the fragmentation grenade back into his pocket.

"Hey Sarge, ya see that 'Semi', four trucks up!"

Evans looked up seeing the large tractor trailer and van ahead.

"Yeah, what is it?"

"It's a reefer men. A refrigerated van. My buddy is drivin' it. When we stop at Ban Me Thout, I'll get us some ice cream."

"Alll-right."

The truck slowed as the convoy began its slow climb. In minutes the rice paddies were gone. The low foothills of the Dai Das had taken their place.

The rumbling convoy reached the steeper mountains and slowed down considerably. Here the road twisted through and up the south side of a small valley that lay beneath huge green-brown peaks.

Evans looked down the steep slope of the valley, envisioning the small stream that he knew would be at its bottom, meandering around gray-brown rocks covered with soft green moss. Gnarled roots washed clean by countless rains would cling to the banks and reach for the gurgling, clear water. He had filled his canteen many times from such a stream.

The truck made a sharp left turn and the road became surprisingly flat. The roar of the engine immediately eased to a low-pitched whine.

Evans glanced up. A soldier in the truck ahead of them suddenly opened his mouth as he looked at something behind them. Evans was about to turn when the sound of a thunderous explosion engulfed them. The ensuing shock wave shook the truck, rattling the windshield and the windows. Evans grabbed his CAR and was about to turn around again, but his eyes caught movement on the ridge above them. He yelled at Amos *"Gun it!"* Then he heard the sickening, unmistakable sound of RPG-40 rockets swooshing through the air.

The truck in front of them suddenly leaped up and tilted awkwardly to its right before disappearing in a red-orange blast of metal, glass, and whirling, killing shrapnel. The soldier in the back was thrown violently into sideboards, then bounced back, lifeless, into the raging fiery inferno.

Amos jerked the steering wheel right, avoiding the burning truck, when suddenly the windshield exploded, showering the confined men. Amos screamed in pain and whipped the wheels back just before going over the steep bank, the right rear tire knocking loose rocks and dirt down the embankment.

Evans had his head down when the windshield shattered. He'd been lucky that none of the glass shards had hit his face.

Amos was bleeding profusely from his cheeks and forehead as he sped down the road past the stopped, burning vehicles. Murderous machine-gun fire from the ridge above raked the road all around them.

Evans saw the green van ahead and screamed at Amos, pointing. "The van! Beside the van!"

The driver understood: The large metal container would shield them from the withering fire above.

Chico had reacted first to the blast and grabbed his rifle, raising it. Before he could place his finger on the trigger, bullets tore through his chest, knocking him over the shocked Howdy Doody. The spraying bullets shattered the wood sideboards and struck with metallic clangs. Black Jack fell back screaming. A large wooden splinter had lodged just below his right eye.

The truck, reaching the protection of the van, slammed to a jolting stop throwing the men and ammo boxes to the front bulkhead. Elkins heard the sickening, snapping crack of his left wrist as his body smashed into the rear sideboard. Bull jerked himself up, grabbing his weapon. Howdy Doody pulled Chico's bloody body over. He was dead. He then grabbed the flailing Black Jack who was pawing his face. Bull quickly leaned over and grasped hold of the black splinter end, and yanked. Only half came out, leaving a blue-black jagged piece still under the screaming man's skin.

Bullets struck the large van like hail stones on a tin roof. Evans jumped to the ground, holding his CAR-15. Amos fell from the cab and ran to the front of the big semitractor, yelling, "Sam! Sa—"

Evans screamed, *"No! No, Amos, No!"*

The ground around the running driver erupted. He jerked backward with the impact of tearing bullets. The lifeless body continued to twitch and jump as still more bullets riddled him.

The silver-haired battalion commander rose from his camouflaged position when the first blast rocked the earth below him. It had blown a two-and-a-half-ton truck over, blocking the road; the second blast threw a small jeep over the cliff, but a wall of rock partially blocked that part of road as well. The vehicles within the *U* were trapped. The supporting unit had run from the protective trees and taken up positions, shooting into the trapped vehicles for a final coup de grace. He was pleased. The ambush had gone exactly as planned. The vehicles had stopped and, one by one, were methodically destroyed, except one that attained protection behind a large van. His men's fire was extremely effective; he saw not a single American return fire. The shooting suddenly stopped; the bugler behind him began his shrill call for the assault.

The Colonel stepped closer and saw Le Be Son and his men pour over the embankment. He felt glad for the young officer below, for he was going to achieve his dream . . . a dream of revenge.

The old commander took one last look, turned, and ran slowly up the hill.

Sergeant Evans crawled over the truck's sideboards. The sickly-sweet smell of blood hit him first. His stomach revolted as he looked down and saw Chico's spread-eagled body lying on the tarpaulin.

"My God!" His body shook with revulsion. The rest of his team were huddled against the truck's left side, seeking protection from the van only two feet away. They knelt in the dark pools of the dead man's blood.

Evans felt helpless. He had an overwhelming desire to cry. His team . . . his men—they were hurt and he could do nothing! He began crawling to them, when miraculously the shooting stopped.

Then the eerie silence was pierced by a shrill bugle call. Every man's eyes swung to their team sergeant, who rose and looked in the direction of the strange sound.

Lieutenant Son ran over the lip of the embankment at the first note of the bugle. The sight before him was glorious: Twisted trucks sat smoking, burning. A thin cloud of dust and smoke was hugging the bullet-torn road. He ran to the right, to the first truck, firing into the cab. He jumped up and swung the door open. Two contorted bodies lay in the seat and on the floorboard.

A squad of his men passed by him, yelling and firing. He jumped down to join them. Ahead, a wounded Yankee was kneeling by his truck, holding his hands up, crying from unseeing eyes. His face was full of glass shards. Le Be Son ran up to him and plunged his thin bayonet into the man's chest. The soldier screamed, clutching at the weapon. It caught Son off balance and jerked him forward. His jungle hat fell backward off his head. The Yankee held the barrel: he writhed and twisted. Son screamed, grabbing the weapon and plunging it deeper, then pulled the trigger. Blood and human tissue splattered him. He jerked the bayonet free and held the weapon up, screaming "Revenge!" as he ran to the next truck.

Evans and the others heard their attackers before they saw them. They had time only to fall to the bed of the truck and push up a few ammo boxes for protection.

The Vietnamese were shooting and screaming wildly as they swarmed down the line of trucks. Evans pushed the safety off, took careful aim and fired. One of the running men spun around and fell to the ground. The others, seeing their comrade fall, screamed louder and ran directly for the truck. Evans and Bull rose up, catching them in the open. Two more of the running soldiers pitched backward. Bull dropped to his knee to shoot at the soldier who had gotten the closest. He snapped off a quick shot, hitting the running man in the head. Before Bull could conceal himself again, a barrage of bullets struck the back of the truck. Bull fell back, hit in the chest, but caught his balance and stood straight up. Crazed with pain, he screamed *"Come on! Come on!"* while raising his M-16 to his hip and firing.

Blood spilled from his mouth as he yelled madly. The running men directed every weapon on him. Bull groaned and fell back, hit again, but kept his balance, shaking his powerful body and continuing to fire until his weapon was empty. Evans jumped up, grabbed his wounded team member, and pulled him down. Bull had broken the assault. The attackers had taken refuge behind the trucks. Bull lay dying; there was nothing Evans could do but cradle his head and listen to his friend's last agonizing breaths.

Howdy Doody, threw two grenades toward the trucks and yelled at Evans that more men were coming from down the road. Evans slowly lowered Bull's head. He knew the attackers would reorganize and try to flank their truck. He would have to move under the van to see them if they tried to go around. He turned to the two wounded men behind him. "Black Jack, Elk, come here!"

Both men crawled forward, knowing their wounds would have to wait. They would have to fight or they would die.

"I'm goin' over the side. If they try goin' around the van, I'll get 'em. I'll be under the van, so don't throw any grenades short. If they rush and you don't hear me firing, you know I've bought it, understand?"

The two men nodded, as did Howdy Doody, who turned, peered over the tailgate, and turned back to his sergeant. "You better go now, Ev. . . . I'll cover."

Evans looked into each man's eyes.

"See you guys later." He held his CAR tightly and bounded over the side, landing on his feet and rolling under the van.

Le Be Son lay waiting for more of his men to work their way up to him. He'd been running when Corporal Tuy beside him suddenly fell. Tuy had been shot in the groin. Son and the others immediately attacked, but were beaten back by deadly fire. Only he and Private Li remained.

Son's arm was hurt. He had been hit by grenade fragments, but the pain was inconsequential compared to the fire inside him. It was them! The men with green faces! He had seen one stand. He wore the camouflage fatigues of the commandos. . . . Them! He sent Li for the others. He knew time was short, but he had to finish them off. He wanted to be able to touch one and lay his mourning band on one of their bodies. He turned and smiled grimly. His men were coming.

Howdy Doody tied a parachute scarf sling securely around Elk's back.

"That ought to do it, Elk. Be glad it's your left hand. You can still load magazines for me and throw grenades if they rush." He looked over at Black Jack, who was watching the road. His face had stopped bleeding, but the ugly black splinter could still be clearly seen under the skin.

"See anything?"

Black Jack ducked slightly and spoke through his clenched jaw. Obviously he was still in pain. "There's a bunch of them about four trucks back. It looks like they're in a pow-wow."

The hatless redhead slowly raised himself up and peered over the tailgate.

Le Be Son pointed to three men. "You go around to the left and throw grenades over the van. We will wait for the explosion before we attack."

The three nodded and ran off. They went unobserved by the men in the truck, but not by Evans, who lay behind the two back tires of the van. He could see them clearly, running hunched over. The first two had their weapons slung and held bamboo-handled Chicom grenades in both their hands. The sergeant aimed and gently squeezed. The first soldier dropped his grenades and grabbed at his stomach. Evans swung the barrel and fired at the second soldier, who was running for cover. The bullet struck him in the back. The third Vietnamese quickly fired from the hip, hitting the ground in front of the sergeant. Dirt flew up into Evans's face, blinding him. He fired blindly, emptying his magazine.

Howdy Doody heard the firing and looked behind him at Elkins. "Ev is dealin', baby!"

Evans blinked his eyes and rubbed them quickly. He then peered around the tires. The soldier he had fired at was standing, pulling the firing string of a Chicom grenade. The soldier raised his eyes and met Evans's glare. Evans brought the CAR up and pulled the trigger. It was empty. He grabbed for his pistol. The soldier tossed the grenade toward him and fell to the ground.

Evans yanked the pistol free, leveled it at the fallen soldier, and fired. The grenade exploded.

"Now!" yelled Le Be Son upon hearing the grenade blast. Eight men broke from the protection of the truck while two in the truck bed raised up and fired to support the assault.

Black Jack yelled "Here they come!" then raised up shooting. Elk readied his M-16 to give to Howdy Doody to fire. The grenade blast seconds before meant one thing: Evans was dead. It had gone off almost directly under the truck. "Mother fuckers!" yelled Elk as he reached down and took out a grenade from his pant-leg pocket and set it down in front of him. *They ain't taking me alive.* "Mother-fuckers! . . . You'll pay!"

Evans's torn body lay twitching. The unendurable pain had passed, leaving him fighting to regain consciousness. He had fired his pistol, when suddenly he was violently thrown back and burning, searing pain overcame him. The jagged fragments had torn into his chest, neck, and face, leaving excruciating paths of destruction through tissue, muscle, and bone. His mind had mercifully relieved him of the tormenting agony and now transmitted only a dull throbbing sensation.

The sergeant opened his eyes slowly. He was in a fog. His body seemed to be floating, unable to right its awkward position. There were sounds, but they were behind the fog and far away. It was uncomfortable. He tried to reach out. Suddenly he was falling . . . falling faster and faster, unable to breathe. The fog cleared, revealing colors and loud sounds, but he continued to fall, faster and faster, as the sounds grew louder. *Stop! Stop!* His body jerked. He vomited.

Evans shut his eyes tightly in agony as his stomach convulsed and a warm, bloody substance flowed over his torn, exposed jaw. *Helen! Helen!* He opened his eyes. He was on his side, looking at the two large tires. His body seemed weighted now and it tingled. He moved his tongue, feeling the loose tissue and shattered lower teeth. The trapped fluid was choking him. He turned his head, letting the blood and tissue drool out to the already soaked ground. Feeling was coming back, as was the stabbing pain.

His left arm was under him, unable to move. He willed his right hand to touch his face. He could hear gunshots and yelling as his hand came up and to where his jaw should have been. It touched his tongue. *Oh, God! No! . . . No!* He moved his hand farther down and pushed the ripped lower portion of his face up. He couldn't scream, only shut his eyes and move his hand to his side and cry silently. *Helen . . . Helen, I'm so sorry . . . so sorry.*

Howdy Doody had shot two of the attacking men. He squeezed the trigger again, emptying the magazine. He turned, exchanging the empty weapon with Elkins's loaded one. He was about to turn back when his eyes suddenly rolled up and he slowly toppled over. Elkins deflected his fall with the outstretched weapon.

"Howdy! What's—" Then he saw the small red hole in the back of Elkins's head. *"Mother-Fuckers!"*

Black Jack fired in short bursts. Incoming bullets hit the tailgate with loud thuds. He didn't care. He was going to die, he knew. The team was finished. The assaulting NVA came in rushes. There were only four left, and they were hiding one truck away. The shooting from farther back made it impossible to rise up for more than two quick shots. It was just a matter of time before more came. He pulled the pin on his last grenade, took a deep breath, rose up, and tossed it. He fell backward; he had been hit in the neck. He could see his blood squirting up, hitting his hand as he grabbed his throat. He couldn't breathe. He rolled over and crawled toward Elk.

Elkins got to his knee and awkwardly raised his M-16. He saw Jack. Jack was trying to speak but could only make a gurgling noise. Jack fell in front of him, his eyes bulging. *"Oh, my God, Jack! Jack!"*

Black Jack bounced and convulsed on the bloody metal floor, his face turning blue and purple as he gasped for air. Finally his body slumped, went rigid, then lay still.

"Jack!"

More bullets slammed into the truck, sending small jolting shock waves through the metal floor.

"Now!" Le Be Son stood and charged straight for the truck, firing. The others followed.

Evans heard the screams and shooting of the approaching men. His right hand reached into his leg pocket and withdrew the round grenade. Holding it somehow made him feel stronger. He moved his shoulder and fell heavily on his back, releasing his left arm. His throat immediately filled with blood. He couldn't breathe. *Oh, Grady, there was so much I wanted to tell you. . . .* His freed left hand came up and pulled the grenade pin.

The screaming was coming closer. *Grady . . . Grady . . . Helen, I love—* He brought his right hand up with the last of his strength and let the grenade roll from his hand behind his head toward the screams. *I love you so, Helen. . . . Grady, I love . . .*

Son was four feet from the truck when the small green object rolled out from under the van in front of him, but he didn't notice it as he jumped for the truck tailgate. The towering mountain peaks seemed to grumble as the manmade thunderclap echoed through its crevices and cannonaded back down into the smoking valley of twisted death.

Corporal Tuy lay in agony. He had seen his lieutenant and two men rush the truck and disappear in an explosion. He knew he was going to die in the dusty road. Suddenly he was jerked over. The men who had been firing support knelt beside him. One stood and ran to a dead American, tore the first-aid packet from his harness, then picked up something else and came back.

"Here, comrade, bite this while we carry you to the embankment."

"Leave me, I'm dying."

The soldier shook his head and folded the lieutenant's lost jungle hat and placed it in the corporal's mouth while the other tied the bandage. They could hear the sound of helicopters coming up the valley.

14

"Okay, clowns, take your time and remember to squeeze, not jerk. I want all the remaining ammo fired up! Remember, you gotta hump back what you don't shoot!"

Sergeant Childs stepped back to a slight rise and faced the long line of men. *"Ready on the right? Ready on the left? Com-mence . . . firing!"*

Childs walked along the rise with his hands on his hips. It had been a good day to be a soldier, he thought. *"Ben!* Goddamn it! You're blinkin' your fat eyes."

"Yo, Sergeant."

Childs moved on, his eyes searching for the slightest error in position or technique. Yeah, it had been a good learning day, he said to himself again as he spun around and began retracing his steps, hands still on hips. The march to the dump had been slow and easy. Once there they had made up a makeshift range and he had given the platoon a quick refresher course on zeroing weapons. It had been a worthwhile class: Most had forgotten. Rock Steady had complained that zeroing wasn't necessary, since most of their ambushes took place within thirty feet of a trail. Childs had grabbed Rock's weapons run the elevation and windage knobs to their extremes, and thrown the loaded M-16 back at the thin soldier.

"Now, *Deadeye*! Hit that can!" He'd pointed to a green C-ration can only twenty feet away. Rock had smirked and aimed with confidence. He didn't even come close; the point was made.

Childs stopped and began rocking back and forth from heel to sole. He knew he was doing the right thing by pushing them. They all complained, but he knew they were proud of themselves. *He* was proud of them too.

The firing began tapering off. Childs stalked to the middle of the rise and waited until the shooting ceased.

"Cease fire, girls! Anybody not done? . . . Clear all weapons and take your mags out. Leave the bolt back! File by me and let me check your weapons! . . . Come on, shitbirds, *Mooove out! You're on your own time!"*

"I've got good news, Lieutenant Sikes. You're being discharged tomorrow.

Bud smiled. "Thanks, Doc. You got a nice place to visit, but I sure wouldn't want to live here."

The doctor walked over to the next patient. Jean followed him, but not before giving Bud a pained look.

A corpsman came through the swinging doors from the emergency room and walked to the lieutenant's bed.

"Hey, sir, we just got one of your guys in the ER."

Bud looked up at the black corpsman, who often delivered the food. "Naw, all our guys went up north days ago."

The corpsman shrugged his shoulders. "This guy got chopped up in a convoy ambush. He's wearin' cammies, so I figured he was one of yours."

Bud's face suddenly turned pale. "You say convoy?"

The corpsman stepped closer. "Yeah, the gooks really wasted it."

Bud spun around in the bed, grabbing for his crutches. Jean saw the lieutenant moving rapidly toward the door. She excused herself from the doctor and walked toward him.

"Lieutenant Sikes . . . Bud!"

He didn't hear her. It took him only seconds to get to the emergency room and push the door open.

A doctor and nurse were leaning over a single gurney, working feverishly. The wounded soldier was lying still.

Bud almost fell over with the weakness he suddenly felt. He moved closer, praying it wasn't one of his men. The nurse changed position, exposing the soldier's pale face.

"Elkins! Oh, God, no!"

The doctor looked up from the man's chest wound. He pulled off his rubber gloves and spoke to the nurse.

"He's stable. Get him prepped for OR. Watch his arm. His wrist is broken. I'll tell Dr. Collier he's on the way."

Bud followed the wheeled cart as the orderly pushed Elkins to the prep area. He gave the nurse all the information he could and then asked, "Can I talk to him? I've got to know about the others."

"He's pretty doped up. The medics gave him morphine."

Sikes's pleading look told her he didn't care; he had to talk to his man.

"Go on, but just for a while."

Bud felt helpless as he leaned over and studied the dirty, bruised face.

"Elkins. Elk, it's me, Lieutenant Sikes."

The soldier's eyes opened slowly.

"Elk. Elk, can you hear me?"

"Yes-s-s, sir-r-r."

He sounded like a record on the wrong speed.

"What about the others? Where's the team?"

The soldier's eyes closed. His mouth opened partially. "They . . . they're . . . gone."

"Where, Elk? Gone where?"

His eyelids half opened before closing again. "They're . . . dead, sir. . . . All dead."

Sikes's body sank. He reached over and clasped the man's hand.

"I'm sorry, Elk. I'm . . . so sorry."

He felt Elkins squeeze his hand.

"We . . . got 'em . . . good . . . sir."

The nurse tapped Bud's shoulder. "That's it, Bud. We have to get him in."

Bud patted Elkins's hand and turned around. Jean was waiting for him. Their eyes met for only a second before he lowered his head and crutched slowly down the aisle past her. Jean joined him, putting her arm around his waist.

They walked silently for several seconds. Bud shook his head and spoke softly. "The team, Jean. The whole damn team."

She squeezed him closer. He stopped, still looking at the floor, then turned and pulled her to him. His tears fell softly on her neck.

"Oh, Jean, Jean . . . I . . . loved them so much."

She could feel the sadness flow through his body, wishing she could do something to ease his untreatable pain.

"I know, Bud. I know."

Rock tapped Thumper's wet back as they walked to the barracks. "I could have run all day, Thump. How 'bout you?"

Thumper rolled his shoulders. "I don't know, Rock. This damn ruck rubbed my back raw."

"Oh, hey, I'll look at it for you. I took a first aid course in school and know all . . ."

"Hey, Grady, I ran good, huh? I can eat regular chow, right?" Ben said.

Grady turned toward the huge, sweaty body. "Yeah, Ben, you get to eat regular, but still no thirds."

"Aw, Grade!"

"No thirds!"

"Okay, Grade. I can hang tough, but I'm tellin' my mama 'bout you!"

Grady grinned. The subject of food reminded him that he had to tell the mess sergeant to save some chow for Evans's team when they rolled in later that night. *Guess I'd better get a couple of six-packs too,* he thought. *Yeah, ol' Ev will wanna rub my nose in it. I'll let him drink most of the beer, and then, when we run tomorrow morning . . .* The sergeant laughed aloud as he pulled the barracks door open.

At dinner Grady and the team sat at the large corner table. As usual, they were joking and laughing, but their laughter abruptly stopped when they saw Major Colven and Sergeant Childs walking toward them.

Grady began to stand, but Colven motioned him back down. All the mess-hall activity had stopped. Something was wrong. Every eye had turned to the major.

Grady searched the major's expression. He shifted his stare to Childs, who clenched his jaw and glanced down.

"Double-Deuce, I wanted to tell you myself. I'm afraid we've just received very bad news."

Grady stared at the major, screaming inside, somehow already knowing.

"Sergeant Evans and his team were ambushed on Highway 19 north of Nha Trang. There was only one survivor. . . ."

No, no, no! Please let the survivor be Ev. Oh, God, please say Evans. . . .

"It's Specialist Elkins. He's seriously wounded."

Colven glanced at the floor before looking back at the team. "I'm sorry, men. I know Two-Four was special to you all. I'm very sorry."

Grady didn't move his eyes from the major, praying that he would smile and say it was a bad joke. He sat unbelieving. It couldn't have been Ev. It couldn't!

Colven grasped Grady's shoulder. "Son, you have to Charlie Mike. I'll be in my office if any of you want to talk."

The team sat staring at their half-full plates. Grady rose slowly, took out his beret, and put it on, pulling it low over his right ear before turning to his men.

"I'll be in the barracks in an hour to inspect your weapons." He took a deep breath and strode for the door.

Thumper looked at the team. "Should someone go with him?"

Rock shook his head. Ben stood and walked out slowly. Sox and Pancho slid back their chairs and walked toward the exit together. Thumper stared at his plate for a moment, then started to rise.

Rock grabbed his arm. "Thump, promise me somethin'."

The large soldier lowered himself to his seat and stared into the watery eyes of his friend. "Sure, Rock."

"If I buy it, Thump . . . if I go down, make sure they get me back, will ya?"

Thumper had never seen that look in his friend's face before. It was a look of desperation. Thumper nodded as Rock continued.

"My ol' man . . . he thinks I'm . . . well, a nothing. I wanna be buried with the full honors I'm entitled to, you know? The shooting squad and all. You know what I mean?"

Thumper nodded again. Rock looked at the table, still holding Thumper's arm tightly. "I want him to know I was a somebody, Thump." He looked back into Thumper's eyes. "It's important to me. Please don't say nothin' to the guys, okay?"

Thumper placed his hand on top of Rock's. "I promise you, buddy."

Sarah changed into her khaki shorts and shirt. She wanted to explore her newfound spot again. Mary Ann sat on the couch, drinking a beer, when Sarah walked out of her room and headed for the door.

"Sarah, did you call that Captain Lowe back?"

Sarah stopped, putting her hands on her slim hips. "He's such a bore, Mary Ann."

"You've gone out with him four times! He thinks you're crazy about him."

"He certainly does not!"

Mary Ann laughed, pleased to see Sarah's irate reaction. "Well, he called for you twice today. He wanted to take you to the club tonight. They've got a floor show in from Australia."

"I detest that wretched club. The officers drink too bloody much and carry on just shockingly."

"He's awfully good-looking."

"Well, yes, he's handsome, but limited."

"Limited? How can you say that. He's a graduate of Harvard Law School."

"He's a bore."

"My gosh, Sarah, what is it you want? What kind of men do you like?"

Sarah began to speak, but stopped when she realized she didn't have an answer. "Uh . . . I prefer men who . . . uh . . . I don't know!"

Mary Ann smiled. "Me neither, except they gotta be big! This girl needs a big man to love this *biiiiig* woman."

Sarah grinned. "What about you, Mary Ann? What about the captain who calls you?"

The dark-haired woman winked. "He's a bore too."

Sarah laughed as she walked out the door and strode quickly down the walkway toward her little valley.

Grady crossed the green grass in six long strides and bounded up to the boulders. He stood staring at the place where he and Evans used to sit, unable to stop the tears that rolled down his cheeks.

Ev . . . Ev . . . He sat down, taking off his beret, looking at the hills across the valley. *Oh, Ev . . .* He shut his eyes and leaned back on the cool rock. Evans's smiling face looked at him.

"Hey, you seen the latest picture of Helen?"

"Is it like the other six hundred you showed me?"

"Look at this one, Grade! See, that's my folks beside her."

"Which one's Helen?"

"Aw, Grade, doesn't she look great?"

Helen is a skinny broad, Ev. I never told you, but I never thought she was your type. I always thought she looked too simple for you. She is so thin, and her long brown hair makes her look even skinnier. You should have had a queen—a real looker. Oh, you dumb shit! Why?

Why you, Ev? You were the only one I could really talk to. You understood, Ev. You knew what to say and . . . Jesus, you had so much to live for! You were going home, back to Helen and your dumb-ass baseball team. You wanted to coach so bad, didn't you? Oh, Ev, I would have taken your place. Hell, I've got nobody, nothing, to go back for.

Grady raised his head and looked skyward as tears streamed down his face.

Please, Lord, take care of him. There has to be a heaven, Lord, there's just got to be a place where he can fulfill his dreams. Please, Lord, take care of him and the Two-Four . . . make them happy.

Grady lowered his head and thought of his team. He needed to be with them. He needed to be with friends. Friends—friends he cared for more than anything in the world. Friends he would have for only two more months.

Grady looked at the spot where Evans used to sit and moved over to it. He wanted somehow to feel his presence just one last time.

Sarah stood motionless in the trees. It was *him*! He had disappeared behind the boulder. Probably sitting, she thought. She remained perfectly still for several minutes, to make certain he hadn't seen her. Then a smile spread across her face. She had thought of a way to get back at him.

Ever so slowly she bent down and picked up a small broken branch. She crept forward, being careful not to step on any twigs. Her heart was pounding with excitement.

When she could just see the top of his head, she raised her arm. He opened his eyes and turned.

She threw the branch high, but he saw a movement and jumped into its path. It struck his chin and fell to the ground.

"Oh, it's you," she said. "I thought you were a sapper."

She was about to laugh when she saw that something was wrong with him. His cheeks were glistening from crying. For a long moment he stood staring at her with a strange, pained expression. Then his eyes narrowed and his jaw muscles rippled. He bent down, picked up his beret, put it on, and began walking down the slope.

"Hey, look, I'm sorry. I didn't mean to . . ."

He rolled his shoulders and kept walking.

"Hey," she cried out in confusion, "I didn't mean any harm. . . ."

She watched the broad-shouldered soldier disappear over the ridge. *Oh, to hell with him,* she thought. He should have said *something* . . . but then she thought she realized what had happened. She had caught him crying, and he had been embarrassed. That must have been it! Oh, why did she have to do that to him? Those sad gray eyes had looked at her and . . . *Damn, Sarah, you're so dumb sometimes.*

On her way back she stopped and turned toward the Ranger compound. She would have to see him, that's all there was to it. Maybe she would see him tomorrow, apologize quickly, and get it over with. Then she would never have to see him again.

Grady crossed the field without looking back. The worst was over. He'd had the initial shock of losing Evans, and he'd learned he could handle it. He pushed open the shower-building door and walked to the sink. He splashed water on his face, then looked into the cracked mirror. The tears were gone. He wouldn't cry again. Sentiment could make you lose your edge. It could get you killed. Evans would be placed in a special recess of his mind where fond memories were kept. Grady had his team to worry about now.

He looked back into the mirror and checked his chin where the branch had struck him. What had she said? She thought he was a sapper? Okay. They were even. Good.

He moved his jaw again and pushed open the door. Why had she been there anyway? Had she been waiting all this time just to get even? To hell with her. He didn't care why she'd been there. Nothing mattered but the team.

Jean walked alone back up the dark road. Just ten minutes ago she had gone down to pick up her lieutenant. It would have been their last night together, and she had wanted desperately to hold him for those final hours. But as soon as she pushed through the ward door, she knew she would be sleeping alone. Bud was sitting beside the unconscious Ranger, who had been wheeled in from the OR earlier. She asked him to go with her anyway, but his face told her the answer before he spoke. "Jean, I want to, but I wouldn't feel right. It's just that . . . I really want to, but . . ."

He didn't have to explain it to her. She knew how he felt. He would feel obligated to stay until Elkins awoke. He wanted to be there so the first thing the boy saw was a friendly face. And she knew the soldier would need it. He was badly hurt, and he was the only survivor of his team. Bud would be there to talk to him and ease his survivor's guilt.

Still, it had hurt her when he declined to come. Like a fool she'd pouted and stomped out. Oh, he'd stood and tried to follow, but she got out of the door before he caught her. Now he would be sitting by the wounded Ranger, tormenting himself about his decision to stay.

Jean stopped at the MP booth and looked up at the white stars that speckled the sky.

She would have to go back to him. Bud wouldn't compromise his affection for the platoon member, not even for her. And for that reason, more than any other, he was special to her. She would go back and be with him. It wouldn't be as though she wanted it, but they would be together . . . at least for a while.

Grady pushed open the barracks door.

The team was sitting at the large green felt table, cleaning their weapons, when he walked in. All their eyes searched his face.

"Any of you shitbirds hungry? I checked with the mess sergeant, and he's got some sandwiches and milk."

Their eyes shifted to one another, then back to Grady, who stood with his hands on his hips.

Ben suddenly hopped up and loomed over the sergeant. "You reckon he's got cake, too, Grade?"

"You didn't run *that* far today."

"Aw, Grade."

Thumper grinned. He knew they were back to normal . . . well, almost. Each of them retained the memories of their dead friends in their own way, but each was now ready to go on. As the major said: Charlie Mike—continue the mission.

The glow from the small fire reflected off the silver-haired commander's face. The remaining men of the assault squad rose and walked into the darkness. The news they had reported had saddened the old man. The joy of success had been dashed by their report.

The deaths of so many brave liberators was like a hot knife touching his skin. He would write the brave men's names in the unit diary and tell of their glorious assault. He would tell of the revenge platoon and their mourning bands. It was good to be old, he thought, for he would not have to make many more such entries. The small American group responsible for the deaths were brave fighters too. He wanted to die as they had—fighting gloriously. Yes, to be placed in the diary with such a death would indeed be a blessing from Buddha. His sons would be honored for many springs.

The Americans—he did not hate them. They were soldiers like his own, young men far from home and filled with blazing passions.

"Commander."

The colonel turned toward the voice coming out of the darkness.

"Commander, the wounded soldier brought back by the assault team is awake. Did you want to see him?"

The silver-haired soldier nodded and walked with the medical orderly.

"Will he live, my friend?" he asked quietly.

"I would have said no earlier. I would not have thought he could possibly have made the difficult trip here, but he is here, Commander, alive, and now, with the blood expander we have administered, his chances are excellent."

The two men squatted down beside the prostrate figure.

"Corporal Tuy, the commander is here."

Tuy turned his head and smiled. The old man patted the soldier's hand, which tightly held a twisted wet jungle hat. "Corporal Tuy, you are a brave liberator. I am proud to serve with you. Tomorrow we will be sending you to the hospital to recover."

Tuy nodded as he brought the hat to his mouth and bit down to ease the pain.

The colonel rose, still looking at his wounded soldier. He would place his name in the diary as the brave survivor who courageously held on to life in order to fight again.

He was about to turn away, but he saw there was something strange about the hat upon which the young man was biting. The commander bent over and looked at the soldier's face more closely. The twisted hat had a strange piece of cloth affixed to it.

Curious, he thought, as he turned and started back to his fire. A scarlet patch. What significance could it hold for the soldier named Tuy? Strange, very strange.

The night had slipped away, and the rays of the morning sun slowly burned off the mist in the valley.

"Company . . . ah-tench-*hut*! Left . . . face! For-ward . . . *march!*"

Sierra Company, Seventy-fifth Infantry Rangers, marched in perfect step, their backs straight, their faces set. A passerby would have stopped and stood, impressed at the ranks of somber men in camouflage fatigues who wore black berets and stepped in regimented unison.

The passerby would stand a little straighter, hold his chin slightly higher, as he watched the passing men, touched by what the Rangers felt: pride—pride in themselves, pride in their unit. It showed in their steps, their faces, their unwavering eyes. The marching echelon radiated camaraderie, friendship, confidence.

"Com-pan-ee . . . halt! Right . . . face!"

Major Colven stood at attention, waiting. Six soldiers stood five paces behind him, holding M-16 rifles with bayonets attached. Six pairs of glistening jungle boots were positioned two feet in front of the group.

The first sergeant marched toward the major, stopped in front of him, and presented a rigid salute.

Returning the salute, the major commanded, "First Sergeant, conduct roll call."

The senior sergeant dropped his salute and executed an about-face, raised a paper in his left hand, and began calling the names of the assembled men. Roll call continued until he came to the last six names. He paused momentarily, staring at the remaining names, seeing the dead soldiers' familiar faces. His hand trembled only slightly as he continued the call.

"Evans, Stanley. Team Sergeant, Two-Four."

There was an eerie silence for several seconds, which was suddenly broken by one of the soldiers behind the major, who slapped his M-16 handguard loudly. He took one step forward, spun his weapon around, and plunged the black steel bayonet into the red earth behind the first pair of boots. He then withdrew the beret from his belt, placed it on the still-vibrating weapon stock, and marched two paces back.

"Murphy, Robert 'Bull.' Team Rifleman, Two-Four."

The second soldier slapped his handguard and stepped forward.

The roll call was complete in minutes. Colven took a deep breath and commanded, ". . . Pa-rade . . . *rest!*"

"Sierra Rangers team Two-Four has been called to a higher command. Their final contact resulted in the ultimate sacrifice of five men. Five Rangers who lived, trained, fought, and now . . . have died together.

"They died on a twisting dirt road in an unnamed valley. They will be buried with honors at homes where families will ask why. It will be difficult to console those loved ones in their grief with words of duty, honor, and love of country. A folded flag is little consolation to a mother or wife. But you men standing here understand love of country. It is not a love for a land called America. It is the love of men in your unit who represent her. You know what it is to do your duty—twenty-four hours a day for the three hundred and sixty-five days you spend here living, laughing, crying, and sharing. You sacrifice by staying and fighting when others have turned their backs on their country. You understand the duty of helping your friends when conditions or circumstances are miserable or dangerous. You know the devotion you feel for your fellow soldiers and the closeness and respect it engenders. You do all this, and the people ask why. Why did they have to die?

"They died, Rangers, for you and me. They died protecting their friends to their left or the ones behind them. They did their best so more like them wouldn't fall.

"No, Rangers, soldiers don't die for great causes or countries far away. They march forward and give their lives for their friends and fellow soldiers, who they know would do the same for them.

"Today we pay our respects to our fallen friends who for the last time will be in our ranks."

The major came to attention. "Company! Ah-tench-*hut*! Present . . . arms!"

Each man's right hand rose sharply, fingers extended, in a final salute.

A bugler stepped forward and brought his glistening brass bugle to his lips. The shrill refrain echoed through the quiet valley. Its sad notes hung and lingered in the still morning air.

A small yellow puppy yelped at the sound and bounded to the feet of her master for protection. She sat whining, not understanding the strange sound. Unseen by the furry animal were the teardrops that trickled and fell into the dust by her wagging tail.

A large muscular man standing between a small Puerto Rican and a thin hawk-faced soldier closed his tearing eyes as he listened to the bugle's sorrowful tattoo.

Kenneth Meeks now understood why his brother's life had not been wasted. The answer . . . was beside him.

Sergeant David Grady knew that his mother would be consoling his friend in the next life as she had always taken care of him, her son, in this one. The thought of them together, the only two people with whom he had shared a special love, seemed fitting. She would know the right things to say. She would smile with that loving smile, and she would understand that Evans was like a brother to him and needed her. *Oh, Mother, take care of him. Please . . . please ease his pain.*

The last note echoed down the valley as the major dropped his salute and commanded, "Or-der . . . arms!"

The first sergeant spun around and faced his major with a salute. "Sir, this concludes the ceremony."

Colven raised his hand slowly, returning the salute. "Top . . . have 'em . . . have 'em carry on."

15

General Glendon Burton leaned over and grabbed his green map case from the backseat of the jeep, threw the pouch over his shoulder, and nodded at his dark-haired driver.

"Thanks, Jack, I'll be back around eighteen-hundred hours. You take it easy."

The young soldier smiled and gave his general a quick salute.

Burton winked and turned for his waiting helicopter, which was parked just thirty meters away. To his left, he noticed beside the runway a small tin shed full of waiting soldiers resting in its shade. They were like the hundreds who waited at all the major air bases for transportation to their units, R&R, or even a flight to Cam Ranh, where they would catch their freedom birds for home.

The general changed direction and walked for the shed.

Bud Sikes rested against the support poles. He had seen the brigadier approaching and rose quickly, saluting.

Burton threw him a quick return salute and looked over the anxious faces.

"Who's going to An Khe?"

Bud and two other men raised their hands.

"Get on my bird. I'm headin' that way."

The men smiled and picked up their gear. The two soldiers ran for the waiting helicopter. Bud, still wearing a partial cast, walked with a pronounced limp.

The general noticed the lieutenant's slow gait and walked back to him to take his bag. He slowed his pace so that the limping lieutenant wouldn't feel pressured to hurry. The kind gesture did not go unnoticed by Bud.

"You're in Sierra Rangers, I see," said the general, eyeing the Ranger patch.

"Yes, sir."

"You're lucky. I can take you right to your doorstep. I'm going to visit your commander."

"Great, sir. Thank you."

The crew chief ran from the helicopter, handed the general a flight helmet, and took the map case and Sikes's bag.

Bud sat on the lip of the bird. He swung his leg up stiffly, stood and took a seat, then buckled in. The general hopped up easily and sat in the jump seat just behind the pilot and co-pilot. In seconds they were up and flying north.

Bud leaned back. He liked the general. That judgment had been made as soon as the general had asked for passengers. He hadn't had to do that; in fact, it was very unusual. The general obviously liked soldiers. His type—the type who cared—was rare. Caring was not a prerequisite for leadership. But Bud felt sorry for the men who only played at the game of leadership—the ones who mouthed the proper platitudes, accomplished the missions, took the glory, but never really knew the men who made the successes possible. Such leaders never really got the respect or loyalty they wanted from their men.

Bud's thoughts shifted from the general to the brown-eyed nurse who had inexplicably torn at his feelings and left a hollow place in his heart. He hadn't thought of himself as a man who could be much affected by a woman he hardly knew. Yet, the auburn-haired nurse with the gentle smile had gotten to him. He missed her. She had come back last night and apologized for her abrupt departure and had stayed with him during his long vigil. They had talked all night, sharing each other's hopes and dreams, and when they parted they felt closer than they had the night before, when they'd made love. The thought of her lying beside him, of her body glistening in the candlelight, caused a warmth to spread through him and intensified the dull ache that ate at his heart.

Bud liked her. It was more than that, really, but any other word would be presumptuous. After all, he hardly knew her.

And, yet, he knew Jean as he knew no other woman, because she had bared her secrets to him.

They were going to see each other soon. They had discussed it excitedly, planning to meet at the in-country R&R center in Da Nang. Jean already had made reservations. Their good-bye was eased by the knowledge that they would see each other again. They would hold each other on a beach far away and have time to learn what it was that drew them together. Maybe when they met, the time they had spent apart would have taken its toll, and the strange feelings would be gone; but now, right now, he longed for the day when he could hold her again.

"Sir, we have a general coming in from Corps. His aide called thirty minutes ago."

"Who's coming, Top?"

The broad-shouldered soldier strained to read the paper he held. "Sir, the first sergeant's got to have his darn glasses to see his small note."

Colven laughed as he hopped out of his jeep and put his arm around the black sergeant's shoulder. "Come on, you old blind buzzard, let's go find the first sergeant's glasses so he can make sense of his chicken scratches."

Sergeant Demand smiled broadly. "You know, you as old as the first sergeant, sir."

"Yeah, Top, but I'm a hell of a lot prettier."

They walked, laughing, into the headquarters building. The first sergeant collected his glasses from his desk and quickly followed the major into his office.

"The aide said a General Burton was flying in and would be here at sixteen hundred hours. He said he was gonna give you some info on an upcoming ball game and also make presentations of some medals. Sir, what's he talking about?"

Colven sat down, leaning back in his chair. "Top, make sure Dove is ready to pick him up. General Burton is the deputy Corps commander. He was my brigade commander at Fort Benning and is one helluva soldier. Don't worry, he's talking about an operation that might come up. The medals are for Sergeant Grady, Meeks, and Lieutenant Sikes."

"Oh, and, sir, we got another call—The Red Cross recreation office. They gonna send some girls over at sixteen hundred hours to make a little visit and eat in the first sergeant's mess."

Colven grinned. "You mean we're not gonna have you serenade us for chow this evening, Top?"

"Aw, sir, the first sergeant wouldn't know how to act unless he got a little hollering in, but I might have to ease off just a bit. I wouldn't want to embarrass them Doughnut Dollies."

"Okay, Top. Troops are in classes now. They'll be done at sixteen-thirty. We'll have a quick formation and present the awards. Call and tell the Doughnut Dollies there's no use showing up till sixteen-thirty. They can talk to the troops in the chow line and then eat with them afterwards. The general might want to eat with us, so make the arrangements."

The first sergeant nodded and walked out as Captain Shane walked in.

"What the fly-boys have to say, Ed?" asked Colven, looking up from his desk.

"Sir, the aviation battalion commander and his ops officer will be over tomorrow to get our briefing. They were very responsive and seemed ready to go."

"What kind of guns we getting?"

"We're lucky. They said we'd have the Warriors as our gun support. They've got the Hotel models."

"Good. What about our TOC? You gonna have it ready for operations in a couple of days?"

"We'll have it ready by tomorrow. Sergeant Ingram and I will get the maps up and have the commo gear installed tonight. We'll be ready, sir."

"Okay, Ed, it's your show. Hey, go down and check the companies training for me. I'm going to be too busy to get away. Let me know how it went at chow."

"Will do, sir."

Colven stood and walked to his window as his new ops officer departed. Bright rays penetrated the thin glass, casting warmth on him as his thoughts drifted thousands of miles away to a rambling house nestled among green pines. Sybil would be digging in her flower beds. Spring was coming. She loved spring; it was her favorite time of the year. The letter in his breast pocket said she was tired of winter. She prayed for spring because it meant he'd be home soon. Home . . . so damn far away. He had missed too many springs with her . . . too many. *We'll have next spring, Syb, and all the rest we'll have together. . . . I promise.*

The helicopter landed gently, and Brigadier General Burton hopped to the ground, holding out his hand to the approaching major.

"Good to see you, John, been a long time since Benning."

Colven shook his hand warmly. "Yes sir. I see you haven't changed any. Still can't keep you in the office."

Before the general could answer, Colven's eyes shifted to the young officer who had swung out of the helicopter. Burton turned as the limping officer began approaching with a broad grin.

Colven blinked and put his hands on his hips, speaking gruffly. "You weren't supposed to be back for a couple days yet, kid."

"Sir, they threw me out. Said I was ruining their image."

The major stared at Bud for a few seconds before shooting out his hand. "Okay, kid, I guess I'll keep ya."

The general thought the young officer might cry, but Sikes lowered his head quickly and took the major's hand without speaking.

Burton clasped Colven's shoulder and asked about his health to allow the lieutenant to recover his composure as they walked toward the waiting jeep.

"Corps is the damnedest place I've ever seen. Why, hell, I've even got a shower and sink in my room. In my room, John!"

"Damn, sir, some might say you're a REMF."

"The hell of it is, they'd be right! Me, a REMF. Shit. John, get me to your place fast. I wanna smell a dirty Ranger and feel like a soldier again."

"Right this way, sir."

They walked to the waiting jeep and climbed in. Sikes couldn't climb over the back tire, so he stood there embarrassed. The general, realizing his predicament, rose quickly and stepped into the small back seat with Colven.

"You sit in front, Lieutenant. I wanna talk to your major."

"But, sir, you're supposed to—"

"Sit down, son. Damn, John, your boy leaves for a vacation and forgets how to obey his generals."

Sikes smiled sheepishly and sat in the front seat. Dove winked at him. As the jeep pulled away Bud adjusted the kit bag on his lap. A small yellow dog jumped from Dove's lap to the bag and sniffed the new passenger.

"What's this, Dove?"

"Aw, it's just a dumb mutt one of the guys pawned off on me. I'm selling it soon as it gets a little bigger."

The puppy tried to open the bag, gave up, and crawled back over to the blond driver.

"You gonna sell it, huh?"

"You bet, sir. I'll tell 'em it belonged to an NVA commander or something. Heck, I might paint a red star on her head for effect, you know?"

Bud smiled inwardly. Dove didn't sound too convincing, especially since his left hand constantly patted the dog's head.

"How's your leg, sir?"

"It's fine. I'll be a hundred percent in a couple of weeks."

Dove briefly glanced at the lieutenant before returning his attention to the road.

"Sir, I'm sorry about the Two-Four."

Bud dropped his head. "Yeah. How's Grady taking it?"

"No sweat with Grady, sir. He's doin' okay. He and the team didn't lose none of the edge. They hung tough."

Bud nodded, understanding. "How's the business?"

Dove smiled. Sikes was cool; he understood his operation. "You know, sir, a little slow. We just got in and all, but the Dove hasn't really gone out yet and gotten serious. He will, though . . . he will. Hey, we're home!"

The jeep pulled onto the dirt road leading to the Ranger camp. The red dust cloud that followed billowed like a miniature thundercloud.

The first sergeant stood in front of the assembling company. "Hurry up, Rangers! This ain't a bird-watchin' tour."

The men quickly fell into a company formation.

"Rangers, we got us a surprise today. In fact, we got two surprises. We got a general gonna give a couple of our heroes some medals, and we got us some Doughnut Dollies come to visit. Now, Rangers, don't none of you embarrass your first sergeant. Be nice! Take two minutes and blouse your boots and look presentable. Sergeant Grady, Meeks, fall out and get up to the major's office. You two is he-roes today!"

Twenty minutes later Lieutenant Sikes, with Grady and Thumper, stood at attention in front of the formation of

Rangers. Major Colven followed the general as they marched out and positioned themselves in front of the awardees. Captain Treadwell began reading the citation as the general took the Air Medal from Colven and pinned it on the chest of Lieutenant Sikes.

Captain Shane, standing behind the formation, turned and nodded to two Red Cross women as they came over from their compound. One was a tall, well-built, raven-haired girl, and the other was a short, pretty blond who held her head up as if she were a princess.

"Mary Ann, why can't we get closer?" Sarah whispered.

"It will disturb the presentation. Now, remember what I told you the first sergeant said: They had five men killed the other day, and—"

"The following award is announced. Grady, David C., Jr. 447-48-6006, Sergeant, E-5, United States Army, Company S, Ranger, Seventy-fifth Infantry Airborne . . ."

"What's going on, Mary Ann?"

". . . awarded the Silver Star by direction of the President of the United States for gallantry in action while engaged in military operations involving conflict with an armed hostile force in the Republic of Vietnam. Sergeant Grady . . ."

"Those three soldiers out front are getting medals," Mary Ann said. "The man in front with the green fatigues is a one-star general. I don't recognize him. He's not with the division. He must be from Corps." Mary Ann gave Sarah a sideways glance. "All the Rangers are here. Which one attacked you?"

"What?"

"Which one attacked you?"

"Oh, the one standing in front of the general."

". . . Sergeant Grady's personal bravery and devotion to duty were in keeping with the highest traditions of the military service and reflect great . . ."

Mary Ann stared openmouthed at the soldier. "You mean the one the general's pinning the medal on now?"

Sarah sighed indifferently. "Yes, that's him."

Mary Ann shook her head in disbelief. "My God, Sarah."

Sarah lifted her head indignantly. "Well, how was I supposed to know he was some kind of hero?"

Mary Ann's breasts bounced as she held her stomach and turned around so as not to be heard.

"What's so funny?"

The presentation ended a few minutes later. The awardees were marched into headquarters to talk to the general while the company was reassembled. Sergeant Ingram escorted the Red Cross women to the mess hall, where they would have a chance to talk to the men while they waited outside.

When the general, the major, and the awardees walked out, Colven told the first sergeant that the general wouldn't be eating with them but that he should take Grady and Meeks down to meet with the Doughnut Dollies.

First Sergeant Demand led Grady and Meeks around a large group of laughing Rangers. The Red Cross women were putting on a routine. They had picked out four "volunteers" and were pantomiming a movie. The men were trying to guess its title by their actions.

Thumper tried to move closer to see the women, but the first sergeant tapped him. "Come on, I'm taking you two inside. Now you two he-roes don't embarrass your first sergeant. I want you to be nice and watch your language."

Grady balked at the door. "Look, Top, I don't wanna meet any bony broads. Hell, the company is gonna give me enough shit as it is."

The first sergeant narrowed his eyes and motioned the two men inside. "You best not cuss around your first sergeant, boy. Now, you two get your food and sit at that corner table. And, Grady . . ."

"Yeah, Top?"

"Don't you embarrass me. Be nice or I'll have you and your team burning manure for a year. I'm goin' to get them sweet thangs for you."

Thumper grinned at his sergeant's discomfort. Grady picked up his tray, then noticed the big man's expression.

"What the hell you smiling at? We're screwed, you know? The guys will be hasslin' us for a month of Sundays."

"Aw, hell, Grade, relax. It'll be nice to talk to some ladies for a change."

"The hell it will."

The two men picked up their food and walked to the far table. Grady sat facing the wall opposite Thumper.

"Thump, this is dumb."

"Will you relax, Sarge?"

Grady looked down at his stringy roast beef, picked up a large piece, and dropped it into his open mouth.

"You better hope Top doesn't see you, Grade. He said wait till . . ."

Grady snickered. Thumper's eyes widened.

"Shit, Grade, they're comin'. . . . They're . . ."

"Hi, I'm Mary Ann."

Thumper shot up, smiling.

Grady rose but turned only slightly toward the voice as he chewed hurriedly his mouthful of meat. He could see the light-blue pinstriped dress and an outstretched hand held out to him. He tried to swallow, but the mouthful was too big. Then he tried to smile over tightly clenched teeth, as though nothing were amiss.

Thumper, seeing his sergeant's dilemma, quickly reached over and grabbed the surprised woman's hand, throwing her off balance.

Grady took two quick chews, turning his back as if coughing. Another feminine voice spoke directly behind him.

"Hello. I'm Sarah Boyce."

Grady quickly chewed again, clenched his teeth, and turned to nod. His gaze swung first to her waist, then slowly rose to her smiling face.

Her! Son of a . . . He choked.

First Sergeant Demand, standing behind the blond, ran to Grady's side, as did Thumper, who bent his sergeant over and pounded his back with a loud slap. The two women stood shocked, against the wall, unable to take their eyes from the poor, gasping man.

Thumper's blow knocked Grady forward, but it did the trick. The first sergeant handed him a napkin, then turned to the women, trying to smile.

"Sorry, ladies. It's been so long since this boonie rat seen pretty ladies. He just don't know how to act."

He turned back to the recovering sergeant, throwing him a scowl.

Sarah stepped toward the first sergeant, smiling. "Oh, no, Sergeant Demand. I know Sergeant Grady quite well." She turned toward the wide-eyed Grady and extended her hand. "Don't I?"

Grady bent over and coughed again.

Thumper and the first sergeant exchanged quick confused glances. Then they turned and stared at Grady, waiting for an explanation. The embarrassed sergeant smiled meekly at the two men and shook the woman's hand without looking at her.

Mary Ann pulled back a chair and sat next to Thumper. "Isn't it nice that old friends can meet again? Now, shall we eat? This big girl needs food."

The first sergeant, still stupefied that the blond had professed to know his team sergeant, forced a laugh and pulled out the chair beside Grady for Sarah, then excused himself and grumbled as he walked away. Small Vietnamese girls who worked in the mess hall set down full trays before the women.

Thumper tapped Grady's foot under the table and shifted his eyes to Sarah and back again, trying to get a response. Grady glanced up and shrugged, looking very uncomfortable.

"I must say, Sergeant Grady, I know I'm a little larger than most women, but that's never made a man choke before."

Sarah and Thumper laughed, but Grady only nodded with a faint smile and quickly picked up his water glass.

Sarah decided to explain. She spoke to Thumper. "Did your sergeant tell you I struck him with a stick yesterday? I didn't have a chance to apologize then, so I'll take the opportunity to do that now." She turned and smiled at Grady, who took another sip of water and nodded.

Mary Ann, seeing Grady's discomfort, began eating and making small talk, but he was still so distracted that he excused himself to get another glass of water.

On the pretense of looking over the mess hall, Sarah turned and watched the sergeant as he walked over to a far table and began talking to a huge, round-faced black soldier, then took some food off the man's plate. He then did something Sarah had never seen him do before: He smiled.

Sarah smiled faintly herself. "He likes them, doesn't he?"

Thumper glanced at Sarah then over to Grady.

"Yep, we're kinda like family. You know, that Silver Star we got today? It's Grady's second; plus, he's got a bunch of Bronze Stars. He's the best there is. We, the team, are really lucky."

Sarah picked up her iced-tea glass. "Does he have any education?"

Thumper's eyes narrowed, and Sarah instantly knew she had made an error, so she quickly added, "I mean, of course, does he have any special training that would prepare him better than the others for the work he does?"

Thumper's eyes shifted from the impertinent blond to his sergeant, who was now turning toward the food line. "Grady has two years of college and is leaving 'Nam in a few months to finish up. Education has got nothing to do with his being a leader. Some just have it. Others don't."

Grady walked back and sat down.

Thumper chuckled. "Ben loaded his tray again, huh? I saw you relieving him of some calories."

Grady smiled. "Yeah, he didn't think I'd check."

Mary Ann quickly put her hands over her food. "Don't take away any of *my* food, Sergeant."

Grady grinned. "Ma'am, a lady as pretty as you shouldn't have to eat in a common mess hall."

"It beats the hell outta our cookies."

Grady laughed.

Sarah was surprised at his genuinely good-natured laugh. It suited him, she thought.

Mary Ann elbowed Thumper in the ribs. "Look, big guy, you don't have to suffer on our account. I know you want seconds. Go on, I promise I won't tell your old mean sergeant, here. Oh, will you get me another piece of pie while you're at it?"

"Gee, Mary Ann, I thought you'd never ask."

She elbowed him again, laughing. "I guess I'd better go with you: I'm afraid you'll eat it before you get back to the table."

The couple departed for the food line, leaving Grady and Sarah in awkward silence.

Grady smiled to himself. Thumper liked Mary Ann, he could tell. They had really hit if off more than Lady Astor and him. *Jesus*, he thought, *she acts like she owns the damn place.*

Sarah was staring at him, obviously waiting for him to speak. He stared back, thinking, *To hell with her. Let her talk first.*

After several long minutes the other two returned.

"Well, have you two gotten to know each other better?" Mary Ann put down her plate of pie, allowing Thumper to scoot behind her.

Sarah glanced up smiling. "Why, yes. Sergeant Grady has been a perfect host." She turned and stared at him with cold eyes. "Haven't you, Sergeant?"

Grady nearly choked again. *Damn, her. I should have hit her harder when I had the chance.* "Sure, if you say so."

Mary Ann and Thumper exchanged concerned glances.

Sarah tensed. "Sergeant Grady, your manners are unimpeachable—except for the minor lack of judgment you showed when you pounced on me, although I'm sure that was quite by accident."

"Miss Boyce, it was indeed unfortunate; however, you've obviously forgotten a few of the circumstances and facts, possibly because you were so distraught at the time. One thing that's puzzled me, for example, is why you were in an unauthorized area."

"Unauthorized area?"

"Yes, of course. And by the way, now that I'm thinking about it, I would like to compliment you on your throwing arm. Ever think of trying out for the big leagues?"

Sarah's face turned beet red.

Mary Ann nudged Thumper and cleared her throat. Thumper reached over to Grady's plate. "Sarge, you gonna eat your pie?"

The ploy worked. Grady broke his stare from the glaring blond and shoved his plate toward Thumper.

Mary Ann quickly took the tray from Thumper and cut the pie in half, taking a portion for herself. "Did I tell you my dad was in the Army? He served in World War Two and . . ."

Sarah leaned back in her chair, obviously not hearing a word, but after a while, an odd little smile touched her lips, as if she'd suddenly had an amusing thought, and she leaned over with a mischievous look in her eyes. "Sergeant, I know you won't believe me, but I really have enjoyed your company. Do you think you and Thumper could come and visit us tomorrow at the center? I would love to show you around. Perhaps later we could go to the movie at the outdoor theater."

Grady fought to keep the surprise he felt from showing. What the hell did she *want*? *God, lady, leave me alone. I know you want something and I'll bet it's to make me feel like a fool.*

He looked at his watch and shook his head, speaking without looking at her. "No, ma'am. I'm afraid I don't have time for that. But I'm sure I can let Thump go. Listen, I gotta go to a meeting. It was very nice meeting you ladies. I probably won't see you again, but I'll always remember this dinner."

He stood and shook hands with Mary Ann, smiling. When he took Sarah's hand, he avoided her eyes. "Sorry about tomorrow, but . . ."

Major Colven walked up to the table as Grady turned. They collided.

"Excuse me, sir. I was just leav—"

"I can't imagine a man wanting to leave such pretty company."

"Yes, sir, but I—"

"Oh, Major Colven, these men are just delightful," Sarah said boldly. "I wonder if you'd mind if we borrowed them for this evening. One of our girls is departing, and we truly need help arranging the heavy cans of ice and stereo speakers and such. We would be indebted to you forever for their help."

Colven smiled at the small blond. "Of course. How could I possibly turn down such a request?"

Grady stared at Sarah, who winked and coyly smiled as if saying "Got ya." He tightened his jaw and excused himself as the women formally introduced themselves.

Damn her blue eyes and sweet talk, he thought. Grady strode straight for the door. She might fool the major, but not him. She'd have to do more than flash those gooey eyes to get what she wanted from David Grady, and as for seeing her that night, he just wasn't going. He would put himself on sick call.

Captain Shane walked in the side door of the mess hall. He did not recognize the lieutenant sitting with Captain Treadwell.

He went to their table and introduced himself. Sikes took his hand and asked him to sit down. Shane liked him immediately. Sikes seemed like an honest, warm person who didn't take himself too seriously. Treadwell had to get back and sign an emergency leave form for a soldier in the First Platoon, so he excused himself and left the two officers at the table.

"You married, sir?"

"Yeah, and I have a little one on the way."

"Hey, great. Congratulations."

"How about you?"

"Nope. I never had the time, although I had the inclination once or twice."

"You got a special girl?"

Sikes almost said no, but his thoughts turned to Jean. "Yes, sir. I guess maybe I do."

Sarah looked over at the smiling Mary Ann. "He's a nice man, isn't he?" she said as Thumper left their table to find Grady.

"Yeah, he's what's called your basic 'good ol' boy.' Now, what's this about needing help?"

Sarah blushed. "Well, Sergeant Grady hardly spoke to me. In fact, he wouldn't even look at me."

"Yeah, I don't think he feels too comfortable around you. I actually felt sorry for him."

"Well, I'm going to get him to talk to me tonight."

Mary Ann started laughing.

"What's so funny, Mary Ann?"

"You! You're unbelievable. Why don't you just forget the sergeant. You have plenty of men interested in you."

Sarah stared indignantly at her friend. "First, because I want that man to apologize for attacking me, and then for his rude behavior today, and then . . ." She was about to say "then I'll forget him," but she caught herself. . . . "then I'll feel better." She pushed back her chair and stood.

Mary Ann rose and walked beside her friend. "I'll bet he doesn't apologize to you."

Sarah turned defiantly. "It's a bet."

The major leaned back in serious thought. General Burton had dropped off a packet for him that he was to keep in the strictest confidence. It lay before him on his desk. The packet contained one small handwritten note and a map, which Colven had spread out and studied for ten minutes. The note simply said the operation was postponed for two weeks but that the area the major was to work was enclosed.

Colven leaned forward again and looked at the multicolored map. It wasn't marked with an AO. The general had told him he would be getting that information later but that he at least wanted him to know where he and his men would be going. Colven shut his eyes and shook his head. *It must be a mistake*, he thought. But he knew the general too well for that. He opened his eyes slowly and reread the bold black letters at the top of the map: CAMBODIA 1:25000.

Thumper and Grady walked across the grassy knoll toward the women's compound.

"Thump, I'll never forgive you for pulling me out of the medic's shack. I'm really not feeling well."

"Aw, Sarge, you just don't wanna see Sarah."

"Thump, that woman is trouble. I've seen her type before at school—rich sorority types, all nicey on the outside and cold and hard as steel on the inside."

The big man patted his sergeant's back. "Well, then, I'd say she's met her match, Sarge."

They marched up to the MP booth.

"Names?"

"Sergeant Grady and Thump—Meeks."

The MP looked at his clipboard. "Here you are, write-ins on the bottom. Go on in."

They walked past the booth, down the entryway, and into a busy courtyard that was strung with colored Japanese lanterns. A dozen uniformed Red Cross women were busy setting up tables and arranging a bar. When the two Rangers strode into view, all work ceased. A short, plump woman with tousled hair approached and introduced herself as Mrs. Sheppard. The other women giggled and exchanged greetings with the two men.

"Ma'am, we're supposed to help with the heavy things, I believe," said Grady. Mrs. Sheppard seemed mystified at their presence.

"There you are!" came Mary Ann's booming voice from across the courtyard. Mrs. Sheppard seemed relieved as Mary Ann walked up and took each of the two men by the arm.

"Mrs. Sheppard, these fellas will set up the dance floor and move the heavy speakers for us. Strong backs and weak minds, you know." Mary Ann kept a straight face for only a second before laughing and squeezing their arms tightly.

The older woman smiled. "Oh, how nice. Well, Mary Ann, dear, if you'd be kind enough to escort these gentlemen . . . And please introduce them to the others for me."

"Of course, Mrs. Sheppard."

She led them into the grassy yard and introduced them around. Then she walked them to the far side of the compound and into the large middle room that was the kitchen and storage area. A stove, a sink, and two large refrigerators sat against the back cinder-block wall.

Mary Ann sighed once inside the room and made straight for the closest refrigerator while talking over her shoulder. "Mrs. Shepard is sweet and well-meaning, but she's a pain. She used to be a dorm mother and never realized she changed jobs."

Both men smiled. Mary Ann opened the icebox door and handed each of them a beer and took one for herself. She looked on the top of the refrigerator and then around the room, searching. "Darn, I don't have an opener."

Thumper reached into his pocket, pulled out his steel pocket demo knife, and deftly opened the woman's beer can.

Mary Ann grinned slyly. "You come prepared, huh, big guy?"

Thumper replaced his knife. "Just like a boy scout, Mary Ann, *always* prepared."

"Well, boy scouts, the party starts in forty-five minutes. It's a surprise farewell for Gail Connors." Mary Ann shifted her eyes to Grady. "Sarah and Gail are at the center and should be here in about an hour." She smiled to herself when she saw the sergeant relax. He had a whole hour before he had to see Sarah again. Poor guy. He really didn't know what to make of her.

Thumper looked around the room. "Where's the heavy stuff?"

"The plywood for the dance floor is against the wall behind you. The speakers and receiver are in my room."

Grady patted Thumper's back. "Well, let's get started. Us strong backs are ready, if the weak mind will direct us."

Mary Ann slugged him lightly on the chest. "Okay, strong backs, follow me!"

First Sergeant Demand paced across the wooden platform twice before turning and facing the audience of Rangers. Behind him was the white painted wood wall used as their outdoor movie screen. The theater was next to the mess hall. The Rangers used the hill leading up to their barracks as their seats. The first sergeant stared at the front row before assuming his usual bellowing position with his hands on his hips.

"Rangers. The first sergeant's movie is a good 'un. I picked it out special. It's called *VD and You* produced by the U.S. Army in cooperation with the whores of Saigon."

The Rangers booed. The bantam soldier smiled, proud of his practiced joke, and raised his hand. The booing ceased immediately.

"I was only kiddin', it's just the cartoon."

The audience booed again, until the standing man raised his hand—silence.

"Okay, Rangers, standard rules for first sergeant's movie. No pissin' on first sergeant's flowers. If you feel a callin', you visit the first sergeant's latrine."

The men booed and hooted for several seconds until the sergeant's hand came up.

"Rangers will not verbally or physically abuse Pete, our projectionist."

"Boo," then silence as his hand rose.

"Who got care packages today in the mail?"

No one raised their hands.

"Now, Rangers. The first sergeant knows everything. If you don't raise yo hands and I got to call yo name off my list, you gonna be burning crap for a month!"

Three hands shot up.

"Who got brownies?"

One hand stayed up.

"You sit with me trooper Rawles. I best try some of yo mama's cook'n'."

The Rangers all laughed at the plight of the embarrassed soldier in the front row.

"Men, the movie tonight is heavy in violence!"

"*Yea!*", yelled the audience.

"Heavy in *sex!*"

Thunderous yells from the men.

"Tonight's feature is . . . *Snow White and the Seven Dwarfs*"

A loud boo.

"Well, how 'bout *Gidget Goes Hiwaiian?*"

"Yea."

"Roll 'em, Pete!" The broad shouldered first sergeant smiled as he stepped down from the platform to get a brownie.

The courtyard and walkways were partially filled with smiling women and field-grade officers. Thumper had faded back slowly as the rank kept coming in. Grady and Thump went to the refrigerator together to get more beer.

"Hey, Grade, we're the only enlisted men in the place."

Grady smiled. "Well, we're also the only Rangers in the place. Somebody's got to keep our end up."

Thumper was a little surprised at his sergeant, who not long ago had been all jitters. "Have you seen Sarah yet?"

Grady's expression changed. "No, Lady Astor isn't here yet."

"There you are!" Mary Ann came in and grabbed Thumper's arm. "You stay near me, big guy, and protect me from this bunch, will ya?" She pushed him toward the door. Thumper looked over his shoulder at Grady and rolled his eyes. Grady laughed and raised his beer can in a salute.

A loud yell suddenly went up near the entrance, followed by clapping. Grady opened his beer and squared his shoulders. *She's here,* he thought as he walked out into the glow of the Japanese lanterns.

Grady had managed to avoid her for five minutes, and he was about to start for the kitchen when he heard the all-too-familiar voice.

"Well, Sergeant Grady, I see you were useful."

He turned toward Sarah and dropped his eyes. He leaned back against the wall and looked down at his beer.

"Yes, ma'am, I guess we were."

"You know, I don't even know your first name." She stepped closer to him.

"It's David, but I prefer Grady."

"I'll call you David. I like it."

He brought his head up slowly and stared into her pale blue eyes. "Do you always do what you want?"

The remark caught her off guard. The only reply she could think of was an honest one. "Most of the time."

He smiled. "I really do prefer Grady."

His smile unnerved her. "Well, if you insist, Grady it is. How do you like the party?" she asked, changing the subject.

"It's very nice."

"I'm sorry there aren't more enlisted men here. I suppose you feel a little out of place."

"Not really." The sergeant showed no emotion except boredom as he shook his empty beer can as if to give her a hint. "Sorry to disappoint you," he added.

Damn him! she thought, and took a deep breath to contain her annoyance. Obviously nothing was going to get to him or penetrate that impervious brain of his, so she decided to get her apology now and be done with it. "Sergeant Grady, I hope you understand that I was apologizing to you this afternoon. I really am sorry I threw that branch at you."

Without realizing it she reached up and touched his chin where she'd hit him and caressed the slight red abrasion mark. Touching him triggered a strange sensation in her that embarrassed her. She quickly withdrew her hand, but not before his eyes suddenly looked at her in a way that made her stomach flutter. For the first time he had looked at her as if he liked her, if only for a second.

She swallowed hard and continued: "You know, I really think you owe me a little apology too."

Grady stared into her anxious face, his eyes twinkling as he spoke. "You shouldn't have been there, Miss Boyce."

Her cheeks flushed as her body tightened with silent rage. "I had every right to be there," she snapped, her previous slow, drawling inflection replaced by a cold, crisp, authoritative retort.

"And I had every right to protect myself."

Sarah fought to keep her shaking hands from striking him. "You call attacking a defenseless woman protecting yourself?"

"I attacked what I thought was a sapper."

"Do I look like a sapper to you?"

"Lady, you could have been Raquel Welch behind that rock and I'd have done the same thing. What I did was justified." He pushed away from the wall but continued to look down at her. Sarah didn't move an inch or blink an eye. "Furthermore, I'm thirsty and need a beer."

"Justified? Justified, Sergeant Grady? You call attacking me justified? I suppose you call your friend's death in this godforsaken country justified too." That afternoon at the mess hall Thumper had told her and Mary Ann about Evans.

Grady's reaction was immediate. His eyes changed from a twinkle to fire and then to hurt. They dropped to his beer can. He spoke in an emotional whisper as he raised his eyes to hers. "Yes, Miss Boyce, the death of my friend was very much justified."

He moved forward, bumping her slightly as he walked toward the kitchen.

She stood there shaking with mortification. *Why had she said it? Oh, why, why, why?*

Dove lay back in the red dirt, eating popcorn, watching Gidget balance herself on a red surf board. Pete checked the reel and looked down at the puppy between them, who was chewing on a meat bone Dove had gotten from the mess sergeant.

Rodriquez leaned over across Pete. "Wow, Dove, you do that, man?"

Dove popped two kernels into his mouth, not taking his eyes from the painted wall. "Sure, Pancho, it's easy."

"Is broads all over like that, man?"

"Sure. How come you think the Dove surfs, man?"

"Dig it, man. I gonna go Hawaii, man. I gonna get me some of them broads, . . . *Oh, man*, the dog is chewin' my boot!"

"Come 'ere, Bitch! Come 'ere. Pancho will make you sick. Ya dumb dog, come 'ere!"

"Shut up over there!"

"Damn, man, she ate up my bootlace!"

For the next hour Grady and Sarah ignored each other completely, although Sarah couldn't stop thinking about him. She had said the wrong thing, she knew, but she was too proud to apologize. Or maybe just too embarrassed. She had really hurt him. She could tell by the look in his eyes and the tone in his voice. But he was so damned arrogant. It was only when he started for the exit that she made up her mind.

Sarah stepped up behind him and grabbed his arm. He turned sharply. "I want to apologize for being so tacky," she said before he could speak. "I just don't know why I say such dumb things." Her voice was trembling and her eyes were downcast. They began to ache. She felt a small tear roll down her cheek.

Grady's hard gaze slowly softened. "You know, Miss Boyce," he said, "your chin should always be up." He smiled warmly, looking deep into her glistening eyes. "You,

Miss Boyce, are a proud tiger, and a proud tiger never apologizes, especially to another tiger."

Sarah smiled feebly and whispered, "You'll never apologize to me, will you?"

He held her gaze for a few moments and then said softly, "I'll say the words you want to hear if you want me to."

Sarah suddenly felt weak. He was going to let her win . . . yet, she had already lost. She knew that now as she sighed deeply and smiled. "Sergeant Grady, will you dance with this old tiger?"

Grady smiled and took her arm. "Miss Boyce, I would consider it a pleasure."

They walked to the dance floor just as "Moon River" began playing.

"One of my favorites," said Sarah as they came together and began dancing to the soft beat.

Grady didn't speak. He was thinking that touching her and feeling her body next to his was dangerous ground and that he'd have to concentrate on something else.

Damn, he couldn't help but think about her. At first he thought her tears had done it, but now he knew it wasn't just that. *Grade,* he told himself, *you're just going to have to admit you liked her the minute you saw her angry blue eyes challenge you, but she is one of those special women you can never possess, can never afford. Her type needs to be picked up in a new car and taken to the finest restaurants. She is way out of your league. It's written all over her. So you'd better get the hell out of here before you get yourself into trouble.*

Even as he decided to go he realized he was holding her tightly and had moved closer to her, feeling her every movement. Damn! He tightened again and backed away from her just as the melody ended. Embarrassed by his lack of control, he didn't look at her as they walked off the dance floor. "Thank you, Miss Boyce. It was very nice. I'm going for a beer. Would you like me to get you a drink?"

Sarah leaned against a support post. "Yes. A gin and tonic would be nice."

She watched him make his way through the crowd. She folded her arms across her chest to stop trembling. Her stomach felt queezy, yet she felt light . . . yes, she thought, delightfully light.

Dancing with him was an experience like none she had ever experienced before. She had felt a need to be close to him and to feel his arms around her. And when he'd relaxed those few moments and embraced her tightly, she had felt his warmth and desire for her. Why had he fought her so? Why would he want to shun such a wonderful feeling?

Grady got his beer and had just poured Sarah's drink when Mary Ann walked up hurriedly and grabbed his beer, gasping, "First aid. Medic!" She took a long drink and gasped again, "Medic." She threw her head in the direction of the aproaching Thumper. "That big ape stepped all over my feet."

Thumper shrugged his shoulders. "Gosh, Grade, I told her this was a combat zone and she could be injured at any time."

"But not to 'Moon River,' you big gazoo," she snapped, hitting him in the chest with the back of her hand and taking another drink of Grady's beer.

Grady laughed and patted Mary Ann's back. "Give him a break, Mary Ann. He's just a strong back, remember?"

Mary Ann smiled, handing the sergeant his half-drunk beer. "Strong back and clumsy feet."

Grady held out Sarah's drink to Thumper. "Will you give this to Sarah. I've got to get back and check the team. Thump, you better stick around in case Mary Ann needs your strong back for cleanup."

Thumper reached for the glass, but Mary Ann knocked his hand back. "Not to him. The clumsy gazoo wouldn't make it two feet." She took the glass and winked at Grady.

"Now, Mary Ann, be nice, or I won't open any more of your beers," said Thumper, taking her arm and walking her to the dance floor.

Grady shook his head, grinning, glad that his friend was having a good time. He turned and made his way to the exit. Once outside he breathed deeply as the night's gentle breeze brushed his face. Thank God, he thought as he walked into the parking lot. For a moment he'd found himself falling for that woman, but when he'd seen a chance to make a getaway, he'd had sense enough to take it.

"Hey!"

Grady stopped and shut his eyes. *Damn her*. He turned with a sigh.

Sarah walked past the MP booth toward him. "I thought we were getting along. And you forgot to say good-bye."

"I never liked good-byes. It's a bad habit, I guess."

Sarah stepped closer. "Why does it have to be good-bye? I . . . I would like to . . ." She lowered her head and shifted her feet as if uncomfortable. "Well, I wondered if maybe we could . . . be friends. I really would like to talk to you and . . ." She shook her head. "I'm not doing this too well, am I?"

Grady, feeling her discomfort, reached out and lifted her chin. "Chin up, Miss Boyce, remember?" He took her arm and walked her toward a nearby jeep. They sat on the hood. Grady leaned back on the windshield and looked up at the stars.

"Beautiful, isn't it?"

Sarah looked up with a smile. "Yes. I didn't realize it could be."

They sat for several moments is silence. In the distance they could hear the muffled crumps of artillery fire. Sarah turned toward the sound. "It's hard to believe there's still a war going on out there. It's so peaceful here."

Grady thought of the many nights he lay awake in a patrol base, looking up at the stars but never seeing them. His mind was always on the mission or his men.

Sarah leaned back on the windshield. "Grady, is the little spot with the boulders and trees special to you for some reason?"

Grady smiled back. "Yeah, it's my spot. Mine and Ev—ah, yeah, it's my spot."

"You and your friend were very close, weren't you?"

Grady sat up. "Yeah, Ev was one of those guys that comes around only once in your life. I'm going to miss him."

Sarah knew it bothered him and tried to change the subject. "What about a girl friend. You have a special girl, don't you?"

"Nope."

"What about your family? Where are they from?"

"I don't really have a family. My dad remarried when I was very young and I didn't get along too well with his new wife or her kids. I moved on when I got the chance."

"Haven't you seen him lately?"

"I went to their new house on leave once. It was a pretty bad scene. We kind of agreed I shouldn't come around. He had a new life and so did I."

Sarah shook her head. "That's sad."

"No, that's life. Look, Sarah, I gotta get back and check the guys." He scooted off the hood. "Were going out soon. It was real nice being with you. Thanks for the company."

Sarah hopped down. "Could we see each other again and talk before you go out?"

"No. We're awfully busy during the prep stage. Maybe when we get back I'll swing by and see you at the center."

Sarah forced a smile, but she knew her questions had been upsetting to him. "Grady, please do come by and see me. I would really like that."

Grady smiled warmly. "Sure, lady, but don't try and feed me any of you-all's cookies: I heard about 'em."

Sarah laughed. "Okay, I promise."

Sarah watched him disappear into the night, knowing he wouldn't come by and see her. It didn't matter. She would go and see him.

16

Rock Steady's bony fingers slowly rolled back the wet pant leg, exposing his pale white flesh. He glanced up to check the trail as he continued pulling back the cloth.

Shit! There it was, gorged, its gray body bloated with his blood. His finger cautiously lifted the corpulent leech. It had its toothlike structures firmly implanted in his leg. The leech had secreted a salivalike substance called hirudin that would prevent the warm blood from clotting.

"Shit!" Rock mumbled to himself again as he looked up and surveyed the trail. He reached into his shirt pocket and withdrew his small plastic bag of chewing tobacco. He popped a small bite into his mouth, chewed quickly, and spit the brown tobacco juice into his hand.

He poured brown, sticky drool over the feeding pest, smearing it carefully around the sucking head. Nothing happened. Shit! He again glanced at the trail. The leech twitched slightly and suddenly shuddered violently, detaching its head.

It shuddered again and fell to the dank jungle floor. It seemed to throb as it tried to turn its rotund body over. It writhed for several seconds before Rock punctured its back with a small stick, causing it to explode.

There, you little shit! Deep crimson blood oozed, inundating the the ground around the lifeless body.

Rock began lowering his pant leg and saw yet another of the grotesque creatures crawling up his boot. It was a thin version of the one he'd just dispatched. He lowered his hand to end its existence but stopped. Instead he picked it up delicately and placed it on the flat side of his Claymore detonator. The light green plastic electric firing device was the stage, the thin inch-and-a-half leech its single actor. It looked like a grayish noodle with sucker heads on both ends as it scooted silently along.

Rock placed a finger over its head to stroke its body. As Rock's finger slowly approached, the actor rose up on its posterior sucker and elongated, trying to attach its head to the approaching finger.

I'll be damned. Rock moved his finger slightly to the right; The leech tilted, following his movement. He moved his finger left; it followed again.

Neat, man. It wants me bad, like the women do. He lowered his finger to play with his new friend.

It was the second break already that morning. Senior Sergeant Van Tran Khanh walked down the trail hurriedly, stopping in front of the three small women seated beside the path.

"Friends, we only have another six kilometers."

The women looked up and smiled. The older one, Director Le Ky Nha, stood. "Sergeant, it is not that we are weak. It is that when we arrive at the camp we will be expected to sing and perform as we did at your camp yesterday. We do not want to displease you."

The sergeant smiled. "It is not your worry. It is just that I have not been fortunate enough to escort a 'happiness group' before."

Le Ky Nha smiled sweetly. She had soothed the young sergeant's worries, as she had for other worried soldiers during the past three months. Their group was from the Viet Bac Normal College and had traveled the long distance from the north to lift the spirits of the liberators. They had made jokes about being the Yankee Bob Hope to their brave soldiers. The traveling was difficult but very rewarding for them all. She and the others had been bestowed many honors by the units they had entertained with songs, dances, and stories. This next camp would be the last for a week before resting in a hospital complex farther to the south. The six escorts were very gracious, and Sergeant Khanh had given them rest each time Nha requested it.

"Please, Sergeant, we may proceed now."

The women rose and lifted their packs, which held the costumes and banners used for their performances. They walked wordlessly for fifteen minutes, the sergeant in the lead. Where the trail forked, Khanh took the left branch, which led to a small stream. Thick bamboo groves lined both sides of the trail, forming a tunnel. He walked several feet into the green darkness, then he paused and looked over his shoulder. At that moment a deafening blast broke the stillness, and the trail and people behind him disappeared in a black cloud. Corporal Phi fell at his feet, screaming. Deafened by the explosion, Khanh couldn't hear him. Suddenly a huge green-faced man rose from the earth and began firing at him. The bullets went high. He fell and grabbed the corporal, dragging him to the side of the trail. Bullets cut the leaves just above his head as he pulled harder, trying to fight through the thick bamboo.

Ben had seen the soldier as soon as he leaped up to fire, his first burst going high. The man fell to the ground out of his line of sight. He raised his weapon to fire again when bullets cracked by his ear, causing him to duck for cover.

Rodriguez aimed carefully and squeezed. The single bullet hit the shooting Vietnamese in the back of the head. He watched as the weapon fell from the soldier's hands and he slowly sank backward, his knees bending awkwardly.

"I get him," yelled the Puerto Rican.

Ben stood and sprayed the area where the soldier had disappeared.

"There's one over here," he yelled.

Rock sprang up and threw a grenade toward the area where Ben had been firing. The explosion shook the ground, and leaves and small branches filtered down like green and yellow snowflakes.

Sergeant Khanh knelt over the corporal, who was trying to get up. They had crawled back and dropped into a small gully that ran to the stream behind them. The corporal had no injuries except for temporary deafness. Khanh got the shaking man to his feet, and they moved quickly down the rocky gully. He could faintly hear the yelling of a foreign voice. He grabbed the corporal and pulled him along faster.

"Security," yelled Grady.

Rock and Ben jumped up and ran to the trail, followed by Rodriguez and Thumper. Grady waited for his men to move into position before standing and jogging to the pathway. Ben and Rodriguez secured their respective ends of the trail as Rock and Thumper moved cautiously toward the crumpled bodies. Grady, in the center, quickly turned a soldier over onto his back. His riddled rice tube had leaked its white kernels into an expanding pool of blood. The dead man's eyes were half open. Dark red holes were scattered over the left side of his face and body. Grady searched the shirt pockets and pants, then pulled off the soldier's pack and emptied it of its contents. He tossed clothes to the side, keeping the plastic-wrapped letters and notebooks, which he threw back into the pack. He picked up the soldier's AK-47 and moved on to the next body. He roughly flipped the corpse over. The gray-clad soldier's head flopped toward him, the gray jungle hat falling off and releasing long black hair that cascaded over the serene face.

"Christ, a woman," he mumbled.

Rock looked up from the soldier he was checking. "This one's movin'." He nudged the face of the groaning soldier. "It's a broad," he squealed as he knelt down and checked the woman's injuries. She had been hit in the legs and side by the Claymore pellets.

"How bad?" asked Grady.

"She'll make it," answered Rock, taking out his first-aid packet.

Grady pointed at Sox. "Tell X-ray we got six enemy KIA, one enemy WIA, and undetermined escaped. . . . We'll be at the PZ in twenty Mikes."

Sergeant Khanh and Corporal Phi sat on a gravel creek bank and splashed the cool water onto their faces. "What happened to us?" asked Phi.

Khanh stood and dried his hands on his pants. "A Yankee ambush. I saw the one who shot at me. He had a green and black face and wore a hat such as ours."

The corporal's eyes widened. "The commandos?"

"Yes," answered the sergeant, bringing his weapon up and checking his magazine. "We will follow the creek down to the black trail and cross to the next valley. We must report immediately."

Phi nodded in agreement and stood. "The happiness group sang like birds, didn't they, Sergeant?"

Khanh took a deep breath and began walking down the bank without answering. He was thinking of having to go back and bury the lovely girls who, only an hour before, had made him so happy.

Grady motioned for the team to move out. They had to move only five hundred meters to a pickup zone they had found two days before. Rock moved to point with Sox and Grady following. Thumper carried the wounded woman, with Rodriguez and Ben securing their rear.

Sox whispered to his sergeant, "Contacted X-ray and told 'em we was skying to the PZ. X-ray said the Bird Dog would be here *ti ti* and the Slick would be scrambled ASAP."

Grady looked over his shoulder, checking the men behind him. Sox suddenly grabbed him. Grady snapped his head back. Rock was frantically motioning them down.

Grady fell to the ground. Seventy-five feet away, three Vietnamese were running directly toward them. The men jogged single file at a slow pace, carrying their weapons at their sides.

"Thank God," mumbled Grady as he realized the men hadn't seen them. The running men veered right, following an old unused trail the team had crossed two days before. Grady shifted his eyes toward Rock, knowing he would wait to fire until the men got within ten or fifteen feet, but Rock suddenly jumped up and ran toward the surprised men, screaming and shooting.

What the—Jesus, he's gone crazy, thought Grady as he stood up and fired.

The lead Vietnamese turned toward the bloodcurdling scream and tried to bring up his weapon. The other two men, unable to stop their forward momentum, ran into each other, giving the screaming maniac a group target. The faces of the stunned men registered confusion and shock as the bullets tore into them.

The wild man ran directly into their midst, swinging his just-emptied weapon at the lone standing soldier. The blow caught the wounded man in the head, making a dull cracking sound.

Grady, running full speed toward the melee, shouted at Ben and Sox to cover him.

Rock was screaming as he shook his arms and legs and tore at his shirt. Grady quickly scanned the bodies and was about to grab Rock but abruptly stopped. "Jesus!" Rock was covered with red ants!

Grady pulled off his jungle hat and began slapping at Rock's flailing body.

"Oh, god damn! Oh, god damn!" squealed the frail soldier as he threw his shirt down and began unbuckling his pants.

Sox ran up and frantically brushed and slapped with Grady. Ben quickly searched the bodies as Thumper and Rodriguez secured the trail.

Twenty seconds later Grady took a deep breath and stepped back from the naked soldier, who was still mumbling and picking ants from his groin.

Sox held up the radio handset. "Grade, we got a Slick inbound. We gotta sky. Quick!"

"Two-zero, this is the Flying Dutchman. Got yellow smoke; going in."

The spotter plane circled over 2-2's PZ watching the Slick begin its flare. The pilot eased the control stick back as he pushed down the collective. The shuddering helicopter landed heavily.

"I'll be goddamned," mumbled the co-pilot as he grabbed the pilot's arm and pointed.

Two Rangers had already climbed aboard, when out of the jungle came a thin, stark-naked soldier wearing only his boots and jungle hat. He was being escorted by a huge black soldier carrying NVA packs and an armload of weapons.

"I can't believe it," yelled the door gunner as the men jumped aboard.

The team sat ready for the immediate lift-off. Instead both pilots had turned and were staring openmouthed at their naked passenger, who acted as though nothing were unusual. The right door gunner broke the spell. "Sirs, could we, like, get the fuck outta here?"

Sarah put down the phone and jumped up, smiling. Mary Ann grabbed her. "Well?"

"They're coming in! They're all okay."

"Thank God," said Mary Ann as she headed for the refrigerator to get a beer.

"Mary Ann, we're on duty!"

The big woman took a long drink. Sarah reached for her beer, taking a hefty swig.

"You don't drink beer," chuckled Mary Ann.

Sarah made a face and coughed, handing the beer back. "You're right." Sarah picked up her bag and hurried toward the door.

"Where are you going, Sarah?" asked Mary Ann.

"I'm going to beat him to his spot. He told me he always goes there to wind down."

"Good luck," yelled Mary Ann as Sarah disappeared out the door.

First Sergeant Demand smiled, thinking about the women who called him every day, wanting an update on team 2-2. He was glad he'd been able to give the girls some good news and get them off his back. He wondered how he could razz the two dummies who'd made such a hit with the Doughnut Dollies. He smiled again, thinking, *I guess it ain't so bad. Those two are good troops, and those girls . . . they sounded so concerned. Well, this time, dummies, you're lucky.*

Grady let the water trickle down his back. Rock and Thumper were under the other two shower heads, and Sox and Rodriguez were drying off.

"Wow, man, I think the Rock done went loco, man. I mean, wow, when he put his 16 on rock 'n' roll and charged, screamin', man, I says, 'Yep, Rock been chewin' grass, man.'"

"Really, there it is," agreed Sox.

"Look, I layed down. I was gonna let 'em get close, you know, when I sees a million fuckin' ants eatin on the Rock. I lay there takin' it, man, grittin' my teeth—look, I even chipped this mother." Rock pointed toward an incisor. "Then I felt them crawling up my balls. Man, that did it! It was rock 'n' roll and *go,* baby! I figured the faster I could kill them bastards, the faster I'd get to them little piss ants."

Thumper looked over Rock's red-welted body. "Looks like those ants ate up about twenty pounds' worth."

Dove drove down the dusty road and handed the blue notebook to Pete with a smile. "Log it, buddy."

Pete looked at his friend and the book in disbelief. "Dove, I've never logged in the book before."

"It's time you learned."

Pete took the notebook affectionately. The puppy between them tried to reach the blue plaything. Disappointed when she wasn't successful, she sat on her haunches and began yelping. Dove reached down and scratched her head and pulled the furry creature into his lap.

Pete turned to the last written page. "My God! My God, Dove! We're . . . you're rich!"

Dove nodded. "That's a lot of REMFs, man."

"I'll say: eight thousand, two hundred and forty-two dollars' worth of REMFs!"

"Now, let's see, we sold fourteen buckles at ten each and eight flags at twelve apiece. Not bad. Those signal guys were hot for souvenirs."

"I'll say. They lined up for the buckles like a chowline."

"We gotta pick up some beer and Cokes, so we'll have a little expense there, and the bill for the flowers we sent to the families of the Two-Four hasn't come in yet, but yeah, we're doing all right. We'll sell a bunch of AK-47s to the Air Force control team this afternoon. They can get them out of country on board the C-130s that base outta Guam, so we'll make fifty apiece on them." Pete began logging the new entries. "Pete, you're gonna be takin' over for the Dove pretty quick. I'm short. I only got twenty-some days left, so you got to Charlie Mike."

"Sure, Dove. I'll do a good job for you."

Dove smiled. "I know you will, Pete. Hey, I gotta show you a picture of the rings I ordered. This company that makes school class rings sent this brochure to me. They make a ring with anything we want on the top, so I ordered one for each of the guys in the company. I figure it'll be a week or so before they come in. It's my present to them."

"That sounds cool, Dove."

"Yeah, I like the idea. Hey, we're gonna pass the engineer unit up here. Ya wanna stop for a while?"

Pete smiled and reached for the bag of buckles.

Grady only picked at his food, unable to eat because of his excitement. The whole platoon was in, and each team had gotten confirmed kills. It was a first. Tonight Childs planned to throw a big party to celebrate. Grady left the mess hall and headed for his spot to try to relax. He knew the party would be a drunken brawl and that he'd better stay away for a while so he wouldn't get caught up in it. He would have to stay sober in order to keep his men from fighting with Rangers from the other platoons and to make sure they all got safely to bed.

He suddenly felt very lonely. He could see Evans's smiling face. *Relax, Grade,* he remembered his friend saying, *you gotta take it easy after a mission and clear your mind. You gotta whole war yet to fight . . . unless, of course, they turn loose the ol' Two-Four.*

Cheese, canned ham, sesame crackers, canned shrimp, brown bread, spread, wine, glasses, corkscrew—yes, the arrangement on the picnic blanket looked perfect, Sarah thought with satisfaction. She looked up and scanned the ridge. He should be coming any minute. *Now, remember, Sarah, be calm. Follow the plan you've been dreaming about for seven days. He'll be surprised to see you here, so be careful of what you say. It's been a week since you've seen him, and, Lord knows, things can change in that time.*

Her heart raced when she saw him. His head was down as if in deep thought. She quickly poured the wine and picked up her glass.

Grady paused at the far end of the little green glade and looked up.

Sarah was ecstatic. It was just as she had dreamed. She lifted her glass and spoke the words she'd been practicing.

"You've kept me waiting, Sergeant Grady."

Grady stood staring at her for a second, then shook his head, turned around, and began walking back to the barracks. In a moment he was gone.

Grady, please . . . please don't, her thoughts screamed. Her body seemed to shrivel as her stomach knotted with emptiness and pain. She sat down, shut her eyes tight, and lowered her head.

She had so much wanted to see him. She had planned for days how she could see him again and not have it look as if she were being presumptuous. She had dreamed about how it would be when he came to his spot and found her there. He would be pleasantly surprised and thank her for the

thoughtfulness and maybe, just maybe, say he'd missed her
or mention how he had wanted to see her again, but . . .

"Hi, lady."

She started, spilling her glass of wine, and spun around.
Grady stood behind the boulders, smiling.

Sarah glared at the sergeant for only an instant before regaining her composure.

"What's for chow?" he said. "I'm starved."

He walked around the boulders and stood a few feet away.
Still trying to hide her excitement, Sarah forced a feeble
smile and held a wineglass up to him.

"Naw. Don't you have a beer?"

She was on her feet in an instant, seething in rage. She
threw the glass, striking him in the chest.

Grady laughed. "Now, *there* is my tiger."

"You . . . you . . ."

Before she could say another word, he grabbed her and
yanked her up into his arms. He was laughing and holding
her tightly as she tensed and struggled to free her hands to
hit him, but he suddenly became silent and gently lowered
her to the ground. He looked into her pale blue eyes.

"I've missed you," he said.

"I've missed you too." She seemed to be lost in his gaze.
Only after a second did she realize what she had admitted,
and she wanted to back away from him; but as if he had read
her thoughts, he turned his back on her, sat down in front of
the food, and said, "What's for chow?"

From behind, Sarah made as if to strangle him; then she
shook her head and her expression relaxed into a smile.

They didn't say much as they ate, but when Grady had
finished his second glass of wine, he looked out over the
valley and said, "You know, Sarah, this wine, food . . . and
your company sure are nice."

Sarah leaned back on the boulder, studying his tanned
face. "So, I'm equal to the wine and food, at least."

"Well, the wine is *awfully* good. . . ." He watched for a
reaction from the corner of his eye.

Sarah hesitated for a long moment, then leaned over and
rested her head on his shoulder and sighed contentedly. "I'll
settle for being equal to the food, then," she said softly.

Her tone surprised him. He had not expected her to give in so quickly. He put his arm around her and gently hugged her closer. "Your company is the best thing that's happened to me in a long time."

She returned his caress and nestled closer.

Grady looked at the valley again, thinking of the last time he'd been with her. She had gotten to him. He knew that. But he also knew it would never work. The place and time were all wrong, and their backgrounds were too different. Why start something that could never amount to anything? He liked her too much to hurt her later . . . or to hurt himself. She was a special lady who needed someone who could give her the things she deserved, things he could never give. No. He would be her friend but nothing more.

When they finally started back, Sarah slipped her arm around his waist and leaned against him as they walked. "You know something, Grady? I . . . I . . . well, I enjoy being with you."

"I know," said Grady, "me too." He wanted to say more but knew he shouldn't.

"Is there any chance we could see each other again? I would really like it if you came by the center so I could show you where I work."

"Sure. I'll come by tomorrow. I'll even bring the big guy to make Mary Ann happy."

"You promise?"

"Sure. I'll have Dove drop me and Thump by."

They walked into the light of the outside compound and stopped short of the entrance.

"Sarah, thanks again. I'll see you tomorrow." He turned and was about to walk away.

"Grady," she said softly, moving closer to him, "could I . . . I've never asked a man to kiss me before, and I—"

Grady grabbed her before she could say another word and pulled her to him, kissing her passionately. She returned his kiss and felt his body shudder at her touch.

He stepped back, embarrassed at his lack of control. "I'm sorry, Sarah. I shouldn't have done that. I . . ."

Sarah lifted his chin. "Sergeant Grady, your chin should always be up. Proud tigers never apologize."

The Deuce Platoon's large green felt table was covered with beer cans that surrounded a huge empty glass bottle, three feet high. The bottle was two feet across at the base, but it narrowed to four inches at the top. The platoon members stood behind the table in various stages of intoxication, trying to imitate Sergeant Childs, who had just snapped stiffly to attention and commanded "At ease" as Lieutenant Sikes walked through the barracks door. Childs motioned the officer to a chair near the table and turned to the platoon.

"It's time we said good-bye to a true member of *the Deuce!*" Childs said. Sikes wasn't actually leaving. He was just transfering to operations, under Captain Shane, but any excuse for a party.

The platoon raised their beer cans and yelled, *"The Deuce!"*

Ben stepped forward, holding a large box, and set it on the table next to the sergeant. Childs reached into the box and held up a fifth of Jack Daniel's whiskey. "This . . . this represents us—the Seventy-fifth Infantry Airborne Rangers." He opened the cap and held the bottle high. "It's good, it's smooth, it's American, and it will definitely fuck you up!"

The platoon hollered and clapped as he poured the whiskey into the large bottle. Rock handed Childs a bottle of Vietnamese wine from the box. The sergeant held it up. "This represents the country we fight in. Its rice base represents the soul of the country. Its bitterness represents the people and the land."

He poured the clear liquid into the bottle and gave it to Rock, then held a dark brown medicine bottle. "This . . . this is blood. It represents that which was spilled by Rangers and our enemies—blood of soldiers who may hate each other but, by God, respect each other!"

He poured in the scarlet fluid and picked up a canteen.

"This water represents the monsoons that soak us and shrivel our bodies."

Emptying the canteen, he held up a bottle of Tabasco sauce. "This represents the heat that drains us. And last, these beers"—six men quickly opened cans as he picked one up—"represent the sweat that pours from us. Rangers of the Deuce, this potion is vile, vulgar, disgusting, . . . and it's *fuckin'* great!"

He half-filled a canteen cup. "Before we drink the jar dry, we commend the first drink to those worms that consume our bodies." He poured some liquid on the floor and yelled, "To the worms!"

"To the worms!" yelled the platoon, raising their beers.

Childs pointed to the bottle. "Every man, get a cupful, and then we'll have a toast."

It took a few minutes to pour the drinks into every conceivable container imaginable—half beer cars, C-ration cans, mess-hall cups, canteen cups, and even a few paper cups.

Childs stood on a chair and raised his canteen cup. "We say good-bye to Lieutenant Sikes: Although he's still—and always will be—a member of the platoon, he leaves the active roll. We bring in and welcome our new team from the dissolved Fourth Platoon, Sergeant Wade and his men, proud new members of *the Deuce!*"

"The Deuce!" the men screamed back, holding their cups high.

Childs raised his cup. "A toast . . . to the old, the new, and the dead, of the baddest fuckin' platoon in the Seventy-fifth Infantry Airborne Rangers—*the Deuce!*"

The small desk lamp was the only light on in the darkened room. Its pale yellow-white radiance reflected off the maps and reports scattered over the desk.

Colven leaned forward from the darkness, his face only partially illuminated. "What do you think, Ed?"

Captain Shane stepped into the light and tossed onto the desk the sheaf of papers he'd been reading. "Based on what the intell reports say, we'd better go in heavy, sir."

"It looks like a lot of activity, that's for sure."

"Sir, I'm not worried so much about what we find as how the hell we get in without their knowing. The AO is full of training, logistics, and base camps. How do we get in without everybody knowing we're there?"

Colven leaned back and stretched. "At my request the aviation unit at Pleiku is making early-morning low-levels over the border as if they were on photo runs, gaining intell. The dinks should think it's commonplace by now." Colven grinned. "I hear from General Burton that the aviation commander is fit to be tied. He doesn't like being ordered to fly over hostile area without rhyme or reason."

Shane looked at his major, surprised." You mean he hasn't been told?"

"No, and he won't be until we get there."

Shane picked up one of the maps from the desk. "This one is really going to be different, sir. We won't be bushin' on small trails. Hell, they'll be ten-to-twelve-foot-wide roads."

"No, Ed, I don't think we'll be ambushing. We haven't got our mission yet, but I'd say we'll be sent in to pinpoint big concentrations of the enemy for a larger invasion force."

"Jesus, sir, you mean we'll be playing advance scout?"

"Yes, I'd say that's the best thing they could do. The large unit will probably be the 173rd or a brigade from the Fourth Division."

"Damn, sir, you're talking about an invasion of Cambodia. Son of a bitch! This is big-time! But the area they've given us is huge. How can a brigade do much damage?"

"That's why they've called the Rangers. We'll find the big stuff, then the units will come and do the dirty work."

Shane put down the map. "Well, sir, forget what I said about going in heavy. If we're going to be reconning, then we gotta go in light and hope to hell the teams don't get spotted till the big units get there."

"That's what I figured too. Oh, we'll be getting two squads of Kit Carsons from Pleiku to help us. These are Rade montagnards and know the area. We'll put one scout in each team to help out. The dispatch I got from Corps this afternoon confirmed their assignment to us, so we'll get them when we get the word to go." Kit Carsons were ex-communists who now fought against the North.

"When are we gettin' the word, sir?"

"I'm not sure. The dispatch said it's coming soon, maybe within days, maybe hours. When it does come, Ed, we're going to get busy fast. That's why I'm telling you about the operation now. The men mustn't know till we get to Pleiku and I brief them. They'll have to be in isolation till we go in. I've told Top and Treadwell, so right now it's just the four of us. When we get the word, four C-130s will land within twenty-four hours to take us and selected aviation outfits there. We'll have only twenty-four hours in Pleiku before we go in. We'll land at Pleiku Airport and truck to here"—he pointed toward the map—"a place called Engineer Hill. It has empty barracks and an operating mess hall. Engineer Hill is a base inside of a larger base. It's a maintenance battalion's camp, but half of them are gone. Treadwell left yesterday to make all the arrangements for billeting. Engineer Hill will be our rear-area camp. As you can see, we're still a good thirty kilometers from the border. We're going to set up a forward base here, at Plei Djereng, an old Special Forces camp only a few miles from the border. We'll establish for-

ward operations there, and we'll keep our Slicks and guns
there so they can react quickly. The X-ray will go in here, on
this mountain next to the border. From there we'll have good
commo."

Shane nodded and picked up the aerial photos. "Sir, this is
going to be big-time. Did you see all the trucks and people on
the roads?"

"I've looked at the photos a hundred times, Ed. Like you
said, this is the big time."

The crickets and darkness had joined to secure the evening. An eighteen-year-old soldier sat in front of his radio,
looking into a mirror and squeezing his third pimple. The
phone rang, startling him.

He looked at his watch. "Damn, who's calling at oh-two-
hundred in the morning?" He picked up the phone as it rang
a second time. "Sierra Rangers. . . . Yes, sir, I'll take the
message."

He picked up a pencil and began writing: *To: Major Colven. Subject: Ball game. Pregame in motion. You have been
activated. Report for warm-up immediately. Signed, Coach.*

"That's the message, sir? . . . Yes, sir. Out."

He replaced the phone and stood up, stretched, and
walked toward the man sleeping on a cot next to the wall.
"Hey, Wiz . . . Wiz, get up, man."

The fully dressed soldier sat up slowly, rubbing his eyes.
"Yeah?"

"Take this message to the Ol' Man."

"Ya want me to wake him up?"

"Yeah. They said it's important and he would want it."

"All right, all right, the Wiz is on his way."

He got up, took the message from the radio operator, and,
yawning, walked to the door.

PART THREE

17

Corporal Trung Ly Vee walked slowly down the bamboo steps of the supply hut and took the path that led past headquarters to the dismount point. Three Czech two-and-a-half-ton Skoda trucks were being unloaded in the *U*-shaped road. He mentally computed how long he'd have to spend inventorying that night. The unloaded boxes were filled with ammunition—no medical supplies or communications parts.

Corporal Vee smiled to himself. *Easy work,* he thought as he walked toward the cadre barracks. He stopped at the third hut, took off his rubber sandals, and climbed the bamboo ladder. A Rade woman tended a small cooking fire in front of the hut. She didn't look up from her blackened brass pot as she stirred. Vee shuffled across the shiny dark bamboo slats and over to his hammock. It hung from a center support pole and a side support railing. He was fortunate: Only four of the ten men who lived in the hut had been able to hang their hammocks. He lay back and shut his eyes.

He had been selected only eight months before when the Party's Central Committee had asked for volunteers from among the students at the Hanoi Polytechnic. He had been in his third year of study in the Electronics Department, and was given no choice in volunteering.

After three months of training at Xuan Mai Training Center at Ha Dong, he was sent by truck to the Laotian–North Vietnamese border, and from there he marched southward through Laos. It was a very difficult trip for him. He was not used to the rigors of a soldier's life. He became exhausted and got sick, so that he had to be left at a way station, where it took him a week to recover his strength. He joined another infiltrating unit and finally reached Cambodia and the northern supply base two weeks later.

Vee turned in his hammock. The camp was a good assignment, a true blessing from Buddha. The camp itself was well away from the fighting. The supplies came in by sea to the port of Sihanoukville and were trucked up Route 3 to Highway 19 and then to the camp. He would take inventory, and on orders he would distribute gear to infiltrating or transportation units, which would haul enormous loads on bikes to field battalions. In the evenings he would read, and listen to the wireless. The radio had reported the overthrow of Prince Sihanouk a month before and told how the South Vietnamese and Americans had declared Lon Nol, the new Cambodian leader, an ally. Vee remembered how he'd shaken with fear upon hearing the news and how he couldn't eat for days afterward. But nothing had changed. Nol proved to be a paper tiger who didn't have enough soldiers to push the liberating forces out.

Then two weeks ago his fear had returned. The supply trucks began coming only in dribbles, and they were always camouflaged with trees and branches. The soldiers of South Vietnam invaded in the south and destroyed several camps like this one. The leaders told them not to fear, that the northern provinces were much too strong for South Vietnamese puppets to attack. Vee listened every night to the Vietnamese broadcast of the BBC, trying to determine the advances of the puppets. The radio spoke many times of some American involvement, but nothing large. It looked as if it would be a South Vietnamese invasion only. He felt heartened by the news; the Americans would stay out. It had been yesterday, when they began building fighting positions and bunkers, that his nervousness struck again and forced him to report to the medical shack.

He was not a coward, but the fear of dying was a disease within him. He had always shunned all sports or any type of play that could possibly hurt him. His father, a radio repairman, had never chastised his son for his weakness. He had told him, "Be proud of your skills; leave fighting for those who like it."

The possibility of using the Chinese automatic weapon assigned to him made him sick. He thought of the gun and abruptly sat up, looking around. He had forgotten it again! He'd left it at his desk in the supply hut. Last week the commander had decreed that all cadres keep their weapons with them at all times. Vee hurried to the door and looked out. He saw no one except the old woman tending the fires. He climbed hurriedly down the ladder and slipped into his sandals. Now, if he could just make it back to the hut without being noticed . . .

Sarah replaced the phone after letting it ring eight times. "There's no answer. What's wrong?"

Mary Ann shook her head. "I don't know. Thump said he'd come by."

"So did Grady."

"Sarah, it's nine o'clock. They should have been here by now. And somebody should have answered the phone in their orderly room." Mary Ann picked up her bag and headed for the door.

"Where are you going?" asked Sarah.

"Come on. We'll surprise them and pick 'em up."

First Sergeant Demand walked through the deserted barracks, stopped at the orderly room, and looked back. Only thirty Rangers from the company remained, and most of them were new students. He had ordered all those left behind to move into the headquarters barracks. He shook his head. He could still feel Major Colven's hand on his shoulder. "No, Top, you can't go. I need you to take care of the school and the camp. Hell, ol'-timer, we'll be back soon enough."

The black soldier had lowered his head. "Come home to me, you Rangers. This old man ain't a soldier unless he's got you."

"Miss Boyce."

Sarah turned, surprised to see a young MP standing beside the jeep. She and Mary Ann had just pulled into the compound parking lot.

"Heavens, Private, you startled me. Yes, I'm Miss Boyce."

"Sorry, but I was to give you this note. A Ranger ran up to the booth about eight or so and dropped it off."

Sarah opened the folded piece of paper and read quickly:

"Hi, lady,

Sorry, I won't be able to see you for a while. We moved out early this morning. I'm having a friend deliver this note for me. Thumper says to tell Mary Ann he'll write her as soon as we get wherever we're going.

Take care, lady. Don't let the sappers get you! I'll try to drop a line too.

Tiger

Sarah handed the note to Mary Ann.

"Leaving? Leaving? Leaving for where?" Mary Ann shook her head.

Sarah got out of the jeep and began walking toward the ridge.

"Hey, where are you going?" yelled Mary Ann.

"I'm going over there to find out where they went."

"But you . . . Wait, I'm going too!"

It was 1100 hours, and the small, crowded briefing room at the camp outside Pleiku was stifling, but the anxious men assembled there didn't seem to notice as they fidgeted in their chairs. They all knew that something big was about to break. Excitement hung in the air like an invisible mist as the men laughed and talked among themselves, trying to ignore their fluttering stomachs.

Sergeant Ingram looked at his list again: *Team sergeants, the Lts., Bird-Dog pilots, Slick and gunship company commanders and their leads, the Air Force liaison, and the Fourth Division liaison—Yeah, they're all here,* he thought to himself.

He nodded to Captain Shane, who then knocked on the door to the major's office. Seconds later Major Colven opened the door and strode down the aisle to the briefing platform. The men stood, searching the officer's expressionless face for a hint about what was to happen.

Colven positioned himself beside a large sheet-covered map and picked up a pointer from the sill before turning and facing the group.

"Take your seats, gentlemen. The reason I have called you here is to brief you on a major operation that will begin at zero-six-hundred hours tomorrow morning."

The pilots exchanged quick glances. They weren't used to such short notice for large operations.

Colven walked to the map and removed the sheet. "We are about to begin the American invasion of Cambodia."

The reaction was instantaneous. Everyone turned and began talking to confirm what had just been said.

Colven tapped the floor with his pointer for quiet before continuing. "We will be the lead American contingent. Our mission is to go into the northern provinces prior to the main invasion, recon, and locate major supply, training, and command bases. Three days from now the Fourth Division will follow and destroy what we find."

Colven pointed toward the map and raised his voice for emphasis. "The Rangers must be infiltrated by air, and they must go in undetected. Our assigned area is roughly a rectangle drawn ten kilometers in from the Cambodian border and forty kilometers down from the Laotian border. Based on aerial photos and intell reports, we have broken the rectangle down into three platoon AOs: The First Platoon has the lower third, the Third Platoon is in the middle, and the Deuce Platoon is at the top. You can see that the terrain gets progressively hillier the farther north we go.

"The Rangers will avoid detection and contact at all costs. They are to travel light and to report *only*! Timing is critical. The teams will go in tomorrow, find the enemy, call in the locations, and get to a PZ by the following morning at oh-eight-hundred. They will be picked up prior to the main invasion force that will be choppered in.

"We will be giving more briefings throughout the day to discuss specifics.

"Gentlemen, this is a tough, dangerous operation"—Colven put his pointer down and lowered his voice—"but I can't think of a better bunch to do the job. I'm proud to be with you, and I'm confident we'll accomplish the mission. Good Hunting."

One hour after the briefing, Sergeant Grady sat on the floor of the Second Platoon's barracks with his team and a newly assigned Kit Carson scout, Fon Tay.

"We're going in light with only two days' rations and water," Grady explained. "We'll carry only two claymores. Thump, you and Pancho take 'em. We'll be going just to the west of Hill 671. From there we'll move around the mountain to the north, then strike east. By the looks of the aerial photos, we'll probably find a camp somewhere in the valley.

"Remember, if something happens and we get separated or have to escape and evade, head due east toward the border. As you can see, the Se San River is actually the border, and all the streams and valleys eventually run into it. From the river you'll be able to signal a passing plane or chopper easily.

"Rock, I want you to carry the silenced Sterling gun this mission."

Rock Steady smiled. He didn't have many opportunities to carry the British submachine gun.

"Pancho, you take care of Fon Tay and ensure he's got everything he needs. Tay is a Rade montagnard and knows the area, so he'll be a big help. I'll check equipment in one hour. Any questions?"

Captain Shane stood in front of the briefing room map talking to Sikes.

"Bud, as you know, this place will be our rear operations base, and here, fifteen klicks away, at Plei Djereng, will be the forward base. Sergeant Ingram, a radio team, and I will be there. Major Colven and Childs will run the rear area. Plei Djereng is only a few klicks from the border, so it's a perfect location for the birds to bed down, refuel, and rearm. Sergeant Ingram flew out there after the briefing and has already set up. Plei Djereng is an old Special Forces camp and sits on a bald plateau. Ingram says the airfield is in good shape and that we are lucky in getting one of the only buildings to use. It's a shack surrounded by a ten-foot earth berm next to the runway. In a couple of days the place is going to turn into a madhouse. The Fourth Division is going to use the camp as a forward base too.

"We're going to put the X-ray in this evening. It's going in on this mountain, on the border.

"The montagnard scouts have been given to all the teams by now, so you'd better check to see they've been taken care of. Questions?"

"How many teams do we have going in tomorrow, sir?"

"All twelve of them," answered Shane. "They'll all be on the ground by oh-nine-hundred."

"Well, sir, looks like we got somethin' to write home about."

Shane smiled. "Yeah, it's not often you lead an invasion."

Corporal Trung Ly Vee and his assistant, Private Ban Thi Luc, sat in the glow of the small kerosene lamp, listening to the wireless. News was good. The South Vietnamese invasion force was bogging down, and the liberators were consolidating positions deep inside Cambodia. That afternoon the political officer had explained that Lon Nol's government was an enemy and that the true government, the exiled Prince Sihanouk's government, had asked for their help. The people of Cambodia were in revolt against Lon Nol and were fighting the Yankee-backed Phnom Penh troops.

Luc smiled upon hearing the announcer say that the provinces of Mondolkis and Ratankiri were under total control by the Communists. He tapped Vee's shoulder. "That's us, friend."

The corporal nodded and leaned back, contented. The rice wine had taken his worries away, as had the good news.

The two men listened for several minutes before turning the dial to Radio Hanoi and listening to the soft music of the People's concert held in honor of Ho Chi Minh.

Vee shut his eyes and thought about the next day's work on the new bunkers. He would not report to the medical shack to be released from the duty. No, tomorrow he would help with construction and be a real soldier. A soldier—no, not really: a technician who happened to be in soldier's clothes and was called a soldier.

Vee opened his eyes and reached down to touch the weapon beside him. He smiled inwardly. He hadn't forgotten it. Maybe he was becoming a soldier after all.

Dove was standing in the middle of the Engineer barracks. His dog sat at his feet, sniffing the strange surroundings.

"How much again for the buckles?" asked a burly Engineer private.

"Ten bucks," answered Dove, yawning. "It was a special unit we hit. They all wore the same buckles and carried flags. We figured they was sappers or some kind of commando unit or somethin'."

Pete spread the last of the five flags on the floor as the other engineers fingered the merchandise. The burly soldier picked up a buckle. "I'll take one for eight bucks."

Dove yawned again. "I'm sorry, ten bucks. You could get twenty for it easy in Saigon." He walked toward the bag of buckles that was sitting on a footlocker.

The thick-shouldered private looked at the buckle again. "Okay, ten."

"Me too," said another soldier. "And I want a flag. Hey, Bob, this is a good deal, man."

"All right. I guess I'll take a flag," said a third soldier.

Dove winked at Pete and sat on the footlocker to collect his money. Pete reached into his pocket and threw the curly-haired blond the small blue notebook, holding another flag out to a buyer. Dove's dog, which had become known as Bitch, scampered over to her master, not wanting to be trampled by the gathering men. She was about to yelp when a hand grasped her around the tummy and lifted her up. Dove put the puppy on his lap, then held out his hand to be paid.

18

Childs walked through the cool morning darkness toward the platoon barracks. It was 0430. He was going to awaken the men and check their equipment one last time. He stopped before opening the door. The blissful feeling of serenity overcame him. He turned and breathed deeply. He always liked the mornings and this would be the last he would have time to enjoy for a while. Once the mission began, he would not be allowed the luxury of enjoying anything. He took another deep breath and opened the door.

His trip had been wasted. The men were already awake, fully dressed and huddled in teams. They were going over the mission.

The sergeant walked through the barracks in silence. The men needed no pep talk or coaxing. Their serious faces and oiled, spotless weapons told the sergeant all he needed to know. They were ready. He walked out the back door and strolled slowly to the operations center.

Bud Sikes climbed into the backseat of the small plane with mixed feelings. He hadn't been in a Bird Dog since his crash landing. The seat felt strangely good. He felt at home as he put on his flight helmet and flipped the radio toggle switches.

The headphones crackled and a familiar voice spoke. "How's it feel to be back, Bud?"

"Feels good, Larry, real good. I've missed it."

"It's a big day, kid. Hope you brought a lot of food. We're going to need it."

"What do you mean, *we're* gonna need it? How come you fly-boys are such moochers?"

Larry Wine was still laughing when he depressed his talk button. "Yeah, the kid is back."

John Colven sipped his second cup of coffee as he stood at the doorway of the ops center, watching the teams file by. The pickup site was just a hundred yards farther up the hill.

Jerry Childs joined his major and leaned against the doorframe. "Sir, we got a call from the Slicks. They'll be here in just a few minutes."

Colven nodded without speaking, still watching his men.

Childs watched the procession for several moments before speaking again, this time quietly. "Sir, is there anything else we can do? I feel so . . . so damned useless standing here, watching them."

The major took another sip of coffee, but his eyes remained fixed on the teams. "Everything is done. The planning, the coordination . . . and the praying. It's time for those young Rangers out there to do the dirty part. It's all in their hands now." Colven turned and looked at his old friend. "And you know something, Jerry? They'll do it. They'll do the best they can, and they'll give everything they've got to accomplish the mission. I love them for that. I only wish I could be with them."

The sergeant nodded, feeling the same pride and anguish. From the distance he could hear the familiar sound of approaching choppers.

General Wayland leaned back in his padded chair and set down his coffee cup. His G-3 stood in front of him, briefing the Fourth Division commander, who was seated to his left, about the Cambodian operation. Wayland glanced at his watch: 0632.

The G-3 was pointing to a map. "As you can see, sir, your lead companies will be air-landed at the Pleiku Airport. They'll move to waiting lift helicopters, which will take them straight into Cambodia. All three battalions of your Fifth Brigade will be in Cambodia by nightfall. We'll also be lifting two artillery batteries of 105 howitzers to fire bases here and here. They will be your indirect fire support."

The fourth division general raised his hand, stopping the colonel, and turned toward General Wayland. "Sir, I don't think there're enough helicopters in the corps to put the whole brigade plus artillery in there in one day."

Wayland shook his head. "I've been given assurances from G-3 Air that there are. He has my permission to use every available helicopter in the corps. All the units are giving up their support to help out."

The division commander began to speak again, but Wayland nodded to his G-3 to continue.

Lieutenant Colonel Henley, the corps G-3 Air, sat in the last row, fidgeting upon hearing his general speak of him. He had told the general a week before that there were not enough lift ships available and that they'd need to plan on putting only two battalions, not three, in on the first day. He tried to explain the turnaround distance from Pleiku and Cambodia and the time needed for refueling The general got angry. He told Henley he had already briefed the plan to "higher headquarters," and he was *not* going to go back and tell them those plans had been changed. In the general's words: "You find those extra helicopters if it means pulling every chopper in Corps, including Medevacs."

Henley shook his head. It was impossible.

Corporal Vee walked tiredly up the steps to his supply hut. Above the entrance was a picture of Prince Sihanouk. Blue and pink plastic ribbon hung from the bottom of the picture. The photographs had been given out the night before, during the political classes. All huts were to have them placed above the doors.

Vee's stomach had become upset when the political officer said that members of the camp would be called upon to help the Cambodians in their revolt against the imperialists' puppet government of Lon Nol. This morning Vee had been assigned to dig a fighting trench and had worked for nearly an hour before being released to his normal duties. Private Luc had just finished issuing equipment to a large group that still stood behind the hut. Surprisingly they were not going to South Vietnam; instead they were heading west toward Phnom Penh, the capital of Cambodia. Vee was sitting at his desk when Luc came back in to make the necessary entries in the equipment log book.

"What is wrong, friend?" ask Luc.

"I'm tired. I'm tired of this war. I want to go home and sit on my doorstep and talk to my neighbors the way I used to do."

Luc smiled and put his hand on his leader's shoulder. "It's not long until Uncle Ho's birthday. Look at this." The bespeckled private reached into his pant pocket and withdrew a handful of dông. "We will buy some rice wine and bricks of sweetened popped rice to celebrate."

Vee stared at the money, openmouthed. "Where did you get such money?"

"Didn't I learn my supply job from the most competent corporal?"

Vee knew Luc must have sold some extra medical supplies to the soldiers. They always wanted more painkillers and medicines. "I had forgotten about the celebration. Yes! We will plan a big celebration for the two of us."

Vee laughed. He was glad to have a friend like Luc. Who else could ease one's mind from the worries that made one so sick.

Grady rose to his knees and nodded at the co-pilot, who was holding up two fingers; then tapped each of his men and scooted out into the ninety-knot wind and placed his feet on the skids. The ground below was a green blur. As the helicopter began its flare, its tail dipped and the blade pitch changed. Grady saw the LZ coming up. "Shit," he mumbled. The ground was too sloped for a set-down. He bent his legs slightly and held his weapon tighter.

When the chopper dropped to within eight feet of the whirling elephant grass, Grady jumped. The team followed. Fon Tay was still in midair when the bird lifted and shot forward. Grady got to his feet and jogged for the treeline. One look over his shoulder told him everyone was all right.

Grady motioned to Rock to move due north and nodded at Thumper to shadow in the slack man's position with Fon Tay.

Rock walked down the gradual descent confidently, knowing there was no danger this high up on the mountain. When they got lower and turned east, he would have to slow down and walk more cautiously. The light L34A1 British Sterling gun felt good in his hands. Its long black silencer made the front heavy and off-balanced, but he had compensated by moving his hands farther forward on the barrel grip.

The triple canopy above blocked out all rays of sunlight. The semidarkness smelled of damp and rot. Huge felled trees decaying on the slope were the only prominent features.

Rock was filled with the sense of power he always felt while walking point—the power of knowing he held death in his hands and would be the first to use it. He loved that feeling. He was a somebody when he walked point. He was the man he'd always wanted to be—respected, tough, and indispensable.

Bud Sikes let out a sigh of relief. Only one more team to go. The infills had gone in like clockwork, and there were no contacts, thank God.

"Stagecoach-Three, are you ready, baby?"

"Three-Alfa, this is Stagecoach-Three. Roger. Hurry, will ya? Your Rangers are eatin' all my door gunner's food."

"Roger, Stagecoach. Take up a heading of 270 degrees. I'll pick you up as you cross the river."

"Roger. We're on the way."

Sergeant Matt Wade looked like an all-American boy: five foot ten, with blond, crew-cut hair, brown eyes, and broad shoulders. He was on his knees between the pilot and co-pilot. He quickly grabbed the back of the pilot's seat as the chopper sharply banked right and began its descent.

Wade turned and looked at his team. "Cambodia, here we come," he yelled excitedly.

The sinking helicopter had to bank abruptly to jockey itself into the small, oblong LZ covered with elephant grass. Wade's team jumped off and ran for the trees. The chopper rose slightly, then veered sharply to clear the high trees in front of it. The door gunner leaned out, watching the tail as they swung around.

"Oh, shit!" he yelled into the intercom as a jagged tree stump suddenly became visible in the blowing grass.

"Left, *left!*"

The pilot, hearing the scream, frantically pushed the right pedal, but it was too late. The tail rotor tore into the soft bark like a buzz saw and suddenly shattered in a thundering crack. The gear box was torn from the spinning tail housing as the splintered blade flew into hundreds of whirling pieces. The main rotor was struck by the tail blade shrapnel and whined as if in agony. Without a tail rotor to counter the torque of the main blades, the chopper spun crazily out of control, corkscrewing itself into the ground.

Wade pressed himself farther into the moist earth, praying the noise would end. For an instant he had thought they were under fire, but he had looked over his shoulder just in time to see the blade disintegrate. He fell to the ground, praying the bird wouldn't burn; if it did, he would be one of its victims.

Finally the dying machine gave off a metallic grinding screech, then it sat motionless. Wade rose up on one knee and yelled for his team to report their status. A door gunner was running directly for him. He looked like an alien from a spaceship with his large helmet and darkened visor. He seemed out of place in the hot yellow elephant grass, thought Wade as he ran to the chopper to help the pilots.

Pfc. Oscar and the guy they called the Russian, although he was actually a Czech refugee, were already helping the shaking pilot and the wide-eyed co-pilot, who couldn't get out of his seat. The crew chief threw his helmet at the wrecked helicopter. "You whore! You goddamn whore!"

The radioman ran up to Wade and handed him the handset. "Sarge, it's Lieutenant Sikes. He wants a report."

Sikes couldn't believe what he'd just seen. He'd flown a lot of missions but had never seen a tail strike before. He looked down, searching as they circled the wreck. "Shit, there's not another LZ anywhere close."

Wade's voice came from the radio. "We're all okay. No injuries. Crew's okay. Over."

"Thank God. You were lucky. I'm gonna fly a little east and see if I can find an LZ. Stand by. Out."

Larry banked the plane on an easterly course. Both Wine and Sikes searched the ground below for light green or brown—signs of a possible open area.

Larry hit the switch. "There we go! One o'clock."

"Damn, that's a good ten, maybe twelve klicks away," said Sikes, staring at the large open area where the forest abruptly ended and the grassy, rolling hills began.

"Two-One, this is Three-Alpha."

"This is Two-One. Go."

"Tell that air crew they're now Rangers. You guys got to hump a ways to get out. Due east, you'll hit an open area in ten to twelve klicks."

"Roger. We'll destroy radios and move out."

"Roger. Call X-ray when you're ready for pickup. We'll be waiting at forward. Over."

"Roger. Out."

"God damn," said Sikes disgustedly as the plane headed for Plei Djereng. "It was going so good too."

Corporal Vee ran up the steps and into his supply hut. Private Luc looked up from his inventory. The winded corporal was trying to catch his breath as he spoke: "We're . . . we're staying here!" Vee said breathlessly. "Sergeant Duan and his unit, as well as . . . Corporal Vinh's, are going west . . . tomorrow. But you"—he took another quick breath—"and I are remaining."

Luc forced a grin, although he would have preferred going, especially after hearing the helicopter fly close by earlier. There would be less danger deeper into Cambodia. "Did you hear the helicopter?"

"Yes, it was to the north of us, probably photographing. Sergeant Phan said it was the puppets' machine because there was only one. Yankees fly with at least two." Vee patted the private's back. "We shall celebrate tonight. I'll borrow a motorbike and go to Phum Lay and pick up good things to eat."

"Do you need dông?" asked Luc, reaching into his pocket.

"Who has taught you all you know, young Private?" Vee pulled out a wad of paper currency and waved it in front of Luc's eyes.

"Yes, it is true. It is you, Corporal Leader—oh, honorable one—who has misguided this poor rice farmer's son to evil ways."

The two men laughed goodheartedly.

"I'll be back soon," said Vee, turning for the door.

Luc stood up quickly and picked up the corporal's forgotten AK-47.

"You had better take this or the political officer will report you." Vee rolled his eyes and walked back for his weapon.

John Colven anxiously paced the floor in front of the large map. Teams 1-1 and 1-3 had reported large concentrations of North Vietnamese, and he knew about 2-1's downed bird, but the other teams had not checked in yet.

Sound came from the green speaker box: "Zero-Six, this is X-ray. Sit rep from Three-Two follows. On high-speed road, location: from Coors, one right, two up. Bad guys moving to the west. NVA and civilians all carrying heavy loads. A few trucks, lots of motorbikes. They're Charlie Miking. End message."

Colven stepped to the map and looked at the red grease pencil dot labeled BEER. One right and two up, he said to himself, as he quickly plotted the team's location.

Ingram rose and looked at the major's plot. "The dinks are leavin' and headin' west. You think they know?"

Colven shook his head. "I don't know, but it looks like they're sure movin' out. You'd better call Corps and then the Fourth and tell 'em what we've learned."

Colven walked to another map and looked at the team's AOs. *Come on, guys,* he thought, *find the bastards.*

"Son of a bitch," mumbled Sergeant Wade to himself, trying to contain his anger. "That co-pilot is a pain in the ass."

The team had been moving for forty minutes since leaving the crash site. Wade had to tell the helicopter crew to throw away three-fourths of the gear they'd wanted to carry. The co-pilot wanted to take his flight helmet, explaining that he had specially painted it. Wade took the time to explain that they had to travel light, silently, and fast. The pilot and door gunners followed his instructions to the letter, but the co-pilot constantly lagged behind, coughing aloud every few minutes. Wade warned him two times, but the third un-muffled cough did it. Wade halted the team and grabbed the startled young warrant officer by his flight-suit collar and pulled his face within inches of his own. "Sir, you fuckin' cough one more time without trying to muffle it, and I'm going to gag you!"

The co-pilot couldn't doubt the menacing tone or cold eyes that bore through him.

Wade released the co-pilot and motioned the others to continue. They had moved only five minutes when he saw the two lead men, the Russian and the montagnard scout, fall to the ground. Instinctively he did the same, but when he turned, the helicopter crewmen were still standing. Wade frantically motioned them down. They slowly complied, except for the co-pilot, who paused to look around to select a clear spot. Wade made a mental note to kill the son of a bitch.

The Russian lay only a few yards from a trail he hadn't seen until it was too late. The ground level suddenly dropped down, but not until he'd reached the edge of the drop-off did he see the path and two NVA approaching down it. The two men hadn't seen him, but it was only a matter of time. There was no place to hide—no trees nearby, only the few ferns in which the Russian lay. They came closer until they were almost parallel to him.

The second North Vietnamese suddenly turned his head, as if he had seen something out of the corner of his eye. The Russian lunged and swung the butt of his weapon, hitting the soldier in the head. The other Vietnamese spun around. The Russian, unable to stop his forward momentum, fell to the ground and rolled. He jumped to his feet and ran toward the soldier.

The montagnard's knife had already made its deadly swipe as the Russian hit the falling body. Hot fluid spurted into the Russian's face, temporarily blinding him as he fought to break free of the lifeless body.

The montagnard knelt by the soldier the Russian had hit and jerked his head up as he brought his knife around. There was no need: His neck had been broken by the blow. The front of his head above the eyebrow was grotesquely flattened. Pfc. Oscar jumped down to the trail to secure the far end as the Russian bent over the first body and pulled the soldier's scarf off to wipe the blood from his face.

Wade looked down at the damage, pushing back his jungle hat. *Good work,* he thought. *Messy but silent.* The helicopter crew gathered close behind him. The co-pilot gagged when he saw the Russian's bloody face.

"Get their weapons, ammo, and packs," Wade told the pilot and crew chief.

The men stared at him unbelievingly.

"Move, *sirs,*" he hissed.

"It's gotta be a supply base," Rock whispered excitedly.

Grady nodded as he counted the hootches and trucks. He rolled onto his side to withdraw his map from his leg pocket.

"Hot damn, Grade, I wish ol' Dove was here. He'd go nuts seeing that NVA flag they're flyin'. Just think of the shit we could sell."

Grady replaced the map, satisfied that he'd pinpointed their location, and looked at the map again.

Grady and Rock were in a banana grove east of camp. The grove bordered what looked like a small soccer field. Directly across from them was a headquarters building, and beside it was a *U*-shaped road where two trucks were being loaded. A row of elevated thatched hootches sat behind the trucks.

"Grade, you see that first hootch by the road? A dude just pulled up on a motorbike."

Grady had seen the motorbike but was much more interested in the way the soldier was straining under the weight of the truck's boxes. *Must be ammo,* he thought.

"Let's get back and call it in."

The corps G-3 brought the reports in to General Wayland and set them down in front of him. "Good news, sir."

The general picked up the papers and began reading. A few moments later he looked up and smiled at the colonel. "The Rangers did it. They found the base camps."

The G-3 grinned. "Yes, sir. It sure saves a lot of time. The Fourth Division battalions will be able to air-mobile almost on top of them."

The general nodded and continued to read. Suddenly his brow wrinkled in concentration. "My God, it says the North Vietnamese are leaving and heading west into the interior."

The colonel shifted his stance. "Yes, sir. Some of the units are probably leaving to take up positions to fight Lon Nol's government troops, but—"

"But, nothing! They're leaving!"

"Not all of them, sir, only—"

"They're leaving, god damn it! You contact that Ranger unit and tell them to stop them until tomorrow, when the Fourth arrives."

The G-3 almost laughed. Then he realized that the general was serious. "Sir, they're only six-man teams. They couldn't begin to stop units of the size they're reporting. Hell, it'd be suicide!"

The general studied his subordinate's face for a moment. "Howie, we can't go in and find the enemy gone." The general rose and walked to the map behind him. "Tomorrow this corps is responsible for launching the largest attack in the shortest period in this war's history. We must have results." The general's voice had risen to a high pitch. His chest heaved as he caught his breath and pointed a trembling finger at the balding colonel. "Contact the Rangers. Tell them to ambush the major roads and stop the North Vietnamese, god damn it!"

The colonel stared at the general without expression. "Yes, sir."

Wayland turned away, clasping his hands behind his back. "Being a commander is difficult. There are many decisions that must be made, many sacrifices." He turned around again and stared at the colonel. "This operation calls for sacrifice. You do understand that, don't you, Colonel?"

The G-3 fought the dryness in his throat and forced another expressionless "Yes, sir" before turning for the door. He paused in the hallway after shutting the door and mumbled to himself, "I understand perfectly."

The colonel walked down two flights of stairs to the communications room and quickly wrote out the instructions. He handed the note to the watch officer.

"Send this out immediately. Priority."

The watch officer read the message as the colonel walked toward the door.

FROM: COMMANDER THIRD FIELD FORCES
TO: COMMANDER "S" CO. 75TH INFANTRY RANGER, PLEIKU

ENGAGE ENEMY FORCES REFERENCE YOUR MESSAGE 121A. DELAY FLEEING ENEMY AS LONG AS POSSIBLE WITHOUT BECOMING DECISIVELY ENGAGED. MISSION IS TO CONTAIN AS MANY ENEMY AS POSSIBLE BEFORE ARRIVAL OF LARGER FRIENDLY FORCE. CONDUCT DELAY ORDER COMMENCING 0800 *TOMORROW*.

The G-3 walked back up the stairs slowly. *I told him I'd do it; I just didn't say when. At least those poor bastards will now have some time to get out . . . I hope.*

John Colven looked at his watch and back at the map. It was getting late—1812 hours. The teams would be moving to their night laagers. They had done well. They had found enough to keep the incoming brigade busy for quite a while. The message he'd received a few hours before from Corps worried him, however. The teams would have to move to positions to ambush the roads, but they would also have to position themselves close to a PZ.

"Shit," he said aloud. He turned toward Childs, who looked up from the report he was reading. "Jerry, I don't like this." He held the message out. "It's cuttin' things too damn close."

Childs stood and walked toward the map. "I know, sir. With us ambushin' at oh-eight-hundred and the fourth not coming in until oh-nine-hundred, we might get into a lotta shit without any help."

Colven shook his head disgustedly and looked at the teams' locations.

"We can't do this delay crap! Hell, it's crazy: The teams don't have the ammo and they're too small for that kind of mission. What we'll do is have the six teams that found camps to ambush wherever the team leader thinks he can do the most damage and yet have time to get to a pickup site."

"What about the six teams that came up dry?"

"We'll have them move to PZs at first light tomorrow. We can pick up a few of them prior to the zero-eight-hundred ambushes."

"That makes sense, John, but it still sucks hind tit. This gun-and-run business is risky shit. We gotta tell those teams to hit 'em hard, throw gas, and get the hell out."

Colven sighed heavily as he turned around. "Jerry, take care of sending out the new orders to the teams . . . just make sure they know timing is critical."

Childs looked into his major's concerned eyes. "They'll do all right, sir. They're probably itchin' to kill some of bastards anyhow."

Colven smiled. "Jerry, I'm glad you're here to keep me straight."

"Hell, John, I'm glad you're here to take the shit if we fuck it up. 'Course we won't, but it's nice to know you get it first anyway."

"Thanks."

"Don't mention it."

Sox whispered the message he'd received from X-ray.

Grady smiled. "Gun and run." They would move just before light and set up at the edge of the camp and open up on the trucks if they were still there, then move to the PZ, which he knew was only a klick farther to the east. He leaned over and whispered the good news to the others.

Corporal Trung Ly Vee lit the kerosene lamp and turned the wick up slightly. Luc turned on the radio and opened the small bottle of rice wine. Vee picked up his pack and placed it on the desk.

"My friend, prices are up, but I was able"—he paused as he reached into the dirty khaki bag—"to purchase some fried pork fat and"—he placed some green-wrapped banana leaves on the table, then reached in again and took out a small package wrapped in red rice paper— "rice sweet cakes."

Luc whistled and unwrapped the pork. "It's too good to be true. You did well at the market, friend."

"Yes," said Vee proudly. "I also bought batteries for the radio and several other small items."

Luc bit into the delicacy, moaning in ecstasy.

The G-3 Air sat up quickly. "What was that unit again?"

"The 299th Aviation," answered the aviation liaison.

"They're at Plei Djereng and Pleiku now?" questioned Henley excitedly.

"Yes, sir." He looked at another paper. "Supporting Sierra Rangers."

"How many birds?"

"Four guns and . . . a total of six Slicks."

"Get them all!"

"But, sir, they're there to pull the Rangers if they get in trouble or—"

"Shit, I'll tell the colonel tomorrow to have those Rangers sit tight, and then they can go out on the choppers that bring the Fourth Division units in, right? Make sense?"

"Yes, sir, it does, but you need to leave them the guns for sure. If they get in trouble—"

"No, I'm going to need them, too, to prep the LZs. Okay, okay, I'll leave two—that's all. Now, we'll want those Slicks to be at Pleiku Airport at zero-eight-hundred, so assign them to us effective zero-seven-thirty tomorrow. You'll contact them first thing in the morning, right?"

"Yes, sir, otherwise there'll be a fight on your hands tonight with the Ranger commander."

"Okay. Let's find some more birds. What's the next unit you've got there on your list?"

The dark An Khe airfield was a restless sea of humanity. The Fourth Division's Fifth Brigade soldiers lay on their rucksacks, trying to sleep and fight the marauding mosquitoes.

The brigade's battalions had been moved in late that afternoon to organize into loads. The next morning they would be picked up by C-130. Most had no idea where they were headed, but it was obviously going to be a big operation. The artillery units had been picked up at dusk by large double-rotored CH-47 helicopters and flown to Pleiku. The rotor wash of the Chinooks was the closest thing to a tornado that man could devise, and it wreaked destruction on the cursing infantrymen's poncho shelters and poncho liners. The gale-force winds covered the waiting men with biting red dust that seeped into everything, even watch crystals. It caked the men's food, weapons, teeth, and dispositions. Most fell to sleep dreaming of inflicting pain and misery—not on the enemy but on CH-47 pilots and artillerymen.

The An Khe Red Cross Center had been empty all day. Mary Ann and Sarah knew their Rangers were involved in whatever was going on. First Sergeant Demand had been closemouthed when they visited him the day before, but Mary Ann had heard from an officer at the Club that he'd heard the Rangers were in Pleiku on some kind of special operation. It was all the girls needed to hear. They had marched into Mrs. Sheppard's office earlier that day and explained that one-third of the division was on its way to Pleiku, and they had volunteered to go along to provide for recreational and morale needs. After all, they'd pleaded, at least one team of girls should go to show that the Red Cross cared and was ready to provide assistance when needed. Mrs. Sheppard had given in easily and had begun making the necessary arrangements.

The women were packing. Sarah boxed assorted games and cards, while Mary Ann bagged stationery and Kool-Aid packets. Suddenly Mary Ann looked up from her bag and laughed raucously.

Sarah glanced up. "What's so funny?"

"You are. Look at you! A couple of weeks ago, you were . . . well, you . . . Sarah, I'm your friend, so I can say it: You weren't really one of us. You were just here filling a space. But now it's like you're a different person. You really seem to enjoy the work now."

Sarah sat on the floor and stared at Mary Ann sadly. "Was I that bad?"

Mary Ann nodded timidly and shrugged. "Sorry. But what's happened to change you? Has it got anything to do with a Ranger sergeant?"

Sarah shook her head. "I don't know. I just know I don't feel the same way about these soldiers as I did before. I guess I'm beginning to feel that I'm really doing something worthwhile. I can talk to these young men and find what they're proud of or what they like and . . . and you know, it makes me feel good when they smile and talk to me about things."

Mary Ann patted Sarah on the shoulder. "Yes, I do. I do know."

Colven sat up. He couldn't sleep. He had had Dove bring a cot up to Operations that afternoon so he'd be close to the radios. He stood and walked to the doorway. As he walked through the door he was surprised to hear a growl. He glanced down and saw a sleeping man rolled up in a poncho liner by the wall. Next to the man stood a small dog. Her low growl brought a smile to the major's lips.

"It's only me, Bitch," said Colven, bending over and patting the playful pup. *Dove, you're a crazy bastard*, thought Colven affectionately. *You're up here looking out for me, aren't you, son? You're taking care of me like you always do . . . like your dog, there, looks out for you.*

Colven shook his head and walked down the darkened hallway to the operations room, where Childs sat at a table playing cards with Johnson, the radio operator.

Childs threw down two cards. "Gimme four."

"You only put down two," protested Johnson.

"I know, but I need four to beat your ass." Childs glanced up and saw the major in the doorway. "Shit, sir, did we wake you?"

"No, I just couldn't sleep. What time you got?"

"Little past midnight. You better get some rest. Tomorrow is going to be busy."

"Anything from the teams?"

"No, sir, it's all quiet. You go on to bed and get some rest."

Colven began to turn but stopped and looked back at the sergeant. "Why the hell are *you* up? You ought to be in bed too."

"Aw, shit, sir, us old NCOs never sleep. Plus, I wanted to win some of Johnson's money."

Colven winked at Johnson. "How much he owe you so far?"

"About twenty bucks, sir."

"You never could play cards, Jerry. You better get some rest before you go broke."

Colven waited in the doorway for his sergeant, and the two men walked down the hall together. Childs saw Dove and the dog by the major's office door and shook his head.

"The beach boy is some guard, ain't he?"

Colven stopped at the door and looked down at the sleeping driver. "Jerry, I like that kid. He reminds me of my son."

The sergeant paused and glanced down. "I know, sir. The damn beach boy kinda grows on you. Get down, ya goddamn dog. Down, damn it!"

The specialist fourth class put down the telephone and re-read the weather report he'd just received. He got up and walked over to the major who was Corps's night-duty officer.

"Sir, this just came in from the Air Force weather people. They said it's a revised report."

The major looked at the paper, then focused on one sentence that caused him to read it a second time. ". . . dense fog in the An Khe area in the early morning hours, burning off in the later hours. . . ."

The major looked up and walked quickly to the phone operator. "Get me the Air Force liaison!" He turned back toward the specialist. "Run over and get Lieutenant Colonel Henley, the G-3 Air. Tell him we got problems and I need his help. He's in the officers' hootch in the next compound."

The specialist could tell the major was concerned by his tone, but why? he wondered. So what if it was foggy? No big thing. He jogged down one flight of stairs and out into the compounds.

19

Bud Sikes shivered as he looked down on the dark green land where white-gray clouds of morning mist nestled in wispy patches. The sun was not quite up, but its rays had begun lighting the eastern sky. It looked so quiet and beautiful, he thought as they crossed over the brown waters of the Se San River.

"Bud . . ." said Larry releasing the floor mike.

Sikes broke from his trance. "What's up?"

"You got some crackers or something? I didn't get a chance to eat."

Bud laughed. "Well, well, you kid the kid about his chow, and now you ain't kidding the kid." He took the box of ginger snaps he had at his side, leaned forward, and tapped the pilot's helmet with the box.

"Ginger snaps! I hate ginger snaps. . . . I hate . . . these ain't bad, though," he said with his mouth full.

Bud leaned back and looked at his map, sighing. *It's gonna be one hell of a day,* he thought, seeing the red pencil marks depicting team locations. He and Captain Shane had stayed up most of the night working out the extraction schedule. It was decided by Major Colven that they would pull teams 1-4 and 2-3 and Wade's 2-1 team at first light. The Bird Dog and helicopters would then return to Plei Djereng, refuel, and wait until the teams blew their ambushes and ran to the pickup zones. He didn't like the idea of the teams' ambushing and then running. It was too risky with only two sets of gunships for support, but Colven had said they had no choice.

Bud took a deep breath and depressed his floor button.

"Stagecoach, this is Three-Alfa. Over." The radio crackled as the Slick pilot answered.

"This is Stagecoach Lead. We're all ready. Are your people standing by?"

"This is Three-Alfa. Roger, take up heading three two zero and let's do it."

"Roger, we're on the way."

0610 Hours

The red edge of the sun was just beginning to appear on the horizon as Salazar turned toward the sound of the helicopter.

"Birds inbound," he whispered to his waiting men, who were barely visible through the violet smoke that swirled skyward. "Get ready!"

Salazar shook his head and slapped his CAR-15 disgustedly. "Not a thing," he mumbled to himself. "Didn't find a damn thing . . . god damn it."

The Slick popped up over the trees and dipped its tail. Salazar yelled over the loud whopping noise, "Move it!"

Bud watched as the Slick lifted, banked left, and turned for the border. *One down,* he thought. *Okay, One-Four, you're next, baby.* "One-Four . . . One-Four, stand by with smoke."

A faint voice came through his headphones, answering, "Standing by."

Larry Wine turned the Bird Dog south and gained altitude. Bud called the other waiting Slick and gunships that were circling a checkpoint six klicks away.

"Stagecoach Three take up heading two seven zero and I'll pick you up in five minutes over the river."

"Roger."

0622 Hours

Jungle Jim Stanley, team sergeant of 1-4, pulled out a smoke canister and held it ready. The day before, they had found a major road but no base camps. They'd moved to a PZ that evening, laagering for the night. Now they stood ready to be lifted out. The radio operator had the handset pressed to his ear and looked up at his team sergeant.

"He says Pop Smoke."

Jungle Jim pulled the pin and tossed the smoke grenade a few feet in front of him. The canister popped, then hissed out a dark yellow cloud.

"Five hundred meters . . . 250 . . . begin flare now. . . ."

"I got yellow smoke. Going in."

Bud watched as the bird flared and began its rapid decent. In seconds it began its lift-off and turned east. As it began to gain altitude the sky around it erupted in red flashes.

"Son of a bitch," yelled Bud upon seeing the tracers arcing up. "They're under fire!"

The radio immediately buzzed with excited voices. "We're hit! We're hit!"

"Bank left. We're rolling in hot."

"The fuckers are everywhere. . . . Break left! Break left!"

The lead gunship fired four rockets toward the red flashes. Suddenly more tracers from two other locations crisscrossed in front of the Slick. It banked and dipped, trying desperately to avoid the fiery streaks that followed its every movement. The gunships' rockets exploded in orange-scarlet bursts, sending up billowing clouds of dark smoke. The second gunship streaked in, and its 40mm cannon pumped destruction into the hidden gun positions. The slick steered hard left, turning on its side before righting itself and gaining altitude. The tracers moved across the sky toward the gunships.

"Gun lead breaking. . . . They're in. . . . We're hit!"

"Lead . . . Lead, break right! You're receiving fire!"

Bud sighed, seeing the tracers stop and the three helicopters climbing for more altitude. None were smoking or showed loss of power.

"Three-Alfa, this is Stagecoach-Three. We took some bad ones. Three of your men and my crew chief are hit. Looks like we lost the chief and one of yours. We're going straight to Pleiku Hospital. Sorry, Three-Alfa."

Bud answered quickly, "Understand two KIA, two WIA, one serious. What's your bird status?"

"We took hits through the belly. We'll have to set down to inspect damage. We won't be back for a while."

"This is Gunslinger Lead. We took hits in the tail and will have to set down at Plei Djereng to take a look."

"Roger," said Bud, leaning back, trying to think what the implications would be on the rest of the extractions. He depressed the switch and spoke calmly. "Stagecoach-Three, Gunslinger Lead, we'll need you back ASAP. We got a bunch of folks depending on you. Give me a call as soon as you inspect your birds."

"This is Stagecoach-Three. Understand. Will do, buddy."

"This is Gunslinger Lead. We'll be back."

Bud's thoughts turned to the speeding helicopter that held the team. The two dead men would be lying on the vibrating floor. The wounded would be lying beside them as the other team members worked feverishly to keep them alive. The roar of the engine would drown out their screams, and the open cabin's wind would blow their blood inward. The floor would be slick and sticky . . . like . . . like . . . He looked down at the plane's floor, and he could see Bob Celeste's coagulating blood on his boots. "Oh God, no . . . no!"

"Bud . . . Bud!"

Sikes shut his eyes and pulled his head up. "Yeah."

"You okay? You got Wade's team talking to you."

Bud could now hear the voices in headphones. ". . . Alfa. Three-Alfa, this is Two-One. Over."

Bud shook his head to clear his mind and depressed the floor button. "This is Three-Alfa. Go."

"This is Two-One. We cannot be picked up. I say again, *cannot* be picked up. We got dinks on the road only three hundred meters away. We'll have to wait."

"Shit," mumbled Sikes before answering. "Give us a call when clear."

"Roger. This is Two-One out."

0710 Hours

Colven paced back and forth in front of the map. The teams that were ambushing were all in position except for team Two-Five. One of their soldiers had sprained an ankle on the way to their ambush position. Colven had told X-ray to inform Two-Five to abort the mission and move to a PZ. It was too dangerous to have a limping man holding them back if they had to run.

Colven stopped and turned to Childs, who was posting the map. "Where is Lieutenant Sikes now?"

"He's at Plei Djereng, refueling. He'll be up again in a few minutes. The choppers are all sitting, waiting for the word to go up. We don't want them up too soon or we'll run into refueling problems."

"Okay, I understand. What about the ships that were hit?"

"They're both flyable and are reporting back."

"Thank God. . . . All we needed was to be short a gunship and Slick."

Childs nodded in agreement, turning back to the map.

0720 Hours

The general was fuming. "You mean not a single C-130 has landed?"

Lieutenant Colonel Henley said quietly, "No, sir, it's still too socked in."

The general slammed his hand on the desk. "How far behind does this put us?"

"I'd say within the next thirty minutes if this fog lifts like it's supposed to. We'll get the first troops on the ground in Cambodia at ten-thirty or so."

The general's face flushed as he turned to the other colonel and pointed a finger at him. "Howard, what are we going to do?"

The G-3 looked up slowly. "We fall back to the alternate plan of putting only two battalions in today, plus the artillery. Tomorrow we put the Third Battalion in at first light."

The general paced in front of them. "There goes the biggest operation of the war. . . . Damn it! Goddamn Air Force wouldn't come in."

Henley smiled inwardly. It was the best thing that could have happened, he thought.

The general turned. His face was still red. "Well, this is just like any other operation, then. Howard, you and General Burton fly out there and show Corps interest.

"Yes, sir, I'll tell the general now. We'll leave in twenty minutes. We'll have to take your bird, sir."

The general didn't hear. He was busy looking through other papers. He looked up at the standing men. "Well, go on."

The colonels saluted and walked out. Both took deep breaths after leaving his office. The G-3 turned to Henley. "I'll tell General Burton he's going to the field. I'll bet he'll be thrilled to get out of here. You call and get the general's bird here in fifteen minutes." Henley nodded and thought of the word *bird*. He remembered he was going to tell the colonel something about choppers, but he couldn't remember what it was. The G-3 walked off, leaving Henley in thought. *Damn, what was it I was going . . .? Oh, yeah, I took the choppers away from the Rangers. That's it!* He began walking down the steps to tell the G-3, but remembered he had to call about the general's helicopter. He turned around and went into the aide's office.

"Harry, call the aviation unit and tell them to send the general's bird over now."

The aide looked up from his magazine and picked up the telephone. Just then General Wayland walked out from his office and, upon seeing Henley, said coldly, "Henley, get into my office and explain to me again why the Air Force wouldn't come in this morning."

"Yes, sir, I need to talk to Howie before he goes and then I'll—"

"Now, god damn it! I'm sending a message to Region Headquarters."

"Yes, sir."

The general turned and walked back into his office. Henley quickly scribbled out a note and handed it to the aide who was talking to the aviation unit, then walked in and shut the door.

The lieutenant hung up the phone and looked at the note, which said:

Tell the G-3 I pulled the Rangers' choppers effective 0730 and that they should get picked up on the 4th's birds when they go in.

Henley

The aide stood before realizing that the secretary wasn't there yet. He couldn't leave the desk because he had to answer the telephones. She'd be in at 0800. He set the note down and picked up his magazine again.

0740 Hours

The helicopters had just refueled when the aviation battalion assistant operations officer walked over to flight lead. "You guys got orders to get to Pleiku and pick up the troops coming in from the Fourth."

The warrant officer shook his head. "No, we're assigned here with the Rangers. They're gettin' pulled out in just a few minutes."

The captain held out a piece of paper. "The message says the Rangers have now been told to sit tight and wait until the Fourth Division troops arrive and come out with the returning birds."

"I'll be damned," said the young warrant. "I wish the goddamn higher-ups would make up their minds."

The captain smiled. "Yeah, I know what you mean. Ours is not to reason why, only to go and fly."

The warrant laughed and yelled to the other crews, "Hey guys, saddle up. We got another mission. The Rangers have been told to cool it until we bring the grunts in!"

The crews hurried to their helicopters and cranked them up. The captain walked over to the gun pilots, who were another hundred yards down the runway at the rearming pad, and gave them the same orders he'd given the others. He then asked the pilots where the Ranger operations was; he wanted to drop by and make sure they knew they wouldn't get picked up until 1030 because of the fog delay at An Khe. The gun pilot who was remaining told him to go across the runway and down four hundreds meters. The captain turned to leave but then stopped.

"Hey, where can I get some coffee?" The pilot reached into the cockpit and picked up his Thermos.

"Right here, Captain. Sit down and have a cup of the worst ever made."

"I don't care as long as it wakes me up."

"Well, if it don't kill ya, it'll sure do that!"

0755 Hours

Grady had moved the team into position along the banana grove and assigned each man his targets. Thumper, who was the farthest left, was to shoot his M-79 grenades into the supply hootch, the headquarters hut, and finally the two fully loaded trucks. Ben, positioned in the middle, was to rake the barracks with his M-60 machine gun as the men streamed out. The others were to shoot at targets of opportunity.

They were all going to fire for two minutes and pull back when Grady blew his whistle. Thumper laid out eight high-explosive rounds in front of him before looking up at his target again. There was a group of ten men lined up behind the supply hut. Six others sat in the back of the loaded trucks, as if they expected to leave soon. He lowered himself down and glanced at his watch: 0758.

Bud Sikes chewed his gum nervously as he looked at his radio toggle switches. He had decided not to call the Slicks and guns out until the teams had initiated their ambushes and begun to move to their PZs. Time was critical. If the helicopters circled while the teams were moving, precious fuel would be wasted. He could not afford to have a team waiting while a Slick refueled. The teams were to call when they were halfway to their PZs or were in trouble. Once Bud got the call, he would scramble the birds.

Bud glanced at his watch and immediately his stomach quivered. He stared out of the Plexiglas at the green morass below, knowing that within seconds death would come violently, quickly turning the morning calm into a living hell. Those who survived would be left with invisible scars forever.

Bud shut his eyes and listened for the first radio messages.

Corporal Trung Ly Vee handed out two medical kits to the newly arrived squad and yelled back inside the hut for two more. There was no response. He shrugged his shoulders at the senior sergeant in front of him and walked up the steps. Luc was not at his desk. He picked up two kits, but then heard his private's voice coming from the front entrance.

Vee walked to the doorway and looked down at his friend,
who was talking to an old woman. Luc, seeing his corporal
in the doorway, pointed at the woman and shook his head in
disgust.

"She says she wants more money for washing our
clothes."

Vee smiled. "Tell her we—" The corporal was suddenly
propelled from the door by a shattering blast. Luc and the
screaming woman fell to the ground as the debris and smoke
quickly covered them.

Thumper rose up and fired again as the rest of the team
raked the running, confused men unmercifully. A truck, hit
in the gas tank and leaking fuel, caught fire and exploded in a
raging inferno.

0810 Hours

The first C-130 landed with a roar and taxied down the An
Khe airfield. Waiting soldiers of the Fourth Division who
lined the runway in assigned loads yelled out a cheer. They
had played the old Army ritual of "Hurry up and wait" long
enough. The men had been told earlier that morning that
they were going to Cambodia, and they now stood ready to
board. Five more of the camouflaged planes circled above
them, waiting to land.

Sarah and Mary Ann sat by a CH-47 Chinook that would
be taking helicopter parts to the aviation battalion at Pleiku.
The two girls chatted with a door gunner as the last of the
boxes was loaded. The crew chief waved for them to load up.
The two women picked up their awkward boxes and ran excitedly to the whining chopper.

"Three-Alfa . . . Three-Alfa, this is One-One. We're fifteen Mikes from the PZ. Over!"

Sikes had monitored all the teams' initial calls of contact
and was circling over the Se San River. He depressed the
floor switch and called the helicopters. "Stagecoach and
Gunslinger, this is Three-Alfa. Over."

"This is Gunslinger. Over."

"Crank 'em up. Teams are almost at PZs. Over!"

There was a long silence before the gun pilot answered again, "Three-Alfa, there must be a screw-up. The Slicks and one set of guns left for Pleiku fifteen minutes ago."

"What? . . . They can't . . . My God, I've got teams running!"

"We're cranking now, Three-Alfa, but it's just me and my wing man. We got word you were not initiating."

Captain Shane, who had been monitoring the radio, quickly picked up the handset and called Bud. "Three-Alfa, this is Zero-Three. I'll . . . Wait, the aviation ops officers just walked in. We'll straighten it out!"

A few anxious seconds passed before Shane's voice came through the headphones. "Three-Alfa, Corps has pulled the Slicks! I say again, Corps has released the Slicks! We've got to contact Corps to get them back. Inform teams of the situation ASAP."

Bud's mind raced with the implications of the horrible news. The teams would be running to PZs that they couldn't use. The Dinks knew they were there and would be swarming, looking for them. Bud felt as if he had been hit between the eyes. He pulled out his map. There were not many PZs available to the teams, which meant they would have to try and run for the border or hide until the birds could come in.

"God damn it!" he yelled, throwing down the map and depressing the floor button. "I need birds *now*! Get me anything, but, damn it, get something. . . . The teams are running, for God's sake!"

Shane spoke coldly into the handset: "Three-Alfa, inform the teams of situation. Get control, Three-Alfa, there is nothing available. I will call rear base and have the Ol' Man get us birds, but you must inform the teams!"

Bud was shaking with rage and was about to answer when an out-of breath-voice came through his headphones. "Three-Alfa, this is One-Three, we're almost at PZ. Need Slick. Over."

Bud felt like crying as he depressed the floor button to tell the waiting team there would be no helicopter.

Luc lay next to Corporal Vee and gently touched his head. Vee sat up and blinked his eyes. The shooting coming from behind the hut made him spin around and lie back down. "What happened?" he asked, shaking his head.

"We're under attack," Luc said. "You were knocked from the doorway by an explosion in the hut, but you have no wounds."

Vee felt himself. He was still numb but happy to be otherwise unhurt. He rolled over onto his stomach and looked in the direction of the firing. He could see flashes from the banana grove some thirty meters away. The headquarters building was on fire, as were the trucks. Dead and wounded soldiers lay everywhere.

Luc, seeing that his friend was alert, crawled backward, unnoticed by his corporal. Vee watched as several men ran from the cadre barracks and were immediately shot down. He looked back at the banana grove. He could make out the distinct flashes of the firing machine gun. From the corner of his eye he saw a soldier run across the red dirt field. It was Luc! "No . . . no, Luc, no!"

Luc fell to the ground and rolled to the edge of the grove.

Thumper had seen the soldier run across the field and swung his weapon around. He couldn't use the M-79 at such short range, so he pulled his .45 from its shoulder holster. The soldier fell ten feet in front of him and slowly looked up as if searching for a target. Thumper rose to one knee and fired. The small soldier was thrown back violently as the bullet shattered his collarbone. A shrill whistle blast cut through the air. Thumper got to his feet and was again leveling his pistol at the man when he saw another soldier running directly toward him. He ran stiffly, his face contorted in fear. He had no weapon, yet kept running until he fell in front of the wounded soldier and tried to pick him up. Thumper stepped closer, dropped to one knee, and aimed at the soldier's head. The young Vietnamese looked up at the huge American. Thumper's finger began to squeeze but suddenly released the trigger.

"Thumper! Thumper, come on!" yelled Ben from behind him. Thumper stared into the large brown eyes of the brave soldier, then raised his pistol and brushed the brim of his hat in a salute. He turned and ran for the others.

Trung Vee watched the large soldier as he disappeared into the forest before looking down at his friend. Luc's shoulder was bleeding profusely. Vee ripped the shirt open and put pressure on the gaping hole to stop the bleeding.

Sox reported the contact and said they were running for the PZ. Then he got the bad news over the radio. He ran faster to catch up with Grady and grabbed him by the shoulder. "No Slick!"

0835 Hours

"Who pulled the Seventy-fifth Rangers' Slicks?" Colven was seething as he talked to the corps duty officer on the telephone. "I said, *who pulled my damn Slicks?*"

The voice on the other end stammered, "Wait, I'll check, sir. Stand by."

Childs stood only a few feet from Colven. Childs was talking on the radio to the aviation unit: ". . . Look, I got teams in deep shit. I need Slicks now! Over."

"Understand your situation, but have no Slicks. Every Slick is committed. Over."

"Do you have any scout ships or log birds? Shit, I'll take anything."

"Roger, we have two Loaches, but they're here for maintenance. Over."

"I'll take 'em. Get them to Plei Djereng ASAP. Look, we're going to straighten out this Slick screw-up with Corps. Be ready to get the Slicks back to us."

"Will do. Understand. Out."

Lieutenant Colonel Henley pointed a finger at the duty officer. "You tell Major Colven, 'By order of the corps commander, that's fuckin' who!' And no, I'm not releasing those helicopters. Those damn Rangers are just going to have to suck it up and wait till the Fourth arrives."

The young major shook his head at the tired lieutenant colonel. "Sir, he's really pissed. He'll ask to speak to the general personally."

Henley's face turned red and he jumped up from his chair. "Tell him he is not available! I got better things to do than argue with a damn major. Tell him that Burton and the G-3 will be out there in twenty minutes or so. Tell him to take it up with them."

The major walked back into the ops center. He took a deep breath before picking up the telephone. "Hello, Major Colven, I'm to inform you—"

Sergeant Matt Wade peered over a gray rock and cursed under his breath. Fifty meters away was a road packed with enemy troops and civilians walking north. He lowered himself and turned to the helicopter pilot who lay beside him. "No way, it's too damn busy to try and cross. We're gonna have to sit tight."

The pilot smiled. "It doesn't matter to us that Slicks aren't available. We couldn't have used them anyway."

Wade spat a brown stream of tobacco juice over his shoulder, "Yes sir, for us maybe, but let me tell ya, the other teams are in deep shit. The Dinks have radios too, and right now are doing their damndest to find our guys."

"Your people can hide."

"Hide! Hide where? You saw the stuff we came through. It's open like a park, and we leave a trail through the damn soft ground. It don't take a hot-shot tracker to find anybody."

The pilot shook his head, "What will they do?"

"My guess is they'll try for the border or try and find some thick vegetation. They'll have to move fast and hope the Dinks don't have units between them and the border.

The pilot looked at Wade, "I just didn't realize how bad it was, sorry."

Wade spat again. "It's about as bad as you can get. I just hope they get some birds fast or . . . or . . ." He turned and peered over the rocks again without finishing. A large Russian Molotov truck was beeping its horn for the civilians to move out of the way.

0904 Hours

Sergeant Lawrence Kramer of team 1-1 never saw the men who lay waiting for them. The first burst of AK-47 caught the young sergeant in the head and chest. The NVA platoon had set up two ambushes in hopes of catching the raider unit that had attacked the base camp four miles away.

The remaining team members never got a shot off. The RTO fell wounded behind a tree and yelled into the radio handset for several seconds until a Chicom grenade exploded within feet of him.

Bud Sikes bolted upright in his seat when the frantic scream came through his headphones. "Oh, God, we're hit! We're hit. Team One-One hit! We're—" Sikes tried calling back for several minutes but got no response.

Corporal Vee helped carry his friend to a truck that had just arrived with an infantry platoon.

"Do you feel better?" he asked as they placed the litter in the back of the truck beside the other wounded.

Luc opened his eyes and tried to focus on the corporal. Vee smiled. "Maybe next time you will learn how to shoot your gun before charging the enemy."

Luc's jaw tightened, then relaxed. "You saved my life. . . . You . . ."

Vee lowered his eyes. "No, no. I'm no hero. I still do not know how I got to you. I was only—" The truck began moving. Vee jogged behind the vehicle for several seconds then yelled, "Take care, my friend."

Luc tried to wave, but the effort was too painful. He closed his eyes and said quietly, "Good-bye. Good-bye, my friend."

Vee stood in the middle of the road, watching the truck for several moments before turning and walking back to the camp. Eighteen bodies wrapped in ground cloths lay next to the smoking headquarters building. The destroyed trucks were still burning and sending ugly black clouds of smoke upward through the trees. A captain from the Forty-third Regiment had taken over the camp and was giving the newly arrived platoon instructions on finding the attackers. Vee was behind the formation of infantry when Sergeant Noi handed him a rifle.

"Corporal Vee, the platoon is sending five scouts and two of our Jari trackers out in front of the platoon. You are to go with them and ensure that the Jari return to the camp if the platoon decides to go farther."

"But, Sergeant, I am not infantry. I have never been in the forest around this camp. I know nothing of—"

"Corporal, you have been ordered! Report to Sergeant Von immediately. You are leaving in minutes."

0926 Hours

Sergeant Randy LePage of team 1-3 lay on a stream bank with his head in the water. He hoisted himself up, letting the water trickle down his neck and shoulders. He wasn't sure if he could move. His body still shook with fatigue from the grueling pace. One of his men had passed out just as they'd reached the stream, and another was in agony with leg cramps. The stream had been a lifesaver. *Jesus, we can't keep this up much longer,* he thought. He leaned forward and dipped his hand into the water to splash himself when shots rang out. He jumped up, grabbing his CAR-15. The montagnard scout he had posted on the bank for security was running toward him, yelling. On the other bank a small, wiry black man, the one they called the Rose, dived for cover in the brush. The sergeant yelled for the rest of his men to get behind a fallen tree that lay next to the stream. As he turned, bullets popped by LePage's ear. He ducked, spinning around. Twenty meters away, two North Vietnamese wearing dark gray uniforms were kneeling at the top of the bank.

LePage fired from the hip. The red tracers hit the ground in front of the kneeling men. He brought the barrel up, and the red streaks disappeared into one of them, knocking him off his feet. The other stopped shooting and fell back out of sight. The team members had reached the protection of the fallen tree. The sergeant ran and jumped over the log, falling on Allen, The RTO, who was trying to get the handset out of his rucksack. LePage got to his knees and pressed himself against the tree as more bullets slammed into the protective wood. He returned fire, yelling, "Rose! Rose!"

The Rose, whose real name was Specialist Flowers, heard the yell but couldn't move. Three NVA were directly behind him, talking excitedly. He lay in a water-filled depression, trying to stay hidden.

Allen had the handset pressed to his ear and was asking for help when a grenade fell within a few feet of him. He yelled, falling back as it exploded. The montagnard screamed and flopped onto the ground. LePage sat stunned, bleeding from his face and hands. Hettinger, the M-60 gunner, fired at the rushing NVA, who had begun their assault when the grenade exploded. His first burst caught two of the sweat-soaked enemy at the top of the bank. Both men were hit in the legs and slid down the bank to within ten feet of the gunner. He lowered his barrel and stitched both of them.

Allen stood up to fire, but bullets tore into the back of his legs. He spun around to see two Vietnamese rushing from down the creek. He fired until his weapon was empty. One NVA was hit, but the other continued his rush and was about to fire when he jerked and spun around, clutching his stomach. Sergeant LePage lowered his smoking CAR and tried to get to his knees.

The fallen tree that had been protecting the team suddenly shuddered and lurched upward in a shattering explosion. The Rose had heard the swishing sound of the RPG-40 rocket and had shut his eyes. The first blast was followed by two similar explosions that shook the ground beneath him. "Son of a bitch," he said to himself as he opened his eyes.

There was no more shooting. The rockets had ended the resistance. Bodies lay torn and unrecognizable. No piece of equipment or weapon was left intact. There would be no trophies for the searching NVA soldiers to claim.

As he slowly crawled out of the depression the Rose heard voices. He peered from behind a tree down into the creek bed. A thin layer of mist hung over the dead like a ghostly cloud. Eight North Vietnamese were busy carrying their dead and wounded to a flat spot directly below him. Within a minute the soldiers were picking over belongings and digging in the soft earth.

Rose put down his M-16 and took two grenades from his pistol belt. He pulled the pins, held down the spoons, and slowly rose up on his knees. He tossed the grenades down the bank, grabbed his weapon, and rolled behind a tree. The grenades blew simultaneously. He jumped to his feet and ran down the bank, firing at four stunned survivors. Two jerked and were flung backward with the impact of bullets. The other two ran. Rose shot one of the soldiers in the buttocks, spinning him around. Rose tried to shoot again, but his weapon was empty. The second soldier was hobbling away and had just reached the creek bed when Rose caught up to him and slammed his rifle butt savagely into his back. The soldier screamed in pain and fell into the water. Rose threw his arms around the man's neck, yanking up as he drove his knee down into the NVA's back. The soldier's neck popped with a loud crack. Rose released the lifeless body, picked up an AK-47, and started to stand when bullets cracked by his head.

The soldier who had been shot in the buttocks had reached a weapon and had shot at Rose on full automatic. The bullets had gone high. Rose stood when he heard the metallic click of the bolt slamming forward in the empty chamber.

The wounded man hurriedly reached down for another magazine. When he glanced up, he saw the black soldier walking slowly toward him. His eyes widened as Rose brought the AK-47 to his hip and fired. Rose kept his finger on the trigger and held the recoiling weapon tightly as he pumped rounds into the other NVA. One soldier moaned as the bullets shattered his kneecap.

Rose emptied the magazine, bent down, and took another magazine from a blood-splattered body. He fired again, putting a bullet into the head of each man.

Rose stood up after putting the last weapon in place. He walked over to the creek and washed the blood from his hands. He had picked up his mutilated friends and placed them side by side. He had stuck their broken weapons into the ground, placing their jungle hats on the stocks. He picked up the AK-47 and the extra magazines and turned for a last look at his team. The small, muscular black soldier's face was repainted with camouflage, and his eyes were dry as he threw his comrades a final salute. The lone soldier walked up the bank, stopped, adjusted his ruck, and checked the Chinese automatic. He straightened his back, took a deep breath, and began his hunt. He headed west, knowing the border was in the opposite direction.

0946 Hours

Captain Shane had received a message from Major Colven telling him that he had two small OH-58 observation helicopters coming to Plei Djereng to help with extractions. Shane now stood in front of the wall map, explaining to Sergeant Ingram his priorities for pulling the teams.

"First we have to pull the teams that are in the most trouble. That means the teams that ambushed and had to run. It looks right now as if we can pull only one team—the Double-Deuce. Teams One-One and One-Three—well, shit, it's too late for them. They're probably dead. Teams Three-Two and Three-Three, according to Bud, are at least an hour away from a pickup site. We'll get the Slicks that bring in the Fourth Division troops to pick up the other teams. The Fourth should be coming in at about ten-thirty."

Ingram nodded in agreement and pointed at the map. "At least we don't have to worry about Three-One and Two-Five. Their AOs are close enough to the border so they'll be able to cross the river."

"Yeah, at least they're relatively safe. Sergeant Wade's team is still in trouble, but he said they hadn't been spotted, so right now our concern is for Two-Two, Three-Two, and Three-Three."

Ingram looked at his watch and shook his head in disgust. "Bastards! Didn't they know we needed those Slicks? So far it's cost us fourteen men. Fourteen! And we still have another thirty minutes until the Slicks are available! How many more will we lose in that time?"

Shane shook his head without answering and walked over to listen to the radio.

Ben shifted the M-60 on his lap and took another long drink from his canteen. Rock passed his half-filled canteen to Fon Tay and turned toward Grady, who was looking at his map.

"What we gonna do, Grade?"

Grady didn't answer for several seconds. Finally he raised his head. "Looks like we're about ten klicks from the river. We'll head straight for it."

Rock looked up at the treetops. "The defoliant sure worked in this area. The tops are all dead."

Grady glanced up and then turned and looked in the direction from which they'd come. "Yeah, and it sure makes it easy for the dinks to follow us. The underbrush is thick because it's getting sunlight. We're making a trampled path."

Rock shook his head in agreement. "Shit, we best get goin' then. I'll—"

Sox suddenly leaned over and handed Grady the handset. "Fella, here, says he's got us some choppers."

Grady grabbed the handset as Rock clapped Thumper on the back. "Hey, we're gettin' out after all!"

Corporal Trung Ly Vee slowed to a stop. He just couldn't keep the pace the trackers and scouts were setting as they jogged through the underbrush. Minutes before they had stopped when they had found an American canteen. Vee had hoped for a rest, but they had continued their grueling pace. He wiped the perspiration from his eyes and watched the seven men disappear into the forest. He couldn't keep up, but he could follow easily enough. The scouts were marking a trail for the platoon, which was only ten minutes behind.

Vee took another swallow from his canteen and began walking the beaten-down path.

1001 Hours

Major Colven paced back and forth in front of the aviation battalion commander's desk as the lieutenant colonel talked on the phone. Colven turned toward the colonel as he concluded his conversation and hung up.

"John, the corps G-3 Air, a Lieutenant Colonel Henley, pulled your birds effective zero-seven-thirty this morning. There was a screw-up of some kind because you were supposed to have received the word too."

Colven slammed his hand on the colonel's desk, "A screw-up! *A screw-up* is what they said? That, sir, is an understatement. It's a goddamn disaster!"

The colonel stood, knowing there was nothing that either of them could do to right the error. It was too late. "John, the first choppers that take in the Fourth are yours."

Colven sighed deeply, and he thanked the colonel for finding out what had happened. He walked for the door.

Dove was waiting in the jeep outside. He had a radio in the back seat and was monitoring the traffic to keep his major up-to-date on developments. Bitch sat next to the radio, listening to its hum and static.

Colven hopped into the front seat. "What's happening now?"

"Sir, the Bird Dog called a few minutes ago. The Double-Deuce is almost at the PZ and should be picked up within a few minutes."

"Good, that leaves only three more teams in trouble."

"Sir, did you find out what happened?"

Colven's jaw and neck muscles tightened as he looked at his driver and nodded slightly. Dove started the jeep and pulled out onto the road. The major's look told him he had found out why, and it also told the young driver that whoever was responsible was going to wish he were dead if his major ever got ahold of him.

The jeep rolled down a road next to Pleiku Airport. Three C-130s were parked and unloading Fourth Division soldiers. Colven pointed to the field adjacent to the runway where rows of helicopters sat. "Those are the Slicks that will bring in the invasion force."

Dove nodded but didn't speak. He was concentrating on listening to the radio transmission from the Bird Dog to Captain Shane. Grady's team had arrived at the PZ and the choppers were five minutes out.

Sarah and Mary Ann threw their boxes into the backseat of the jeep and climbed aboard. "Will you take us to where the Rangers are, please?" asked Sarah sweetly.

The driver pushed back his jungle hat and scratched his head as if confused. "Ma'am, I was sent down here from the Red Cross office and told to pick up two Doughnut Dollies. They said I was to bring you back. They have some rooms assigned for you and—"

"Could you take us by the Ranger unit first?" asked Mary Ann impatiently.

The nineteen-year-old soldier shook his head. "I can't do that, ma'am, 'cause I don't have the foggiest idea where it is. I only drive around the airbase here, and it's all aviation units mostly."

Sarah got out of the jeep. She spoke over her shoulder, "Mary Ann, I'll call the Red Cross office and get the number of— Look!"

Mary Ann turned just in time to see a jeep drive by. She didn't see the passengers' faces, but she saw the black berets. "Who was it?"

"Major Colven!" shrieked Sarah, jumping back into the jeep and poking the driver. "Follow that jeep!"

The soldier shook his head. "I . . . I don't know. I'm supposed to—"

Mary Ann stood up in the backseat and leaned over the driver's shoulder, grabbing the steering wheel. "Move over, I'm driving."

The soldier hopped out and started to climb into the backseat when Mary Ann popped the clutch and left the startled man in a cloud of dust and gravel.

Double-Deuce had been at the bomb crater for several minutes. It was half filled with green stagnant water, and uprooted trees lay along its sides. Five meters from the hole were gray skeletonlike stumps, emaciated and twisted with torn tops. Still farther away stood trees that had been mortally damaged, their branches bare like oaks in winter.

The Bird Dog circled overhead. Sox sat on the lip of the crater and held the handset to his ear. Orders came to stand by to pop smoke. Grady stood up and told the team to start moving in. Fon Tay was posted ten meters in front of Ben and Rodriguez, who lay behind an uprooted tree. The montagnard was watching the path they had made. When he heard Grady, he stooped to pick up his pack. A branch snapped, and Fon Tay looked up. He only had time to wince before the Jari tracker, kneeling fifteen feet in front of him, fired. Fon Tay was flung back against a tree and was shot again. Ben jumped up and swung his M-60 toward the sound. Bullets filled the air around him, one hitting his shoulder and knocking him down. Rodriguez came up firing and caught the tracker changing magazines. The Jari screamed as he fell to the ground, hit in the thigh and hip. The Puerto Rican ducked as the uprooted tree cracked and splintered with the impact of additional automatic fire. He screamed frantically at Ben, who was rising again to shoot. Rodriguez fired a burst but was suddenly thrown backward, hit in the face. Ben had just grabbed his M-60 when Rodriguez fell on him. The huge soldier shook with anger as he rolled his friend off and stood up. A remaining Jari tracker and an NVA scout ran toward the uprooted tree, thinking the defenders were dead. Their eyes widened in horror as a huge dark skinned apparition rose from behind the tree and leveled a short-barreled machine gun at them. Ben squeezed the trigger, methodically pulling the barrel from left to right. The deadly spray of lead ripped into the rushing men, violently jerking their bodies in a grotesque death dance.

Thumper and Rock had been on the other side of the crater when the first shots were fired, and they'd rushed to try to flank the attackers. Grady crawled to a thick jagged stump as bullets raked the ground around him and cracked over his head. Sox crawled into the crater and cautiously rose to spot the incoming fire. He was immediately struck in the neck and fell back into the water, gasping. Grady pulled the pin of a grenade and tossed it toward the shooting. When it exploded, he jumped up and ran to a nearby tree. He took out another grenade, pulled the pin, listened for an instant, tossed it, and fell to the ground.

Thumper peered around the tree trunk and saw two NVA scouts lying beside each other, shooting toward the crater. He brought up his M-79 and fired. The spin-stabilized grenade landed beside the closest soldier, exploding and knocking the scout over onto his stunned comrade. Rock stepped out from behind Thumper and pumped half of a magazine into the two men, finishing them off.

An eerie silence hung with the misty cloud of gunsmoke over the crater area. Grady stood up and was about to yell at the others to report when he heard a moan coming from the crater. He ran for it and jumped in, sinking to his knees in muck. He waded over to Sox, who lay against the bank, clutching his throat.

Grady felt a tingle of relief when he saw that the radioman's eyes were open. "Move your hands so I can check it out," he commanded.

Sox closed his eyes and dropped his hands away. Grady let out a sigh of relief when he saw the wound. He smiled as he unsnapped Sox's first-aid pouch. "You're lucky, buddy: It took a hunk out of the side of your neck muscle, but it didn't hit the artery."

"Grade! Grade, Ben and Pancho are hit!" yelled Thumper. Grady hurriedly placed a bandage on the wound. "Hold this tight," he said, taking Sox's hand and placing it on the dressing. Then Grady got to his feet.

Rock and Thumper were searching the foliage. Ben had said he'd heard something there and had gone to investigate.

Grady ran up to Ben, who was holding a dressing on the large muscle above his collarbone. Ben shook his head. "I'm okay. Check Pancho. He looks bad."

Grady knelt beside the small man and turned him over. Rodriguez uttered a loud moan. Rock and Thumper instinctively turned toward the sound. A wounded NVA scout, hiding in the dense vegetation, used the distraction to fire. Rock saw the movement from the corner of his eye and began to swing the light submachine gun around, but he suddenly felt heavy. His right side felt as if it had been hit with a baseball bat. He could see the shooting soldier but couldn't make his body respond to bring his weapon around. His mind fought through the pain and focused on the enemy soldier. His left arm jerked the weapon around, and he fired. The NVA scout's head snapped back and his jungle hat floated momentarily in midair before falling on his lifeless body. Rock toppled over.

"Rock's hit," yelled Thumper, running to his friend's side and turning him over.

"Shit," mumbled Grady, lifting himself off Rodriguez. To protect the Puerto Rican, Grady had fallen on him when the shooting had started. "How bad?" Grady then yelled, lifting Rodriguez's head to inspect the wound.

Thumper tore open Rock's shirt and quickly assessed at the damage. "He'll make it! The bullet ricocheted off his rib cage and lodged in his arm."

Grady examined the Puerto Rican's face. The bullet had entered through the chin and exited from the lower jaw. The sergeant quickly put his fingers into the semi-conscious man's mouth and raked out the broken teeth and splintered bone so he wouldn't choke, then leaned him forward so the blood wouldn't block his breathing.

Sox examined the radio and shut his eyes. The bottom of it had two bullet holes, which meant he had to have been on his stomach when it was hit. The only time he'd been on his stomach was when he had crawled into the crater. He knew that had the bullets not hit the radio they would have hit him in the head. Painfully the radioman bent over and kissed the dead radio. Then he heard the helicopter approaching.

The gunship flew over the crater at treetop level. Sox quickly picked up the smoke canister, pulled the pin, and tossed it behind him.

Grady heard the chopper and yelled to Sox to tell the lieutenant to bring the first Loach in. Sox tried to yell back that the radio was hit, but the effort was too painful. He held the bandage to his neck and ran to where Grady was kneeling.

"No radio," he whispered hoarsely to Grady, who was wrapping a bandage around Rodriguez's jaw.

Grady stood and yelled, "Thump, you and Rock stay where you are and secure the path." He looked toward Ben. "Those small choppers only hold three or four people. When the first bird comes in, you, Pancho, and Sox get in. Me and the others will take Fon Tay's body out in the second chopper. Can you pick up Pancho and get him to the crater?"

Ben nodded and leaned the small Puerto Rican forward.

Corporal Trung Ly Vee was far behind the Jari trackers when he heard the firing. He fell to the earth and hid, shaking. He lay listening to the shooting and muffled explosions, telling himself to get up and move. When the firing stopped, his guilt overcame him. He stood up with tears in his eyes and walked slowly forward. When the shooting began again, it seemed very close. He lay down and continued crawling, determined not to be a coward and shame his ancestors. He knew they were watching him. The shooting stopped abruptly, and he could hear helicopters in the distance. He continued to crawl, knowing that the venerable ones would be pleased.

The small helicopter jockied into the small PZ and set down, one skid extending over the crater. Grady helped Ben support Rodriguez as he set him in the back of the chopper. Ben climbed in, but Sox stayed beside Grady. "Go on, Grade. I'll get the next bird."

Grady shook his head, yelling over the roar of the engine, "Get on." He turned toward Ben. "Take care of Pancho. See you—"

The pilot yelled at him, interrupting, but Grady couldn't hear what he'd said. He stepped closer as the pilot yelled again, "No more birds. The other Loach had a red light—hydraulic trouble."

Ben and Sox began to crawl out of the chopper, but Grady raised his CAR and pointed it at them. "Stay *on*." Turning toward the pilot, he commanded, "Get out of here!"

Ben stared into Grady's eyes as the helicopter lifted. There was so much to say, but only their eyes could express the deep friendship they shared. The chopper began its forward momentum. Ben held his thumb up. Grady smiled and returned the gesture just as the bird cleared the treetops and disappeared.

Pulling a map from his pocket, Grady yelled, "Thump, bring Rock. We gotta move."

Vee watched through the trees as the small helicopter landed. The view was partially blocked by trees, but it was an experience he would remember forever. He crawled closer as the machine churned the air. When the machine lifted off, the forest again became quiet. Suddenly he heard a foreign voice. Vee lay quietly, looking through the vines. A huge green-faced man rose from the ground twenty meters away. As Vee brought his rifle up slowly and aimed, his target bent over. Vee looked quickly to the side of the gun and saw that the big man was helping another soldier stand up. Vee aimed again at the larger target and pushed the safety off.

The green-faced American hefted his comrade to his feet and turned, looking at the path. Vee began to squeeze the trigger just as the larger man looked in his direction. Then Vee lowered his rifle. The big man turned, and supporting his comrade, began walking.

Vee brought his hand up and touched the edge of his hat in a salute. The man who had spared him would himself be spared. His act of mercy had been repaid. Vee smiled as he raised his rifle, aimed it high, and fired until empty. He'd now be able to say he shot at the Yankees. He crawled back ten meters, jumped up, and ran back in the direction from which he'd come.

Vee slowed to a walk, feeling good inside. He knew the venerable ones understood and were proud.

20

The three men splashed through the stream and fell heavily on the far bank, trying to catch their breaths. They'd been running for ten minutes, since the bullets had cracked over their heads. Grady and Thumper had half carried, half dragged Rock, who, despite his painful wounds, had gritted his teeth and remained silent.

Grady motioned for Thumper to guard behind them while he turned to inspect Rock's wounds. "We're gonna have to bind you up tight to keep pressure on the bandage."

Rock, pale from the exertion, nodded weakly. Grady opened his rucksack and pulled out his poncho. Cutting two strips from it, he wrapped one around Rock's chest and another around his arm.

"We gotta lighten up," Grady whispered to Thumper. "It's a good ways to the river."

Thumper pulled off his pack and began tossing out unneeded gear. Digging a hole in the creek bank with his hands and knife, Grady buried the excess items.

"We'll go up the creek. Stay in the water and don't step on the bank or mossy rocks," said Grady as he helped Rock to his feet. "Are you going to be able to walk?"

Rock forced a weak smile, "It ain't that bad. I can hang."

Grady patted his pale friend's shoulder. "Just take it easy, buddy. Thump, you take point, and use Rock's Sterling."

Seconds later the three men walked carefully up the small, meandering creek, heading east.

Pete handed the blue notebook to Dove. "I see you sent some money to Zit Towmey's ol' lady."

Dove put the notebook in his shirt pocket and picked up his whining dog. "Yeah, a week ago. Like I told you before, we gotta take care of our own. It's a good thing Zit stayed in An Khe, or he'd never have gotten to go."

"You don't have to try and fool me, Dove. I know you told Top to hold him back, that you were taking care of getting him to R&R."

Dove eyed the bespectacled private for a moment. "You listened at the door, huh?"

"Of course. I'm the company clerk. I have to know everything."

"See, Pete! See, you're perfect to take over for ol' Dove. You're smart like me and . . . and slick. Real slick!"

Pete laughed but noted the concern in Dove's eyes. He asked quietly, "Anything else on Grady?"

Dove kicked at a rock and bent over to let the dog go. "Naw, but I'll bet they're skying for the river. They'll make it. I know they will. You know Grady. He's the best. He'll get the guys back."

"What about those Red Cross girls who pulled in just after you did. They know some of our guys?"

Dove squatted down by his jeep and played with the pup. "Yeah, it was a pretty bad scene. They're the ones Grady and Thump had me deliver a message to before we left An Khe."

"Then they heard about the team too?"

"Yeah, the major told them. The blond sure took it bad. They're driving down to see Ben and the others at the hospital."

"How is the major taking it? I mean, the teams' getting hurt so bad and all."

"I'm worried about him," said Dove with a frown. "He's feeling helpless. He tries to keep it inside him, but I know he's hurting real bad. He's flying out to Plei Djereng as soon as he visits the guys in the hospital. Damn REMFs sure fucked this one up."

"I'm sorry, Dove. I . . . I know it bothers you too."

The curly-haired blond looked up and forced a smile. "I'm not worried. They'll make it."

Captain Ed Shane jogged down the steps of the shack toward the airfield. The once quiet, out-of-the-way Plei Djereng airfield had become a beehive of activity. The Fourth Division was moving in their support units and had already set up several large tents to house their operations center and briefing area. Hundreds of people were busily working, setting up tents and stacking equipment. A convoy had arrived from Pleiku and, combined with the new inhabitants, had churned up a huge red dust cloud that billowed over the base, turning everything within its choking mist a rust color.

Shane entered the Fifth Brigade's operation tent and walked over to the brigade S-3, who was annotating a map.

"Sir, I'm the ops officer for Sierra Rangers. I wanted to brief you on the current situation and coordinate the choppers that will be released to pick up my remaining teams." The preoccupied officer didn't look up until the captain said *released*.

"Yeah, the first flight. Well, it's all taken care of. The aviation battalion commander has already taken care of it. In fact, those birds should have gone in"—he looked at his watch—"five minutes ago. You Rangers sure did a helluva job finding those camps. Sorry to hear about the screw-up."

Relieved that the coordination had been taken care of, Shane thanked the colonel for his concern. As he turned to leave, the Fifth Brigade commander and General Burton walked in. Burton held out his hand. "Good to see you, Captain. The colonel briefed me a few minutes ago on your company's status. I guess some of our people didn't talk to each other. I've got the G-3 calling back to Corps to find out what happened."

Shane shook hands with the general and lowered his head, trying to hide his anger.

The general placed his hand on Shane's shoulder. "In big operations such as this one, things like this happen. It's sad, Captain, but it's true. Men who thought they were doing their best to make this operation work made a mistake. The mistake killed. There is nothing that can be done now, but don't ever forget it. One day you'll be planning such an operation, and this experience may help save others. I know it's not much, but it's all there is."

"I understand, sir."

"Good. We have a battalion from the 101st Airborne Division coming in tomorrow, and we're going to need your unit's help. There's a meeting here in an hour to discuss the operation, and I'll need you here."

"Yes, sir. But Major Colven will be the one you want to talk to. He'll be coming out after he visits the hospital."

"Fine. Have him come and see me as soon as he gets in. How many teams you still have in trouble?"

"Three, sir."

Captain Jean O'Neal sat at her desk, annotating a patient's files, when a corpsman pushed open the swinging doors and walked into her office, holding a mailbag.

Jean looked up as the corpsman set down several letters for the patients.

"Sorry, ma'am, no letter from your lieutenant Ranger today."

Jean smiled. "Burke, you probably read all the mail, don't you?"

The corpsman smiled before his expression became serious. "He's probably busy, ma'am, with that Cambodia invasion and all."

Jean's eyes widened and she stood up. Seeing her reaction, he quickly said, "I'm sorry, ma'am, I thought you knew. The notice went out this morning. You should have got one. It says we're to be prepared for overfill patients from Pleiku, and it lists the units that are taking part."

Jean remembered the notice, but she hadn't read it. Where had she put it? She quickly went through the stacked papers on the corner of the desk, finding it midway down. Not breathing, she read down the list. When she saw it, her heart seemed to stop. Sixth from the bottom was Seventy-fifth Infantry, Airborne Ranger, S Company. Jean put the paper down and shut her eyes. *Oh, Bud, please take care of yourself. Please, please.*

Bud Sikes turned in his seat and looked down at the large field below. There was no visible enemy guns, so he called team 3-2 and told them to pop smoke as soon as they arrived.

By the time he and Larry Wine picked up a Slick and two gunships over the check point, 3-2's radioman was calling to say they'd arrived at the PZ and were standing by.

Bud let out a breath and gave the Slick the heading. *At least we'll get these guys out,* he thought as he watched the chopper begin its descent.

Only fifteen minutes before, he'd had a call informing him that four Slicks had just delivered a load of Fourth Division troops and were now assigned to the Rangers. Bud had needed the good news after hearing about Grady's team. He told the lead he'd use one bird to pick up 3-2 and send another to get 2-5. Wade's team, 2-1, was located too near an NVA position for safe extraction.

Bud made a mental picture of the PZ to determine the best approach for the bird. The PZ was large and shaped like a golf-course dogleg. It looked as if it had been cleared for farming and was at least forty meters wide and one hundred meters long. He looked down at the helicopters below him. A gunship led, followed by the Slick, with another gun following.

"Steer right," commanded Bud.

When the birds were on line with their unseen PZ, he depressed the transmit button. "On course. You're three klicks out."

Sergeant Le Quang Lich sat on the small hill behind his heavy machine gun. The air above him had been filled with the sounds of helicopters and planes all day. He'd been assigned to the post for three months and had never heard such activity before. He knew it meant the puppets, or maybe even the Americans, were invading. Privates Hy and Ngoc sat next to him.

Private Ngoc turned toward the sergeant. "What are our orders if a helicopter flies within range?"

The frail soldier smiled. "We will let them pass. We don't want to draw attention to ourselves. Remember, it is our responsibility to protect the hospital below us."

The private nodded. He, like the others, had been a patient at the underground hospital. They'd been assigned to the gun position as soon as they'd recovered enough to stand watch. Sy Ngoc liked this gun position because it sat higher than the other three located around the small hill. From here he could see the open field five hundred meters distant that could be used as a landing place for helicopters. The sergeant in charge was a frail man. Some said he had poison within his body and that was why he was never assigned back to a unit once he recovered from his wounds. He was a kind leader and explained how the guns worked to his new crews every day. "I must make sure you know what to do when the time comes," he'd tell them.

Sy Ngoc looked attentive as the sergeant pulled back the cocking handle, chambering a round in the big gun. He glanced at Huu Hy, who was adjusting the 250-round belt of ammunition.

"Remember," the sergeant said, "you are my feeder. Keep the belt straight as the gun pulls the ammunition in. Should you take my place as shooter," he said to Ngoc, "the trigger-locking lever must first be raised like this, with the left thumb, and then you can fire with the right thumb."

Both men nodded. They'd heard it many times. In fact, Ngoc had fired one of the Russian SG-43s before. He'd been trained on the gun before leaving to go south. It would be impolite, however, to show he knew more than the leader, so he always said nothing and was attentive.

As the sergeant was pulling himself out of the gun position, he heard helicopters approaching. "This may be the time, friends. Hear how the sound is—" He saw the glint of the helicopter's windshield. It was coming at treetop level from his left, and it flew directly over the open area. Then came a second, the tail of which suddenly went down in a rocking motion as the machine began descending. He had hoped they would fly over and no battle would be fought. But his orders were clear. If a helicopter landed, he was to destroy it. He aimed through the large round sights and depressed the trigger.

Sergeant Redican of team 3-2 ran for the waiting helicopter at half speed. He wanted to make sure the others got on first. He was within ten feet of the chopper when the left side of the chopper's windshield shattered. The helicopter shuddered and seemed to screech. Two team members in the door were thrown backward like puppets on strings. Redican knew the helicopter was being hit, but he couldn't hear the shooting because of the horrible screeching and grinding of the dying chopper's engine. He turned and began running back to the trees as fast as he could.

The co-pilot was hit in the hand but didn't move. Pieces of Plexiglas and instrument panel jumped and flew through the air in front of him as he remained frozen to the seat. The pilot, who'd been killed in the first burst, had slumped forward, held by the shoulder harness. The helicopter was being torn to pieces around him. He knew that, but he also knew he was being shielded by the pilot's seat and body. If he moved, he'd die.

The self-sealing fuel tanks were not designed for such a beating, and in seconds aviation fuel spurted from them. The wounded left-door gunner lay back on his seat. He smelled the flammable fluid and knew it was just a matter of time. Suddenly the fuel ignited and flames engulfed him. His terrified scream lasted only a second before an explosion tore him from the seat and flung him skyward.

Sikes released the floor switch when he realized he'd been screaming into the radio. As soon as the chopper had landed, he'd seen the seven tiny figures run toward it. Then he'd seen the light green specks of the tracers race through the air. Sikes never heard a word from the pilot as the helicopter sat for what seemed to him at least ten seconds before exploding. He kept yelling to the pilot, "Get up! Get up!"

The gunships were talking excitedly to each other on the other frequency as Sikes watched.

"Slicks hit! From where? Where?"

"My four o'clock. Green tracers. Heavy machine gun."

"Roger. I'm going in hot."

Sergeant Le Quang Lich saw the dark-green helicopter bank left and aim its blunt nose directly at him. He turned the barrel quickly from the burning helicopter and began firing. The helicopter spit smoke as it came toward him, and he could hear a whining swoosh above the noise of his gun. The ground shook in front of him and smoke billowed up, but he kept the helicopter in his sights and kept shooting as it passed over to his right.

"I'm hit, Lead! I'm hit. Oil pressure gone."

"Keep it up! God damn it. Keep your nose up."

"Won't respond. We're going in."

Sikes watched in horror as the smoking gunship rocked crazily. It fought upward, then slowed, then hung suspended, then fell.

The second gunship had seen none of it. It was bound on a course of vengeance and had already unleashed six twenty-pound rockets.

Sikes could hear the pilot screaming, "Get 'em! Get the fuckers!"

The door gunners were leaning out and shooting with their mounted M-60 machine guns. Red tracers streaked out and disappeared into the small hill.

Private Ngoc lay at the bottom of the gun position. Sergeant Le Quang Lich lay on top of him, dead. The sergeant's bloody hand fell on Ngoc's face as Ngoc turned and pushed upward. When he finally worked himself free and rose from the pit, he found Private Hy's smoking, torn body. It stank horribly from the punctured intestines that lay scattered over his chest. Two men ran up and grabbed Ngoc's arms, pulling him away from the position. They set him on the ground, quickly checking him over for wounds as the helicopter sound grew louder. All three men looked skyward. The green machine whirled by, shooting at the ground to their left.

Ngoc tried to get to his feet and fell back. One of the soldiers grabbed his arm and stood him up.

"Come, comrade," the soldier said, pulling Ngoc along. "We must help the patients. The hospital will be under attack soon."

Ngoc shook his head to clear the pounding as they pulled him toward the entrance. He looked back one last time. The hill was covered with a light mist of smoke, dust, and death that lingered in the air and made it difficult to breathe. Five minutes before, it had been a beautiful day. Now the war had come and spread its evil hand over the hill. He ducked his head and entered the dark entrance.

Redican had felt the heat of the exploding helicopter on the back of his neck as pieces of the helicopter flew past him. He got up quickly after the blast and ran farther into the protective trees before turning toward the burning chopper. No one else had escaped. The gunships had flown directly over him, firing their rockets and shooting their machine guns. A few moments later he heard one of the choppers hit the trees behind him. He ran toward the sound, hoping he could help the crew. When he arrived, a pathetic sight awaited him. The gunship was caught like a fly in a web in the huge branches eighty feet above. It was on its side, burning. Three smoking bodies lay on the ground, shattered from the fall. A fourth hung suspended from the gunship by a safety strap still attached to his waist.

Redican ran back to the PZ. He took out his flare pen gun and fired it skyward.

The remaining gunship began gaining altitude after making a pass over the burning helicopter.

"Three-Alfa, this is Gunslinger-Two. We've been hit but seem to be okay. The bastards have at least two more gun positions on the hill, but we're all expended. We're going to—*hey, a flare.*"

The gunship banked hard right and over the PZ.

Bob Redican waved frantically as the bird sped above him.

"Three-Alfa, we got a friendly on PZ. We're going in."

Sikes hit the floor switch. "What about gun positions?"

"Three-Alfa, we received no fire on pass. I think the guns are too low on hill to observe PZ. We're going in low and fast.

Sikes watched as the gunship flared and dropped into the grassy field. In what seemed like only a second the chopper lifted up and shot forward, staying low over the trees.

"Three-Alfa, we got him. He's one of yours. Crew chief is asking him about the others."

"Roger, Gunslinger. I've got an Air Force controller coming over, and he's got a pair of fast movers to deal with the hill. You better get back and check out your damage."

"Roger. We're leaving now. Your man says there were no other survivors. Make sure they get 'em, Bud. Blow that fucking hill away!"

Bud watched the lone helicopter turn east, then looked down at the PZ where five Rangers, eight crewmen, and a montagnard scout had died. "We'll get them, Gunslinger. I'm going to make sure of it."

Captain Shane and Sergeant Ingram listened to the radio solemnly as Sikes reported the loss of the team and the two helicopters. Ingram picked up the handset and called Engineer Hill to relay the bad news. Shane slowly stood and walked over to the map. He picked up a blue grease pencil and circled team 3-2's PZ location and placed the letters KIA(5) inside the circle. He looked at the other two blue circles of teams 1-1 and 1-3 and shook his head. "Killed in action," he said to himself as he backed away from the map. Ingram put down the handset and looked at the new circles.

"Sir, we need to put something up for Grady and his two men."

Shane stared at the map for a moment before picking up a red grease pencil and circling the PZ the chopper had used. He paused before writing MIA(3) in the center of the circle.

The first F-4 Phantom streaked in, releasing its five-hundred-pound "snake eye" bomb. The iron projectile's retard fin section blew back, slowing the descent as the jet pulled up and began its turn. Sikes watched the olive-drab bomb glide downward and disappear into the trees. A second later the small hill shook violently. A dark brown cloud of debris rose through the trees as the second plane began its attack.

Colven saw the two men as soon as he opened the ward door. They were standing in the middle of the aisle, listening to a small nurse, who was admonishing, ". . . And furthermore, you men are not assigned to this ward. You should be . . ."

Ben looked up and saw the major and walked toward him, brushing past the surprised nurse.

"Any word about Grady, sir?" asked Ben anxiously.

Colven shook his head. "Nothing yet. What about you? How you doing?"

"I'm okay, sir. I'm—"

"Major, really!"

Colven turned toward the nurse, who walked around Ben, her hands on her hips.

"Major, please, all visitors are to report in at the desk before—"

"How you doing, Sox?" asked Colven, ignoring the irate first lieutenant.

Sox nodded slightly and motioned toward the bed where Rodriguez lay with tubes running from his nose to plastic bottles hanging beside the bed.

"Major, I must insist you and these men—"

"How is he doing, Lieutenant?" asked Colven, interrupting the nurse as he walked over to the bed and looked at the bandaged face of the Puerto Rican.

"Major, please! I'm talking to you. You are supposed to check in before coming in here. This is the critical ward."

Colven waited patiently until the nurse had finished.

"How is he?" he asked again.

The lieutenant shook her head, realizing she was fighting a losing battle. "He just came in from surgery and he's still under sedation. He'll be sent to Japan this afternoon for further surgery, but the worst is over. He's stable now."

Colven patted the soldier's bare chest and turned toward the two men. Sox dropped his eyes to the floor and spoke in a raspy whisper.

"Sir, I didn't know it was the last bird until it was too late. I . . . I didn't know. I never would have . . ." His words trailed off as he brought his hand up to wipe away the tears.

Ben shook his head. "Grady made us go. We wanted to stay with 'em, but he—"

Colven put up his hand. "Stop it! Both of you! Sergeant Grady did exactly what he was supposed to do. I want both of you to keep your heads up. You didn't run out on your team. You did what you were told. When this Ranger"—he motioned toward Rodriguez—"wakes up, I don't want him seeing two down-in-the-mouth soldiers feeling sorry for themselves, you understand?"

Sox sniffed back the tears and straightened his back. "Yes, sir."

Ben closed his eyes and nodded without speaking.

Colven put his hand on Ben's arm. "Look, there are two women outside who are waiting to see you guys. They're the Red Cross girls who Grady and Meeks knew, and they're not taking this too well. I want you and Sox to talk to them."

Ben looked into the major's eyes. "Sir, Rock was wounded. They got to be moving pretty slow. We're gonna get them out soon, aren't we?"

Colven stared into the large brown eyes and answered softly, "We're going to do our best."

Colven motioned for the nurse to follow him to the door. He spoke to her quietly as they walked down the aisle. "These men are like brothers. I would appreciate your letting them stay together until Rodriguez is shipped out. It's very important to both of them."

"Major, it is highly irregular and . . . well, okay, this time, Major. I think, under the circumstances, it wouldn't hurt anything."

"You must be Ben."

The hulking soldier turned and smiled at the small blond. "And you must be Sarah, and you gotta be Mary Ann."

The two women shook hands with Ben and Sox. Ben could see that both girls had been crying.

"You know, Ben," said Sarah, "I feel I know you two quite well. Grady has told me so much about you." Sarah fought to keep her smile as the huge black man chuckled and then winced in pain at the effort. A shoulder bandage was taped across his massive chest and neck.

Sox's neck was held rigid by a brace and was bandaged heavily on the right side. He moved his shoulders stiffly to look at the women and spoke in a whisper. "We've heard a lot about you girls too. Grade said never to eat your cookies."

Mary Ann laughed and held out a bag of chocolate-chip cookies. "Well, then, I guess you don't want these."

"He mighta told you that, but not me," said Ben, taking the cookies. He started to thank Mary Ann, but saw Sarah's smile vanish when she turned toward Rodriguez.

"Oh, Lord, no," she said softly as she walked toward his bed and stared at his pale, bandaged face.

Ben put his arm around her shoulder. "He's okay, Sarah. They gonna fix him up like new, honey."

Shaking, she spun around and buried her face in his chest. "Oh, Ben, will they make it? I have to know. Will they get out of there?"

Patting her back and trying to hold back his emotions, he answered, "They gonna be fine. Them boys be back real soon, honey. Real soon."

John Colven sat in the Fifth Brigade's stifling briefing tent as the brigade S-3 briefed on the current situation.

". . . We now have one and a half battalions in, with the other half expected to close within the hour. The artillery units are also in, but resupply of ammo is only by air and is not up to full combat stockage yet. The infantry battalions have captured a supply base, here, and a training base, here. The Third Battalion will go in here tomorrow," he said pointing to the large map.

"Casualties have been light. Tomorrow all infantry units will conduct search-and-destroy operations in their assigned sectors. Once the First Battalion goes in, a battalion from the 101st Airborne Division will be air-mobiled into three company-size blocking positions on major avenues of escape, here, here, and here.

"Region headquarters has given us the 101st Battalion especially for this mission. With the 101st in those three locations and us pushing toward them, we should be able to capture several hundred trucks. The enemy will be effectively blocked from using the roads. The enemy soldiers will, of course, be able to escape using multiple trail systems, but they will have to leave their heavy equipment or destroy it.

"Gentlemen, this concludes the briefing. Major Colven, would you please stay a few minutes? The rest of you gentlemen are excused."

Colven remained in his chair as the rest of the officers filed out. He didn't like surprises, and being asked to stay was a surprise. He saw the brigade commander and General Burton rise from their front-row seats and walk toward him. Quickly he stood up.

"Sit down, John," said Burton as they approached and took chairs beside him.

"John, it's been a bad day for you," said Colonel Mac-Donald, the brigade commander. "I'm sorry."

"Yes, sir, it was an extremely bad day."

The colonel took a cigarette pack from his shirt pocket and offered cigarettes to both of them. They both refused.

"Major Colven, as you have heard, the region headquarters has given us three rifle companies from the 101st. I'm going to need your help in watching those companies' asses. I'll need some of your Ranger teams to go in three or four klicks behind them to make sure no large NVA units from deep in Cambodia try to overrun one of their blocking positions. You're going in strictly to watch their backs."

"Sir, that's a big area," said Colven, looking at the map. "You're going to need at least two teams behind each company, for a total of six. I only have four operational teams left, and they just got back today."

The colonel rubbed his eyes and sighed deeply before resuming. "John, believe me, I hear what you are saying, but we're stuck. This is a big stateside show. The President went on national television today and told the American people we're here. The big brass are pushin' hard for results. We have you to thank for our present success, but I can't have a company wiped out by the enemy or the invasion will mean nothing. Yours is the only unit that has the expertise and radio equipment to get the job done in the time I have."

"How much time is that, sir?"

"Tomorrow, noon."

"I guess we don't have a choice, do we, sir?" asked Colven, turning first to General Burton and then to the colonel.

"No, John, I'm afraid not."

"Okay, sir, but god damn it, I can't have what happened today. I have got to have the aircraft to support us."

"I've talked to my 3 Air, and he is waiting in your area right now with the aviation liaison to work out the arrangements. You'll have what you need."

Colven looked at the map again. "It's a shitty war, isn't it, sir?"

"Yes, John, they don't get much shittier than this one.

The Rose stepped from behind the large tree where he'd been hiding, and fired. Four North Vietnamese soldiers, who had been squatting beside a creek and filling canteens, died quickly. The expressionless black soldier released the trigger and pushed the magazine release. The empty thirty-round magazine fell into the creek as he walked through the water and inserted a new one. He bent over and picked up a just-filled NVA canteen. He took a long drink before removing his jungle hat and pouring the rest of the water over his head. He shut his eyes and let out a deep breath as the water trickled over his short, curly hair and down his camouflaged face.

Grady untied the poncho strip gently. The blood-soaked bandage stuck to the plastic as he pulled it back. Rock lay white-faced and sweating as Grady put on a new dressing and rewrapped the poncho strip. Next he untied the arm strip and examined that wound.

"The bullet is right there. I need to get it out, Rock."

The pale man nodded and turned his head. Grady took a razor blade from the small medical kit and examined the bullet further. It was lodged like a thick splinter in the biceps. He could see its base when he raised the skin that covered the wound.

"Thump, I'm gonna cut the hole back a little ways and try to push the bullet out. What do you think?"

"Rock, buddy, it's gonna hurt like hell. You'd better bite on something," said Thump.

Rock forced a smile. "Just like in the movies, huh?"

Thumper took off his parachute scarf and put a wadded-up corner into Rock's mouth. He leaned forward and held him down, then nodded to Grady, who made a quick incision and pushed with his thumb on the tip of the bullet. Rock's arm and body were as taut as steel. Pus and clear fluid mixed with blood oozed out of the hole. Slowly the bullet began to come out.

Colven, eating peaches from a C-ration can, was addressing Shane. ". . . So, that's it, Ed. Tomorrow, we pull Wade's team at first light and then get ready to put us in."

"Sir, you don't need to take a team out. I'll do it, and you run operations here."

Colven dipped the plastic spoon back into the can, trying to fish out the last slice floating in the heavy syrup. "Naw, you've been running the show and know the plan inside and out. It's better that you handle it. I'm pulling everybody from Engineer Hill to make up teams, so you'll have only Ingram, Dove, and Pete to help you."

"Damn, sir, taking the radiomen and supply people to make up teams is risky."

Colven gave up trying to spoon out the slice and raised the can to his lips to drink the sweet fluid. "It's all we got left. There's no other choice."

"How you doing?" Thumper asked quietly. He brushed the hair from Rock's eyes.

"I'm hangin' tough. You did a good job with the albumin needle. 'Course, I coulda done it better with my schooling and all, but it wasn't bad."

Thumper smiled and pulled the poncho liner up to Rock's chest. Grady watched his two men as they lay on their packs, waiting for night. He would listen awhile longer, he thought, as he pulled out his pistol and inspected it.

Checking his watch, Sergeant Matt Wade turned toward Simmons. "Make sure everybody is ready. We're moving out in one hour, when it gets darker. I want everything packed now so we don't leave anything."

Simmons nodded and crawled toward the Russian. The helicopter pilot tapped Wade's shoulder. "How far we gonna travel?"

"Only a couple of klicks, sir. It's all wide open, so moving won't be a problem. The birds will come in tomorrow at first light."

"What happens if they don't come? We'll be stuck out in an open field. We'll been seen."

"Not in the tall grass, we won't. Anyway, it beats the hell out of staying here. At least we'll have a chance out there and won't get any of your birds shot up."

"Okay, Sarge. Hey, thanks for everything. I mean, dragging us around and all. I know it wasn't easy."

"You know, sir, you oughta get out of them choppers and join the Rangers. You don't look half bad with a camouflaged face," retorted Wade with a grin.

"I'm not that crazy," mumbled the pilot as he lay back down.

Shutting his eyes, Grady placed his hand over Rock's and gently squeezed. Rock smiled in the darkness and returned the squeeze. He closed his eyes and tried not to think of the pain. His side throbbed and his arm ached. Quietly he pulled at a corner of the sweat rag around his neck and put a balled-up piece into his mouth. The pain came in small waves, and there was no way to be comfortable. Instead of squeezing Grady's hand, which he held loosely, he bit the cloth. Grady needed his sleep.

A wave hit him, and his jaw contracted. *Oh, God. God, help me through this night. Please, Lord, help me.*

21

Matt Wade awoke and sat up stiffly. His mouth felt like sandpaper. It was still dark, but the luminous glow of his watch told him it was time to get ready.

"Simmons. Simmons, wake up, troop."

The still body moved slightly. "Aw, shit, Sarge, I was just screwin' Tina Louise."

"Huh?"

The damp poncho liner flew back as Simmons sat up. "Yeah, I took her on a picnic and just lay her back on my poncho liner and spread her—"

"Poncho liner? Shit, Sim, the Army has done warped your mind if you're dreamin' about bangin' on a poncho liner."

"Hell, Sarge, I'm a lifer like you. Don't lifers always do it on poncho liners or with jump boots on?"

"Wake up the others. We're getting outta here, you crazy shitbird."

Rose swayed in the blue NVA hammock, listening to the sounds of the jungle as the new day began. He reached down for a plastic bag of peanuts he'd taken from one of the men he'd killed the day before. He popped a few into his mouth. They tasted strange, not like American peanuts, but not bad.

He ate several handfuls, then sat up and washed down the taste with half a canteen of water. As he packed his gear, he hummed the Supremes' "Stop! In the Name of Love." His body moved in rhythm with the tune.

He stood and hefted his pack. "Stop,"—he put his hand up like he'd seen Diana Ross do on television and sang the words as he acted out her motions.

He glanced down and checked his weapon without missing a beat and began walking west.

Grady stared at the sleeping soldier. "Doesn't look good, does he?"

Thumper shook his head and whispered, "He didn't sleep well at all."

Grady gazed at Rock for several more seconds before getting up. "We'll let him sleep and rest up today. I'm afraid he'll never make it if he doesn't get some strength back. Make sure he eats when he wakes up. I'll take first watch, and you can relieve me in a couple hours."

"Sure, Grade. You really think we can chance it? Staying here, I mean."

Grady's eyes shifted to Rock. "We gotta chance it or we'll lose him, and I don't plan on losin' anybody."

"Two-One, we're inbound. Don't need smoke. I have a visual on you."

The lead gunship roared over as the first Slick dropped its tail and began its landing, followed closely by another. The happy passengers ran to the birds and quickly jumped on. In seconds the choppers lifted off and banked to the east.

Matt Wade sat back on his ruck and let out a deep breath, feeling the hundred-pound monkey of responsibility crawl off his back. He felt totally relaxed for the first time in days. Suddenly he realized he had to spit. He'd forgotten to get rid of the wad of tobacco before hopping on. "Damn it," he mumbled as he leaned forward to the side of the speeding helicopter. The ninety-knot wind took the brown spittle and carried it straight back to the unwary door gunner, who was leaning out inspecting his M-60. The gunner raised his head at the sound of rain hitting his helmet, but all he could see through the visor was a dark substance streaking across the tinted plastic and obscuring his vision. He raised his gloved hand to clean off the strange fluid, but it stuck and smeared the visor even more.

Seeing what had happened, Wade immediately leaned back and tried to look innocent. He knew the second he'd spit that it had been a mistake. The thought raced through his mind that the gunner might turn the 60 around and drill him right there or, worse, order him off the aircraft in front of God and everybody.

Wade took a deep breath and smiled to himself. *That's ridiculous,* he thought. *He's probably had worse blown on him—hell, blood and puke and Lord knows what else.*

The sergeant turned his head slightly and looked from the corner of his eye to confirm that the gunner had taken the incident in stride. He saw only a blur before he was temporarily stunned by a hand slap just above his ear. Matt shook his head, cleared his vision, and looked up at the irate door gunner, who stood over him, yelling, "Don't ever do that again, asshole!"

Wade meekly shrugged his shoulders. He was happy the gunner hadn't thrown him out.

Sergeant Childs stood in front of the large wall map in the operations room. The team leaders sat facing him, holding individual maps to mark their areas of operations.

"Our mission is to watch the asses of three rifle companies that are sitting on high-speed avenues of escape. Those avenues are also avenues of approach, which means a dink company or battalion could come sneaking in and do a damn-damn to those guys from the rear coming out of the interior of Cambodia. As you can see by your maps, it's a lot of area to cover behind each company, so we're puttin' in two teams behind each one. Three-Three and Two-Five, you guys are going to the south. Two-Three, Salazar, you and Major Colven's new team, Two-Six, will go in the center, and team One-Two and Gino's new team, One-Five, will go in behind the northern company. You are there to watch, god damn it! No shoot-em'-ups. Go in ready to fight, but don't engage unless you are compromised. The radio frequency to the 101st companies is on the board, and there'll be guns and fast movers on standby. Mission is to last three days. Any questions? . . . That's all, then. Be prepared for pickup in two hours. Good luck, good huntin', and Charlie Mike."

Thumper fed Rock the last bite of the Lurp. His color was coming back, and he complained the whole time Thumper was feeding him. "Damnit, I can feed myself. I ain't no baby, I—"

"Shut up and eat. Sarge said to make sure you eat, so I'm making sure; plus, I don't want you movin' your arm for a while. Tomorrow you're gonna need your strength. We're going home."

"How far is it, Thump?"

"The river is about eight klicks from here. We should make it by tomorrow evening, moving slow and careful."

"Then what?"

"We'll shine a mirror or flash a panel at the first thing that flies over. We'll be out day after tomorrow for sure. Hey, you'll get your second Purple Heart, so you'll get a rear job, huh?"

Rock grinned. "Yeah, I'll be a supply puke and screw up all you dudes' records. I can hardly wait. It's lucky for you guys I took accounting and business management courses in school. Why, I'll have the whole system reorganized and . . ."

The Rose was humming as he slowly walked down a well-used path. He glanced down at his feet. The NVA sandals were surprisingly comfortable. They didn't rub his feet nearly as badly as his boots had. He tossed a few more peanuts into his mouth and began humming a new tune.

Damn, he couldn't remember the words to the song. He shifted his AK-47 to the other hand and continued walking. *How's that mother start now?* "The western world . . . it is explodin' . . ."

Bud Sikes was flying to the second checkpoint to pick up Colven and Salazar's teams for infill. He had just put in 3-3 and 2-5 and had informed Captain Shane that both teams had good commo with X-ray. He nibbled a chocolate-chip cookie as he looked out of the window for the circling helicopters. There had been a slight delay as one of the Slicks landed at Plei Djereng to pick up the major. Dove had packed his commander's equipment and brought his weapon, so all the major had to do was hop on.

Larry Wine broke the silence. "What time's the 101st going in again?"

Bud glanced at his watch. "In about an hour."

"You think the plan will work? I mean, trapping the heavy equipment?"

"Yeah, Larry. Intelligence says there's a lot of stuff in there. With the 101st blocking the roads, they sure can't carry it out. The terrain is too rough. The Fourth begins their drive toward the 101st companies at fourteen hundred, so we'll know pretty quick."

Colven jumped from the chopper and ran for the protective trees. The helicopter cleared the treetops and shot forward as he fell to the ground. Dove fell beside him as the others closed in, forming a wheel. Dove had volunteered for the mission, although he had only a few days left before rotating home. Colven sat up and put on his jungle hat as Johnson motioned that he'd contacted X-ray.

Childs whispered to the major, "How's it feel to be on the ground again, John?"

Colven winked and patted the stock of his CAR-15. "Just like old times."

Rose crept closer, watching the gray cloud of smoke directly to his front. He could see four ponchos strung above four hammocks and a small fire protected by a fifth poncho. Three NVA squatted by the fire, preparing to eat. Rose scanned the area for the fourth soldier and noticed the bulge in the most distant hammock. His eyes then swept past the camp, searching for other smoke trails or ponchos. There were none.

His lips quivered in a smile as he checked the Russian weapon's selector switch to make sure it was on semiautomatic. He raised the weapon and began humming the song that had been on his mind, "Eve of Destruction."

He crept slowly forward. The NVA's crackling fire muted his footsteps and his soft singing.

One of the soldiers looked up. Rose fired a long burst and spun and fired into the wiggling blue hammock.

He walked over to the closest soldier, who lay on his side, moaning and trying to roll over. The bullets had passed through his arm into his chest. Rose lowered his rifle with one hand and fired at point-blank range. He turned toward the hammock and saw that the lower portion was turning deep crimson. He placed his smoking weapon against the closest body and checked what was in the blackened cooking pot resting in the coals. Rice. Chopsticks lay neatly spread on green banana leaves, and a jar of *nuoc mam* sauce sat unspilled next to one of the dead men. The black soldier sang aloud as he reached for the rice pot, ". . . on the eve of destruction."

Deft brown hands rolled the cigarette tightly and placed it between dampened lips. The stainless-steel Zippo ignited with the first pass of a calloused thumb. Captain Min Coi Nha bowed his head slightly, brought the flame to the extended cigarette tip, and inhaled. The pungent country tobacco filled his nostrils. He smiled as he closed the lighter top. The engraved inscription was American. He'd taken the lighter from a dead Yankee in the Plei Trap Valley in 1966, when he was a platoon leader. His platoon had ambushed a patrol close to the banks of the Se San and killed them all. He'd had the inscription interpreted later and had written it down. The paper had been lost years ago, but not before he'd memorized the words:

To: Sgt. Jack Nolan
Co. A 1/12, 4th Infantry Div.
"Go get 'em."
        Connie

"Fourth Division," he said to himself as he exhaled a white cloud of smoke. The radio had reported that it was the Fourth Division that had invaded the camps and bases just seven miles from where he sat. He looked down at the squatting man bent over the old yellow map covered with plastic. The man's face was horribly scarred on the right side, and he had no hair on the top right portion of his head from where a scar, looking like folds of old skin, ran down the right side of his face to his jaw and neck. Only a small opening for the eye was left. Captain Thi Hue Phong had been fortunate in surviving a napalm attack. He was a blessed one. It was his third near-lethal wound, yet he was here, commander of First Company, ready to attack again. The scarred-faced one was fearless and was known throughout the district, as was their battalion commander, Colonel Dinh Thu Dang. The two men were legends.

Captain Nha squatted down. "What orders do you think we will receive?"

The scarred face looked up from the map. "We will fall back and sharpen our claws." His smile was cruel, for only one side of his mouth could move. "We will leave tonight, I'm sure, and wait until the Americans leave. Then we will return." He shifted his eyes back to his map. "The reports indicate that a brigade-size force came in with the two battalions yesterday, going here and here"—he pointed to the map—"and then the other battalion going in today, here." He looked up at Captain Nha, commander of the Third Company. "They are from the Fourth Division, you know."

Nha took the cigarette from his mouth and exhaled the smoke through his nostrils. "Yes, friend, it is like old times, but now we withdraw, not fight. Remember when—"

An excited voice at the entrance interrupted him. "Comrade Leader, excuse me. An urgent report has come in."

The scarred captain motioned the soldier over and extended his hand without getting up. The soldier quickly crossed the bamboo-matted floor and handed the thin rice paper to his commander. Nha watched the eye inside the grotesque socket shift from side to side and abruptly stop.

Phong leaned over the map and traced a line with his finger. He looked up slowly. "My friend, you may have the opportunity to fight after all."

Nha leaned forward and looked at the spot where his finger was pointing. "What has happened?"

"The Americans have air-landed a new force behind us."

"How big?"

"It looks as if it is only one company, by the number of flying machines."

Nha smiled. "Only a company?"

The scarred one nodded, stood, and slowly walked to the doorway, lost in thought.

Nha looked at the spot where the new force was reported. They were only five miles to the west of them, blocking the road.

Colonel Dinh Thu Dang sat in his battalion headquarters in the village of Phum Ban Kon, twenty-five kilometers from the border. Reports were being radioed in every few minutes. He posted the latest on his wall map and turned toward his deputy commander.

"The Yankee intentions are very clear. They have three battalions in my area, one in the north, one in the center, and one in the south. Now they have brought in three companies and placed them in blocking positions ten to twelve kilometers away from each of the battalions. Undoubtedly the battalion soldiers will sweep toward the companies and try to clear the area in between."

He studied the map for several moments and turned, smiling, toward his deputy. "I will call Captain Nha's Third Company and Captain Phong's First Company and tell them to leave their heavy equipment and infiltrate around the single company that blocks the road. They will join us"—he paused, looking closer at the map—"here, tomorrow, four kilometers behind the Americans. We will then make our attack the following day and wipe out the blocking position."

The deputy stepped closer to the map and looked at his colonel's markings. "Comrade, should you not leave a squad to slow the advance of the approaching Fourth Division battalion, and perhaps another squad to snipe at the soldiers in the blocking position? That would focus their attention away from us."

The colonel smiled. "Nguyen, you are a devious devil dog. Your thoughts are excellent! Radio the First and Third immediately and have them carry out our plan."

Rose had reoutfitted his gear. He held a new AK-47 assault rifle with a folding aluminum stock and aluminum magazines. His pack was stuffed with food. Strapped to his waist was a K-54 pistol. He backed up, looked at his handiwork, and smiled.

He'd stacked the bodies on top of each other, resting each man's chin on the head of the man below him. If someone walked down the trail, they'd be shocked to see four faces staring at them like a ghastly miniature totem pole.

"Mutha-fuckers," said Rose aloud as he walked by the bodies. "You done met the Rose! Jeremiah Flowers done killed your ass. The Rose, he's a cool dude. He's cool."

The black soldier looked over his shoulder at the bodies one last time, adjusted his jungle hat, and narrowed his eyes. He was ready to hunt again. The Rose was on the prowl. A small inner voice spoke to him and pleaded, "Get some, Rose. Get some more!"

"I would like to bid one."

"One! No, Sarah," said Sox in an irritated raspy whisper.

Sarah glanced at her cards again before looking at the laughing woman who sat beside her. "Stop it, Mary Ann. I've never played spades before."

Ben reached over and patted Sarah's hand. "That's okay, Sarah honey. Don't let that professional cardplayer bug you."

He shifted his gaze to Sox and frowned a warning. Sox glared back, unimpressed.

"Easy for you to say, man. She ain't your partner, and you're winning!"

Mary Ann laughed louder and stood up. "We have to be going, guys. We have a program to put on at the aviation battalion. We'll see you again tomorrow."

All four walked to the door. Sox leaned toward Mary Ann and nodded toward Sarah. "Mary Ann, teach that girl about spades, will ya? She's killing my image."

Sarah put her hands on her hips. "No more cookies for you guys for that remark, mister."

Ben loomed over Sox. "Apologize, *now*!"

The small dog was tired. She had run to every soldier who had approached the ops shack, only to return to the shade under the shack where Sergeant Wade's team lay.

"What's wrong with that dumb dog?" Simmons asked Oscar.

"Aw, the poor mutt is looking for Dove, I guess. Sergeant Ingram said Dove dropped her off here when the Ol' Man got on the bird to go out."

"You think she needs water?"

Simmons reached for his canteen. "Hell, I'm out. You got some?"

Oscar leaned forward, opening his ruck, pulled out his plastic two-quart canteen, and poured some into his hand. "Come here, Bitch, baby. Here's water, baby. Come here, Bitch."

The small dog trotted over to the soldier and lapped up the clear liquid from his hand.

Oscar patted the pup as it drank. "Dove be back real soon, doggie, real soon."

Sergeant Wade took the parachute scarf from his neck and dipped it into the canteen cup of water. He patted his eyes with the wet cloth and replaced it around his neck. "Damn dust," he said as he threw the rest of the water out the door of the hootch. Water trickled down his face, leaving reddish streaks. Sikes and Shane sat at the table, sharing a chili Lurp. Wade sat down on the floor and looked across the room to the map on the far wall. *Shit,* he thought as he looked at the circles indicating teams 1-1, 1-3, 3-2, and 2-2. *Jesus—Grady, Rock, and Thumper missing and the rest of the teams dead.*

Wade shut his eyes and put his hand on his forehead. *My God, it must be a bad dream. It's gotta be.* He opened his eyes and saw the circles again. *Son of a bitch!* He got up and walked out the door, stooping under the hootch and sitting against one of the wood pilings. The Russian looked up at the sergeant from his reclining position and rose up on his elbow. "Is the information correct about the loss of our comrades?"

Wade shut his eyes and nodded.

The Russian lay back and said softly, "The Rangers, they die an honorable death. They die killing their enemies, and they die with their friends."

The small dog left Oscar's side and walked over to Wade, sniffing him for several moments. Dissatisfied, she walked back to the steps and lay on her stomach, awaiting her master's return.

"What do you think, Jerry?" whispered Colven.

"You're right, John. I saw the dust kick up when the motorbike went by. It's got to be a road, but I don't see any place to get closer. It's just too damn open."

Colven rose to look again and lowered himself. "This spot is okay during the day, but at night we're gonna have to get closer to hear what's going on down the road."

"How about setting up a base camp back in the draw behind us, and we'll send two out here during the day and two more out at dusk to get close to the road for the night?"

Colven smiled. "Okay, Jerry. Set it up. Dove and I will take the first shift. Send him on up, will ya?"

Childs nodded and whispered "Will do" as he backed out of the large ferns.

Grady sat down by Rock. "You feeling better, huh?"

"Yeah, Grade, thanks for the rest. It hurts, but not like yesterday."

Grady crawled over to where Thumper was cleaning his pistol. "You got any chow left?"

Thumper looked up casually. "Yeah, I got one Lurp."

Grady whispered so Rock couldn't hear, "I've got one too. You go ahead and split yours with Rock, and tomorrow we'll all split the one I have."

Thumper eyed his friend. "You didn't eat a bite today. You'd better split yours with him."

Grady smiled. "You're bigger than me. You need more food."

Thumper shook his head. "I'm not hungry."

"Well, me neither."

"If you dudes are talking about food, I ain't hungry. You stuffed me so full of Lurps, I'll probably fart all night and keep everybody awake," said Rock in a loud whisper.

The two men looked at each other and smiled. Grady took out his Lurp and threw it to Rock. "Put in a lot of water. It's gonna get split three ways tonight."

Captain Min Nha lit a cigarette with the Zippo and continued walking. They had left their camp several hours before and were now skirting around the Americans' blocking position. Nha glanced at his watch. Only another hour of daylight left.

Muffled rifle fire caused him to stop and turn. It was one of his squads sniping at the American company, but by the sound of the chattering AK-47s, it sounded as if his squad might have gotten lucky and ambushed a patrol. He didn't hear the distinctive sounds of M-16s returning fire.

Nha stepped off the trail to listen and watched his men as they filed by. He inhaled deeply on the cigarette, holding the smoke momentarily before exhaling. He did not like having to destroy the trucks before leaving the camp, but it could not be helped. The colonel's plan was a good one, so all was not wasted. Perhaps he could obtain another Yankee lighter and maybe a watch. The Yankees were so rich, they all wore watches. Yes, a watch would be excellent compensation for the trucks he had to destroy.

The captain stood listening for a few more minutes before joining his men. He leaned forward slightly and quickened his pace to find his radioman.

Rose swayed gently in his NVA hammock. He smelled rain in the air and had strung a rubber poncho above his hammock. He let out a deep breath and relaxed. He shut his eyes and made a promise to himself: Tomorrow he would get some more.

22

Midnight

Grady was awakened by the silence. He opened his eyes, but he had to blink to make sure they were open. He stared into deathlike blackness so thick and dark, he felt relief at the sound of his own breath.

Sitting up slowly, he reached out to touch Thumper but abruptly stopped when he heard a faint patter. *Damn! No, not now, not . . .* The first drop fell, striking his outstretched hand. A single raindrop, a delicate, seemingly inconsequential thing, but he knew it was a germ of an evil plague—a plague nurtured in the jungle incubator and multiplied by billions. Its onslaught would inundate and decompose everything, including man. A plague that drenched and permeated, leaving nothing untouched.

Fatigues and boots would become weighted instruments of torture that chafed and rubbed, turning wet, wrinkled skin into festering, oozing agony. Unmerciful night would bring the shivering cold that made a man's jaws fatigued from uncontrollable chattering. The body would become paralyzingly numb and refuse to respond to the simplest command.

Not rain. Not now, not the damn rain.

Morning

"All teams, all teams, this is X-ray. Be advised, no aircraft can fly—I say again, no aircraft can fly—due to bad weather.

Advise extreme caution. Do not—say again, do not—become engaged. . . ."

Grady threw back his glistening wet poncho and adjusted the boonie hat he had pulled down over his ears. Thumper, hearing the sergeant, lifted his head and pulled his poncho back. Rock lay next to him with his poncho liner over his head.

Rock raised his head from the camouflaged liner. "You know, Thump, one day you'll make a heck of a mother for some lucky guy."

He sat up gingerly and glanced toward Grady. "I think the big guy's gone queer. He stayed within kissing distance all night."

Thumper whispered, "Just because I had a headache last night, honey, doesn't mean you have to be bitchy."

Rock put his hand out, and Thumper easily pulled him to his feet. "Okay, Thump, I still love ya. Let's go, huh?"

The three men quickly packed their few possessions and repainted their faces and hands with the two-color green camouflage stick. Cold rain drizzled through the thick canopy in a fine mist.

Rock shivered as he tested his movement. Not bad, he thought. His arm was as sore as a boil, but the sling Thumper had made from his parachute scarf would help keep his arm immobile and ease the pain. His side ached, but if he walked stiffly and didn't twist or bend, he could hang tough.

Grady motioned for Thumper to take point, and in seconds the men were moving east.

Rose had let a group of ten NVA pass by ten minutes before.

They'd been moving at a half run down the trail. He'd heard them long before he saw them, giving him time to hide. Why were they running? he wondered. Were they running *from* something, or *to* something?

Childs hunched over, trying to keep the rain out of his cold Lurp. Water trickled down from his chin as he spoke to the major. "No birds up in this shit, huh?"

Colven sighed heavily. "No, probably won't be until this stuff breaks. See or hear anything last night?"

Childs tried to control his shaking hand as he brought a spoonful of the cold food up to his mouth. "Naw." He took the bite and chewed a moment. "It was quiet. When the rain hit, we couldn't hear a fucking thing. A division coulda marched down that road and we wouldn't have heard 'em."

"If it keeps up, we'll have to move closer."

The soaked sergeant shook his head. "Fuck, John, I was only five feet off that bastard. You can't get closer without sitting in the damn middle of the road."

Colven smiled at his tired friend. "Okay, Jerry, you'd best try and get some sleep. It's gonna be a long day."

Dove tapped the major on the shoulder. "Sir, it's our turn to watch."

Colven let out a deep breath and turned toward the young Pfc., who was putting another plastic bag around his blue notebook. "Okay, son, let's do it."

Shane and Sergeant Wade watched Bud Sikes pacing the floor. "Relax, Bud," said Shane. "It isn't your fault we got shitty weather."

Sikes stopped and pointed to the map. "I don't like it! I don't like it one bit! The 101st company in the center and the Fourth Division's center battalion both gettin' hit at the same time and nobody else seeing anything. I don't like it. The dinks are up to something."

Wade looked at the map. "How many did the company lose, sir?"

"Four KIA and three WIA," Shane answered tiredly. "A squad walked into an ambush just outside the perimeter. The Fourth's Battalion lost two KIA and two WIA to snipers and lost five more to a booby trap. This morning a point man was shot dead as he walked out of their night perimeter."

"Are they gonna sweep today as planned?" asked Sikes.

Shane walked to the open door and stared out into the rain. "No, they're going to wait until the weather breaks so they can use guns and fast-movers. The artillery fired up most of their rounds last night and can't get a resupply in until the weather breaks."

Bud shook his head disgustedly. "I'm tellin' you, it stinks! The major and Salazar are hangin' in the breeze if a force comes marchin' down that valley. No gunships, no artillery, nothing!"

Shane turned from the door and exchanged glances with Wade. They both knew Sikes was right, but there was nothing that could be done.

The small dog was covered with red mud. She lay shivering, watching the muddy path. The Russian sat under the building and watched as the dog raised her head as a lieutenant splashed down the path toward the shack. She got to her feet and waited at the bottom step, sniffing the air as the lieutenant sidestepped her and bounded up the steps.

The dog lowered her head, walked back, and lay down, resuming her vigil.

The Russian crawled over and dragged the filthy animal out of the rain and began wiping her off with his parachute scarf. "You must stay out of the rain, little one. The Russian, he will take care of you. You are lucky, my small friend"—he rubbed the dog's head affectionately—"I have decided to care for you until your master returns."

Simmons looked over from his reclining position. "Russian, that dog don't like no foreigners."

The Russian shot him a cold stare. "What do you mean? We are all foreigners, as you say. This animal is the only native."

Simmons propped up on one elbow. He knew he'd hit a nerve. He liked arguing with the Russian because his accent sounded strange. "Yeah, but Russian, you're *foreign,* foreign!"

The Russian, realizing Simmons was taunting him, grunted and continued patting the dog.

Beads of water fell off the brim of Dove's jungle hat, but he didn't notice. His eyes were fixed on the large unit of NVA walking down the road. Their heads were down, and they had weapons slung with the barrels pointed toward the ground. Dove counted each as they passed by. Their shimmering ponchos were being pounded by the rain, causing a unique sound that he could hear distinctly from fifty meters away.

Colven lay beside him, relieved that the large unit was moving to the west, away from Bravo Company of the 101st, which was only a few miles away. He watched as one of the soldiers stopped and raised his poncho high over his head. A second later he could see the distinctive yellow flash of a lighter or match and then a small, whitish cloud rising from the elevated poncho. Then the soldier was back in the ranks and moving.

Colven envied the man for being able to enjoy the simple pleasure. He wiped the water from his eyes with his wrinkled hand. His soaked hat was dripping and trickling cold water down onto his face.

Rose heard them coming and quickly lay down five meters off the trail. *I'll be damned,* he said to himself, slowly rising and putting his hands in the air. Three startled GIs spun their weapons around, pointing them at the filthy soldier.

"Red-Six, this is Red-One. Over."

"This is Six. Go."

"Red-Six, we found a GI. . . at least we think that's what he is. He says he's a Ranger. He's wearing NVA equipment and got one of them folding-stock AKs."

"Red-One, hold him. I'll be right there."

Two Fourth Divison soldiers had their weapons pointed at Rose when the captain walked up.

Rose was heating water in an NVA canteen cup. "Sorry to bother you, sir," he said. "I'd like to borrow some heat tabs, then I'll be on my way."

The captain stared, unbelieving, at the soldier who was pouring a coffee packet into the heated water. "What unit you with?"

Rose took a sip of coffee and glanced up. "I'm with Sierra Rangers, sir. I'm Charlie Mikin'."

Salazar let out a deep breath as he reached for the radio handset. An NVA company had passed behind them only seconds before, heading for the west. The company of ninety men had come out of a stream bed behind them and walked to the road fifty yards in front of the team's position. Still shivering, Salazar depressed the side bar. "X-ray, X-ray, this is Two-Three. We have sighted . . ."

The cigarette smoke didn't seem to want to leave the protection of the gray jungle hat. Captain Nha put away his American lighter and raised his head, allowing the smoke to escape from under the brim. Two soldiers were busy stringing a poncho shelter over him as the rest of his company made shelters and started fires. That night they had slept only a few kilometers from the American company and had left at first light. The terrain was difficult and had slowed them considerably. They had finally come to the road and marched only a kilometer when a battalion runner, sent by Colonel Dang, met them with the message that the assembly area for his company and for Captain Phong's First Company was to be at a fork in the road only two hundred meters distant. The colonel would be coming in the late afternoon, and he would bring the Second Company and his headquarters. They had moved to the wide fork in the road and begun setting up camp under the huge mahoganies.

Nha inhaled deeply on the cigarette and glanced at his watch: 0930. It would be some time before the commander arrived, he thought, as he blew out a light cloud of smoke.

Excited voices caused him to look up. The First Company was marching down the road toward them.

Nha rose and smiled as the scarred-faced commander approached. He shook his poncho before ducking under the cover of Nha's hootch. "The weather is foul, my friend," said Nha, squatting by his pack.

Captain Phong took off his poncho and squatted beside Nha. "Yes, comrade, my old bones felt the rains coming days ago. So this is our assembly area."

A soldier splashed through the mud and set down a small tray with cups and a pot of tea. Captain Nha passed a cup to Phong and poured as he spoke. "Yes, the old warrior will join us this afternoon to give us orders for the attack."

Phong sipped his tea and leaned back on his pack. "The weather is with us. The American planes are grounded."

Nha took the cigarette from his lips and stared at the scarred face for several moments. "Don't you tire of it? Of the constant moving and fighting?"

Phong stared into the rain. "I have been fighting for six years. I will probably fight another six." He turned, looking at Nha. "*Tire* is a word for those who believe there is such a thing as rest. My friend, there is no rest. There is only fighting and moving until we die. Such words as *tire* are only for the young who dream." He looked back at the rain. "Commanders such as us gave up our dreams long ago."

Colven handed the radio handset back to Dove and put his map back into his pocket. "You know, Dove, it's a helluva note watching an NVA company go by and you can't do a thing about it."

Dove nodded and tried to relax his taut, shivering body. "Jesus, sir, I counted ninety of them. Two damn companies in less than an hour. Sir, I'm too short to watch that many dinks."

Colven smiled. "Well, let's just hope they keep moving. According to the map, there's a fork in the road about a klick up. Both lead to Highway 16. If we had air, we could find out which road they took and bomb the shit out of them."

Dove looked up at the gray mist and shook his head. "Too bad this stuff won't break. I sure would like to call that air in—kinda my parting gift, you know?"

"How long you have?"

"Ten days, sir. Ten days, then back to the world. Hot damn, the world. . . ."

"Flowers, Jeremiah, Spec-4 of One-Three, sir," said Ingram, repeating the information he'd received only seconds before. "We call him the Rose. Alpha Company of the Thirty-fifth called in to Brigade Ops minutes ago. They found him while making a sweep around their perimeter. I guess they think he's crazy. The message said he refused to go with them, and he had to be placed under guard to be taken in."

Shane shook his head. "I guess the others are dead, huh?"

Ingram nodded. "He was the only survivor."

"This goddamn weather!" Shane shouted. "Can't even get that kid out of there. Think he's crazy? Crazy? They'll treat him like shit, you know? Poor kid. Rose alive, and I can't get him back to his own kind. *Shit!* The old man has got his ass hanging out with NVA companies all over the place, and I can't do a fucking thing. Nothing! No artillery, no air, no nothing!"

"Feel better, Captain?" Ingram asked with a half smile.

"*No!*" Shane turned and stared out of the door, mumbling. "Crazy. My God, we're all crazy to be in this fucking place."

Sarah sat in the open doorway, holding a Styrofoam cup filled with strong coffee, and watching the rain beat down on the asphalt street. She knew that the rain would hurt chances of a plane or helicopter spotting Grady, but he was going to make it, she was completely convinced. She had willed it. He would come back, and she was going to tell him what she'd never told any man: that she loved him. What else but love could it possibly be? It hurt too badly to be anything else.

Sarah leaned back and shut her eyes. She had always liked the rain. There was something soothing about it—like a cozy fire, or waves breaking on a moonlit beach. She thought about how it would be with him when it rained. They'd listen to the soft patter on the roof, lost in their thoughts, content. Her body warmed, thinking of him next to her in a comfortable bed. She so desperately wanted to hold him close.

She sipped her coffee and glanced over her shoulder at Mary Ann, who sat at a desk, staring at the ceiling. Sarah knew Mary Ann felt the same way about Thumper. Sarah walked to the desk and turned and looked back at the rain. "I've always loved the rain. But now . . . it's keeping them away from us, you know."

Mary Ann stared out of the open door and answered softly, "I know."

Grady wiped beaded drops from the plastic-coated map and started to reach for his compass when he heard a series of sounds: "Psst. Clink. Psst. Clink." He jerked his CAR up, pushing off the safety. The sound was Thumper shooting the silenced Sterling submachine gun. Grady ran four steps and found Thumper crouched over, his weapon smoking and readied.

Grady slowly walked forward, keeping one eye on Thumper's back. He took several more steps and suddenly saw the ferns to his right fall over. He raised his CAR. A shirtless NVA soldier was crawling on his hands and knees, looking over his shoulder at Thumper. Grady lowered the CAR and pulled out his pistol. In seconds the silencer was in place. The soldier had stopped because he'd found a slight depression in which to lower himself and hide. He lay flat and then turned his head, as if sensing a presence.

The two men held each other's gaze for just an instant before the bullet struck, hitting the soldier in the forehead. The man's hand twitched involuntarily as Grady flipped the body over and confirmed his shot.

"He's the last one, Grade," Thumper said when he came over.

"What happened?"

"I walked on top of them. There're three more back at their little camp. This one popped out of the bushes behind me. He musta been takin' a crap or somethin'. I didn't get a shot at him."

"That was close, buddy," said Grady, bending over and taking a pistol from the soldier's hand.

Thumper stared at the pistol for a moment. "Why didn't he use it?"

Grady shook his head as he eyed the big soldier. "You know, if I saw you creeping up on me, I'm not sure I'd trust a small pistol to bring you down either. Come on, show me that camp. Maybe they left some food."

The two men entered the camp, only to find Rock already sitting by their fire, eating a ball of rice. He tried to speak, but his mouth was full. He motioned to the full pot and rubbed his stomach as he tossed each man a leaf-wrapped ball of the rice. Grady pulled back the leaf and took a quick bite. It was delicious. The cooked brown kernels were mixed with vegetables and slivers of fish.

"Christmastime," Thumper whispered as he unwrapped the banana leaf.

Dove lay under his poncho, trying to sleep. Colven was already dozing a foot away. It wasn't dark yet, but Childs and Johnson had moved to their position on the road while they could still see. Dove's body heat, trapped in the rubber poncho, slowly began to warm him. *Short!* he thought to himself. *Short! Ten days and a wake-up, and the Dove will be on that freedom bird. The beach, baby, here I come. I'm gonna lie back in the hot sand and let the sun burn up my jungle rot. I'm never gonna get cold again in my life. I can take the heat, but this damp cold kicks my ass. First day back, I'll just get some rays and drink some beer and make it with Monica or Faith or . . . what was that chick's name who bummed out that time? She was a friend of Split Toe from Black Beach. Alice. No, Arden . . . Al . . . Alicia . . . Shit, short! Who cares? Ten days and a wake-up!*

Grady swore under his breath as he looked at the swollen Se San River before him. He turned and glanced back at the tracks they'd made and swore again. Their trail from the kill site would be easy to follow.

Thumper motioned Grady toward him as he knelt in the mud.

"This trail has had a lot of traffic on it," Thumper whispered.

Grady nodded and motioned for Rock. He whispered to both men, "We can't go back, and we sure can't cross here. It's gonna be dangerous, so be on your toes. We gotta move down the trail and find us a place to cross. Thump, you take point. I'll take the rear. Rock, you gotta—"

Rock held up his M-79, opening the breach. "No sweat, Grade. I'll hang tough and won't slow you up. I know what's gotta be done."

Grady exchanged a worried glance with Thumper but smiled at Rock. "I know you will, Rock. You always do, buddy, but be careful. If you get tired, tell us."

"No sweat, Grade. Let's go. We've only got an hour of light left."

The scarred-faced man looked up into the canopy. The rain had slackened, but huge drops still fell around him with loud splats. He dipped another piece of pineapple into the salt-and-sugar mix and placed the fruit in his mouth, savoring the taste. He squatted alone near the small fire. The heat of the burning branches caused his wet pants to smoke. He backed up slightly; it was too hot for his sandaled feet. He dipped the last piece from the coconut shell, popped it into his mouth, and stood. He still walked with a slight limp that favored his left leg. When the weather was damp and cold, his old wound was particularly aggravating. He moved from campfire to campfire, talking to the old veterans who had been with him for many years. The newer soldiers were ignored. Only when they had proven themselves over time would he speak to them. The veterans smiled as he approached, and they talked as equals. The newer soldiers backed away from the fire, showing respect, huddling together, listening. They hoped one day to be "honored ones" too.

The ugly brown water swirled and bubbled, eating away at the red clay bank only a few feet from Rock's face, where he lay motionless, praying. Thumper had dived to the ground only seconds before. Rock slowly lifted his head enough to turn his face toward the trail. The engorged, rushing river blotted out all other sounds as it tore at the land unmercifully as if maddened by its swelling. Feet, some in canvas-boots, others wearing rubber sandals, passed by several yards away. Rock moaned silently and involuntarily tensed his body for the impact of bullets that would surely come. He had no way to fight back, no way to have a last angry, dying squeeze of the trigger. He'd gone down so fast, he hadn't had time to position Thump's M-79, which he was now partially lying on. When the warning yell and bullets came, he would only be able to shut his eyes and hope it would be quick and painless and that Thump or Grady would exact the toll.

They kept passing. He could see nothing but the dark- and light-green broad-leaved vines that surrounded him. His toes and hip were dug into the side of the slight incline of the bank, holding him perilously close to the edge of the muddy water. His left toe was losing its hold in the soft mud, and his hip struggled to compensate for the loss. His body was slipping downward. The soldiers kept passing, agonizingly slowly. His left boot and lower leg slowly disappeared into the brown liquid that tugged gently at his body. He released the 79 and dug his hand into the soil, grabbing at the precious earth and roots that could save him. Intense knifelike jabs shot warning tremors through his left arm that made him want to scream out. He bit his lip and held on. The sweet, warm taste of blood seeped over and down his tongue as his brain commanded his body to survive. The tug on his lower body grew more intense. He could only shut his eyes and lower his head to use his chin as yet another anchor in the wet leaves and earth. He could feel the ground beneath his groin giving away like Jell-O melting as he slipped. *Jesus, sweet Jesus, I'm going . . . I . . .*

His body was suddenly jerked upward. Rock's eyes snapped open and he saw the grinning face of Thumper, who'd pulled him out by his wet, bunched fatigue shirt. As Thumper leaned forward and released him, he whispered almost inaudibly, "No fair swimming without me, buddy."

Rock turned toward the trail and saw nothing. They'd passed. He couldn't speak, and his lip throbbed where he'd bitten through it. He tried to smile but couldn't. His body was still rigid with fear.

Grady, several feet behind them, motioned for them to move out. Thumper reached down and gently pulled Rock to his feet. Water rolled out of Rock's pants legs and gushed in little streams from the vent holes in the insteps of his boots. He hurt everywhere, yet he felt almost blissful. The big man moved ahead a few paces, turned and winked, and began walking into the fading light.

Childs saw a flicker. Rising to one knee, he stood and looked around. *Holy shit,* he thought, *must be twenty fires, no more than four hundred meters to the west. What the hell? Who the hell is it?* He tapped Johnson's shoulder and whispered, "Look to the west and tell me what you see."

Sikes sat in the corner of the small shack. Scattered, dried mud on the floor lay in geometric shapes where it had fallen out of the patterned jungle-boot soles. The single Coleman lantern hissed and threw strange shadows on the walls. Sikes thought of Jean. It'd been a while since he'd taken the time to think of the brown-haired girl. He pictured her half dressed in her fatigues. A slight smile cracked his lips. He closed his eyes and leaned his head back and thought of the first evening he'd made love to her. The memory of the love-making was clouded, but her smiles and affectionate caresses were crystal clear in his mind.

Shane sat in a folding chair, looking at the weather report. He shook his head slowly as he read. Ingram sat across from him, watching his reaction, knowing the report called for more rain that night and the following morning, with only a fifty-percent probability of clearing by noon the next day. Wade lay on the floor next to the door, asleep, his wide-brimmed jungle hat pulled over his face. There was nothing to do but wait.

Dove saw the fires when he got up from his warm poncho to relieve himself. He groped around the ground for a rubber poncho and tapped the body underneath. Colven swung up in one movement, seeing nothing but blackness.

"Sir, there's campfires out there!"

Colven threw the poncho back. "Where?" he asked flatly.

"Stand up and look to the west, sir."

Colven got up quietly and stood for several seconds, then moved a few paces into the darkness. He stepped on Winters, who uttered a low moan.

Dove smiled. He, too, had stepped on Winters, a few minutes before.

The three men lay huddled under a dug-out place under a fallen tree only ten feet from the trail. Grady lay awake, listening to the raging river flowing past as the others slept. The ground in front of him was sprinkled with iridescent specks that glowed like miniature stars. He was thinking of Sarah. He could see her walking across the grass in the bright, warm sunlight, holding her head high, with pride, as she always did.

Then suddenly she was gone, and another woman appeared. She was thin and had long auburn hair that flowed to her waist. The young woman was walking onto a hot, dusty baseball field. Young laughing boys were running out of a dugout with their elated coach. The coach was Evans. He was laughing with his usual deep laugh and holding an equipment bag. The brown-haired girl stopped in front of him and said softly, "I love you." Evans pushed back his ball cap and leaned forward, kissing her.

"Ev. Helen, I . . . I . . ." Their images disappeared in the darkness as Grady mumbled and opened his eyes. The iridescent specks sparkled.

Ev, Ev, you were right. I know what you were trying to tell me. I really think I understand now. Sarah has taken a piece of me, and . . . I've never felt a pain like it before. It's an ache, a tormenting ache, that only she can end. I want her, Ev. I want to hold her and make her happy. I want to see her laugh and hear her voice, feel her closeness. I want to be a part of her. Damn, Ev, you didn't tell me it would hurt so bad. You didn't tell me how . . . Oh, Ev, I miss you. I need you to tell me, to help me with this. I don't want to lose her. I don't know what to say or do to keep her. I don't think it will ever work, but, Ev, I have to try. I have to.

The black skies rumbled, unleashing another torrent of wet hell. The rampaging Se San tore at the clay banks. Grady felt Rock shivering and moved closer and put his arm over the shaking man's shoulder. A second later Thumper's huge arm also wrapped around him.

Unseen by both concerned men was the faint smile of the wounded, wet man, who, although cold and in pain, felt strangely good inside. He knew he had friends—friends who cared about him. He'd never known concern or love until he'd come to this sad land. In the States men were too busy competing with each other. They lived in a world of competition for jobs, position, money, women. But here, here in this world, they competed only for survival. One man couldn't do it alone. It took all of them together, believing and trusting one another. It brought them so close that one thought more of the others than of himself. It was as if they had all become one. He knew the warmth of the two friends would be gone in the morning, but the spot they warmed in his heart would be with him forever.

23

The small dog rose from the red dirt next to the sleeping Russian and growled. Her hair rose on the back of her neck, and she took two cautious steps forward, sniffing the wet air. The soldier who ran up the muddy steps never heard the animal's warning bark over the sound of the rain beating on the tin roof of the shack.

Ingram looked up tiredly at the Fourth Division private first class. "Yeah?"

"The brigade operations officer wanted me to confirm the info you-all sent last night about one of your teams seeing fires."

Ingram got up slowly and walked to the map. The soldier pulled a piece of paper from his pocket and read "Grid YD956042."

"Yeah, it's a good copy," said Ingram, after plotting the coordinates. "Team Two-Six is only five hundred meters away. They're going to sneak over this morning to find out what it is."

The soldier nodded, refolded the paper, and walked out into the rain as Captain Shane came up the steps.

Shane shook the wet poncho before lifting it over his head. "Who was that?"

"Brigade duty runner confirming the grid we got last night from the major."

Shane sat a steaming canteen of coffee in front of the weary sergeant. "After staying up all night, I thought you could use it." Ingram winked as he lifted the cup to his nose and inhaled deeply. "Ahhh, the benefits, the benefits, of the U.S. Army."

As Thumper squeezed Rock's wound, yellow pus oozed out. Rock bit on his shirt-sleeve, his huge tears mixed with the water that had penetrated his boonie hat and trickled down his face. Grady, watching the trail, was holding the British submachine gun.

Thumper rebandaged the arm and side wounds with the last clean bandages and then inspected Rock's swollen lip. "Your lip is infected already. I told you to brush your teeth every day."

Rock merely nodded, his eyes still watery.

Grady handed the Sterling to Thumper and picked up his Colt Commando. "We're crossing that mother today," he said, looking at the flooded river.

Thumper nodded. It was too dangerous on this side. Grady stood and motioned toward the south.

Soon the three men were on the move, sloshing through the wet soil, their feet sinking several inches with every step.

Rock gritted his teeth, pushed his swollen lip out, and fixed his eyes on Thumper, who was stalking ahead. The pain was coming back in his side, and his arm throbbed with every heartbeat. *I'll make it,* he said to himself. *I've been worse off. Why, when I played football and I . . . Oh, shit, I've never played football, or gone to college, or done anything that I've told the others I've done.*

Guilt swept over him, but the pain washed it away with sharp pangs that almost made him cry out. *I'll make it. I'm a Ranger. I can tell people that and not be lying. I'm gonna walk up to my old man's trailer and beat on his cheap-ass door. When he comes out, I'll stand there in my dress greens with my beret and Corcoran jump boots. I won't yell or scream at him. No, I'll just say nice and quiet, like, "You said I was a bum. You threw me out 'cause I was a nothin'. You said I was a punk who'd be nothing but a fuckin' hippie. Well, I am something!"* The vision of his father slapping him and kicking him as he lay on the floor, begging for him to stop, flashed before his eyes. Rock had been thrown out of high school for assaulting a teacher who'd called him "an unteachable tax burden." *The asshole,* thought Rock, as he stepped over a felled tree. *Just because I couldn't remember*

*those countries and capitals, he called me dumb. I'm glad I
hit the bastard.* He hadn't told his dad of the incident and of
the one-week dismissal from school, afraid he wouldn't understand. He'd gotten up every morning as if going to
school, but instead had gone to the pool hall. The third day
the school had called his father at work and said they would
give Rock a chance to come back early. When he'd come
home, his dad had met him in the doorway and knocked him
to the trailer floor. *Fuckin' punk, he called me! A worthless
punk who wasn't going to amount to anything, just like him.
The bastard threw me out, said he wasn't wasting another
cent on me. Well, you sorry old bastard, I am somebody! I'm
gonna make it! I'm gonna go back and show you. I'll make
it!*

The soldier's pain was pushed back into another chamber
of his mind as he saw his father's wild eyes as he slapped
Rock again and again. *I'm gonna make it! I'll show you!*

Childs, Colven, and Dove crawled through the decayed
wet muck. It clung to their clothes and bodies, and it
darkened their fatigues to a blackish brown. The NVA camp
was only twenty meters ahead when they stopped. Colven
parted some ferns and peered through. One look confirmed
his suspicions about the fires seen the night before.

Colonel Dang sipped tea from a fragile cup. Speaking to
his three commanders, he said, "We shall bloody his nose,
get his attention, and strike the death blow from his blind
side. We have done this maneuver many times, haven't we?"
he asked the scarred captain.

The captain nodded and chuckled with his grotesque half
smile. "Yes, comrade Leader, many times."

Colonel Dang turned toward Captain Nha who was in the
process of lighting a cigarette with his Zippo. "Comrade
Nha's Third Company and Comrade Niep's Second Company will attack the Yankees' right flank after Captain Phong
makes a feint attack on the Yankees' front. We will fire only
twenty mortar rounds before Comrade Phong begins his
feint attack. Your two companies will wait until I radio you
to begin the main attack."

The two men nodded in acknowledgment. The commander took another sip of tea and walked to the open door
of the small montagnard hut he was using as his temporary

headquarters. The rain fell lazily from the trees above. He turned and spoke quietly to his three company commanders. "The rain will help us. They will not be able to bring their air support to bear on us, but their new artillery base is within range. We must strike quickly, comrades." He moved closer, staring at them intently. "Captain Nha will lead a scout element ahead to find a suitable assembly area and attack position. The rest of us will leave in six hours. Remember, we must strike quickly and violently. I will see you all here tonight, and we will recount our great victory."

The colonel closed his eyes. "That's all, friends."

The three commanders rose and left silently.

Thumper positioned his back against a huge felled tree, then raised his legs from the brown water and placed them against a ten-foot log that had lodged in a jam. Grady rose from the water and got into a similar position at the other end of the log. Thumper gave a signal, and both men pushed with their legs. The log responded by moving slowly away from the jam. The men angled their legs and pushed the tree out toward the river's main current. Rock, up to his chest in water, handed Grady and Thumper their weapons. The rucks had already been secured to the tree. Rock grabbed a limb and hooked his leg over a submerged branch. Within minutes the section of the old mahogany bobbed like a cork in the middle of the Se San. Thumper and Grady had planned to propel the log across the river by kicking their feet. That didn't work. Once in the current, it was all they could do to hold on. The swiftly flowing water shot them down the raging river. Thumper could see Rock struggling but couldn't do anything to help him. The bobbing log jumped and twisted, causing them constantly to reposition their already tenuous holds. Rocks's arm and side wounds were reopened and bleeding. He screamed out uncontrollably when the log jumped, slamming him on his injured side. His mind was blurred with pain. His hands and arms slowly released their hold.

Thumper could see him slipping down. "Rock! Rock! Hold on! Rock, god damn it, hold on!"

Grady could hear Thumper yelling but couldn't see over the log. "Grady, he's going! Jesus, he can't hold!"

Grady took a breath and slipped under the water. He could feel the bottom of the log and then the other side. He surfaced only two feet from Rock just as Rock's hands released the log. Only the injured man's leg hold kept him from being swept away. Grady reached out and grabbed Rock's shirt. He pulled him in with one hand while holding on to the log with the other.

"Rock, you gotta help hold!" he yelled into Rock's ear. "Rock! Rock, hold on!"

Rock could hear a voice through the fog in his mind. Peace would not come. *I have to answer the voice*. He opened his eyes, and the pain returned immediately.

"Agh!"

"Rock, you gotta hold on!"

Rock's hands rose from the water, touched the log and slowly moved upward.

The river made an abrupt right turn several hundred meters ahead. "Grade, we gotta try for the bank," he yelled. "When I say kick, give it all you got." The muddy water swirled and boiled as they neared the bend.

"Now," shouted Thumper.

The two men kicked frantically. The current ran directly toward the bank and then tumbled to the east. By their efforts the two men managed to manipulate the log to the outside of the current just before it made its turn. With the rushing water behind, pushing the log in the slower outer current helped the men's efforts to break the hold of the river. They ran aground in shallow water several yards from the bank.

Thumper waded back to Grady and helped him to pull Rock in toward shore. All three struggled in the chest-high water that made every step an effort. The bank was too steep to climb, but just touching dry land made them feel better.

Grady supported Rock against the bank while Thumper waded back to the log and unstrapped the rucksacks. Rock's arm bandage was gone and the white skin around the mud-filled wound was wrinkled and unnatural-looking. He leaned against the bank and took deep breaths to relieve the pain.

Grady noticed for the first time that it had stopped raining.

Thumper waded up and handed Grady his ruck. "We'd sure never make it in the Navy, Grade," he whispered.

"You got that right," Grady answered, putting on his ruck.

"How's Rock?" Thumper whispered.

Grady shook his head. "We gotta get him to dry land and clean his wounds."

Thumper nodded and began wading down the bank, holding one hand against it to balance himself in the thick mud. Grady held on to Rock's waist to support him as they followed.

"Let's go, Bud. The weather is clearing!" Larry Wine yelled from outside the shack.

Sikes sat up, grabbed his flight helmet, and reached for his goodie bag. He stopped himself when he remembered that the bag had been emptied days before.

Captain Shane stood at the door as Bud walked down the steps. "Bud, check in with the major first and see where the closest PZ is."

Sikes shot him a thumbs-up and disappeared down the path.

Shane walked to a table where Ingram stood talking on the phone. "Roger. I'll tell him the good news and contact the teams and inform them of the artillery. . . . Roger. Thanks again, sir. Out." He hung up the phone and smiled at the captain. "They're resupplying the artillery base within the hour, so the teams will have artillery support."

"Great!" said Shane, clapping his hands. He went to the door to look up at the heavens. "Thank you," he yelled at the sky. "Thank you, Big Ranger, for stopping pissing on us!"

Captain Nha addressed the ten men before him. "We are going to make a reconnaissance." He reached into his pocket, took out the GI lighter, and lit a cigarette. "I will select the attack position and our assembly area when we arrive. After the reconnaissance I will leave Senior Sergeant Niep's scout section in the attack position to keep me informed of the Americans' movements. I will return with the others and lead the company." He took a deep drag on the cigarette and adjusted his rifle sling. "Sergeant Niep, lead us. We'll take the road for several hundred meters, then begin our sweep around to the right of the American position."

The sergeant nodded and commanded his lead scout to move out. Nha fell in behind Sergeant Niep as the single line of men began their march to the east.

Dove ate the last bite of his rice-and-chicken Lurp. The crawl up to the NVA camp and the crawl back had drained him. After they'd returned and called in the information, he'd fixed the Lurp and chowed down. His full stomach and the break in the rain had combined to make him feel better as he lay back on his rucksack. He closed his eyes but quickly opened them again to search for his major. Colven was seated only a few feet away, eating a C-ration can of pears. Satisfied that his boss was all right, he closed his eyes again.

Wonder how that dumb dog is doing, he thought. *Hope they're feedin' her good and keepin' her out of the rain. Hell, before I leave, I'll get fifty bucks easy for her.*

The tap on his shoulder made his stomach jump to his throat. It was not a normal tap. It was too hard and too short to mean anything but trouble. He spun around and confirmed his suspicion. The face of Johnson told him without words. Dove's hand instinctively gripped his weapon tighter as Johnson turned and faced the road, his weapon ready. Dove glanced to his right and saw Colven lying flat on the muddy ground and looking toward the road. Dove couldn't see anything, but by the actions of the others he knew they were watching something. He pushed the safety off silently and waited.

Captain Nha was watching the sergeant in front of him. The road had been very muddy. Since leaving it, the walking had become easier. His mind was on how he would position his company for the attack. He didn't see Sergeant Niep suddenly, frantically motion to his right and raise his rifle.

Childs had been watching the road with Pfc. Winters when the small NVA unit had appeared, walking to the east. The unit had stopped for several seconds before moving off the road and heading almost directly for their position. They'd had just enough time to crawl back and warn everybody before the lead soldier appeared. The scout had veered back to the left and hadn't seen the Rangers' position as he approached, but Childs knew it would be just a matter of time. They were passing too close not to be seen by one of them. The lead soldier turned to check the others when his eyes caught the unnatural shapes of the prone men. He had time to motion with his free hand and try to raise his weapon before the loud staccato sound of the Ranger M-16s filled the forest.

Captain Nha never heard the firing or saw the enemy as he was knocked backward into the soft earth. He tried to rise, but his legs felt as if they were caught in a vine.

Childs pressed the release and let the empty magazine fall. He quickly inserted another. The initial burst of the team had knocked down five of the enemy. He rose and could see only the five men they'd already hit. *The others must have run*, he thought as he got up and hurried back to Colven. The major had just given the radio handset to Johnson.

Colven spoke calmly: "Sikes will be over us in a few minutes, but we gotta get out of here. That camp will be on top of us."

Childs rolled over and yelled to the others, "Lighten your rucks, but don't throw away any ammo or frags. We're gonna be runnin'."

Captain Nha raised himself to his elbows, only to fall back in the mud. For the first time he felt the stabbing pain. It shot through his lower back and almost blacked him out. The bullet had passed through his hip and exited from his back. His right hand, in the mud at his side, lay in a pool of blood.

He forced his hand to his hip to feel the entry wound , but instead his fingers touched the lighter in his pocket just below the oozing hole. His hand slipped back into the warm crimson pool. His eyelids became heavy. He fought to keep them open, knowing that if he allowed them to close, he would never open them again. The pain was now gone. He could feel nothing as he stared at the tree limbs far above.

Suddenly the canopy turned a brilliant green, and rays of golden sunlight burst through small openings in the leaves. The sun. *The ancient one had returned to reign over the land*, he thought as he struggled to hold his eyes open. A single teak leaf drifted down from above. He watched it float and sway softly before finally kissing the earth beside him.

Slowly, very slowly, he began to close his eyes. He was now ready for his long rest. Like the leaf he, too, began to float on his last journey.

"Two-Six is running!" yelled Sikes into the radio transmitter. "Scramble the guns!" He released the floor button and searched the ground for a PZ. They had heard Colven's message saying they were in contact and running south. The plane had just arrived and was circling over the location Colven had called in as their patrol base.

Bud sighed and said thank you to the heavens when he saw two large fields only a few kilometers away. The fields were almost adjacent to each other and separated by only one hundred meters. Bud estimated them to be at least a half kilometer long and thirty meters wide. He'd seen many such open areas while flying. They were montagnard fields, used in times of peace for co-op farming.

Bud stepped on the floor switch. "Two-Six, Two-Six, this is Three-Alpha. Over."

"This . . . is . . . Two- . . . Six. . . . Over," said the out-of-breath RTO.

Sikes recognized the voice as that of Johnson. "Inform Six you have a Papa Zulu two klicks due south from your contact location. Be advised I've scrambled guns and your pickup bird. They should arrive on station in ten Mikes. Keep me informed, and report once you've arrived at Papa Zulu."

"Roger."

Colonel Dang received the news without a show of emotion. He had not heard the firing, although the report said the ambush had occurred only a half kilometer from the Third Company's assembly area. Four men had been killed, including Captain Nha, and one was seriously wounded. The radio report had said the killers were American and that two platoons of the Third Company were now in pursuit. He knew the American trail would be easy to follow in the soft earth. He walked to where his operations captain had his map spread on a folding table. "We must assume the Americans have called their superiors about our location."

The captain nodded in agreement. "Yes, comrade Leader, and we can expect Yankee helicopters to arrive soon. I suggest we become seeds in the wind."

Dang sighed. "It is sad, my friend. It was such a good plan. Contact the companies and have them disperse immediately."

The captain walked to the open door. "Corporal, get me the radio operator quickly!"

Grady reached down wearily and tried to lift Rock back to his feet. They had found a place to climb the bank, only to discover that they were on a small island with the river on one side and a sea of mud on the other. After a few minutes rest, they had no choice but to try to cross the brown quagmire. They went fifty feet in twenty minutes and were left exhausted. The mud sucked them down with every step and refused to release them without their first rocking back and forth to break the suction. Thumper and Grady took turns helping Rock, but it was just too much for the weakened soldier.

Grady took off his ruck and pulled out his poncho. "Thumper, we'll lay Rock on the poncho and drag him across this crap."

Thumper helped place Rock on the rubber sheet and tiredly looked up. "How come you didn't think of this sooner?"

"They don't pay me to think, boy, just kill. How come *you* didn't think of it?"

"I'm a mere Pfc. Hell, I just follow my leader."

"Well, *your* leader got his ass in a sling this time, didn't he?"

"Yeah, he sure did. I'm not ever letting him forget it, either."

Grady smiled weakly. "You ready?"

Thumper nodded, and both weary men began pulling.

Dove stopped and looked back again before crossing the wide, grassy field. As the last man, he wanted to take one last precautionary look. He had seen nothing and he was about to run, when three NVA broke into view twenty-five meters away. He quickly raised his M-16 and took aim, but his heavy breathing wouldn't allow a good site picture. Holding his breath, he aimed and fired. The lead running soldier grabbed his shoulder, spinning around. The two other men fell to the ground before he had a chance to fire again.

Dove hurriedly crawled backward a few feet, jumped to his feet, and sprinted across the field. He was halfway across when the air above him cracked and popped with AK-47 bullets passing near his head. He ducked and zigzagged toward the far side. Childs was off to his right on his knees, waving at him. Dove headed straight for him, running full speed. His lungs burned and his legs seemed weighted and rubbery. He ran past Childs and fell into the protective vegetation with a crash and roll. Colven rushed to him and turned him over.

Dove was white. His chicken Lurp had come back up and was dribbling out of his gasping mouth. He jerked his head sideways, knotted up, and threw up more yellowish vomit.

Colven looked him over for wounds and then slapped his leg. "Goddamn, you're slow!"

Johnson fell beside Colven, holding out the handset. "Sir, I've called in the situation to Lieutenant Sikes, and he wants to talk to you."

Colven grabbed the handset. "This is Six. Go."

"Six, the guns haven't come on station yet. Can you hold?"

Colven looked over at Childs, who was quickly organizing the small team into a defensive position. "Roger, we can hold for a while. Are there any more PZs close by?"

"Roger. There is another field one hundred meters due south of you. Break. What strength is the enemy?"

"Don't know. So far, receiving only light, sporadic firing. We are on the south side of the field and have excellent fields of fire and—"

The air suddenly buzzed and cracked with incoming bullets. Colven rolled behind a tree and brought the handset to his mouth. "We're gettin heavy fire now—must be a platoon."

Childs had positioned two men behind trees facing the field and had just moved Dove behind a fallen trunk when the volley came. He fell beside the curly-haired blond and peered cautiously over the log. "God damn it," he said, jerking his head back and yelling to the others. "Get grenades ready. They're going to rush!"

He knew what the NVA planned to do. He'd seen it too many times before. They would lay down a base of fire, keeping their heads down as a squad assaulted. He had to stop the assault force before they closed on top of them. The only answer was grenades. They could toss the grenades with a flick of the wrist without exposing themselves. "Don't throw till I say!" the sergeant yelled as he pulled out two grenades from his belt. "Throw one, then wait two seconds and toss another."

The fire suddenly increased. Childs peered over the log and dropped back down. "Get ready!"

Bullets hit the trees with splintering thuds and pops. Childs looked over the log again as a line of ten men broke from the far woods and ran toward them, shooting. They were halfway across the field when the sergeant yelled "Now!"

Six grenades sailed out into the ankle-length grass, followed by six more two seconds later.

Colven rose just as the first grenades exploded. The M-33s were devastating. Only three men continued the attack. The rest lay dead or wounded. The second blast violently knocked the remaining three men down in front of Childs's position.

Dove rolled from behind the log after the second explosion and was shocked to see how close three of the NVA were. Two of them were wounded and were trying to get up. He snapped off two shots into each of them. The rest of the team finished off the others who were lying farther away.

The firing from the other side became sporadic and inaccurate. Pfc. Winters rose and screamed wildly, "Left! Left!"

Childs rolled away from the log and brought his weapon up. Seventy-five meters to his far left was a large group of NVA running across the field, flanking them. He fired a burst, as did the others, but hit only a few. The incoming fire began to increase again.

One of the Americans, a Spec-4 named Kutchma, was trying to get into a good position to shoot, when he suddenly jerked and spun over on his back and clutched his head. A second later his body jumped again with another hit and lay still.

"They're flanking us, sir!" yelled Childs as he changed magazines.

Colven tapped Johnson. "We got birds yet?"

"No, sir. They're another couple minutes out!"

The major yelled to Childs over the shooting, "Throw a smoke out to cover our withdrawal. We're running south to another PZ!" Childs unsnapped a green canister from his belt and pulled the pin, tossing it in front of them. Within seconds a yellow cloud engulfed them.

Colven jumped to his feet. "Move! Follow me!"

Winters turned Kutchma over before leaving. He was dead. The men ran, crouched over, trying to catch the major. Childs threw a gas grenade and started to run, but he suddenly pitched forward, hit in the back of the arm. When he tried to get up, he lost his balance and fell again. Dove glanced over his shoulder and saw the sergeant struggling.

He ran back to the stunned man and, grabbing his waist, lifted him up. "Come on, you old bastard, let's go!"

Sikes saw the yellow cloud just as his radio crackled. "Three-Alpha, this is Gunslinger Lead. Whatcha got for us?"

Bud slammed his foot on the floor button. "Got a team in contact and running. Hurry, baby!"

He flicked the dial back to the team. "What's your situation now? Over."

An out-of-breath voice immediately replied, "We're . . . running to another PZ. They're on our ass!"

Colven weaved through the trees at a full run. He could see light ahead and in ten more strides burst out of the forest and into the green grass. He turned and waited for the others, pointing to the other side and yelling, "Over there. Go! Go!"

Winters and Johnson were halfway across when Dove passed by the major, supporting Childs, who was grimacing in pain. The major dropped to his knee and watched the rear as the men ran to the other side. When Dove and Childs disappeared into the trees on the far side, he rose and ran after them.

Colven made a quick inspection of the small perimeter and then sat with Johnson behind a large mahogany on the edge of the field. To his right and five yards back were Dove and Childs. Winters was to his left, watching their flank. Overhead the gunships circled menacingly. Johnson spoke into the headset and handed it quickly to Colven. "Lieutenant Sikes, sir!"

Colven placed the handset to his ear. "This is Two-Six. Go!"

"We're gonna try it. Mark your location, and the guns will make a rocket pass. After the second gun fires up the treeline, the Slick is coming in," said Sikes quickly.

Colven took a deep breath. "Okay, Three-Alpha, we've seen no enemy since arriving in new location, but I'm sure they're there. Be careful."

"Roger. Mark your location. Here we come."

Colven threw out a smoke grenade and told the others what was planned. "Now, stay down when the guns pass. There'll be rocket shrapnel everywhere. When the second gun finishes its run, follow me."

The noise of the beating chopper blades became louder, and a few seconds later the earth shook and roared with the impact of the twenty-pound rockets and mini-gun. Dove looked up. He could see the tops of the trees on the far side of the field disintegrating in large puffs of smoke. The first gunship banked hard left just as the second gun began its firing. The rockets hitting high in the trees sent the whistling hot fragments in every direction. A branch fell from above Winters and landed several feet away as the second bird began to bank. The team ran toward Colven, who was already two steps out onto the field. The Slick was flaring and coming in fast. Colven turned and dropped to his knee and yelled to the others, "Get on! Get on!"

The bird hit the ground hard forty yards away, and the men ran for it at full speed. The right door gunner was waving frantically for them to hurry. Colven waited for Dove to pass and followed as rear security. The screaming engines and whopping blades beating the air were sounds from heaven, thought Winters, as he leaned into the sixty-knot winds that pushed against him. He was ten feet from the bird when bullets tore through his body, killing him instantly. Another Ranger twisted and fell, hitting the ground and rolling several feet in front of him. The others kept coming, their eyes wide and their mouths open as they ran, while the ground around them was kicked up by the impact of bullets. The left door gunner saw the flashes from the treeline to his left rear and spun the M-60 around, firing.

The pilot was yelling into the radio, "My rear, left one hundred meters!" The turning gunship acknowledged and lowered its nose for a run.

Childs, his own arm throbbing, knelt beside Johnson, who'd been hit in the ankle. With his good arm Childs jerked him up to his shoulder and ran for the shaking chopper. Bullets stitched across the metal tail, making a pinging noise as Dove turned to find his major. Colven was running behind him. Dove began to turn when Colven's face suddenly grimaced and he fell. Dove's momentum carried him several steps farther before he could stop and turn around.

Childs threw Johnson into the chopper when he saw the major fall. The door gunner was screaming, "Get in! God damn it, get in!"

Colven had been hit in the thigh. Blood spurted straight up in a shooting stream. Dove ran back to Colven, lifted him by his shoulder, and began dragging him to the chopper. The first rockets fired by the avenging gunships swished out of their pods and streaked for the ground.

Colven yelled, "Leave me! Leave me!"

Dove pulled harder, straining. Childs ran to help despite the screaming door gunner. He got four feet from the major when Dove doubled over and fell on Colven. The rockets exploded a hundred meters away with a loud crack. The door gunner, still screaming, unplugged himself from the radio cord and jumped from the bird. Childs grabbed Dove and tried lifting him with his good arm. The door gunner ran up and picked Dove up, putting him over his shoulder, and ran, staggering, back to the chopper. Childs grabbed Colven and helped him to his good leg. Supporting him, he hopped toward the screeching aircraft. Dove lay on the floor of the vibrating bird, clutching his stomach. Colven pulled himself in beside him. The chopper whined louder, shuddered, and lifted off. The left door gunner was hunched over his smoking gun, firing the last of his ammunition.

Grady reached down and grabbed Rock under the arms and lifted with the last of his energy and then started up the small rise. Their first step took them out of the mud onto firm ground, but the footing was awkward and slippery. He slipped and fell back into the mud. Thumper took a deep breath. He stooped, grabbed Rock, and lifted the thin man to his shoulder. He dug his foot into the bank and started climbing. Grady put his hands on Thump's buttocks to help keep him from sliding. Upward they went, slowly, taking small steps, with Grady supporting the best he could. Thumper took two more steps and topped the bank. He went to his knees, lay Rock down on the firm ground, and fell facedown next to him in exhaustion. Grady crawled over the bank and collapsed beside them.

Colven pulled Dove's hands away. The two small bullet wounds looked inconsequential, but the destruction inside was untold. Childs grabbed the major and yelled at him to sit back. Colven sat next to Dove, who was looking up at him. Childs quickly wrapped his belt around the major's upper leg and tightened it. Colven leaned over to Dove while the sergeant worked quickly to stop the bleeding.

"You should have left me."

Dove's eyes looked hurt. Colven half smiled. "You're really something, you know that? I don't think I've ever told you."

He took his driver's hand and squeezed it gently. Dove tried to smile but gasped and coughed, spitting up blood. Colven quickly wiped it away with his hand.

"Hang in there, son. You'll make it. You got a plane to catch in a few days."

Dove's eyes blinked several times. His face was a pale white, his neck turning a deep yellowish color.

"Sa . . . sa . . . sir . . . are you okay?"

Colven leaned closer. "I'm fine, son. Don't talk. Save your energy."

Dove's eyes filled with tears that trickled slowly down his face. "I . . . I feel like . . . like I gotta puke, sir."

"I know, son. I know. Hang in, now, please. You gotta hang in."

Childs finished tightening the tourniquet on Colven's leg and moved over to Dove, pulling up his shirt. His stomach was bloated and had a yellowish-purple tint. The sergeant looked at Colven and shook his head.

Colven cradled Dove's head in his lap. "Hang on, son."

Dove released the major's hand and let it fall to his chest. He moved his hand slowly to his shirt pocket and fumbled with the buttons, trying to open the flap. Colven reached down and unbuttoned it for him. His fingers slid inside and pulled out the plastic-wrapped small blue notebook.

He looked up at Colven, his eyes widening. "Don't . . . don't let . . . don't let a REMF get Bitch."

Colven nodded. "I won't, son."

Dove raised his shaking hand, holding the notebook. "Give it . . ." He gasped and shut his eyes, grimacing. A few seconds passed and he opened his eyes again. "Give it to Pete . . . for me. . . . Tell him . . ." His body tightened and he coughed, spitting up deep-red blood. Childs moved beside Dove's head and wiped his mouth with his parachute scarf. Dove opened his eyes again and looked up at Colven. "Tell him . . . tell him to . . . Charlie Mike." His breath came in short gasps.

Suddenly his body seemed to relax, and his hand fell to the floor. Colven cradled the blond driver to his breast, and his tears fell on the pale face of the young soldier.

"I'll tell him, son. I'll tell him."

Childs released Dove's wrist after searching for a pulse. "Sir, he's gone. I'll take him."

He got to his knees to lift the soldier from the major, but Colven shook his head and clutched the boy closer.

"No . . . no, Jerry. I wanna hold him awhile."

Childs sat against the back of the pilot's seat. His arm throbbed. He brought it up to his chest and looked at the bandage that Dove had tied earlier. He looked again at Colven, whose tear-filled eyes stared straight ahead as he rocked back and forth, holding the dead soldier. Then he let his arm fall to his side and he looked down at the unmerciful land below.

24

How's he doing?"

The rotund nurse glanced up from a patient's file and tossed her pen down as if annoyed by the interruption.

"You again."

The Ranger captain had been in twice the day before during her shift and once already that morning. Each time she'd told him his major was too sedated for visitors.

She cracked a small smile. "Come on. He's awake. I'll take you to him."

"How bad is it, Lieutenant?"

The nurse pointed to her upper right leg. "The bullet entered the back of his leg and exited here, through his quadricep. The doctors had a helluva time cleaning out the bullet and shattered bone fragments. He'll probably walk with a limp for a long time, but he's lucky he can walk at all."

They walked down the ward's long aisle to the last bed. Colven lay with his leg elevated. When they approached he turned his head and blinked his eyes groggily.

"How you doing, sir?" asked Shane, leaning over the bed.

The major's eyes widened in recognition, and he tried to sit up.

"Whoa, there, Major," said the nurse quickly, stepping in front of Shane and putting her hand on Colven's chest to push him back gently. "You lie back and I'll crank you up. I don't want you moving around too much."

"Ed, how are the teams?"

Shane could see the anxiety in his commander's eyes. "They're all out, sir. Bud pulled the last two yesterday."

"Yesterday?" Colven looked at his leg. "How long have I been here?"

"Two days, sir."

Colven shut his eyes and tried to remember the past events. He remembered holding Dove and . . . *Oh, my God! Dove.* He opened his eyes quickly. "How're Childs and Johnson? They were hit too."

"They're in the next ward over and both fine, sir. Sergeant Childs has been here several times to see you, but—"

"Everybody make it in all right?" asked the major, interrupting and sitting up higher in the bed.

"Yes, sir. We had no contacts after yours. Oh, the Rose, from One-Three, turned up. Some Fourth Division guys found him."

"Did he think there were others?"

Shane's expression changed, and he shook his head. "No, sir, I'm afraid not. We recovered most of the bodies yesterday afternoon. General Burton had ordered the recovery of all the dead and a search for the missing. Sergeant Wade's team and a platoon from the Fourth flew in on the recovery mission and brought them back. We . . . we recovered all but three, sir."

"Who?" asked Colven, shutting his eyes.

"Sergeant Grady and his two men weren't found, so they're presumed dead or captured."

Colven opened his eyes and looked up slowly. "What's the final count, Ed?"

Shane paused before answering. He didn't want to tell him the gruesome statistic. "We had twenty killed, sir, eight wounded, and three missing, presumed dead or captured. We also lost four montagnard scouts and ten crewmen from the aviation battalion."

Colven held Shane's gaze for several seconds before dropping his head. "So many . . . so damn many. Where's the company now?"

"We're all at Engineer Hill, but we're leaving for An Khe first thing tomorrow. General Burton has ordered us back to refit and rest for a couple of weeks. We got a bunch of cherries in, so we'll be back to operational strength soon."

Colven nodded dejectedly as he stared at his leg. "I . . . I guess I'm out of it now. I didn't want to leave this way."

"Well, you did survive after all!" boomed a voice behind them.

Sergeant Childs walked up to the bed, followed by Ben and Sox. Colven brightened when he saw their familiar faces.

"How you doing, Jerry? And who are those AWOL Rangers you're towing around?"

As Childs started to answer, Shane stiffened and commanded, "At ease. Make way for the general."

The other men turned around, surprised to see General Burton approaching.

"Relax, men," he said, coming up to the bed. "John, how are you?"

Colven tried to sit up a little straighter, but the general put his hand on Colven's shoulder and spoke gently.

"Easy, John. You gotta get better quick so you can run this outfit."

Colven's eyes clouded. He was embarrassed at his show of emotion in front of his men and dropped his head. The others felt his discomfort and exchanged glances.

The general raised his hand. "Now, whoa, John. You don't think this wound is knocking you out, do you?"

Colven looked up, blinking his eyes.

The general smiled. "You're going to An Khe to recover. I've talked to the doctor. Hell, I need you to refit the company and get 'em on their feet."

Colven put out his hand and took the general's. "Thank you, sir. Thank you." His eyes began to tear again.

Burton patted Colven's hand. "John, thank *you*, and I thank your Rangers. Nobody knows, or probably ever will, what you and your men did." The general looked around at the others. "Well, looks like you got a bunch of well-wishers, so I'll say good-bye." He shook Colven's hand firmly. "I'll see you in An Khe in a couple of days."

Colven, choked with emotion, was unable to speak. He knew Burton had understood that he couldn't leave the company . . . not when they were down. The general had given him time, precious time to build them up, physically and mentally, to fight again.

Jean stood reading a dirt smudged letter from Bud. He sounded dejected. The tone of his letter was clear; the Rangers had been hurt badly, and he was terribly frustrated at not being able to help his major and the others because of the rain. It was the first letter she'd received from him since finding out the company was involved in the invasion. Val had placed the letter on her bed, and when she'd first seen it, her stomach had done somersaults. She sat down on the bed to read it for a second time, feeling his pain and frustration. He so wanted to see her again, he wrote, and was very sorry he couldn't join her on the in-country R&R, but . . . she glanced up at her packed bag on the desk. She was leaving the next day for her trip to China Beach R&R center in Da Nang. She'd tried to change the date but couldn't because of others reservations. She had to go tomorrow or not at all.

Jean closed her eyes and ran her hand over the bed where they'd made love. She'd dreamed every night about him and of the times they were going to share in Da Nang. She'd pictured them walking, hand in hand, along the beach barefoot, talking, laughing, and later . . . loving. She lay down and put the stained letter beside her. Thoughts of him—the quick smile, the gentle touch, the way he laughed, and the funny way he held his head when he was angry all passed through her memory and spread a warmth through her that almost made him seem close.

The small beetle stopped. Its antennae moved cautiously, feeling again the huge obstacle that blocked its path. Satisfied, the antennae lifted slightly, and the creature began its climb. Like a miniature tank, the hard-shelled insect crawled up and over the folds and ripples of faded camouflaged material.

The man tried to open his eyes. The first attempt failed. A combination of dirt and sweat had dried to form a mud cake that made his eyelashes stick to his skin. On the second try, the thin skin of the eyelids folded partially back, revealing hundreds of enlarged pink-red veins that crisscrossed. The tired brown eyes moved to the side and then down, searching.

The insect continued its journey across the chest of the prone man. It reached the edge of the left pocket and started down. Slowly the eyelids began to close. The inconsequential rustle of another moving person brought the eyelids open again quickly. Thumper turned his head toward the sound. Rock lay two feet away on his side. His face was pained.

"Leave me here, Thump." His lips had barely moved with the words. "You'll never make it with me."

Thumper tried to smile as he answered, but the effort surprised him. Instead his lips only partially opened. "Can't, Buddy."

Rock searched the dirty face across from him for an explanation.

Thumper shut his eyes and spoke slowly. "I promised you I'd get you back."

Rock's eyes widened, remembering the promise in the mess hall at An Khe. "I ain't holdin' you to it, Thump. You gotta leave me. I ain't gonna make it, and I can't stand the thought of you guys not makin' it 'cause of me."

Thumper opened his eyes again. "We gonna make it, and we gonna make it together."

Rock saw the determination in his friend's face and knew arguing with him was futile. He knew he was going to die. The infection in his arm and side was spreading. He was too weak to walk. Thumper and Grady were taking turns carrying him, and the effort was draining them. They would all die—all die because of him. He felt for the M-79, but remembered he'd lost it in the river days before. He turned over slowly.

Grady lay asleep with his hat pulled over his eyes. Rock reached out and touched the wood and metal of Grady's pistol handle. He glanced over at Thump, who'd turned over to get some more rest. Gently, Rock pulled the pistol out of the holster. His hand shook with weakness as he worked it free and lay it on his chest.

I gotta do it. It'll kill them if they gotta keep carrying me. They'll get weaker and never make it. Grady had lost the map in the river, and the compass was water-damaged. They'd navigated by the sun the few times they could see it through the canopy. There was no food and only a few rounds left. Shit, they'd never make it with him. His hand tightened around the grip. His index finger slipped over the trigger. He turned the pistol toward his face. *I ain't a bum, you bastard! You shoulda helped me, not kicked me out. You ain't gonna know it, but I was a somebody . . . a real somebody!* He brought the barrel closer and lowered his forehead on the cool metal. His finger began to squeeze. *I wanted to see your face. I just wanted . . .* His finger pulled farther

back . . . farther. . . . The crack of a twig behind him instinctively caused him to duck and spin the pistol around.

The startled loinclothed montagnard threw his empty
hands into the air. "Me friend. Me friend."

Thumper jumped up at the sound of the frightened voice
and leveled the deadly Sterling at the brown man's stomach.
Grady slapped twice at his holster before glancing down and
realizing his pistol wasn't there. He cursed loudly and frantically searched for his CAR-15. Finally grabbing the
weapon, he brought it up toward the babbling voice, flicking
off the safety. Five feet away stood the small, pathetic montagnard. His eyes were wild with fear. His hands were held
out in front of his shaking body, and he was pleading, "Me
friend. Me friend."

Ben gently placed his hands on the women's shoulders.

"They . . . they called off the search." He clenched his
jaw and stared straight ahead. "We're leavin' for An Khe this
afternoon."

Sox stood behind him, looking at the floor and trying to
hold back the tears he couldn't control.

Mary Ann leaned against Ben, sobbing. Sarah shook her
head in disbelief but, seeing Sox's anguish, walked over to
him and put her arm around his shoulder.

"It shoulda been me," he mumbled. "It shoulda been
me!"

Sarah had never felt so crushed. She had really believed
they would make it. She held on tightly to Sox, dreading
their leaving.

Mary Ann looked up at Ben with puffy eyes. "Is there . . .
is there a chance, Ben?"

Ben shook his head sadly. "Time is against 'em, honey.
They might have been captured, but knowin' them, I don't
think they'd let that happen."

Sarah stiffened and backed away from Sox. "Until it's official, there's hope! There's still hope!"

Mary Ann stared into Sarah's eyes and saw the fire of un-
yielding determination. But there was fearful uncertainty
too. Mary Ann quickly nodded. "Of course there's hope.
My Thumper may be a klutz, but they don't come tougher!"

Sarah patted Sox's shoulder. "Weren't you telling me
about the last time everyone thought they were dead?"

"Yeah, but . . . yeah . . . yeah. Everybody thought they'd bought it for sure. Yeah . . . there it is." His face brightened. "They got outta the last one, Ben!"

Ben patted Mary Ann's shoulder. "We ain't counting 'em out, is we?"

Both girls smiled, wiping their tears away. "Come on," said Mary Ann, "we must say good-bye to the others."

Ben led the way through the door. He could still see Grady's face during those last moments at the chopper. The image of his sergeant standing in the dissipating smoke, looking at him with a knowing smile as the helicopter lifted off, broke his heart. He talked to the women with that same kind of smile, but inside—deep inside—he cried.

Morning

"He won't come to!" Thumper had tears in his eyes as he looked at the pale skeleton of a man. "Rock, Rock, we're gonna make it, you hear me? We are! We heard choppers cranking this morning—cranking, Rock! We're almost there!"

The frail body didn't respond. Thumper reached down and picked up Rock's arm and gently lifted him over his shoulder. He stood and stared at Grady. "I'm taking him out. We're going home. I promised him."

He turned and began walking, but staggered and fell to his knees. Groaning, he rose. "We're going to make it!" he screamed. "We're going home, Rock."

First Sergeant Demand completed his morning rounds and began walking back to the orderly room. It was good to have his Rangers back. They were down and they didn't smile much, but they'd snap out of it. He saw it in their eyes. He walked through the door and saw Pete going through a heavily wrapped box.

Pete looked up at the first sergeant, sniffing back his tears. "It's the rings—the rings Dove ordered for the company."

The wiry soldier took the small blue ring box Pete held out and opened it. It was a fourteen-carat-gold college-style graduation ring. A small diamond glistened in an oval starburst on the top. Around the starburst was the lettering 75TH INFANTRY AIRBORNE RANGERS. On one side were parachute wings and on the other a diving eagle with the American flag in the background.

"It's something, ain't it?"

Pete nodded, brushing away the tears. "Top, that was his going-away present to the company, and, well, now we're gonna have a lot left over. Including his own."

The first sergeant placed his hand on the shoulder of the red-faced clerk. "See to it every man gets his, and make sure they all know who it came from. And the others—well, son, I think Dove would have wanted us to send them to their loved ones."

Pete nodded. "Yes, Top, you're right."

Demand walked into the office and stopped at the window. He could see a group of Rangers sitting on the grass in front of the barracks, shining boots. *My God*, he thought. It was bad. The boots were for the ceremony that afternoon. There were so many of them. He was going to wait until Colven and the other wounded arrived. He'd made arrangements to have the hospital release them for an hour for the ceremony. It was important that they be there.

Mary Ann put the phone down and turned toward Sarah. "We're going to An Khe."

Sarah nodded without speaking. They had called requesting to be with the Rangers during their ceremony. Major Colven had suggested it the night before.

"I guess it's over, Sarah."

Sarah shook her head. "No, not until it's official."

Colonel Dang sat at the bamboo table and sipped tea from his treasured cup. He placed the cup down carefully and looked up at the scarred face across from him.

"We're leaving for the outskirts of Phnom Penh. It's the beginning of the end for the puppets there. We will destroy them."

"My friend, your rhetoric is wasted on this old one. I will follow regardless."

The older man smiled. "I know, friend. We have been through much." He sighed. "The committee has ordered this new campaign to the east, and I have found it difficult to

become enthused. I had hoped my words would sound more
. . . more inspiring."

The scarred captain spoke with no expression. "Inspiring
words have won few battles. But do not worry, my leader,
about inspiration. Our soldiers will go, and go willingly. We
have so many young ones now. They ache to do their part."

The old man shook his head. "We have lost so many, and
yet, they keep coming, filled with such . . . such commitment." He reached into his pocket and withdrew the silver
lighter given to him days before by the new commander of
Second Company. "Captain Nha would have wanted you to
have it. He respected you greatly." He pushed the lighter
over to the far side of the table.

Captain Phong recognized the Zippo immediately. His fingers traced the indentation of the engraving as he spoke to
his commander. "The Americans, they are filled with commitment also."

Dang nodded. "Yes, my friend. It is a feeling known to
both our armies."

The commander rose and walked to the map hanging on
the wall. "This is our plan for the move east. . . ."

"What the hell is that?"

"What?"

"That," said the T-shirted pfc., pointing down the hill.

The specialist got up from the shade of his poncho hootch
and looked where the newly arrived soldier was pointing.

Three hundred meters down the barren hill, the forest sur-
rounding the huge plateau had been cut back, leaving only
scrub brush. Beyond the scrub, the huge, double-canopied
green monsters loomed. The specialist noticed nothing unusual and was about to say so when he saw movement. He
took a step closer and shielded his eyes from the hot afternoon sun.

"It ain't dinks," he said, peering intensely. He could see
only the heads of men moving behind the piles of stacked
brush. "Get on the horn and see if we got patrols out," he
ordered excitedly.

"What is it? I mean, *who* is it, Jay?"

"I don't know!"

The men below negotiated the stacked brush pile and
broke into the open. A large, hatless camouflaged soldier,
carrying a man over his shoulder, was starting up the hill.

His head turned down as he leaned into the climb. A small loinclothed montagnard was next, followed by a third soldier.

The specialist yelled, "Sergeant! Sergeant McCoy!"

McCoy, twenty yards away, stood up. "Yeah?"

"Sarge, we got company!"

The final name was called and the last soldier plunged the bayonetted rifle into the earth. The rifle swayed slightly as the soldier withdrew the black beret from his belt and placed it over the butt of the weapon. He reached down and snapped the leash around the black trigger housing, stood, executed an about-face, and marched to the waiting line of men.

The small yellow dog was confused. She could smell her long-awaited master but couldn't see him. She looked at the black beret above her. It was his. She could smell it, but where was he? She strained on the leash as the shrill bugle began its mournful wail.

Sarah reached for Ben's hand as the first notes filled the valley. The twenty pairs of polished jungle boots glistened in the afternoon sun. A slight breeze rocked the black berets gently on the stocks of the M-16s.

Major Colven lay on a stretcher, as did Johnson next to him. They had been propped up to see and pay their last respects. Colven wiped the tears from his eyes and felt the new weight on his hand. He stared at the gold ring. The last notes of the lone bugle echoed in his ears as he dropped his hand to his side.

The phone rang several times in the empty orderly room. The young Ranger student standing outside the door, watching the ceremony, cursed under his breath and went inside to pick it up.

"Sierra Rangers. . . . No, sir, they're involved in a ceremony right now. . . . I'm sorry, sir, I was told not to disturb them until after . . . Sir, I understand, but . . . Yes, sir. I'll take the message and see if they want to come in. Let me get a pencil. Stand by. . . . Okay, go ahead. . . . Damn, sir. Never mind, I'll get 'em!"

First Sergeant Demand stood in front of the twenty men who had placed the weapons as Captain Treadwell read a prayer.

The young student ran across the grassy field. The first sergeant saw him coming from the corner of his eye. "You're screwing up my ceremony."

"They're comin' in! They're okay!"

The black sergeant turned toward the breathless soldier. "Slow down, boy. What you sayin'?"

"Sergeant Grady and Pfc. Meeks are coming in. The general is flying them in now. The captain on the phone wants to talk to—"

"Come on!" The sergeant broke into a dead run for the orderly room. The formation of solemn men had their heads bowed as the sergeant broke through the door.

Captain Treadwell finished his prayer and turned to command the first sergeant to dismiss the troops, but saw that he was not there. Captain Shane, who'd seen the sergeant leave, stepped out to take his place.

Treadwell commanded, "Captain, dismiss the company."

Shane threw a crisp salute and was about to open his mouth, when he saw the first sergeant running toward Treadwell. Shane could see he was excited, so he waited.

Treadwell listened to the excited man, then said with a smile, "You tell 'em, Top."

The senior sergeant grinned broadly and came to an abrupt position of attention and saluted. Treadwell returned the salute and stepped to the side.

The first sergeant faced the formation of curious men. "Rangers, it's a sad day to say farewell to our fellow soldiers, but the good Lord has a special place for Rangers in heaven, and one day this ol' first sergeant gonna be up there to help keep it squared away. The Lord, old Sky Six, he takes, but, Rangers, he gives too. And today he's given us back three men we thought might have joined Him. I just received a call: Sergeant Grady, Thumper, and Rock Steady have been found. Two of them are flyin' in to the An Khe hospital in a few minutes on the general's helicopter. Thank you, Lord. Thank you!"

The last words were never heard. They were drowned out as the sergeant took off his beret and looked skyward, smiling. The roar that came from the ranks of yelling, laughing men was deafening. The formation turned into a shambles of soldiers patting each other on the back, shaking hands, and hugging.

Sarah fell against Ben, her legs weak. Mary Ann and Sox hugged each other silently and grabbed Ben and Sarah.

Sox whispered hoarsely, "I knew it. I knew it."

Colven watched as the pandemonium broke out. Lieutenant Sikes knelt beside him. "Sir, are you okay?"

Colven nodded. "Yeah, kid, I'm fine." He looked at the laughing, happy men and turned back toward Bud. "Looks like we got a company again, don't it, kid?"

A lone soldier walked up to the row of boots and weapons, stopping at the last M-16. He unleashed the small dog and lifted her to his face, nuzzling her. "I'm sorry, little one, but he won't be coming back. The Russian, he is a poor substitute, but he will try to be your friend."

General Burton looked down at the two filthy, bearded men who had been sleeping during the entire flight on the floor of the whining chopper. He'd been at Pleiku when word came that three Rangers had walked out of the jungle at a fire base next to Plei Djereng. He'd met the Medevac when it had landed at the Pleiku Evac hospital. The young soldier they'd pulled out first was in very bad shape. The other two, lying before him now, stinking of old sweat and rot, were tired and weak but otherwise fine. It had been rough on them to leave the friend they called Rock. The doctor had told them their team member had a fifty-fifty chance of recovering and that he would be shipped to Japan within hours to meet his special needs. The general had offered to fly the two men to the An Khe hospital to recuperate and be near their friends. Only reluctantly had they left, and then only after the doctor had told them they wouldn't be allowed to stay with their fellow Ranger. Burton had the pilot radio ahead that the men had been found and were coming to the hospital.

The co-pilot motioned to the general to look ahead. He saw the huge boulder mountain that was the prominent landmark of An Khe. The general leaned over and tapped the closest sleeping soldier.

Grady looked up, temporarily disoriented. He quickly glanced around for the others. Thumper lay beside him, his arm over Grady's leg. Grady's sudden movement jerked Thumper awake, and Thumper instinctively reached for his weapon.

The general held out his hand and spoke over the noise of the engine. "Take it easy. You're almost home now." He smiled and motioned out the side door as the bird began its descent.

Sarah closed her eyes and tried to relax. It was impossible. Her stomach tightened again as someone yelled, "That's it! The general's bird!"

Lazily the olive-drab helicopter descended. Sarah, along with the rest of the Second Platoon, had been trucked up to the hospital helicopter pad. As the bird touched down gently, those gathered around the pad turned their backs to avoid the stinging bits of sand and gravel kicked up by the rotor wash. The audial pitch changed, and the artificial wind quickly died.

The helmeted crew chief hopped out first, followed by a large soldier who held on tightly to his small submachine gun. His feet touched the ground, and he quickly turned to help the other bearded, hollow-faced soldier.

Ben and Sox stood four feet away when the two filthy men turned toward the crowd. For an instant no one moved. Then, as if on signal, the men ran toward each other. Sarah stood watching with Mary Ann. Ben picked Grady up in a bear hug and jumped up and down. The others had gathered around and were slapping Thumper and Grady on the back. All were talking and yelling at once.

Sarah felt strangely uncomfortable. She was in the midst of a man's world of camaraderie that was understood by the men alone. She lowered her head, feeling she shouldn't be there. She turned her back and tried to fight back the tears. His Rangers always came first. He'd said as much in his own way every time the two of them had talked. But then she noticed that the yelling had stopped. A warmth spread through her as she'd never felt before. She knew before she turned around. Everyone was staring at her, smiling, as Grady walked slowly over to her. She couldn't speak or move.

He raised his dirty hand and touched her chin. "Tigers always keep their chins up, remember?"

She looked into his eyes and let out a sigh. "It's about time you returned."

They grabbed each other at the same time. The crowd of men yelled and hooted and gathered tightly around. Sarah closed her eyes in ecstasy as she was lifted by his strong arms.

Mary Ann, who stood in Thumper's strong embrace, looked over and winked. Sarah laughed and gave her the thumbs-up.

A light evening breeze blew in from the South China Sea and blew whisps of auburn hair over her eyes as she stared out over the darkening water. A small wave rushed over her bare feet and quickly receded, crumbling the sand away around her toes. Sighing, Jean brushed back her hair and continued walking down the white sand beach. It was her second day at the R&R center and her second evening stroll alone along the shore.

She walked slowly, listening to the gentle slap of the breaking waves upon the beach and the faint sound of music as it drifted over the dunes from the distant recreation center. Her thoughts were of a young officer who had stolen her heart. She shut her eyes to be with him.

"Beautiful, isn't it, Jean?"

She spun around when she heard the familiar voice and froze.

"Oh, Bud, Bud!"

He stood smiling at her. "Sorry I'm late, but I . . ."

She ran and jumped into his waiting arms. "You're here, really here!"

Bud kissed her softly and whispered, "I couldn't break a date with a pretty captain. I . . . I, Jean, I missed you."

She pulled him closer and kissed him passionately promising herself never to let him go again.

Three Months Later

The passenger rolled up the car window, shivering.

The cabdriver glanced into the rearview mirror. "Ain't used to the cold yet, huh?"

"No, not yet, sir."

The cabby shook his head and looked back into the mirror. "I ain't no 'sir,' Sarge. I'm just a 'hey, you.'"

The new sergeant smiled and looked out the window at the cold October day.

"Okay, Sarge, you're here. You sure you don't want me to pull on in?"

"No, this is fine. I wanna walk in."

The cabby rolled down the window as the soldier opened the door and stepped out. "Hey, you sure you want to do this, man? I mean, the meter is running and everything. Don't you wanna take more time?"

The sergeant adjusted his black beret and looked down at his shining, spit-polished jump boots. "No, sir, this is only going to take a minute."

The cabby rolled up the window and mumbled as he watched the soldier walk down the gravel driveway. "Crazy GI. Well, he's a Ranger. That explains half of it." He'd been in the Army himself in 1966 and had been to Vietnam, but he hadn't told the sergeant because it would have started one of those 'What unit were you with?' routines. Yeah, he'd been there and knew enough to know that the soldier had seen a lot of action. His ribbons were big-time—a Silver Star, a Bronze Star for Valor, and two Purple Hearts. The sergeant had been to Japan, so he must have been hit pretty bad, which probably explained why his left arm didn't sway as he walked. The cabby wondered why he wanted to stop at this trailer park.

Rock walked up the steps to the old trailer, pausing at the last step. The neighborhood hadn't changed much. The fourteen-foot wide trailer that used to be next door was gone, but everything else looked pretty much the same. He walked up the last step and raised his hand to knock at the door but stopped. The hate he'd felt for so long just wasn't there any longer. Lowering his hand, he turned around and slowly walked back down the steps. *It's over. It wouldn't serve any purpose now,* he thought.

At the bottom of the stairs he glanced back for a final look and began walking toward the cab.

The trailer-house door swung open. "Hey, you lookin' for me?"

Rock stood frozen, his back to the familiar voice, afraid to turn around.

"You . . . you got news about my boy?" asked the voice, pleading.

Rock turned around slowly. The weathered face of the old man looked confused at first, and then his eyes widened in recognition and began to fill with tears. His frail body shook with emotion as he ran down the steps.

Rock found himself opening his arms to accept the crying old man. His words seemed strange. He hadn't said them in two years. "Dad . . . Dad . . ."

The cabby sighed heavily and opened the door. He walked slowly around to the back and opened the trunk. He pulled out the sergeant's duffel bag and threw it over his shoulder, then shook his head and began walking toward the small trailer house.

The orderly room door opened and Ben strode through.

Pete looked up from sorting the mail and smiled broadly. He stood, putting out his hand. "Congratulations. Ben, I heard you were accepted for the seminary."

The big soldier grinned and took the clerk's hand. "Thanks, Pete. Here, I brought you some summer sausage that Grady sent us."

"Gee, Ben, thanks! Hey, this is the good stuff."

"You know Grade: He always goes first class."

"How's Grade doin', Ben?"

"Real good. He's in school and . . . Down, Bitch! Down! Pete, you gotta control this fat thing. She almost got the sausage."

"I can't, I don't speak Russian. Come here, Bitch. Come here, baby. I'll be glad when the Russian gets back from R&R. She's been into everything. Sure is gettin' big, isn't she?"

"Sure is. Come here, Bitch, you can have a little bite. . . . That's good, huh? Grady said in his last letter that Pancho would be gettin' outta the vet hospital next month."

"Great! Is he going back to New York?"

"Yeah, he's got a job in his brother's garage."

"Good. You heard from Sox?"

"Yeah, he's learning to be a disc jockey and got himself a girl friend. He said he was waitin' on me to get back so I could be his best man."

"Sox's gettin' married? I don't believe it. But I didn't believe it when I heard Rock reenlisted and was going to drill-instructor school, either."

Ben laughed. "The Lord truly works in mysterious ways."

Pete chuckled, imagining the thin soldier standing with his hands on his hips and wearing the notorious Smokey-the-Bear hat, yelling at new recruits.

Ben cut Bitch another small piece of sausage and bent over to feed her. He looked up at the clerk with a serious frown.

"Pete, the reason I came over was to let you know Thump and I talked to Slats. His dad passed away, and, as you know, he's going home on emergency leave. Pete, that kid ain't got no money. He's sent it all home. I don't think he's got enough to eat regular on his way out there. Thump and me tried giving him some, but—"

Pete held up his hand and bent over to pat the dog. "Don't worry about it, Ben. It'll be taken care of."

Ben grinned knowingly as he stood. "Thanks, Pete. We appreciate it. See you at chow."

"Ben?"

"Yeah."

"Don't say anything to anybody, okay?"

The big soldier turned in the doorway and winked. "Sure, Pete, just like always. We'll just keep it in the family, huh?"

Pete pulled the blue notebook from his shirt pocket and looked up with a faint smile. "Yeah, Ben, in the family."

June 1982

The umpire jerked his hand up. "Stee-rike!"

"Strike? Strike? That was outside!"

"Please, honey, don't get excited. Remember your condition."

"Mother!"

"Your mother is right. Let me do the yelling, and you just sit quietly."

"Oh, Daddy. It's the last inning with two outs. Your grandson is—"

"Ball!"

"Good eye, son! Way to watch! Your grandson is up, the winning run is on third base, and Mother says 'don't get excited'?"

The small blond-haired batter backed up and looked at his coach for a signal.

The coach just smiled and winked.

"Your mother and I wouldn't be so worried if you at least lived near a decent hospital. This small town is nice, but—"

"Ball!"

"Good eye, Ev! Hang tough! Clobber it! Daddy, it's another month before I'm due. Don't worry. Come on, Ev! Little bingo, honey!"

"Baby, Ev needs to bring his elbow up; he's got it too low."

"Well, Dad, why don't you tell the coach. After all, you are his boss."

"I've never been his boss, and you know it. He's as hardheaded as you are. He runs the damn company and all I do is play golf. I'm going to—"

"Stree-rike two!"

"Strike! My God, Ump, that was high! You see that, honey? That was high."

"Settle down, now, Dad. Don't get excited."

The distinguished, silver-haired man looked at his daughter's smiling face and shook his head. "Sarah, your old dad can still look after himself."

The ten-year-old pitcher nervously wiped his hands on his pants and glanced over at the runner on third.

The young batter choked up on his bat as the small crowd of parents screamed and yelled at their teams. The pitcher nodded to the catcher and began his windup. The crowd became silent.

The ball sailed toward the plate, and the blond batter swung. The crowd gasped at the sound of the crack. The hard-hit ball rolled between the shortstop and the third baseman, but the left fielder caught it on the run and threw it toward home. The fans were frozen in anticipation as the white sphere arced upward, descended, bounced, and was caught by the catcher. The runner slid in a cloud of dust and collided with the catcher.

The umpire tossed his arms out. *"Safe!"*

Half the crowd became hysterical. The other half sat unbelieving and stunned. The boys from the home dugout screamed and ran to the runner, who still lay on home plate, in shock.

"He did it!" shrieked Sarah, pounding her father on the back before turning to hug her mother.

The blond batter took off his helmet and walked slowly toward the dugout. The elated coach stood waiting for him. The boy looked up with a smile.

"Dad, is that the way you used to do it?"

David Grady eyed his son and said quietly, "No, Ev, you do it better."

The boy's smile became wider. The coach grabbed the surprised boy and lifted him, hugging him.

Sarah watched, somehow feeling left out of their joy. She dropped her eyes. Then a familiar voice yelled, "Mom! Mom!"

She looked up and saw her men looking at her with big grins, holding their arms out with their thumbs up. Sarah closed her watering eyes. She was filled with so much love that she felt weak. She opened her eyes and raised her hand, pointing her thumb skyward.

December 1982

The huge barren oaks and sweet gums seemed to shiver in the cold morning's grayness as the northwest wind blew across the Potomac. A large silver tour bus came to a stop beside the stark trees.

An attractive, trim hostess buttoned her coat as she spoke to her passengers. "We will first visit our capital city's newest landmark, the Vietnam Memorial, then proceed to the Lincoln Memorial. Those not accompanying us, please be back on the bus in thirty minutes. Please watch your step as you exit."

A couple walked past the bus as the passengers filed out and followed the black-haired hostess.

Sybil Colven held her husband tightly as they walked past the group of tourists. She knew he was troubled, although he didn't speak of it.

He had come home from his last tour those many years ago as he had done the previous times: quietly and filled with an uneasiness that only time, love, and patience had finally erased. He had thrown himself into his new assignment at the Ranger School at Fort Benning, and his smile had returned. Later, at Fort Hood, as a battalion commander, she'd seen him as happy as she ever had. Then the last tour had brought on the end. Time at the Pentagon was said to be necessary for his career, but instead finished it. Within the ugly gray confines of the huge building, he was no longer a soldier but a bureaucrat, pushing paper instead of troops.

His heart and soul were not in the job. He retired, realizing his days of soldiering were over. His longing dissolved with the changing Georgia seasons. He found a new life—a happy one—teaching at a small college.

Then, three weeks ago, the quiet and uneasiness of past years had returned. She had come home after shopping and found him watching the evening news. He had been crying. The television screen had shown thousands of men marching down Washington, DC, streets during the Vietnam Memorial's dedication parade.

Her husband had looked up at her and said in a whisper, "I should have been there."

The weeks had passed with him in quiet turmoil. Then, two nights before, he'd awakened her from sleep and told her, "Syb, I have to go to the monument. I need to go."

"Ladies and gentlemen, the memorial we will be seeing was established by the Vietnam Veterans Memorial Fund as a tangible symbol of recognition from American society. The memorial is located in Constitution Gardens and was designed by Maya Ying. The polished granite walls point to the Washington Monument and the Lincoln Memorial, bringing the Vietnam Memorial into the historical context of our country. Each wall is two hundred and forty-six feet and eight inches long. At the vertex the walls are ten feet high and gradually decrease to one and a half inches in height. The walls contain a total of 57,939 names of men and women who died or are missing in our nation's longest war.

"Two-point-seven million Americans served in the war, and three hundred thousand were wounded. Seventy-five thousand were permanently disabled, and approximately 1,300 remain missing or unaccounted for. For those of you who have loved ones or friends on the memorial wall, the names are arranged chronologically in order of date of the casualty. A directory at each end of the site will help you find the exact location. We will be here for fifteen minutes, and . . ."

The couple stopped, letting the hostess and her group pass. Sybil looked up at her husband and patted his arm. "Go on, John. I'll wait over there on the bench."

He looked at her as if he did not want her to go, but nodded in understanding and released her arm. Sybil walked to the bench and sat down. She knew he would want to be alone. He'd been alone in his grief for all these years. He had never once talked about the men who had died and for whom he had cared so much. He spoke only of the good times but never of the dead. It was as if he didn't want to share them with anyone else, and it hurt her inside. It hurt to know he loved them so much but couldn't share their memory.

She watched him as he walked down the gradual slope toward the black wall. He still had a slight limp, but the years had been good to him. She couldn't help but smile, thinking of her son's visit a few months before. He had challenged his "old man" to a tennis match, and his father had beaten him soundly.

Her smile vanished as she saw John reach into his pocket and withdraw the piece of paper he'd written on the night before at the motel. It was the list of names, the names of his men—the dead she never knew.

"Ladies and gentlemen, the black granite was quarried in Bangalore, India, and cut and fabricated in Barre, Vermont. The names were grit-blasted in Memphis, Tennessee, and are approximately fifteen-thousandths of an inch in depth. The wall is composed of seventy separate panels, and . . ."

John Colven found the name of his sergeant who had died in 1965 during his first tour and walked to the next panel to find the few names he remembered from his tour in 1967.

Sybil watched as her husband turned for the third time and walked down to the eleventh panel. She knew the last names on his list would be there. They would be his Rangers.

Colven found the first name—a soldier killed in Cambodia—and began to tremble as he recognized more of the inscriptions. It was like yesterday in his mind as he saw them flip their thumbs up at him and grin behind the camouflage paint. Kramer, Lippert, Angelina, LePage—each name tore into his heart like a knife. Allen, Bridges, Kutchma, Winters. His eyes stopped at the last name on the forty-third row. He felt weak and his eyes blurred with the tears he'd held back for so long. Raising his hand, he touched the cold stone and ran his fingers over the inscribed name: Joseph P. Dove.

"Dove, son, I've missed you." He shut his eyes and saw the curly-haired blond's smiling face as he pulled up in his jeep as he'd done so many times. "I'm sorry, son. I'm so sorry. I'd forgotten you. I had forgotten all of you. I put you out of my mind. I wanted to forget it all and live my life without the memory. Son, I was wrong. I can't forget you, because . . . because, you see, I loved you. I loved you but I never told you. Oh, you knew it, and I knew you loved me, too, but we never said it. I guess maybe we didn't really have to."

Colven opened his eyes and looked up at the wall of names. "You're with your friends again, you know. You're all together."

"John?"

He turned. Sybil looked at him with concern. "Are you all right?"

He stared into her eyes for a moment and smiled. "Yes, I had just forgotten some old friends for a while." He took her arm and looked back at the wall. "You see that name? Joseph P. Dove. We called him Dove. He was like a son to me. He had a little dog named Bitch and was . . ."

Sybil Colven held back her tears and listened to his words. They were the words she'd waited to hear for twelve years. They were the words of love about men she desperately wanted to love too.

The hostess stood at the entrance of the memorial as her group looked over their shoulders toward the wall.

". . . Yes, and tragically, upon their return home, they received virtually no recognition for their service and sacrifice due to the domestic controversy over the policy in conducting the war. The memorial is a symbol of this nation's honor and recognition of the men and women who served. It is dedicated to honor the courage, sacrifice, and devotion to duty and country of all who answered their country's call."

Sybil kissed her husband and smiled as she reached into her purse and took out the gold ring he'd given to her twelve years before. His eyes watered again as he took the ring and slipped it on lovingly. He turned and threw his men a final salute and whispered the words he hadn't thought of in years: "I'll Charlie Mike."

GLOSSARY

Airborne Personnel or equipment dropped by parachute.

Airmobile Personnel or equipment delivered or inserted by helicopter.

AK-47 A Soviet-Block produced semi-automatic or automatic 7.62mm assault Rifle, known as the Kalashnikov AK-47, easily identified by its distinctive popping sound.

AO Area of Operation.

Arty Artillery.

Assets Aircraft Support.

ARVIN (AR-VIN) the South Vietnamese Army. Sometimes referred to as "Little People."

AWOL Absent Without Leave.

Azimuth A direction in degrees from North, a bearing.

Ballgame An operation.

Base Camp An administrative and logistical camp for a unit, usually semi-permanent and contains unit's support elements, i.e., mess hall, supply.

Baseball Baseball-shaped grenade, 2½ inches in diameter.

BDA Bomb Damage Assessment.

Beaucoup French for big or many. We pronounced it Boo-Coo.

Berm Parapet around fortification on buildings.

Bird Helicopter or plane.

Birddog L-19, Light fixed-wing observation airplane. O-1A or O-1E.

BN Battalion. 400 to 600 men in U.S. Unit. 200 to 500 NVA battalion.

Boonie hat Soft jungle flop hat.

Boonie rat Infantrymen grunt, dogfaces, line doggies.

Boonies The bush, jungle, field.

C's C-rations, canned meals.

C-4 Plastic explosive.

C-130 Air Force medium cargo plane.

CAR-15 Colt Automatic Rifle . . . Colt Commando submachine gun, same as M-16 but shorter.

C&C Command and Control.

CH-47 Chinook, a large twin-rotor cargo helicopter.

Charlie Mike Continue the Mission.

Cheap Charlie Stingy or Cheap.

Cherry New Troop.

CHICOM Chinese communist, weapon or equipment made in China.

Clacker Electricell detonating device for claymore mines.

Claymore Fan shaped light weight anti-personnel mine, detonated electrically. Plastic cased with a C-4 charge behind a plastic wall of steel balls.

Co Company.

Cobra AH-1G Huey Cobra Helicopter Gunship—Snake.

Commo Communications.

Conex Large corrugated metal container.

C Rats C rations.

CS Riot control gas.

Daisy chain To attach one claymore to another by det cord, firing one also fires the other. No limit to number of claymores that could be attached in this manner.

Det Cord Detonating cord for explosives, used in daisy chaining in ambushes.

Didi (*Dee Dee*) Vietnamese to run, move out quickly.

Dinks Derogatory expression for Vietnamese, enemy and friendly.

Doughnut Dollies Red Cross girls.

Escort Armed helicopter flying escort.

Extraction Withdrawal of troops by air.

FAC Forward Air Controller, Air Force spotter, to coordinate artillery or Air Strikes.

Fast Movers An Air Force F-4 Phantom Jet.

Frag Grenade. Also a term to mean "kill a lifer."

Freq Frequency.

Green   Used to mean safe.

Gook   Derogatory term for enemy or any oriental person or thing.

Gunship   Armed helicopter.

HE   High explosive.

Heat Tabs   An inflammable stick tablet used to heat C's or boil water for Lurps.

Hootch   Your bunk, whether a room or poncho.

Horn   Radio handset.

Hump   To walk carrying a rucksack or to perform tough duty.

Insertion   Placement of soldiers in AO by helicopter.

Jody   Bastard who takes your girl when you're gone.

KIA   Killed in action.

Klick   Kilometer.

Lifer   Career soldiers.

LOH (loach)   Light Observation Helicopter.

LRRP *(Lurp)*   Long Range Reconnaissance Patrol.

Lurps   Long Range Recon Soldiers or lightweight freeze dried food packet.

LZ   Landing Zone.

M-16   Rifle used by U.S. soldiers, weights 7.6 pounds.

M-60   U.S. light machine gun, fired 7.62 bullets.

M-79   Single shot 40mm grenade launcher.

Medevac   Medical evacuation by helicopter.

MP   Military Police.

Nap-of-the-Earth   Flying as close to the ground as possible.

NCO   Noncommissioned Officer: Sergeant.

No sweat   Easy.

Number one *(Numba one)*   The best, first place, the highest.

Number ten *(Numba ten)*   The worst, loser, the lowest.

Nuoc nam   Tangy Vietnamese sauce.

NVA   North Vietnamese Army or soldier.

OD   Olive Drab.

OJT   On Job Training.

On Station   Gunships, Slicks or fast movers in position for mission or operation.

OPS   Operations—Tactical Operations Center.

P-38   C-ration can opener, small and folds, comes in C-ration case.

PZ   Pick up zone.

R&R   Rest-and-Recreation vacation.

Recon   Reconnaissance.

REMF (Rim-ph!)   Rear Echelon Mother Fucker.

Rock-n-roll   Firing full automatic.

RPD   Soviet bi-pod mounted, belt fed light machine gun similar to American M-60.

RPG   Russian made anti-tank grenade launcher.

RTO   Radio Telephone Operator.

Ruck, Rucksack   Backpack issued to infantrymen.

Same-Same   The same as, or to do likewise.

Sapper   Enemy soldiers trained in demolition and infiltration.

Sit Rep   Situation Report.

Short-short timer   A soldier who has little time left in country.

Sky   To leave or move out quickly.

Slackman   The second man behind the point man.

Slicks   Lift helicopter, Hueys.

Snakes   Cobra gunships.

Tee Tee   Vietnamese, small or little.

TOC   Tactical Operations Center, Operations.

TOP   First sergeant of a company.

USMA   United States Military Academy.

Ville   Village.

VHF   Variable High Frequency.

Wake-up   Short timer expression "four days and a wake-up" (going home).

Waste   Kill.

WIA   Wounded in Action.

WIMP   Weak Incompetent Malingering Pussy.

World   U.S. of A.

X ray   Commo site.

XO   Executive Officer.

About the Author

Leonard B. Scott is a career Army officer who served in Vietnam with the 173rd Airborne and 75th Rangers as a Rifle Platoon Leader, Patrol Platoon Leader, and Operations Officer. His combat decorations include the Silver Star, Purple Heart, and Combat Infantryman Badge. His hometown is Minco, Oklahoma. He now lives with his wife and children wherever the Army assigns him. He is also the author of *The Last Run*.

MOVING, ACTION-FILLED WAR STORIES OF UNMISTAKABLE AUTHENTICITY